DANGEROUS ENDS

DANGEROUS ENDS

ALEX SEGURA

POLIS BOOKS

The following is a work of fiction. Names, characters, places, events and incidents are either the product of the author's imagination or used in an entirely fictitious manner. Any resemblance to actual persons, living or dead, is entirely coincidental.

ISBN 978-1-943818-25-9
eISBN 978-1-943818-69-3
Library of Congress Control Number: 2017931155

First hardcover edition April 2017 by Polis Books, LLC
1201 Hudson Street, #211S
Hoboken, NJ 07030
www.PolisBooks.com

POLIS BOOKS

ALSO BY ALEX SEGURA

Silent City
Down the Darkest Street

For Andrea and Rebekah

"There's something ugly about the flawless."
—Dennis Lehane, *Sacred*

"Defer no time, delays have dangerous ends."
—William Shakespeare, *Henry VI*, Part I

PART I:
SHOOT OUT THE LIGHTS

INTERLUDE ONE

Havana, Cuba
February 23, 1959

Diego Fernandez set his drink down and wondered what kind of song they'd play at his funeral. He watched as a few drops of rum rolled down the side of the glass onto his large mahogany desk. He hoped it would be something festive and fast. Not a somber ballad. No, something that would get the blood pumping and people moving. *Un canto festivo.*

The house was quiet. He'd ushered Amparo and Pedro off to his parents' home in Santiago that morning. They'd be safe there, at least for a while.

It was a few minutes past midnight and his visitors were late. Diego's hands were shaking. He wove his fingers together and propped them under his chin. He was usually asleep by now. He was an early riser. His job—as one of six assistants to the Attorney General of Cuba—was a task he took with the utmost seriousness. He was first in the office each morning and often the last one to leave. It was his work ethic, not his smarts or personality, that was responsible for his professional success. He was a quiet and humble man. He put kindness toward others above all else. He had spent years creating a life for himself and his family. A life built on honor and hard work.

But Cuba was changing. Castro and his band of guerillas had toppled Batista's corrupt regime and left the country in disarray. People were scrambling to escape, like roaches fleeing an overturned garbage can. Families were sending their children away—alone—to start new lives in the United States and sometimes beyond.

Diego's world was unraveling fast. Yet he continued his routine as best he could. Instead of well-kept lawns and bustling storefronts, he now drove past burning cars and looters on his way to work at *El Capitolio*. The casinos were empty. Just a few weeks before, they'd been the heart of Havana. At night, Diego kept his gun on the bedside table, always within reach.

The bastard Fidel and his Marxist friend were working their way through every corner of Diego's homeland and making it their own. The romance and heroism of the mountain-dwelling rebels' fight against the fat upper class was fading, and a darker, more predatory vision was taking its place. At least it was for Diego. He already had a good life and he was a man of service. Even as his world collapsed in a cloud of smoke and gunfire, Diego did the one thing he knew best: he went to work. He provided for his family.

The door to Diego's study swung open and the three men entered, all dressed in military fatigues, their leader sporting a slight, knowing smile on his tan face. His two men remained on either side of the doorway as Joaquin Dreke took a seat across from Diego, his old desk the only thing separating them.

"Diego, you knew I was coming," he said. "Che asked me to handle this personally."

"Yes," Diego said. He refused to waste any more breath than necessary on this man.

"As you know, I am here on special dispensation," Dreke said. "I now oversee *La Cabaña*. I took time away from my duties there to come visit you this evening, Diego. It was not an easy journey, as you can imagine."

La Cabaña a fortress-like prison that now housed the majority of government officials the new Castro regime had deemed traitors—was Che Guevara's pet project, and Dreke was Che's favorite lapdog. Castro had tasked his second-in-command with the job of eliminating those who had broken *la ley de la sierra,* the law of the mountains, either by throwing them in jail or by obeying the frantic chants of the masses—¡Paredon! —to put them against the wall, where they would be shot by firing squad.

"I know," Diego said. He started to slide his hands under the desk but stopped when one of Dreke's men—the chubbier one to Diego's left—shifted the rifle in his hands. Diego swallowed.

"Good, good," Dreke said. "Then you must also know that the attorney general is dead, and his other assistants are—well, how do I put it?—in transitional roles in the new government."

Diego met Dreke's eyes. They were wild, hungry—like tiny black holes pulling anything close into their orbit. The smile remained on his face.

"Yes," Diego said, trying not to show how much his hands were shaking as he laid them on the desk, palms down. "I grieve for their families."

Dreke stood and raised his arm in one, smooth, reptilian motion. The sound as his fist slammed into the desk, scattering Diego's papers and knickknacks, made Diego jump back. He took a quick breath as Dreke stood over the desk, his eyes wild and smoldering with anger.

"Do not grieve for those *chivatos,*" Dreke said. "Do not grieve for traitors."

Diego tried to respond but couldn't form the words.

Dreke pulled a rumpled piece of paper out of his shirt pocket and slapped it down in front of Diego. It was a list of about thirty names, hastily written, the ink smeared from Dreke's fingers.

"You are in charge of the Department of Justice now," Dreke said, his voice low and hoarse. "Those are names of men who have grown fat and sleepy thanks to Batista. Who have stolen from the blood of our *madre patria*, Cuba. Who have taken advantage of those who are now in charge."

Diego scanned the list. He knew some of the men. He had heard of others. It was an odd collection—businessmen, politicians, retired military. The only thing they had in common was a strong and vocal hatred for Fidel Castro, Che Guevara, and their "revolution."

Diego let the paper drop back onto his desk. He looked up at Dreke.

"What are you asking of me?"

"Sign the paper," Dreke said. "This request comes from above me—above Che."

Diego looked at the sheet again. He saw nothing but a list of names. "What would my signature add to this?"

"These men will be executed at dawn tomorrow," Dreke said. "The Department of Justice will decree this. You're all that remains of the past. This is your chance. The war has been won and now we must purge this island of the parasites that made it weak. Do not underestimate the generosity we are showing you."

"No."

Dreke let out a quick, humorless laugh, like combat boots walking over shattered glass. "No?" he said. "Take a moment to think over what you are saying. I will not ask you to sign again, *compadre*."

Diego closed his eyes and said a quiet prayer. When he opened them, nothing had changed. The piece of paper remained on his desk. Dreke still stood over him. Two armed men still waited by his door.

Diego thought he saw Dreke nod, but couldn't be sure. The man turned, his long dark hair flailing as he moved toward the door. He made a quick motion with his left hand and the two men followed him out of Diego's study, like a school of fish reforming around an unexpected chunk of coral reef. Before walking through the door, Dreke glanced at Diego. Like a man who knew exactly what would happen next, Dreke's voice was serene and languid.

"You chose poorly."

As the door closed, Diego covered his face with his hands and wept.

CHAPTER ONE

Pete Fernandez hated days like this.

He groaned as the middle-aged man's flabby, naked torso grew larger in the digital camera's lens. "*Cabron,*" he cursed under his breath as he zoomed in on the man's bobbing, sweat-glazed chest. Whatever he charged for this, Pete thought, it was nowhere near enough. There were often times when being a private detective could be exciting—sexy, even. This was not one of them.

He moved the camera away from his face and shifted in the front seat of his beat-up Saturn SL2. He'd bought the teal four-door used—they didn't make Saturns anymore—for less than a thousand bucks. The car was as nondescript as possible, which was ideal for this line of work.

Pete slid his empty coffee cup into the car's holder and brought the expensive digital camera back up to his eyes. It'd been a gift from his friend Dave Mendoza, who owned the used bookstore where Pete rented a tiny back office. Dave was a trust-fund guy with a lot of money to burn. Pete was a broke private detective with a lot of time on his hands.

He tried not to think about the last time Dave had to help him out of a jam. Most of those memories were thankfully lost in a haze of cheap wine and little sleep. But the ones that did crop up, usually right before bed or during a mundane task like fixing a sandwich or pumping gas, sent a wave of shame and guilt over Pete that threatened to envelop him like a palpable fog. These days, Pete spent most of his time chasing deadbeat dads for child support money and snagging people on insurance fraud. He found the monotony soothing—most of the time.

The El Dorado Hotel was a few blocks off Alton Road in Miami Beach. In the mid-eighties, it had been a monthly rental spot for retirees and people not yet ready to commit to an actual mailing address. These days it was a rundown crashpad that was more shithole motel than tourist destination. Not the worst place Pete had ever seen, but that wasn't saying much.

Today's target was Elvis Arenas—a hair-gel soaked minor league sports agent with the moustache of a used car salesman and a hairpiece that resembled a bloated rat. Arenas was well liked in the community and the kind of guy who loved rubbing shoulders with the Miami sports media and talking up his minor league clients. He was a loud talker with a subpar success rate, but he'd parlayed it into his version of the American dream: a Botox-loaded wife, two kids, a one-eyed Shih Tzu dog, and a big house in West Kendall.

The camera's zoom lens allowed Pete to peek through a sizable crack in the hotel room's cheap pastel curtains. Currently, Arenas was unbuttoning his shirt while a lady in a black negligée—who was not his wife—crouched on all fours on the hotel bed, swiping at him like a cat. A wide shit-eating grin dominated Arenas's oily, pockmarked face.

The camera made a series of beeping sounds. These photos, though enough to have Mrs. Arenas consolidate her still-active facial muscles into a frown and file for divorce, weren't enough to fully seal the deal. Pete had done this kind of thing often enough to know he had to get shots of Arenas *in flagrante delicto*, or simply put, red-handed. Otherwise, there would be just enough wiggle room for a savvy lawyer to work their magic. "She was my client's cousin. He was just changing before they went to lunch." It was Pete's job to make these things airtight.

Things started to get airtight pretty soon. Once Arenas and his lady friend were gearing up for round two—about five minutes into the whole episode—Pete had enough. He hated this part of the job—sharing the info he'd collected. But it made him money, and it meant he could be his own boss for at least another month. Mrs. Arenas would pay well. She'd be angry, of course. First at Pete—yelling and cursing. The "kill the messenger" cliché was pretty accurate, Pete had discovered. Then she'd realize Pete was actually on her side and her anger would subside, replaced by depression. By then, Pete would be on his way home with a check to cash.

He stared at the hotel window. Now, without the camera, he couldn't see anything. It was just another room with a barely noticeable crack in the curtains.

It had taken Pete a while to realize that the life of a private investigator wasn't always about chasing mob assassins and serial killers—things he'd dealt with early on. And that was fine. His father, Pedro Fernandez, had been a Miami homicide detective. A real hero. He didn't remember his mother, who'd died during childbirth. Years ago, Pete had been a journalist whose quality of work had gone south as his alcohol intake spiked. This job—whatever it was—had saved his life and given him direction. He was grateful for it, even on days like this.

He felt his phone vibrate and checked the display. Kathy Bentley. She was Pete's sometime-partner when it came to his PI work. She was also, aside from Dave, one of Pete's only friends.

"Good morning," Pete said.

"Well, you're very cheerful," Kathy said. Pete could hear the wind in the background. She was in the car, on her way to or from a press conference or meeting.

"It can only get better after what I had to deal with this morning."

"What was on today's menu? Dude faking an injury for a settlement? Cheating spouse? Missing dog?"

"Option B," Pete said. "The headline will write itself: 'Attention-starved sports agent found canoodling with college sophomore.'"

"Sounds thrilling."

"To what do I owe the honor of your call?" Pete said as he backed his car out of the hotel parking lot.

"I need your help."

"That's a good start," Pete said, turning onto Alton Street and heading toward the highway. "Tell me more."

"Not over the phone."

"Ah, mysterious too."

"Meet me at my apartment in an hour," Kathy said. "I promise it'll be worth it. And don't be late."

CHAPTER TWO

"This is a terrible idea."

"Shush, will you," Kathy said as she pulled her Jetta into the parking lot of the Everglades Correctional Institute. "You agreed to come this far. Don't sour yourself on the whole thing before we get through the door."

They stepped out of the car and Pete let out a long yawn. It was a few minutes past seven in the morning and the Miami sky was more clouds than sun. They walked the short distance to the visitor's entrance, where a line was already forming. Pete's head was throbbing and he knew the headache would only get worse. He hadn't slept much in the last few days since Kathy had pitched him her idea.

Kathy had been hired to write a book about Gaspar Varela, a former Miami-Dade narcotics officer who'd been convicted of viciously stabbing his wife, Carmen Varela, to death a decade earlier in their family home. The story had dominated the Miami headlines, serving up a potent mix of blood, sex, amateur detective theories, and a tabloid-ready fall from grace. The city couldn't look away from the tale of a Cuban immigrant cop who'd gone feral and slaughtered his own wife while their daughter, Maya, was at a sleepover. Despite limited, circumstantial evidence, Gaspar Varela was found guilty of murder in the first degree and sent away for life. Since then, the case had spawned hundreds of Reddit threads, a "Free Gaspar" podcast, and an in-the-works docu-series. Kathy's book would be written in tandem with Varela, and would offer true crime fanatics a chance to get his previously untold version of the events. The book could be a financial boon for Kathy, as the Varela camp would be unable to profit from the sales due to Florida's iteration of the "Son of Sam" laws that prevented convicted felons from making money off of their crimes. Beyond the dollars and cents, it was a hell of a scoop for Kathy, and she wanted Pete along for the ride.

After about a half hour of waiting in line, they reached the entrance to the prison, where an officer handed them forms to fill out and took their photo IDs. They were soon ushered past the front desk and into a secure room. They emptied their pockets and walked through metal detectors. Before they could pass through what Pete presumed was the final door, another officer met them.

"Pete Fernandez and Kathy Bentley," the officer said, not looking up from his clipboard. He looked overheated, sweat collecting on his brow. "Names sound familiar."

"Fernandez is a pretty common name," Pete said. He'd had this conversation before.

"No, no," the officer—Wintle, according to his badge—said as he finally looked at them. "You're that guy. The private dick."

"Is there a problem, officer?" Kathy asked. She'd heard this conversation before too.

"Not yet, ma'am," he said, locking eyes with her. Pete could feel Kathy backing down next to him. She needed to get past that door.

Wintle scrunched up his nose as he looked them over. "You were caught up in that serial killer mess last year," he said, smiling. He was proud that he'd figured it out. "Shit. That was some big news. Wish we'd gotten the chance to put that sonofabitch in here."

"Yeah, well, me too," Pete said. He met Wintle's eyes, hoping the prison cop would let it drop.

"But you had to put some bullets in him, I guess, huh?"

Kathy squirmed next to Pete.

"It was self-defense," Pete said flatly.

Wintle let out a slow, humorless laugh. "Sure as hell was," he said. "You got that guy good, man. Wish I could have seen his face."

He tapped his pen on his clipboard twice and nodded to them.

"Funny you're coming to see Varela. Guy never gets visitors," Wintle said. "He's waiting for you at number seven."

"Number seven?" Pete said.

He felt Kathy grip his elbow and whisper into his ear.

"Let's go."

The Varela case had it all: murder, alleged police corruption, and mysterious, half-baked theories that pointed toward Varela's possible innocence. During the trial, his defense team had tried to convince the jury that two bloodthirsty thugs had murdered Carmen Varela. They had stormed the Varela home, overpowered Gaspar, and murdered Carmen, leaving Gaspar unconscious but alive.

The defense's story hinged on one Janette Ledesma—dubbed "the woman in the orange dress" by the press. Gaspar told the police that he saw a woman in an orange dress in the house immediately after the attack, which was also supported by an officer who responded to Gaspar's 911 call. The officer confirmed a woman fitting Ledesma's description was seen leaving the scene, but the officer could not say he saw her in the house—a point the prosecution focused on during the trial. Ledesma did, in fact, work as a home health aide in the Varelas's neighborhood.

Later, Ledesma told the police that she'd seen two men, clad all in black, rush out of the Varela home. But instead of trying to help the Varelas until the police came, Ledesma said she'd gotten scared that the assailants would return, and had fled the murder scene. It was only upon hearing the Varela story on the news a few days later that she decided to come forward.

Unfortunately for Gaspar Varela's defense, Ledesma collapsed on the stand, recanting her initial statements while getting picked apart by prosecutor Calvin Whitelaw—who hammered Ledesma on her checkered criminal history, drug arrests, and numerous inconsistencies between her testimony and the various statements she had made to the police. Instead of saving the case for Varela, her testimony all but destroyed it. Though the physical evidence against Varela had been minimal—some fibers from his wife's nightgown were found on his body, and his blood seemed to have intermingled with hers in a way that pointed to a struggle—Whitelaw capitalized on the defense's bungle with Ledesma, and painted Varela as a detached husband and father with a temper who was more interested in enjoying the Miami nightlife than in working on his marriage. Whitelaw also reframed the defense's key evidence—Varela's bruised body, which was meant to show that Varela was a victim as well—as proof that Carmen Varela had tried to fight off her husband as he stabbed her. The fact that Carmen's brother, Juan Carlos Maldonado, owner of GrocerEase, a failed e-grocery app and website service, testified against Gaspar didn't help matters. Maldonado claimed his brother-in-law was not only a womanizer and prone to violent outbursts, but also a pill-head who popped Quaaludes like candy.

The defense tried to introduce evidence that supported the home invasion theory—an unidentified thumbprint, unaccounted-for shoeprints, and the absence of a murder weapon—but these facts were just white noise to a jury still reeling from the one-two punch of Ledesma's and Maldonado's testimonies. It didn't help that the judge clearly favored the more seasoned and smooth Whitelaw, a veteran of high-profile Miami murder cases, over Varela's inexperienced and bargain bin attorney, Jackie Cruz. With his shock of slicked-back white hair, athletic build, and penchant for lyrical oration, Whitelaw was the rare combination of spectacle and substance. By the end of the trial, it was clear to anyone watching that he'd won over the mostly white jury. Cruz, for the most part, held her own. But her lack of big trial experience showed at key moments, and she was unable to recover from the collapse of Ledesma's testimony. After only a few hours of deliberation, the jury found Gaspar Varela guilty of first-degree murder.

Since then, Varela had exhausted his appeals and built a cult-like following of supporters and zealots outside of his prison cell—led by his own daughter, who had dedicated her adult life to proving her father's innocence. It was Maya who had approached Kathy with the offer: *Write a book with my father. Explain his side of the story. Help an innocent man go free.*

The opportunity was perfect for Kathy—a newspaper brat, who'd most recently worked as the daily news columnist for Pete's old paper, the *Miami Times*. The job had once belonged to her father, Chaz Bentley, a legendary Miami reporter and unrepentant drunk. Pete had first met Chaz a few years back, at the tail end of Chaz's own gin-soaked journalism career. Chaz had sought Pete out in an effort to find Kathy, who had been kidnapped by one of the deadliest mob killers in Miami history. Pete managed to locate Kathy, but Chaz wasn't as lucky, ending up on the wrong side of the killer's silenced pistol.

Maya, a successful residential real estate agent who'd put her career on hold to help her father, had told Kathy that she hoped the book would help exonerate her father in the eyes of the public and media. But she also hoped that, by reviewing the existing evidence, they'd find something new that might merit another trial, and another chance for her father's freedom. That was where Pete came in. Having exhausted their appeals, the Varela camp's last chance was to unearth significant and previously unseen evidence that would open the door for them to file a post-conviction motion that would allow a judge to consider a new trial for Varela—no mean feat.

After a few hours of hemming and hawing, Pete relented—he

would meet Varela, get a feel for the situation, and decide if he was in. This was enough for Kathy, who had already processed the paperwork they'd need in order to visit Varela the following morning.

"I still haven't said yes to working on this," Pete whispered as they walked through the cramped visitor's area. Pete saw every kind of encounter in the span of a few feet—the grieving mother, the young wife and child, the fellow gangbanger, and the confused friend. Where did he and Kathy fall? Opportunists? Justice seekers?

Varela was seated on the opposite side of the bulletproof glass at cubicle seven. He looked relaxed and used to the procedure, the telephone that would allow him to talk to Pete and Kathy already at his ear. There were two phones on the opposite side. Varela seemed calm but alert, his eyes scanning them as they sat down. Kathy picked up the phone and waited a second.

"Thanks for coming," Varela said. His voice was low and smooth. He looked weathered and worn from a decade in prison, but Pete could still see glimpses of the man Varela had been: handsome, well spoken. "I've been looking forward to talking this out."

"Well, that's good," Kathy said. "I'm, uh, I'm glad we made it. I assume Maya outlined what we were thinking?"

Varela pursed his lips and let his eyes drift over to Kathy. Kathy was a good-looking woman—fit, blond, and naturally tan from time spent on Miami Beach. In her mid-thirties and real, Kathy had no trouble turning heads in Miami, a town built on fake, well, everything. It'd probably been years since Varela had spoken with an attractive woman who wasn't a lawyer or a cop.

"Yes, she did," Varela said. He glanced at Pete for a second. "I'm intrigued by the idea. I think a book can definitely help raise awareness. Lord knows we need it. There's so much to this case—so much that hasn't been brought to light in court or in the eyes of the law—it could really help."

"Of course," Kathy said. "But I have to be clear about one thing:

I can't promise this book will be a puff piece, or something you can use to prove your innocence. I'm going to do my research, talk to the people involved, and, thanks to the access you're providing, form my own conclusions."

Pete tensed up. Kathy had outlined her Varela strategy to him on the ride in, but it felt much more sudden in real time. This was supposed to be the closer. So much for that.

Varela stiffened. Pete couldn't tell if he was upset. He couldn't really read him at all. The silence hung over them for a few seconds, like a business meeting reacting to an off-color joke.

"Are you going to introduce your friend?" Varela asked, motioning with his chin to Pete.

"Oh," Kathy said in relief. "This is Pete. Pete Fernandez. He's a private detective who will, ideally, help me with the book, like I mentioned. You know, interviewing witnesses, reexamining the case evidence, and—"

"You caught that serial killer," Varela said. "And the other guy before that—the Silent killer? Silent…?"

"The Silent Death," Pete said. "That was the guy's nickname."

"Right," Varela said. "I heard about both—even in here. Maya brings me the paper when she can. You're a brave guy—if the stories are true."

"Depends on the story," Pete said. He was trying to be funny, but the joke sounded more defensive than he'd hoped.

Varela nodded and turned his attention back to Kathy. "I'm fine with the idea," he said. "I get that you have your ethics. But I want you to know I'm innocent. I did not kill my wife. The evidence the state has is weak—a joke. If my idiot lawyer hadn't put that woman on the stand, we may have won.

"They made me look like a crazy person. A line of psychiatrists said I didn't have a psychotic bone in my body or a violent temper, but that evidence was disallowed. I had dozens of friends and relatives eager to explain that there was no way I killed my wife. But everything we tried to do was shot down by the judge. The appeals have been even worse."

Varela let out a long sigh and smiled wryly.

Pete wasn't convinced. A part of him felt bad for Varela. The idea of being incarcerated for any amount of time for a crime you didn't commit seemed surreal to him, even though he knew it happened more often than it should. His own dealings with the Miami Police Department had shown him enough corruption to believe it possible. But if Varela was guilty of the crime, he was just getting what he deserved.

Varela seemed to notice the awkward silence.

"So, yes, let's do this," he said. "I'm out of options. I hope you and your friend here can discover enough to make a new case." He looked from Kathy to Pete and then back to Kathy. "Otherwise, I'm going to rot here until I die."

They made tentative plans to reconvene with Varela for a more formal interview once they reviewed the case files. But, like most of Miami, they were familiar with the basics of the case already.

The story of Gaspar Varela was a part of Miami lore. Pete had followed the news from the time Varela was found next to his dead wife, through the conviction, and even after, during his initial appeals. Although Varela was dismissive of the physical evidence—and he was right that the case was mostly circumstantial—the jury had connected the dots and found that there was enough to convict him beyond a reasonable doubt. And the appellate courts had upheld Varela's conviction every time.

Establishing Varela's motive had been more challenging for the prosecution to prove. Beyond the vague explanation that Varela "had a dangerous temper," Whitelaw mostly avoided it during the trial. They tried to paint Varela as a drug-fueled party animal looking to escape the constraints of his marriage, growing more desperate as time passed. That, coupled with his volatile temperament, led to the death of Carmen Varela. It was a flimsy motive at best, and one that the prosecution wasn't able to support very well. From what Pete had gleaned by reading news reports during and after the trial, there were few people who had a genuine dislike for Varela. Still, some cracks appeared after the murder that would come back to haunt Varela's attempts to point to his sterling character. A woman's claim she had an affair with Varela drew some tabloid headlines, and there were rumors that Varela was trying to get a lucrative book deal before the verdict was read. Varela also didn't win any new fans after an awkward, creepy TV talk show appearance that made him seem more cunning and attention-hungry than innocent. These missteps and the prosecution's intimations of marital discord were just enough to make the jury think that maybe Gaspar Varela wasn't the nice guy his lawyers made him out to be.

But just because you're a jerk doesn't mean you're a killer, Pete thought.

"What's going on in that little skull of yours?" Kathy asked as she fumbled through her oversized purse, looking for her car keys. They'd just stepped out into the scorching Miami sun. It was approaching one hundred degrees and Pete felt a sheen of sweat form under his gray polo.

"Trying to wrap my head around this thing," Pete said. "I'm curious to hear Varela's take on what happened, when we have more time with him. How do you feel about it?"

"I'm leaning toward guilty," Kathy said, finally discovering the collection of keys at the bottom of her bag. She yanked them out triumphantly before turning to Pete. "But I do believe his case was botched from the get-go."

"Oh?"

"I don't know for sure," she said. "Although the 'crazy thugs' story never rang true to me, there's more to it, guilty or not."

Pete nodded. He wasn't certain of a lot of things about the case—including whether he wanted to be involved. His life had become fairly mundane and he'd gotten used to it.

As they made their way down the long walkway that led visitors to and from the prison, Pete noticed a figure approaching them. It was hard to make out much with the blazing sun in his eyes, but he could tell it was a woman. She seemed to be waving at them.

"You expecting someone?" Pete asked.

"I think it might be our benefactor," Kathy said.

As the woman got closer, Pete noticed she was young—late twenties—with dark brown hair, and attractive. She was carrying a large canvas bag over her shoulder, which appeared to be full of books and manila folders stuffed with papers. She reached them about halfway down the walkway and extended her hand to Kathy.

"Kathy, hi, so glad to see you here," she said.

"Glad to be here," Kathy said, not bothering to introduce Pete. "The talk went well. I think he's on board. We'll circle back to him soon for a longer chat."

"Excellent," the woman said. Her smile looked natural and soft—the kind one reserved for old friends. "That's great. What a relief. I know he can be a tough guy to talk to."

Pete cleared his throat.

"Oh, right, I forgot you haven't met," Kathy said. "Maya, this is Pete Fernandez, the detective I mentioned to you. Pete, this is Maya Varela, Gaspar's daughter. She's the one who reached out to me—us—about the book."

Pete tried to give her his best I'm-not-a-creep smile and moved to shake her hand. She sidestepped him and went for a hug. Pete returned the embrace with surprise.

"Nice to meet you, Pete," she said, her breath hot on his neck. She let go and took a step back. "Sorry—I'm a hugger." She laughed. "And I'm really glad my dad is on board with this. I think it'll help the case so much. I can't even begin to thank you."

Pete felt his face getting warm. He managed to get out a quick, "Nice to meet you too."

A few seconds passed. Finally, Maya shrugged and took another step toward the prison.

"Well, I have to talk to my dad," she said, still smiling. "We need to go over what his options are."

"For what?" Pete asked.

"For his motion," Kathy said. "Right?"

"Yes, right." Maya nodded. Her shoulders sank a bit. "The truth is he doesn't have many options. He's burned through all his appeals, so the only thing that can save him is another trial. That's part of the reason we're working with you guys. We need some kind of information no one was aware of that proves he's innocent."

"We're going to get started right away," Kathy said. "I sent you our payment info, so let me know if that's okay."

"Oh, I'm sure it's all fine," Maya said. "I'll send over the memo— recapping all the discovery stuff—to you tonight. Once you talk to dad's old attorney, she can get you all the files from the original trial. I've already let her know you'll be reaching out."

Her eyes had gone distant, as if she had just now realized the enormity of their task. Pete felt bad for her. She looked at him and a brief smile returned to her face. Pete nodded. He wasn't sure what else to do.

INTERLUDE TWO

Havana, Cuba
February 23, 1959

Diego Fernandez waited ten minutes. It took that long for his breathing to return to normal, and to feel like he could get up and support his own weight. He stood and peeked out the window of his study. The street seemed clear.

He walked to the master bedroom and searched under the bed—his body flat on the floor like a fallen sheet of paper, his arm reached for the dark bag. He tugged at the strap and dragged it out into the room. He didn't bother to check what was inside, instead hoisting the heavy knapsack over his shoulder. He had to hurry. The time for subterfuge had passed—he had his wits, a bit of luck, and his prayers. Those things would save him from being the next name added to Dreke's kill list.

Diego hurried down the house's main hallway. His head throbbed, bubbling over like a pot left on the stove too long, overcome with worries and fears he'd only experienced in nightmares and his darkest moments. When would he see his wife and son again? What now? He couldn't dwell. He had to run.

The bag was heavy, making his run more intense and taxing. He was wheezing and gasping for breath. Diego was a strong man. He tried to stay in shape. No, this wasn't physical exhaustion. He was scared.

He paused at the front door of his large, four-bedroom house, the one he'd never imagined they'd afford, much less live in for a decade—the house where his young son had been raised. He knew a bullet could be waiting for him when he opened the door and stepped outside. He rested one hand on the doorknob. With the other hand, he opened the curtains that covered the narrow window to the left of the front door.

It was dark outside. He wouldn't be able to see them until they could see him.

Diego grabbed the coatrack next to the door and put one of his favorite hats on top. He draped his coat around it. In the dim light of the house, it didn't resemble anything human, but it wouldn't have to for very long. He crouched down, crawled to the door, and put his hand back on the doorknob. In one movement, he swung open the door and moved out of the way, thrusting the coatrack out into the moonlight like a bedraggled scarecrow.

The grandfather clock in the living room announced the seconds, each one dribbling out like drops of water from a broken faucet. The seconds became a minute. Diego let out an exhausted sigh and started to stand up.

That was when the bullets came.

The gunfire tore into his coat and splintered the front door, knocking the coatrack onto the floor. Diego stayed down. On his belly now, he crawled further into the house, his hands clawing into the carpet as he dragged himself away from the doorway. He felt his nails bending back and breaking. A bullet whizzed by his head.

The hardwood floor signaled that he was out of the front foyer and in the living room—which was open and not any more secure. The gunfire had stalled once the coatrack fell. Maybe they thought he was dead? Diego waited, praying he would hear the peel of tires as his assassins sped off.

Instead, he heard voices—and they were getting louder. Closer.

He got up and ran. He could hear the footsteps. He wasn't sure how many there were, but they were coming fast.

He cut through the kitchen, which was long and spacious. Diego hated his house now. He hated the cluttered dining room and he hated the eat-in kitchen that had too many chairs. He heard the men behind him—they were in the house now. He heard a bullet being fired into his ceiling.

The back door of the house was to the left of the kitchen and opened up to the backyard and the main driveway. He saw right away that his car would be useless—the rims of the wheels were touching the pavement, the tires slashed and flat. He could keep running, but that would only give him a minute or two at best.

The car horn came in a quick burst, the kind of noise you'd shrug off if you heard it on the street any day, like a gust of wind rustling the trees. Diego looked up to see a dark blue Chevy cruising down his street. Pepe Cardenas, his friend and neighbor, was driving. Diego looked back at his front door and saw it was still open. He couldn't hear the men anymore, but that didn't mean they weren't behind him.

"What the fuck are you waiting for, *cabron*?" Pepe said, his hand motioning for Diego to cut through the driveway and get in.

Diego ran around the car to the passenger side, slamming the door behind him.

"You are in serious trouble, Diego—" Pepe started to say as his body lurched forward. Diego saw Pepe's skull burst open from a gunshot, blood and brains and bone spreading onto the steering wheel and windshield like a spilled plate of beef stew. The car continued to move forward. Diego let out a pained scream. He tried to duck down, tried to avoid the second and third shot that shattered the back and side windows. He could feel the wetness in his eyes as he positioned himself on top of his dead friend, Pepe's head resting on his shoulder, what was left of it dripping and sliding over Diego's white dress shirt. He tried to get solid footing but he couldn't, trying to stay low and evade the killers but also keep the car moving.

"Fuck, Pepe, fuck, fuck, fuck," Diego said. He couldn't think.

He slammed his right foot down onto the gas, feeling Pepe's own foot under his. It sent the car hurtling forward. The gunshots continued, but seemed farther away. Diego didn't dare look back. He positioned himself on top of Pepe, sitting on his lap, his hands on the steering wheel, sticky with blood and brain matter. The radio was still on. Elena Burke's smoky, soft voice sang about loves of loves, blood of her soul, and sharing a breath with someone she cared for. Diego tried to keep his eyes open, tried to look through the blood and tears, and focus on the darkened streets of Havana—and making a path toward freedom.

CHAPTER THREE

Pete leaned back in his chair and felt the sugar-heavy, caffeine-loaded *cafecito* kick in. It'd been two days since their visit to Varela—and Pete was feeling anxious. He had been pestering Kathy to meet up and discuss the case, but she was mired in freelance writing for the *Times*.

Pete, on the other hand, had lots of free time. His other cases had dried up. His work as a private detective was rarely consistent. The money he scraped together during the busy spells was rarely enough to pay the rent and the other bills that came with adulthood.

Pete's office was a cramped, closet-like space in the back of the Book Bin. It was also free, a detail not lost on Pete. When things got tight, as they often did, Pete made a few extra bucks riding the register at the bookstore. Most of the time, that entailed just sitting around and looking at old books.

The International Café was a small restaurant down the street from the Book Bin. It was a tiny, home-style Cuban joint—big portions, no frills. The *ropa vieja* was flavorful, the staff was friendly, and the music took him back to the days he'd sit in his father's kitchen and watch him prepare a homemade meal of *vaca frita*, *arroz con pollo*, or *bistec empanizado*.

The slow week had allowed Pete to spend most of his days reading whatever he could find on Varela. The case had spawned a number of trashy, cash-grab "true crime" books after the verdict came down—but none of them did more than scratch the surface, taking the obvious route and portraying Varela as a philandering, druggie psychotic waiting for the right moment to go postal on his wife.

Maybe it was that simple, Pete thought as he closed the casefile he'd been reading and slipped it into his backpack, slung over his chair. He motioned to the waitress for his check.

Pete didn't pay any mind to the jingle of the door chimes. The International Café was always busy.

"Don't you have work to do?"

Pete looked up. An older man in a worn suit and tie stood before him. He was pushing sixty but looked fit, if a little tired.

"Don't you?" Pete said, smiling. The man sat down across from him and extended his hand. Pete shook it.

"Robert Harras," Pete said. "What the hell have you been up to?"

"Trying to enjoy my enforced retirement," Harras said. He looked around until he found a waitress and, with a nod, let her know he wanted a menu.

"I don't get out here enough," he said. "Might as well eat something. Though my doctor is gonna kill me if she finds out."

Robert Harras had been an FBI agent for twenty years. Harras and Pete had been on opposing sides of the same investigation a year ago—hunting down a serial killer named Julian Finch. Harras and his partner, Raul Aguilera, were running the official side of things while Pete ran his own, independent case. When Pete and Kathy discovered Harras's partner was actually working in tandem with the killer, their two lanes came crashing together—and ended with Finch and Aguilera dead and Harras severely wounded.

Pete and Harras had spent most of that investigation at odds—the grizzled agent trying to fend off the pesky, wannabe private detective and his reporter friend. Pete's relationship with Harras was not what one would consider low key.

Harras placed his elbows on the table and scratched at his gray beard. "We need to talk."

"Okay, let's talk."

"You're working for Varela, right?" Harras said.

"Is this when you warn me that I might be getting into something dangerous?" Pete said. "We've been through this before."

Harras smirked. "It's not like that," he said. "I'm working for him too. In fact, we're partners on this."

"What?"

"It's not what I wanted exactly either," he said. "But Varela and I go back. Our cases overlapped a lot years ago. We had to run traffic between the Bureau and Miami PD pretty often. When he heard his daughter had hired you two, he wanted someone with a … more seasoned touch on the team."

"You're kidding," Pete said.

"I'm not kidding," Harras said. "Look, I get this is your thing. You and Kathy are the point people on this. But Varela brought me on as a consultant to help the investigation. I have a lot I can contribute to this if you'll let me. I have contacts. I have years of experience. I may be retired, but I'm not completely out of the loop. I hear things."

Harras raised his hands in mock surrender. "You don't have to listen to anything I say here," he said. "But I had to find you and say it."

"Well, you found me," Pete said. "We just met with Varela and he didn't mention anything about this. And I'm not keen on going back to where we were last time—with you treating me like a pain in your ass while I end up solving your case for you."

Disappointment flickered across Harras's face.

"Fair enough," he said. "This case you're on—Varela. It's not as simple as he probably wants you to believe."

"I don't really know what he wants me to believe," Pete said. "Do you?"

"It's not just about what he did or didn't do," Harras said. "There are layers."

"Layers, huh?" Pete said.

Before Harras could respond, the waitress approached their table. She set down some utensils and a water in front of the retired detective. In fluent—if a bit stilted—Spanish, Harras ordered a side of black beans and rice and an avocado salad.

"That's pretty healthy," Pete said.

"Tell me about it," Harras said. He tapped his heart. "Gotta keep this thing going for as long as I can."

Harras looked around, checking to see who was seated nearby. Satisfied, he leaned in toward Pete.

"I knew one of the first cops to respond to the Varela scene—guy named Tino Vigil," he said. "And I know on good authority it was a mess."

"How so?" Pete said. "And where's this Vigil guy? Can I—we--talk to him?"

"Ate his gun a few years back," Harras said. "Sad case. He was part of a crew with Varela and his partner, Posada, and another kid, Graydon Smith—young guns of the Miami PD narcotics squad. Look at them now, huh? Smith was also one of the first officers to arrive at the Varela home. It was chaos.

"The scene wasn't just a mess as in blood everywhere—it was completely contaminated," Harras said. "Things were not the way they should be if what they said happened really did happen."

He took a long sip of water.

"From what Vigil told me, he had just made it to detective, so he wasn't the lead on the case. And he got there late. Guessing you've heard about the Ledesma lady?"

"The lady in the orange dress?"

"Yeah, her," he said. "Vigil was the cop who saw her first.

According to him, he reported it to his supervisor on the scene. They didn't do much."

"Why not?" Pete said. "I don't understand—why are you coming into this now? Were you investigating the case before?"

"Not officially, but I was poking around. I'm not like regular people. I don't have hobbies. I don't take vacations. I don't have a family. So when a big story breaks around here, I tend to get curious. And the Varela case made me very curious. Now, back then, Varela thought he had a handle on it. He didn't need my help. He had a hotshot young attorney and everything was going to be fine. Not so much, as you already know.

"So here I am, sitting around my condo, going through my old case notes—it gets the gears turning. Then I hear you and Kathy are working on this. Next thing I know, I'm getting a reluctant call from Varela's daughter, asking me to join the team. I figured it'd be better to touch base with you directly instead of both of you being blindsided the next time you talk to your boss. Our boss. I also figured you may want some historical perspective from an old law enforcement guy who has a few decades more experience than you in general, and at least a few years more hands-on knowledge of this case in particular."

"That's very kind of you," Pete said. He was trying to hold back his anger. He wasn't sure if he was more upset at not being told Harras was coming aboard or at the fact that, deep down, he agreed with the move. "So you talked to this Vigil guy before he offed himself? What happened?"

"I interviewed him a few times, informally," Harras said. "He seemed scared to report anything and had bigger problems to deal with. I took some notes down and filed them away until recently.

"One thing he did tell me was that the crime scene was a shitshow, like I told you. This guy, Varela, he was a gold-star kind of cop. Not a blemish on his record. The entire department was caught with their dicks in their hands. They came across like amateurs. Varela had a lot of friends. You've probably met a few already."

"Nope," Pete said.

"You've read the discovery files, right?" Harras asked.

Pete didn't respond. He was playing his cards close to the vest. But the truth was, he hadn't even gotten to the files yet. He felt amateurish, dueling with the older agent.

"Okay, I get it," Harras said. "I can't blame you. It's been months and I show up again, sniffing around your case. But you know me. Things are different than when we first dealt with each other. I'm retired. The only horse I have in this race is my own. Varela brought me into this to be me, not to be competition for you and your pal, Bentley. I don't have the energy to chase this down alone. But I can help you.

"I knew Vigil. I knew Varela, Posada, Smith—everyone. I worked my cases down here while they worked theirs. And I know you're getting into something more complicated than interviewing old witnesses. I'm not just crashing your party to make your life more difficult."

"I'll take your word for it. That's all I can do at this point," Pete said. "But yeah, let's talk then. Why'd Vigil eat his gun?"

"I'm not sure," Harras said, his voice lower. "I knew he was going through some stuff, but it was still a surprise. He'd seemed fine—well, fine enough—the last time I'd seen him. Few weeks before."

"Who should I have met with already?" Pete said.

The waitress brought Harras his food and he leaned back as she placed the plates in front of him.

Harras took a few quick bites of his salad. He used his fork like a spear, yanking the food into his mouth. He talked between bites of lettuce and avocado.

"*We* need to start with Posada," Harras said. "Like I told you, he's been buddies with Varela since they were rookies. They were partners for a long time, in narcotics. Varela was the golden boy and Posada was his sidekick. Not as golden, but not as corrupt as some of the cops on the force back then. The other amigo, Smith, is a guy you want to talk to as well. Posada's protégé, boot-licker."

"Weren't they all corrupt?" Pete blurted out.

"Everyone except your dad, right?"

Pete bristled at the comment, but understood where Harras was coming from. Though his father had spent decades as a cop and was seen by many as a shining example of the best the department could offer, Pete had experienced the corruption and dirty dealings of the Miami Police Department firsthand—even from his father's old partner.

"What else?" Pete said.

Harras took a big forkful of rice and beans. A bit of black bean sauce trickled down the side of his chin for a second before he caught it with his napkin.

"I'm done talking," Harras said. "Now we're going to enter the show-and-tell part of my presentation, partner."

"What do you mean?"

"Got anywhere you need to be today?"

"I've got plans in the evening," Pete said.

"This won't take long," Harras said. "Want to check out the crime scene?"

"What?" Pete said. "How would we get access?"

Harras pulled out a pair of silver keys from his jacket pocket and jingled them.

"Don't worry about that," he said. "Consider this your first day of class. Finish your *café* and let's go."

Harras had offered to drive, but Pete decided to follow in his own car. He needed some time to himself, to mull over what had just happened. He thought about calling Kathy, but decided to wait until he learned as much as he could from the older detective. He wasn't averse to working with the man, but while they'd ended up as allies during their last case together, it hadn't been an easy road. Harras was no-frills, old school, and results-oriented. He'd made it clear he wasn't interested in Pete's instinctual and sometimes impulse-driven method of detection. In a way, Harras reminded Pete of his father, minus a few layers of polish. If he could swallow his pride long enough and keep Kathy's temper in check, they might learn a few things from the guy.

Harras's black Escalade cruised down Bird Road, past the dilapidated Bird Bowl and a few Cuban chain groceries—Sedano's, Varadero—before making a left on 107th Avenue. After about ten minutes, Harras took a right on Sunset Drive. The houses they passed became bigger, newer, and cleaner. The further west they drove, the more cookie cutter the scenery became. Targets. Best Buys. Walgreens and Wal-Marts surrounded by TGI Fridays and Olive Gardens. Miami was a growing city—more like a hive of smaller, more distinct cities than one large metropolis—that didn't stop expanding. Even West Kendall, the area Pete now found himself driving through, wasn't the fringe anymore. No, that came further south, past Homestead and further west, where the Redlands kept growing, expanding and gentrifying too. The thing about Miami was, no matter how bad things got downtown or in the city's poorest or most concentrated areas, there'd always be people willing to move there—to enjoy the weather, the food, and the culture. Even if it meant a longer drive and less time spent in the actual "city." A tropical paradise spread over the bottom of the state.

They drove past 127th Avenue and Harras made a quick right onto 127th Place—a small, curving street that led them into a collection of identical brown and beige townhouses. Harras pulled into the third one, taking up half the driveway. Pete pulled in next to him.

The house seemed well kept. The lawn was mowed, the small garden near the walkway that led to the front door looked tended to. Pete doubted they'd learn anything from the crime scene—too much time had passed.

He followed Harras inside and a chill slid over him. The house felt still and quiet, the air dense, dank and mildewed, like they'd just entered a long-sealed mausoleum. There was no furniture inside. Aside from a few boxes near the far wall of what must have been the living room, the entire house seemed abandoned.

"Nobody home?" Pete said.

"It's been a hard sell," Harras said as he looked around. "There were a few tenants here who lasted a while. But no one's stuck around for more than a year or two."

"Why do you have the keys to this house?"

"This case," Harras said, pacing around the living room, "has, ah, bugged me for a while."

"How so?"

"It just doesn't add up," Harras said, turning toward the southern wall.

"But it's not an FBI case," Pete said.

"That's true," Harras said.

"So, you're not supposed to be working it, retired or not," Pete said.

"Also true," Harras said. "But now I am, so it all evens out."

"Funny how these things happen," Pete said, a touch of bite in his words.

"This is where the couch was," Harras said, ignoring Pete's jab. "Varela said he was sleeping here when the two male intruders broke into the house—average height, armed, and wearing black masks." He motioned to the door, as if signaling for them to come in. He then turned toward Pete. "He didn't wake up immediately—he said he heard a noise from the bedroom—his wife screaming out, 'Why? Why are you doing this to me? Gaspar!' That's when he got up."

"Why was he sleeping on the couch?"

Harras pointed at Pete and nodded. "Excellent question," he said. "But a question we've never gotten a good answer to—at least not from Varela. He claims he dozed off while reading a novel on the couch, and that his wife went to bed early. Plausible. But his reading glasses were in the bedroom, and the book was on his nightstand, also in the bedroom."

"Could he have forgotten?"

"You ever slept on the couch when you lived with a woman?" Harras asked.

"Once or twice," Pete said.

"I'm sure you'd remember why, right? So, while Carmen is screaming in the bedroom, and, according to this version, being stabbed to death, one of the intruders approaches the now-awake Varela and—" as he spoke, Harras turned his body around to face where the couch had been over a decade before "—swung something at him."

"Something?" Pete said.

"Varela's story varies," Harras said, moving closer to Pete. His face was flushed. "In his first comments to the police the night of the murder, he claimed it was a club. Later, it became a bat. Now, it could have been a large stick.

"Varela tried to get up—remember he'd just been hit in the back of the head," Harras said, stepping toward the hall, continuing his reenactment. "But before he could get very far, he said someone else—hard to see in the dark, but clearly a man and clearly strong—came down this hall and struck him down, hitting him across the face."

"With one blow?" Pete asked.

"A few, at least," Harras said. "He knocked him out. Or Varela said he did. By the time he woke up, the house was empty—some time had passed."

Harras walked a few paces away from the south wall and toward the door. He pointed to his feet.

"This is where Varela claims he saw Janette Ledesma—or someone who looked a lot like her—when the person walked in and turned on a light," Harras said. "She was wearing a bright orange dress. Varela claims he tried to get up after regaining consciousness. Ledesma, according to Varela, came in through the open door and ran to him. She looked over the scene, panicked, and ran out the way she came in without more than a frightened yelp. A few moments later, Vigil sees her outside of the Varela home. That was the only confirmed sighting. Other cops who were there first—like Graydon Smith—didn't see anything."

"I'd imagine it was dark," Pete said. "Since all this went down in the early morning."

"Probably," Harras said, not sounding convinced. "This area wasn't as developed then as it is today. But if I were to sleep here tonight and turn off all the lights, I'd be able to see pretty well."

"You have slept here, haven't you?"

Harras gave Pete a smile before he continued.

"After Ledesma ran off, Varela was able to get up and wander to his bedroom," Harras said, his words slowing down, like a car trying to avoid a dark shape in the street, unclear on what it was. "Where he found his murdered wife.

"She'd suffered multiple stab wounds," Harras said. "And by multiple, I don't mean one or two. I mean thirty or forty. She was covered in blood. Long slashes all over her chest and back. She put up a fight. It was not a clean kill."

Pete walked toward the room but stopped short of going inside. He let his eyes wander into the empty space and tried to imagine how the bedroom had looked a decade ago. What pictures did they have on their nightstands? What art hung on their walls?

"You don't buy his story," Pete said, almost as much to Harras as himself.

"I believe parts of it," Harras said. "I think there's a lot going on. I also think there might be things that even Varela doesn't know. But I'm pretty sure it didn't happen the way they explained it at the trial. Still, the crazed gang idea smells funny to me. But gang murders aren't a new twist in Miami. Look at *Los Enfermos*."

Harras was referring to one of the deadliest street gangs in Miami. a cabal of bloodthirsty knife-wielding killers, pro-Castro assassins, and drug dealers who had found a way to plague the city—to varying degrees of success—for years.

"What about them?" Pete said.

"I'm just saying that, conveniently, his story is vague enough that it can be pinned on anyone," Harras said. "And I know parts of it are pure bullshit. That's what bothers me."

"What parts do you believe?" Pete asked. Harras seemed somehow older, having aged years in the past few minutes they'd spent in the empty, musty house.

Harras reached the front door and turned to Pete before walking out.

"Let's save that talk for when the three of us get together," he said. "Got time for another stop?"

Pete hopped into Harras's car for the second trip, which took longer than he'd expected. They didn't talk much on the way. Harras blasted some Miles—*Bitches Brew*. By the time they got on Le Jeune Road and crossed the 836 Expressway, Pete had an idea of where they were heading. Once the Moorish architecture started to crop up, he knew for sure. Opa-Locka.

They turned on Ali Baba and Pete was struck more by the state of disrepair the neighborhood was in than by the style of architecture. The streets were decorated with abandoned cars and piles of garbage. Kids no older than fifteen stood sentry on every other intersection, corner boys already dipping their toes into a life of crime because they didn't see any other option.

Harras parked in front of a pale green house on Burlington Street, off Ali Baba. The house, like many of the others on the block, seemed abandoned. The paint looked worn and faded. Harras didn't move to get out of the car. He turned the volume down on the stereo and acknowledged Pete sitting next to him.

"This is where Janette Ledesma died."

Pete watched as a group of kids scurried past the house, tossing a ball back and forth as they ran.

"She was beaten severely by her boyfriend, a guy named Gilbert Fermin," Harras continued. "But that didn't kill her. At least not right away. Instead of going to the hospital, Ledesma came back here to her house and got high. Couldn't help herself, I guess. She fell down at some point—she'd gotten up from the couch, probably to get a glass of water. She fell and slammed her head against the dining room table. No one found her until a week later. This was four or five years ago."

"Jesus."

"At least that's what the police report says."

"What do you think happened?" Pete asked.

Harras grimaced as he looked out of his car's windshield. Pete guessed that the deaths weighed on him. Not just the ones they were looking into now, like Carmen Varela and Janette Ledesma, but in general. He'd seen too many crime scenes and too much blood.

Harras kept his eyes on the windshield.

Pete waited, expecting him to say more. But nothing came. The car had started to get hot—the air conditioning was off and the afternoon sun was burning through the vehicle. He swept a hand over his face.

"What do you think happened in there?" Pete repeated the question.

Harras closed his eyes for a second and let out an almost silent sigh. Pete wondered if the older man was straining for some kind of peace. A kind of serenity that had eluded both of them for years.

Pete felt like he could finally see him for what he was—a veteran agent who'd been retired before he felt ready, stretching to keep the rush coming, like an aging ballplayer desperate for one more chance to get on the field. An ex-agent looking to get a few more notches in his belt before things went fully dark.

"I think there's a third party here—there's someone who maybe isn't Varela, who isn't us, who doesn't want this resolved the right way," Harras continued. "Janette Ledesma was a druggie, an informant, and a liar. She was also a mother, had a job, and was someone's daughter. She was the wild card in this whole scenario, and I would put all my pension on the fact that someone wanted her off the board."

"Even with the case closed?"

"Nothing's ever fully closed," Harras said. "As long as there was room for a retrial, for any kind of revisiting of the case, she was in play."

Harras was quiet as the sounds of the neighborhood seeped into the car. Car horns, thumping hip-hop blaring from a house down the block.

Harras pulled the car out and started to move down the street. He didn't say anything else on the way back.

The sun was fading as Pete drove down Bird Road, heading home. He replayed Harras's description of the crime in his head. The older detective had spent a lot of time thinking about the case and had clearly looked through more evidence than Pete or Kathy had. They'd be able to catch up as soon as they could get their hands on the defense case file, the trial transcripts, and copies of all of Varela's appeals. Pete made a note to talk to Kathy about it. He'd texted her after he and Harras parted but hadn't gotten a response. Before anything else, Kathy, Harras, and he needed to spend some serious time together, laying ground rules for the investigation.

He turned north and after about twenty minutes in middling traffic, drove into the Villa Verde Apartments parking lot. The buildings that made up the complex were painted in a garish green and yellow, but aside from the color scheme, Pete liked his place. He rented a modest two-bedroom that housed his secondhand furniture, concert T-shirts, books, and records. He parked his car in his assigned space and walked up the three flights to his apartment. He made a beeline for the air conditioner controls on the wall near the entrance, turning down the temperature.

Pete yanked off his shirt and tossed it on the floor of his bedroom, missing the growing pile of dirty laundry. He closed the curtains to the sole window in the room and let himself plop on the bed. He was tired. The excursion with Harras had taken something out of him. Harras intimidated him, and with the detective working the case, Pete felt superfluous. He didn't like that.

Pete closed his eyes and thought of Maya. He was attracted to her. There was something about her, beyond the physical—something simmering beneath the pleasant exterior. A drive and persistence that Pete found appealing. She'd spent the majority of her adult life trying to exonerate her father, even though the courts and public opinion had already convicted him. She'd probably learned enough about Florida criminal law to become an attorney herself—and for what? Her father was still wasting away in prison, few believed him, and his options were dwindling. Pete wasn't sure he'd be able to do the same if he were in her shoes. He had to look into Maya's background. He filed the thought away for now. He still had a lot of catching up to do on the case first. A murder this old and with such history and publicity would require hours, maybe days, of research before they could conduct their first interview with confidence.

After a few minutes, he opened his eyes, yawned, and stood up. Pete changed from worn jeans and a short-sleeved button-down into shorts and a faded blue Springsteen T-shirt. It was getting late, but his appetite was nowhere to be found. He was restless, though. He needed to do something.

Pete walked into the living room and turned on the record player. He rifled through the box of albums under the tiny shelf where the console rested. He wanted something he didn't have to think about. Something he could let the needle hit and not worry about skipping tracks or the backstory of each song. Pete thought too much—about music, books, his life. After years of clouding his brain with alcohol, he was still getting used to the clarity and constant brain activity sobriety provided. He liked it—most of the time.

He pulled out the faded, off-white album sleeve. The cover to Neil Young's *Comes A Time* looked almost like a picture that had fallen out of one of his grandfather's old photo albums from Cuba— yellowed, sometimes gray snapshots of an earlier time. Pete pulled the vinyl out and placed it on the player. He dropped the needle with care and turned the volume up a smidge. He rarely played his music too loud. The opening, lazy strum of the title track came through the record player's not-so-great speakers, followed by Young's nasal, childlike vocals. The album reminded Pete of driving around the frigid north of New Jersey in the wee hours, leaving a sports arena after a long game, and rushing home to finish filing a story or feature, a dozen beers sloshing around in his head, the car stereo cranked up to the max, his windows down, and the wind hitting his face to keep him awake. He remembered the sadness he'd feel—turning the car off with a few tracks left to go—and then the creaking steps to their apartment, his halfhearted attempts to be quiet, and Emily's sigh as she rolled over in bed, annoyed at being woken up but not eager to get into an argument.

He should have known then that it was over. Before his father died and they had to uproot themselves and come back to Miami. Before he'd settled for a job as a copy editor at the *Miami Times*—a gig he had hated and tried to ignore as much as he could. Before he found himself trying to solve a missing persons case just because he was bored and lost, and had given up on having a life that meant anything.

His phone chimed on the kitchen counter.

Pete walked over and scanned the display. It was Jack.

"Hello," Pete said.

Jack had been sober for over a decade. For the last year or so, Jack had helped Pete navigate the challenges that come with quitting drinking, the ways to repair the damage he'd caused in the past, and how to handle himself in the present—and how to avoid the pitfalls that could lead to another drink and a deep dive into darkness Pete was not sure he'd survive.

Pete went to AA meetings. Jack was his sponsor, though they'd never had a formal conversation about it. They chatted regularly and went to meetings together. Pete found the simple tasks that helped keep the meetings going—the "service"—also helped him stay grounded and sober. By stacking chairs, making coffee, or talking to other alcoholics like him, Pete was able to focus on something selfless for a few minutes. It helped disentangle his life, which had been anything but simple in the years before he stumbled into his first meeting. It had been a life on the verge—of being broke, heartbroken, destroyed—like a boulder careening down the side of a steep mountain, with little hope of stopping. The anxiety, only dulled by drink, paralyzed him daily, leaving him in a state so frantic even the most trivial situations sent him into a panic. On most days, Pete was lucky if he could get himself out of bed and to work.

"Petey boy, how goes it?"

"Not bad," Pete said as he walked over to the record player and turned the volume down. "Working on a new case."

"Yeah? Good one?" Jack was a bit older than Pete. He reminded Pete of the youthful uncle he never had as a kid.

"Seems like it," Pete said. He pulled out a chair from his rickety dining set and sat down. "It's still early. Kathy hooked me up with it."

"Good, good," Jack said. "You gotta keep busy. You hitting the seven thirty on Miller?"

Pete hesitated. As much as he loved the program, his brain still hated the activity of it. Sometimes going to meetings felt like a chore, but, deep inside, he knew he needed it. Especially today, when he found himself tired and confused, his brain on overdrive. That was when his kind were most susceptible.

"Wasn't planning on it," Pete said. "Not gonna lie."

"That's a shame," Jack said. He wasn't the pushy type. But Pete knew when he didn't approve. "I'm heading over in a bit, if you want a lift."

Pete slid a finger over the dusty table and looked around his empty apartment. Over the past year, he'd made it his own—decorated, filled it with his things. But it was still just a space, and he was alone, with not enough to do.

"Yeah, I'll go," Pete said. "Meet you outside."

Jack's car reeked of cigarettes and air freshener. Even with the window down, the patchouli odor stung Pete's nostrils. The car—a beat-up copper-colored Volkswagen Golf that seemed to be a century old—creaked down Bird Road toward Pete's apartment. It was almost nine in the evening.

"That was a good one," Pete said, trying to strike up a conversation. Jack had been quiet on the way to the meeting and most of the way back.

"It's always good," he said, keeping his eyes on the road. His voice sounded distant. "Better than when we were drinking, right?"

"Right," Pete said.

Jack pulled into Pete's complex and left the engine running. He tapped his fingers on the steering wheel. Pete waited. Sometimes it took Jack a little bit to get to what he wanted to say.

"I'm worried about Martin," Jack said. His eyes gave Pete the once-over. Martin was another one of the guys Jack sponsored. Martin hadn't been sober very long and had relapsed a few times. He was having trouble sticking with the program.

"Yeah?"

"Yeah," Jack said. "He strings a few days together, then disappears, and when he comes back, I know he's been out there. He's not talking about it either. I know he's hanging around the wrong crowd. He's struggling."

Pete cleared his throat. He knew where this was heading. Pete wasn't a sponsor. He didn't feel like he was ready to mentor anyone about how to stay sober—he'd had enough trouble trying to keep his own head straight.

"Anyway," Jack said. "I was kind of hoping I'd see him tonight."

"Yeah, it'd be good to see him," Pete said. He reached for the door. Before he could open it, Jack put a hand on his shoulder.

"Everything good with you?"

"Yeah, for the most part," Pete said. "This new case is gonna take up a lot of my time. It's complicated."

"Don't let it affect what matters most," Jack said. He said it casually, but Pete got the message. Don't let work distract you from your top priority: staying sober.

"I won't," Pete said, stepping out of the car. He lingered by the open door. "I'll give Martin a call too. Maybe he needs to hear from different people. Get reminded a bit."

"That'd be good," Jack said.

"I'll catch you later," Pete said before closing the door. Jack waved as he backed his car out of the space and turned out of Pete's complex.

Pete felt his phone vibrating as he took the steps up to his apartment. Kathy.

"Yes, ma'am?" Pete said, his tone jovial. The high that came from going to a meeting—discussing his own struggle with fellow drunks for a short time and connecting with himself—was hard to top. It reminded him why he kept coming back.

The feeling disappeared a second after he heard Kathy's voice— weak, flat, and in shock. She was in trouble.

"Pete ... I, um, shit, I don't even know where to start," Kathy said. Pete could barely understand her. She sounded like she was calling from a tunnel.

"Hold on a second, what's going on?" Pete said. He had turned around and was heading to his car. "Where are you? Are you okay?"

"Fuck," she said, her voice low, raspy. "He just left. He said he was going to kill me. He had a gun pointed at my head and said I was going to die."

CHAPTER FOUR

"**H**e said to leave things alone … to stop poking around."

Kathy's story came out in a series of long, rambling sentences, as was her way when under duress or anxious. She had been clear with Pete from the moment she got in his car: *Do not call the cops*. She didn't want to file a report. All she wanted was to go somewhere safe and sleep.

Her voice wavered a bit as she spoke. She'd curled herself up on the passenger seat of Pete's car as they drove back to his apartment. She was staring out the window, her eyes unfocused and wide.

Kathy'd taken the afternoon off from her other freelance work and had driven downtown to the office of Calvin Whitelaw. Now retired, he still had an office where he did some consulting work—including trying to stomp out the remaining vestiges of Varela's appeals process. Whitelaw was a Miami legal legend—known as cutthroat, meticulous, hard-nosed, and his own biggest fan. He rarely lost, even when there was little to no evidence to work with. The

Varela case was a perfect example—no murder weapon, no motive, circumstantial evidence, and a few questionable character witnesses. Still, Whitelaw made it work.

She hadn't had an appointment. Standard Kathy.

"The meeting was a clusterfuck," Kathy said. "I waltzed into his office and sped by his ancient secretary. That was the easy part. Once I got in to see him, everything went to shit."

She fiddled with the strap of her seatbelt. Her breathing had calmed down a bit and her eyes seemed more focused.

"He was pissed off, of course," she said. "'Who the fuck do you think you are?' and, 'What the fuck' this, or, 'Why the fuck' that. Guess he wasn't used to being surprised."

Traffic was light on the way back home. It was a weeknight, and for a party town like Miami, the streets were quiet—especially the further west Pete drove. The Miami evening was lit by traffic lights and the neon signs that decorated every corner bodega, cookie-cutter restaurant, and dollar store they could see. Soon they were a few blocks from Pete's apartment.

"We talked about real stuff for maybe a minute," Kathy said. She straightened up in the seat as Pete pulled the car into his complex. "Then security showed up. I guess his secretary wasn't that slow, even if she did look like a mummy. The guard was nice enough, but he did the whole grabbing-my-elbow thing I hate, so once he did that I lost my shit."

Pete slid the car into his parking space and turned off the engine. He didn't move to open the door. He could tell Kathy wanted to keep talking.

"So I pulled away from the rent-a-cop and it freaked Whitelaw out," she said. "I mean, before, he was all in control and angry, but now he seemed to think I was nuts, which I figured could work in my favor.

"That's when he finally started talking, after I was being led away by this security guy," she said. "He told me to just leave things be, that the court had decided and Varela was guilty, and I should just try to find another case to make money off. He called me a two-bit Anne Rule. What a prick. Anne Rule is fucking amazing."

Pete could see Kathy's color returning with each word. Her anger was helping.

She let out a dismissive sigh. "The nerve of that guy, right?" she said, turning to Pete for the first time since they'd parked. "I've been a reporter for years—longer than I'd even want to count—and this guy thinks I'm some amateur trying to make a buck?

"Anyway, the conversation itself was a waste of time," she said. "I walked out of the office and told the guard to go fuck himself and that I was going to press charges for how he handled me. Bullshit, of course, but still.

"By now, it was late. I was alone in the garage, trying to remember where I'd parked. After a few minutes of wandering around, I find my car. Not even paying attention, of course. Just pulled out my keys and started to get the hell out of there. It was getting late. Somehow I'd been there for almost an hour, and I'd gotten there toward the end of the workday to begin with. So, it was dark. I didn't look around my car."

She started to stammer more. She was searching for the best way to explain what happened next. She swallowed.

"Then I felt something—something cold on the back of my head—and somehow I knew, I just knew it was a gun," she said. "Maybe I could feel the shape or I was just thinking the worst. At first I thought—for that split second before I heard his voice—it was the guard. You know, feeling emasculated and pissed off because I'd made his stupid day more annoying."

She trailed off. She didn't want to talk about this.

"Then what happened?" Pete said. He tried to be as gentle as possible.

"He, ah, he—well, it wasn't the guard," she said. "His voice was low, real growly and low, like a baritone singer who'd swallowed a lot of glass. Something out of a cartoon. He said to mind my fucking business and leave things alone. That I didn't know what I was getting into. Give back the money and leave things be …"

She opened the passenger side door without a word and stepped out into the night. Pete did the same and tried to catch up with her. By the time he did, Kathy had lit a cigarette and was looking out onto the quiet street.

"You okay?" Pete said.

"Relatively, yes," Kathy said. "I think you can understand, right? Let's visit that hovel of yours."

Once inside, Pete motioned for her to take a seat by the dining table. He went into the kitchen and returned with two cups of black coffee. Kathy took hers and nodded thanks.

"So, yeah, pretty fucking scary," Kathy said. "Even for tough-as-nails reporter Kathy Bentley, I guess. You'd think this would be old hat for me by now. Especially after all we've been through.

"At some point, the guy with the gun left," she said. "I'm not sure when. I tried to keep it together, even with the gun at my head, because fuck this guy. I don't think he expected that, which is lucky for me. But he was pretty on-message with his threats: Varela was guilty, we would be hurt if we tried to get him off, and I was a stupid bitch. He'd obviously practiced the speech before the gunplay. After a few minutes, he'd had enough of threatening to murder me, I guess, and he left. I didn't even bother to get a look at him or try to figure out who he was. I was just glad he was gone."

"What did you do then?" Pete said.

"Nothing," she said. "I was just sitting in my car, trying to breathe again, to calm down enough to drive out of there. The parking lot was pretty full—of cars, at least. I wasn't really paying attention. But then I heard a tapping on my window and I freaked. I yelled. It was crazy. I didn't know I could get that loud."

Pete inched his chair a bit closer.

"Who was it?" he said.

"It was Whitelaw," she said. "The absolute last person I expected to see. He seemed concerned—you know, in the weird, creepy way people with no emotions show concern. 'Are you alright, miss?'

46

Probably thought I was having a meltdown. Which I kind of was. I mean, I'd just had a gun pointed at me.

"So I told him what happened," she said. "Maybe not the best idea, but he actually showed he was a real human after all. He offered to call the cops and hung around until I was sure you were on your way. Not what I would have expected. I didn't get anything else out of him, but at least he showed a shred of humanity."

"Life is weird like that," Pete said.

"Fuckin' right it is," Kathy said, a dry laugh escaping her mouth.

"What did Whitelaw say then?" Pete asked. "Anything you could use?"

Kathy's eyebrows popped up.

"Anything *I* could use?" she said. "Having second thoughts?"

"Well, things have gotten a little more complicated," Pete said.

"Oh Christ," she said. "What now?"

"I ran into our old pal Robert Harras earlier," Pete said. "And he had some interesting info."

"Okay," she said. "Quit stringing me along and spill, bro."

"He's on the case," Pete said. "Varela pushed for Maya to hire him and help us."

"What? Like an equal partner?" Kathy asked. She'd stood up and started pacing. "That's not cool at all. I'll have to check our contract, but I am not giving that guy any of our money. They'd better be paying him on top—"

"Not an equal, I don't think," Pete said. "But definitely part of the team. The term he used was *consultant*. Someone to help us navigate the investigation process. He and Varela go back a ways."

"A babysitter," Kathy said. "Fucking great. Well, look, this is even more reason for you to excise your little teen demons and decide if you're doing this with me or not, because I am not pairing up with Harras alone."

"I'm in. I can't let you work this alone and get all the glory," Pete said. "Though I'm not sure what I think of Varela yet."

"Well, neither am I," Kathy said. "But that's not the point. We get to write a book about the case. We don't have to write it a certain way."

"Varela's paying us, though," he said. "It's hard not to feel like there's some kind of expectation there. Especially with all the access he's promised."

"I'm sure there is," she said. She'd taken her seat again, the Harras news a small distraction. "But that's their problem, not ours. I just need to know you're with me on this, though."

Pete rubbed his eyes. It was getting late. He was usually in bed close to eleven. He could feel his body winding down. But circumstances were different now. He had work to do.

"I'm with you," he said. "Let's worry about the rest."

"Whatever," Kathy said.

Pete's phone rang. He didn't recognize the number. Normally he'd ignore such a call, but he answered anyway.

"This is Pete."

"Yo, hey, man, it's Martin," the voice on the other end said. "Martin from the Miller Drive meeting on Wednesdays. Jack gave me your cell."

Martin. Jack's sponsee. The one Jack was worried about.

He raised a finger to Kathy and walked to his bedroom and closed the door. He ignored her annoyed look.

"Hey, Martin," Pete said. "How's it going?"

"Eh, not so good," he said. "I'm, uh, I'm just calling to keep my mind off things, you know? Trying to stay focused."

"I hear you," Pete said. He was pacing around his small bedroom, trying to keep his voice low enough to avoid Kathy's sensitive ears. She knew Pete was in the program, but he didn't feel the need to immerse her in the details of his recovery.

"I've been trying to keep it together, man," Martin said. "Been going to meetings, been reading the Big Book, you know, the whole nine yards. But one of my boys texted me last night and wanted to get together and, shit, I know what that means. I know what he wants to get together with, you know?"

"Yeah, I know," Pete said. "You have to protect yourself from that. Remember, people, places, and things. You have to change your habits."

"Man, I know all those sayings," Martin said. He sounded annoyed. "It's easy on paper, easy at a meeting, but damn, I need a release."

Pete let the conversation go quiet for a beat before responding. He knew what Martin was dealing with. Recovery was tough—even on a good day. He knew you had to remind yourself of the bad times or you'd be prone to fall back into them.

"That's the down side of being sober, man," Pete said. "You can't hide. When life gets tough, you have to face it. But that's good too. You push forward. You remember where you were the last time you picked up?"

"Barely, man, barely," Martin said. "Probably on the street, belly-up in an alley or getting my ass kicked out of a bar. I don't even know. Shit."

"Keep that fresh in your head," Pete said. "Because that's where you'll end up if you pick up again. You don't get a training period and you don't get to ease back into it. You start right where you left off."

Martin was quiet on the other end. Pete wondered if he'd hung up.

"You right, you right," Martin said. He cleared his throat. "It's tough, though, man. I don't do anything anymore. Just work, go to meetings, read. Shit is boring."

"It gets better," Pete said. He wasn't sure what else to say. "You have to keep at it. You know what they say—don't quit before the miracle happens."

Martin laughed for a moment.

"Yeah, man, I could use one, a miracle," he said. "I'll leave you alone, Pete. Thanks for talking to me. I needed that. Glad I'm not the only one with a brain working overtime."

"You got it," Pete said. "Let's get a coffee or something this week."

"Coffee it's gonna be, man," Martin said. "'Or something' got me in trouble for too long."

They laughed and Pete hung up. He looked at his phone for a moment before sliding it into his front pocket.

When he walked out into the living room, he found Kathy curled up on the chair, her knees close to her chest as she scrolled through her phone. She seemed much better than when he picked her up.

"How was your super-secret call there, buddy?" She didn't look up as she asked. "Because I was pretty bored out here while you were having phone sex in your room."

Pete ignored her and took his seat.

"What's next?" Pete said.

"We need to do is meet with Varela's attorney," Kathy said. "I called her when we got hired and let her know we'd like to talk. Her secretary is 'trying to fit us in,' as they say."

Pete leaned back in his chair. Kathy had gotten a second wind, but Pete didn't feel up for talking through the case until the wee hours.

His phone vibrated again. A text message. He looked at the display. Another unknown number.

"You're popular tonight," Kathy said.

Pete checked the message.

Hey Pete, it's Maya Varela. Sorry for the random text, but are you free for breakfast tomorrow?

Pete started typing a response.

"Are you even listening to me?" Kathy asked, her voice sounding like a long whine.

"Gimme a second, I just got a text from our client's daughter," Pete said.

"Oh, right," Kathy said. "She asked me for your number. What did she say?"

Pete: Sure, sounds good. When/where?
Maya: You pick the place. 10am too late? :)
Pete: La Carreta on Bird. See you at 10.

"She wants to have breakfast," Pete said, putting his phone away. "That's weird."

"You're blushing."

"No, I'm not," Pete said. "She probably wants to talk about the case."

"I'm sure that's it," Kathy said. She'd gotten up and plopped herself on the couch. "Can we do something fun now? Put on the TV. I need to turn my brain off for a little while. Surely there's a *Law & Order* marathon going on somewhere."

Pete followed her to the couch and sat on the opposite end. He grabbed the remote and flicked on the television. The screen came to life. It was late, and the local news was on. A young reporter named Hansel Vela appeared, reporting live from what looked like an abandoned field. The banner at the bottom was not subtle: *Vicious Murder in Peacock Park*. Pete turned up the volume.

"Authorities have yet to identity the body," Vela said, his slim, tan figure surrounded by the fluorescent camera light, the shadowy park creating an ominous backdrop. "But Channel 10 News can confirm the victim, a man in his mid-to-late thirties, was found stabbed to death right here in Coconut Grove's Peacock Park, his body left on the outskirts of this wooded area. A late-night jogger made the discovery and alerted the police. While the murder bears the familiar signature of *Los Enfermos*, a dangerous and violent street gang that has made a mark on the city over the last decade, Miami PD are refusing to call this a gang-related slaying. We'll have more info right here on 10 as this story develops. Back to you, Brad."

Pete pushed the power button on the remote and the screen went black.

"Too stabby a day for you?" Kathy asked before standing and stretching.

"Not in the mood for more depressing tales from the streets of our town," Pete said.

Kathy walked over to the dinner table and hooked her purse over her left shoulder. "What are you going to do now?"

"Nothing, I guess," Pete said. "Get ready for bed? I assume you need a ride back to your car."

"Eventually," she said, a sly smile forming on her face. "But I have an idea."

"That's always problematic."

"Let's go," she said as she walked toward Pete's front door. "You're driving."

"**H**obie Beach? Is this a joke?" Harras said as he slammed his car door and walked toward Pete and Kathy.

Hobie Beach *was* a joke—especially when compared to the pristine, postcard-ready shores of Miami Beach. A bay beach on the south side of the Rickenbacker Causeway, Hobie Beach was a destination for those who didn't have the patience to drive on to Key Biscayne, Virginia Key, or Crandon Park. The bay waters were calm and soothing, and, on a good day, Hobie could serve as a nice contrast to the crowded and trendier beach spots that were sprinkled across the Miami coast. Most nights, though, it was a place where teenagers went to feel each other up and drunks stopped to down a six-pack or two before heading home. Pete had managed to be a member of both groups at different times in his life, so he was no stranger to the bottle and cigarette butt littered sands of Hobie. It wasn't the cleanest, but it was mostly desolate in the late hours of the evening, making it a quiet and incognito meeting spot.

Pete and Kathy waited for Harras to reach them on the beach, a few feet from the water. Further down, Pete could see a few dark cars parked next to each other. In the closest one, he noticed two shadowy forms moving back and forth in the backseat. Young lust always found a way, he thought.

"Welcome to the offices of Bentley, Fernandez … and Harras, I hear?" Kathy said as she extended her hand to him.

"News travels fast," Harras said, shaking her hand. "But let's cut the polite stuff. It's late, I'm old, and we're at Hobie. This is not how I envisioned my evening, or our first formal meeting."

"Where's your sense of adventure?" Kathy said. "You're not *that* old. You look pretty spry for a retiree."

Harras sighed and looked at his watch. "Let's get on with it."

It was late enough that the humidity had lightened a bit. Paired with a nice beachside breeze, their encounter could almost be described as pleasant, had they been meeting under different circumstances.

"I wanted to meet up and lay down some ground rules," Kathy said. "I got the ball rolling on this and drafted Pete over here. You, on the other hand, were tacked on."

"I'm not trying to steal your thunder," Harras said, his voice strained. "So we can skip the posturing and cut to the actual work, if that's fine with everyone."

Kathy frowned. Harras had undercut her argument and Pete knew his friend was at a crossroads. Either she could press the conflict and ruin the case—and the financial potential it held—or she could swallow her pride for as long as this effort took. Pete knew logic eventually would overcome ego with her, after a brief skirmish.

"One thing has to happen ASAP," Kathy said, shifting her eyes from Pete to Harras and back to Pete. "We all need to be on the same page in terms of information. That means we need to see what you've seen," she pointed at Harras, "like, soon. While we wait for that to happen, we still have to push forward."

"Agreed," Harras said.

Kathy's eyebrows popped up, pleasantly surprised at Harras's quick assent.

"I'm already talking to Maya tomorrow," Pete said. "I don't envision it being the be-all, end-all interview, which is why I think I can take the first round myself. Then we can connect and figure out a plan for the second round."

"I'm not loving that," Harras said. "But in the spirit of team unity, I'll roll with it. Just be sure you do what you say—and no more. I don't want to meet up and find out you ran down the entire witness list while on a rogue trip."

Pete nodded.

"I'm hoping to get some time with Varela's original attorney," Kathy said. "I put in a call before we knew our team had been promoted to trio. I'll keep you posted on when that's supposed to go down."

"I'm flexible," Harras said.

"What about Maldonado?" Pete asked. "Maya's uncle? I'm curious to get his take on this. He testified against his own brother-in-law. Not unheard of, I guess, but it jumped out at me."

"Your instincts are good," Harras said. "I say go for it. I'll put together some notes on the murder itself—the kind of weapon used, crime scene, who went in, that kind of stuff."

"Cop crap," Kathy said.

"You know as well as anyone, that stuff's important. It'd also serve us well to sit down for a few hours and go over everything—files, old evidence, the works, but I'm hoping you knew that," Harras said. He cracked his knuckles. "Okay, we done here?"

"I move to adjourn the first official meeting of the Terrible Three," Kathy said, waving her hand ceremonially.

"Let's keep in contact," Pete said as he handed Harras his card. He returned the favor and turned away from Pete and Kathy. "So we all know the same info as it happens."

"Smart," Harras said as he reached his black Escalade and opened the driver side door.

Pete and Kathy started to walk toward Pete's car, a hot breeze slapping them as they made their way from the dirty beach to the worn-out parking lot, two weathered soldiers trudging toward their next battle.

Pete waved and they watched as the older man got into his car and backed out onto the causeway. Pete pulled his phone out of his pocket and scrolled through the notifications display, checking for any emails or news on the case. One alert—not an email or social media update, but a breaking news flash via the *Miami Times* app Pete kept on his phone, mostly for nostalgic reasons—grabbed his attention.

He looked at Kathy across the roof of his car as she tied her long hair into a ponytail. His eyes were wide.

"Holy shit."

"What?" she said.

"That murder in the Grove," Pete said. "The guy found stabbed to death in Peacock Park?"

"What about it?"

"It was Rick," Pete said. "Rick Blanco."

"Emily's Rick? As in her ex-husband?" Kathy asked, her face scrunching up in confusion. "What the hell?"

Emily Blanco, *née* Emily Sprague, and Pete had a history—to put it mildly. Years ago, Pete and Emily had shared a life—engaged, living together in New Jersey, and planning their future. That withered away after the sudden death of Pete's father, which led to a move back to Miami, and the marked increase in Pete's drinking. Since then, she'd married and seemed to have found the stability she lacked while with Pete. But just a year prior, Pete had found himself in her orbit again, letting her stay with him while she tried to divorce Rick after discovering he'd been unfaithful. The roomies situation had been a bad idea, and resulted in a brief but troublesome reunion for Pete and Emily—one that saw them together again romantically and also got her tangled with a deadly killer Pete was trying to apprehend. She'd survived, barely. They hadn't spoken since.

Pete scrolled through the short *Times* story—it had little info beyond naming Rick as the victim, describing him as a "Homestead businessman respected by the local community." Pete flicked his phone off and slid it back into his pocket.

"*What the hell* is right," Pete said.

They got into the car. Pete waited a second before starting the engine, letting his eyes wander over the expansive black water, fighting off the creeping feeling that this death wouldn't be the last he'd see in the coming days.

CHAPTER FIVE

"**W**hy are you doing this?"

Pete looked up from his plate of fried eggs, ham, and potatoes and met Maya Varela's stare. She'd barely touched her breakfast, which was quite the feat, considering they were at La Carreta, one of the best Cuban chain restaurants in Miami. They were near the front of the place, in a booth a few steps from the main register and dessert display. They sat across from each other, Pete's Sweat Records canvas bag taking up the spot next to him. They'd danced through ten minutes of small talk, two fireflies circling the same dwindling porch light, before Maya got down to business.

"Pondering a sip of coffee?" Pete said.

"No." She let a slight smile peek out. "Doing this. This case. Working for my father."

"Honestly? At first, it was because Kathy asked me. I was bored. I've been kind of bored for the last year or so. Sometimes in a good way—like, I don't have any major problems or concerns that aren't of my own creation. Sometimes in a bad way—like, I don't know what I'm doing with my life beyond peeping at guys cheating on their wives and taking photos."

"So you see this," she said, waving her hand around, "as a way back to the big time?"

"I'm not sure I'd describe my previous cases as 'the big time,' " Pete said. "I just thought it'd be more interesting than stakeouts and finding missing relatives or pets."

"I just need to know," Maya said. Her smile from a moment before had faded away. "Because I'm trusting you and Kathy with my father's life, really. His chances for freedom are close to zero. If we don't find anything—any evidence to give him another shot at trial—he's as good as dead."

"Tell me why he didn't do it."

"What?"

"I'll be blunt, at the risk of sounding like a moron," Pete said. "But I'm just kind of confused. Why would a good cop kill his wife? What was the motive?"

"There isn't any," Maya said. "He didn't do it."

"Who did it, then?"

"My father says he saw two people in the apartment before he was knocked out."

"You believe him?"

"Of course I do," she said, her face contorting.

"I have to ask you these questions," Pete said. "If you're going to pin these great hopes on Kathy and me, we have to know everything you know."

"Okay," she said. "Like what?"

"Walk me through it," Pete said, leaning back in his chair. "Tell me why he's innocent."

Maya hesitated. Her eyes scanned the table, as if looking for a sign, a cue that would prompt her to continue. Her mouth became a thin, short line.

"They were the perfect couple," Maya said. "Only I know that for sure, because I was there. I know it. I lived it. They were the perfect parents and they were very much in love. They were the best. He would never want to hurt her."

"That's nice, but it doesn't exactly close the door on his guilt. Did they ever fight?"

"You're not much for sentimentality, are you?" she asked, some bite in her voice. Her eyes had glassed over, no tears fell. Pete felt a pang of regret for pushing so hard. But he had to.

"I'm quite the sensitive guy, once you get to know me," Pete said, easing up. "And look, I'm sorry. I know these questions are not easy, but I can't imagine I'm the first person to get tough with you about the case."

"You're far from the first person to get tough with me," she said, her head tilting, as if trying to look at him from a better angle. Yep, she was annoyed. "I've been working my ass off for the past ten years to get my dad out of prison. You just got here. That's why we're meeting. To see if you really want to take this case, or if you're just riding the money train your friend Kathy gave you a ticket for. I need you both invested. I won't have anyone coasting."

Pete put his utensils down next to his plate. They made a clanking sound as they hit the table. He didn't meet her eyes. As good as the food was, he'd lost his appetite.

"Maybe I don't care what happens to your father," Pete said. "Or you, or anyone you care about. That's possible. But you hired Kathy, and she's a hell of a reporter—a great writer. She'll do your dad justice. I can't say it'll be the exact kind of justice he wants, but she'll write a fair, balanced book that will give readers the real story—as far as she can tell. You must have vetted her, right?"

Maya nodded.

"And Harras," Pete said.

"What about him?"

"That was a neat trick you and your dad pulled," Pete said. "Tacking him onto the team without even checking with us. Great way to build trust."

Maya sighed. The meeting was not going as she'd planned. Pete could relate.

"That wasn't my call," she said. "I'm sure Robert filled you in. My father wanted someone he knew and trusted working on this, even if just consulting. I know you and Kathy have a history with Harras—maybe a not-great one, but you know each other. So, yes, I vetted Harras and I vetted Kathy. Of course."

"Okay then," Pete said. "And she suggested me. Kathy and I aren't rookies. I'll admit, we've never worked on something this formal. But we've looked under rocks and made uncomfortable calls and put pieces together. I don't think I need to prove anything to you. I don't have to show that I'm committed. I am. Trust me on that. But you also have to let me do my job. And a big part of that job involves us trusting each other and your allowing me to ask you questions that might not make you feel all warm inside. If you have faith in us, we'll deliver."

Maya crossed her arms over her chest and sighed. "Fair enough," she said. "We'll do it your way. Go ahead. Ask me whatever you want."

Maya's story was organized—she'd told it before and she knew which notes to hit and when, like a veteran politician dishing out her favorite stump speech.

She had been close to her mom; they had sometimes been more like best friends than mother and child. She'd been a good kid, for the most part. She was studious and active at school, she played soccer and took dance classes. She had friends and sleepovers and pizza parties. Her mother taught her how to deal with teenage heartbreak and crushes. Her home was warm and she never wanted for anything. It felt like a mirage now, she admitted. Like an old movie you remembered fondly but couldn't really explain in detail. A memory fading into smoke over time.

She remembered the months leading up to the night of the murder. She'd been preparing for her senior year in high school at

Our Lady of Lourdes—a private school on 142nd Avenue. The three of them made up a fairly typical Cuban immigrant family: they were Catholic, middle class, living on her dad's cop salary while her mom stayed home. Pete wasn't surprised she ended up at Lourdes, though the tuition must have eaten into their finances. Maya hadn't been keen on it being an all-girls school, she said with a smirk, but she got used to it.

As she told her story, the temperature of their conversation cooled a bit. They got back to their food, falling into a rhythm of talking that he found comfortable and soothing. Pete allowed himself to push past the dark story that had brought them together and to appreciate Maya for a moment. The way her eyes would close slightly as she said something funny or how her tongue peeked out between her teeth as she smiled or how she'd push the long strands of brown hair away from her face as she spoke. Her subtle features and easy smile came together to form something uniquely beautiful, like a scenic photograph that lingered in your memory long after walking by. Pete was having a hard time paying attention to what she was saying. He had to drag himself back and focus on the conversation and the fact that this was a job, not a first date.

She laughed a bit while she reminisced—about her mom's terrible love for Billy Joel, how her dad whistled old Celia Cruz songs while driving, the kind of meals they had together as a family every night. Carmen Varela was not a perfect woman, on this Maya was clear. She was a worrier, she was obsessive about keeping a clean house, and she could be strict, especially when it came to curfews and Maya's hanging out with her friends. There were times Maya felt smothered, but that was normal. They argued, but what teenager didn't clash with her parents, much less her mother? As she got older, Maya had come to appreciate her mother's rules, discipline. Carmen Varela had instilled a fierce and independent spirit in her daughter—how to stand up for herself and not settle. Though they were sometimes at odds, Maya made clear her mother was always there for her. Whether it was for a bad high school breakup, a flunked test, or sports injury,

DANGEROUS ENDS

Carmen Varela was front and center for her daughter. Maya spoke of her mother with warmth in her voice, lingering over small details to savor the memories.

Despite some bumps, it sounded to Pete like Maya's childhood had been fairly normal—almost idyllic—until the murder. He couldn't say the same about his formative years. He longed for a way to erase the lonely childhood nights spent waiting for his single father to get home from his job as a Miami police detective, trying to figure out how a dead body got that way. The round robin of babysitters, after-school programs, and friends kept tabs on him while his father made a living. It wasn't until his father realized that his own son had veered toward petty crime himself that he took up the reins of Pete's life, shadowing his son like a stealthy predator, watching his every move until Pete was old enough to go away to college. Pete realized that Maya had had all that he'd ever wanted until it was violently yanked away—her mother dead and her father in jail for the killing.

Maya's memories of the night of her mother's murder were hazy. She had been at her friend Stephanie's house for a sleepover, partaking in bad movies, junk food, and gossip. She did recall the following morning—the visit from the police, letting her know her mother was dead. She remembered falling to her knees, feeling them slam into the ground as her eyes fluttered before she passed out. She remembered waking up minutes later, still on the floor, surrounded by Stephanie, her parents, and the two officers. That was when it became real. It couldn't be chalked up to a nightmare or a daydream gone haywire. Her mother was dead.

She believed her father's story right away—she never considered it possible that he could lie, much less murder her mother. The rest happened fast too—the arrest, the trial, Janette Ledesma, and then her uncle Juan Carlos disowning them after months of support. Maya's story ran parallel to most of what Pete had read on his own. As each word left Maya's mouth, she seemed to get more tired, more defeated, like a wind-up toy sputtering out. This was her—mostly unplanned—life story and life's work, and there was a good chance

61

it would end in abject failure. It was already entering its last lap, no matter the outcome.

Maya tapped her spoon on the side of her water glass. Pete looked up at her.

"You there?" she asked.

"Yeah, just thinking," Pete said.

"What about?"

"What's your theory?"

"Theory?" she said.

"What do you think happened?"

"Well," she said. "I believe what my father said. That's the truth."

"That two masked men barged into your house, beat your dad up, and killed your mom?" Pete said. "I get that. But that doesn't cover an important part of it all: Why?"

Pete rapped the fingers of his left hand on the table.

"Your father was not a controversial guy," Pete said. "He was a cop in good standing, had a nice house and family, and aside from the rumors and other garbage that seemed to percolate when the trial was revving up, lived pretty much under the radar."

"What's your point?"

"Why would someone go to the trouble of murdering his wife? It makes that angle, unfortunately, harder to believe," Pete said. "That's what I need to wrap my head around. I need to know what you think the motivation was. That will help us figure out where to start digging."

Maya glanced at her watch for a moment. She was stalling.

"The only theory that I think holds any weight," she said, her words coming out in a slow, thoughtful rhythm, like a lazy drumroll, "is that someone my father put away wanted to get revenge, so they went after my mother."

"Do you have any names?" Pete asked. "A list of people your father arrested that we can cross-reference? That would be helpful."

"Yes, yes, we should," Maya said, pulling out a pen from her bag and jotting something on a napkin. "I'll make sure you get that."

"Who else do I need to talk to? Who else can convince me your dad's not a killer?"

Maya looked away for a moment.

"Well, Orlando would be good," she said. "Orlando Posada worked with my father. They were best friends. He's like an uncle to me."

"Has he been helpful to the case?"

"He's basically the only person who's stuck with me since the beginning," she said. "He believes absolutely that my father is innocent."

"What's his story?"

"Well, he used to work with my dad, they were partners," she said. "He was a cop. Not anymore. He retired after he was shot on duty. He does security work, runs a pretty big firm. He helps me when he can. He's a good man. He's put a lot of money into this whole thing."

"Will he make time to talk to me?"

"I'm sure," she said. "I can ask him."

"What about your uncle?" Pete asked. "Juan Carlos Maldonado?"

Her face went blank for a second. "What about him?"

"Should we talk to him?"

"I'm not sure what you'd get from him, to be honest," she said with a dismissive scoff. "He betrayed us. Betrayed my dad. Made up lies on the stand to make sure he went to jail. He's a con artist."

"Always good to get the other side, no?"

"That's trite," Maya said, fiddling with her fork, not looking at Pete. "But yes, sure. I'm curious to hear what *Tío* Juan Carlos has to say."

Pete motioned to the waitress for the bill.

"All done?" Maya asked.

"Feels like it," Pete said. "I think I got what I needed—for now. I'll connect with Kathy and Harras and we'll keep you posted."

"So, you're in? Even after this breakfast?"

"Yup," Pete said. "I'm in. Even after this."

Maya responded with a soft smile.

"Good," she said. "I think you three will be a huge help. I'm glad you agreed to meet with me too. I wanted to get to know the detective who'll hopefully exonerate my father. Anything you need, let me know."

The waitress came by and placed the bill next to Pete. Maya began to reach for it.

"You can let me get this one," Pete said, pulling out his wallet. "I'm on the clock after we walk out the door."

"Fair enough," she said. "Maybe we could do this again."

Pete laughed as he slipped two twenties into the bill holder.

"Do what again? Ask you questions that'll make you angry and defensive?"

"Well, maybe not that part," she said, her eyebrows popping up. "But the rest wasn't terrible."

"*The Rest Wasn't Terrible—The Pete Fernandez Saga.* I could see that on the *Times* best-seller list."

"Don't sell yourself short," Maya said, grabbing her bag and sliding out of the booth. "Some guys don't even get to think about 'the rest.' "

Pete stood up. He wasn't sure how to respond. He could swear his client was flirting with him. He took a last sip of water and motioned toward the door.

She brushed past him as they exited the restaurant, and Pete got a whiff of her fancy perfume—he couldn't place it. She looked back at him after a few steps and smiled.

"You coming?"

The sun shone behind her, giving her an ethereal, angelic glow. For a second Pete felt like forgetting everything else and just spending a few hours sitting around laughing with someone. It'd been so long since that happened.

He stopped himself before his mind could wander back too far, a roll of film spinning off its spool, to things he'd screwed up or left unfinished. To people he no longer spoke to. He wanted to say something now, something meaningful that she might think back to years from now. But he knew those words weren't coming, and if they did, it'd be hours from now, long after they'd parted.

"Yeah," he said, moving toward her. "Just enjoying the view for a second."

After walking Maya to her car, Pete headed toward his own, on the north end of La Carreta's lot. Pete looked out past the strip mall to the streets that stretched from Westchester toward Kendall and beyond. The city was pulsing with life, horns honking, people chattering in Spanish and English, Pitbull blasting from one car as Taylor Swift boomed from another. Even out here in the suburbs, Miami was vibrant, as if propelled by the swamp-like heat. He let himself appreciate the landscape for a second before the May weather became truly unbearable.

As he approached his car, Pete heard a light, consistent tapping, which alternated with the more identifiable sound of footsteps behind him. Pete turned around and saw a man—past fifty, with salt-and-pepper hair, wearing dark, impenetrable sunglasses, gray jeans, and a black button-down shirt. He had a gold half heart on a chain around his neck. The man seemed surprised Pete had noticed him. He was only a few feet away and seemed unaffected by the heat. In fact, he looked downright cool. He was also blind. He held his white-tipped cane up a few inches from the ground.

"Can I help you?"

"Pete Fernandez?" the man said. His voice was gruff and low.

"Who're you?" Pete asked. He was tired of surprise run-ins.

"Orlando Posada," he said, stepping closer to Pete. "Sorry if I caught you by surprise. I usually don't do that."

Pete extended his hand, then pulled back, realizing his mistake.

"You did, but that's fine," Pete said. "I was going to look you up eventually. Just didn't expect you to find me first."

Posada straightened up before responding.

"Well, I'm a friend of the Varelas," he said. "Just wanted to let you know I can help if you need anything."

"I definitely plan on taking you up on that," Pete said. "And pardon me if this comes off as ungrateful or rude, but how did you know I was here?"

"Maya said she was meeting you here," Posada said. "My driver pointed you out, and I followed the sound of your steps. Sorry. I can tell that's a little odd. I know she just left, so I figured now would be a good time to chat."

"What about?" Pete asked. He was getting frustrated. "Were you hanging around, waiting for our meal to be over?"

"She asked me to come and hang out," Posada said, shrugging. He was smiling like a lawyer for the other side, waiting to close a deal. He looked around, as if trying to catch a glimpse of Pete. But Pete knew that wasn't possible. "Like I said, anything I can do to help. I'm not great at first impressions. But Maya and her father are very important to me."

Pete sized up the older man.

"That's good," Pete said. He knew he should wait, to talk to Kathy and Harras, to agree on a line of questioning, but the opportunity had presented itself. He had to take it. "Do you have time to chat now?"

"Sure," Posada said. "But let's find a place where I can get some food."

"You don't strike me as a hot dog guy," Pete said as he watched Posada weave a loaded chilidog into his mouth.

Arbetter Hot Dogs was a Miami institution. Everything from the fading exterior to the '50s-style sign and the burnt-out plastic tabletops screamed *old*. But the place wasn't looking to win any beauty contests. It was about the food, and their food was simple: mouth-watering and tasty hot dogs. From the outside, on the corner of Galloway and Bird, it looked like a building lost in time, a relic from a previous era that had managed to avoid remodeling or being absorbed by a chain. Pete knew the place well, as it was just a few blocks away from the house he grew up in.

"This is a rare treat," Posada said, dabbing at his mouth with a napkin, the rest of the dog placed gingerly on the paper plate in front of him. They'd arrived during a lull, before the lunch crowd mobbed the front counter and a free table was closer to fantasy than reality.

"So, you're the detective Maya brought in to save her father," Posada said.

"Along with a few other people," Pete said.

"Yes, yes, I worked with Robert Harras on a few cases back when I was on the force," Posada said. "And Kathy Bentley is well known, I mean, if you read the paper. Though, I guess you're no stranger to attention either. That serial killer business seemed pretty messy."

"That's one way to put it," Pete said.

"I'm sorry," Posada said, placing his hands on the table, palms up. "I don't mean to be glib. I imagine that was an excruciating time for you. I'm here to help Gaspar however I can. I'm doing my best to help Maya fund this last-ditch effort. So, I'm at your service."

"Well, I'll be honest," Pete said. "I wasn't planning on interviewing you today, or alone."

"That's fine, son," Posada said, shrugging. "We can do this another time."

"Well, no, I mean, as long as we can follow up later," Pete said.

"Of course, of course. Whatever you need."

Pete pulled out a small notebook from his back pocket and began flipping through the pages. He found a blank one and set it on the table as he clicked his pen.

"Tell me about Gaspar," Pete said. "What was he like to work with?"

"Well, I'm not sure where to start," Posada said. "We were partners. Close friends. Like family. He was my mentor. I owe him my career. He was very welcoming, from my first day on the force. Jesus, I must have eaten dinner at his house more often than in my own crummy apartment. I'm still baffled that we're here, in this place, talking about clearing his name."

"What about his wife? Did you know her well?" Pete said.

"Oh, yes, of course," Posada said. "We were all close. I felt like Gaspar was a brother and Carmen was my sister. I learned a lot from both of them."

"What was it like working in narcotics?" Pete said. "I'd imagine trying to stay clean back then wasn't easy."

"Stay clean?" Posada said, lifting his chin. "I guess so. There was a lot of corruption. There's still some now, from what my friends on the force tell me. But it was really up to you, as a person and a cop, to determine what kind of officer you wanted to be. Gaspar and I did our best to stay on the up-and-up."

"Did Gaspar ever strike you as someone with a temper?"

"Not particularly," Posada said. "And of course, I think he's innocent. But I also don't know what happens behind closed doors, within a marriage."

"Now you sound like you're on the fence."

"Not at all," Posada said, shaking his head. "I'm just being realistic. You're going to need something really good to get this opened up again. I'm not sure it exists. This case has been looked over exhaustively by greater minds than you or I, no offense."

"Still worth a try, I think," Pete said.

"Yes, definitely," Posada said, crumpling up his paper napkin and dropping it on his tray. "Narcotics was very corrupt, you're right. You must have heard a lot about being a cop back then from your father. I didn't know him well, but I knew he was one of the good ones."

Pete's head buzzed. He'd spent many hours at his father's desk in the Miami PD Homicide Division, finishing homework or just biding his time until it was time to go. He didn't pay much attention to faces or names back then—too caught up in his own teenage drama and concerns. He regretted that now.

"What do you remember about the night of Carmen's murder?" Pete said.

"I remember getting a frantic call," Posada said, his words coming out at a more thoughtful pace, as if slowed by time, "from Maya the next morning. Very early. She was shattered, totally heartbroken. I could only get the barest of facts from her. Eventually, I made my way to the house, then to Gaspar at the police station. It was pure madness. The press was chasing every angle, the police were bumping into each other at the scene, in the station, and the entire family was in shock. 'How could this happen?' That's what everyone was thinking and saying for weeks after. We're still saying it today."

"I know you worked narcotics mainly before your, um, accident," Pete said.

"Before I was blinded—you can say it," Posada said, a humorless smile spreading across his face. "It's my reality."

"Right, okay," Pete said. "So, I know you didn't work homicides, but I imagine you've had your fair share of suspect interrogations. Correct?"

"Yes, of course."

"You saw Varela fairly soon after he was taken into custody," Pete said, winding toward his question, like a predatory cat gauging how close he could get to his intended prey. "So it was all pretty fresh and raw for everyone."

"Yes, like I said, I saw him at the station. We spoke in person a few hours after he was brought in," Posada said.

"Right," Pete said. "So, if you can think back to that moment, the second you first saw him in the interrogation room—tired and worn out from a long night, his wife dead—what was your first thought? Not as his loyal friend, looking to protect someone who's like a brother, but as a cop."

"I thought he looked like a guilty man."

INTERLUDE THREE

Argentinian Embassy in Havana, Cuba
March 15, 1959

The office was empty except for the tiny cot by the window and Diego's stack of books and notepads piled neatly by the foldout bed. It was midday and the Argentinian embassy was bustling. Or so it sounded from inside the office that had served as Diego's home for a little over three weeks. Three weeks since he'd barreled through the front doors, his shirt soaked through with his friend's blood, his eyes wide with fear, and without a word to explain what had happened.

They'd ushered him in and calmed him down. He wasn't sure how he'd survived. Perhaps the thousands of *Padre Nuestro* prayers had something to do with it. He liked to think so.

Very little was decided about Diego's fate the night he arrived at the embassy. Or the next day. He begged them to protect his family, even though they weren't in Havana. Castro's reach was long. The embassy people nodded and took notes.

After a few days, he was given the freedom to wander the building. He felt like a ghost, floating around the massive building. He found it hard to focus. He thought of his family. He repeated his plea to the low-level diplomats assigned to keeping tabs on him. *Help them. Save them.* Had they survived? He weighed his options. He hadn't heard of Castro's rancor spreading to the families of his enemies, but it was still early. He wouldn't put anything past him or his viper-like sidekick, Che. They would do whatever it took to tighten their grasp on the island. On his home.

After a week, an older man, a high-ranking diplomat stationed in Havana, came to see Diego. His family was fine. They were staying with his wife's brother, Rolando, in Pinar del Rio, on the southwestern tip of the island. That was the good news. But Diego's sigh of relief only lasted for a second.

He had to leave. The diplomat made that clear. They were not going to make a habit of housing enemies of a government they were still trying to have relations with. Castro was putting pressure on them to turn Diego over, despite their denials that he was even in the embassy. There was a plane leaving for Miami in a week. Diego had to be on it.

Now, Diego sat on the small cot and bowed his head. He'd spent three weeks in exile, tucked away in his own country. Diego muttered a prayer to the *Virgen* and let a few tears stream down his face, now covered with stubble. The knock on the door was strong and brief.

"Come in," Diego said. He wiped his eyes and stood.

The diplomat was dressed in his usual attire—a tailored black suit and a colorful, almost garish tie. His green eyes were dulled by his glasses. He was clean-shaven and refined. He pulled out a nearby chair and sat across from Diego.

"You leave for Miami tomorrow," the man said. Not a question or a request.

"Yes, thank you," Diego said. "Thank you."

The diplomat walked into the office and to the window by the bed. He tugged at the blinds. Diego stepped back like a vampire—frightened by the light and the possibility that something deadly awaited him on the other side. The diplomat seemed unfazed. He let the sunlight filter into the room, shining on the dusty office and the mess Diego had managed to make in less than a month. He motioned for Diego to come closer.

He didn't see them at first, his vision blinded by the bright sun. He felt like a convict finally being paroled. The shapes—of cars, streetlights, and pedestrians—soon came into focus. Two, in particular, were very familiar.

His wife clutched at their son, Pedro. They both looked at the window. They knew Diego was there. Amparo didn't hold the gaze. She looked around every few moments to see if they'd been caught, if anyone had noticed the sobbing pair of people just standing outside an embassy for no apparent reason. Pedro's eyes didn't waver. The seven-year-old met his father's gaze. Diego moved closer to the window, pushing the diplomat aside. He rested his open hands on the glass. He opened his mouth, but felt the man's hand on his shoulder.

"Don't yell," he warned.

Amparo seemed to notice the diplomat. She whispered into Pedro's ear and their son raised his hand—a wave. Slow, pained. She mirrored his hand's movements with her own. Diego waved back, the seconds dragging as he watched them. They shared a long, slow motion goodbye. Diego tried to remember each detail of their faces—his wife's dimpled smile, his son's furrowed brow—everything. He had to remember everything.

The blinds closed. The diplomat grabbed his elbow and gently prodded Diego away from the window.

Diego fell to his knees. The tears came now. But not as singular, unique droplets of regret, but what felt like a tipped-over bucket of anguish, the hot tears meshing together as they rolled down his face. He felt his mouth open. He felt his throat burn as he screamed his wife's name. He heard the diplomat run to the door and yell for help.

CHAPTER SIX

Pete pulled out his notepad and looked at the address for Juan Carlos Maldonado that he'd scribbled down during his meal with Maya, before his run-in with Posada.

Maldonado had never publicly explained the reasons for his falling out with Varela. Instead, he went quiet, letting his testimony speak for itself. Pete was hopeful he could at least get a sense of what caused him to flip so fast.

Pete backed the car out of the space and turned right on Galloway Road, heading south. He yanked his iPhone out of his pocket and tapped a preset number. He waited for the other end to pick up.

"Want to go golfing?"

The Miccosukee Golf and Country Club was a sprawling, lush chunk of greenery embedded in Kendall suburbia. The club had once been a local hangout catering to nearby residents looking for a pool and clubhouse to bring their kids to in the summertime. In the intervening years, the Miccosukee Indian Tribe had purchased the land and—thanks to some savvy political maneuvering—managed to have it designated as part of the tribal lands. That meant that the space was now officially part of another country. It also meant local residents were up in arms about things like property values and who got to visit their quiet, unblemished neighborhood.

The main entrance to the country club was a quick turn-off from 147th Avenue, on Kendale Lakes Drive and across the street from a small neighborhood park. A long driveway led up to a manned security gate, where members swiped their cards for entry and nonmembers were politely turned away. Pete looked at Kathy before turning off on a side street and parking the car.

"We're going to have to get creative," Pete said.

"Also known as 'My name is Pete Fernandez and I never have a plan,' " Kathy said.

She got out of the car and looked toward the country club's driveway. Pete could tell she'd had a rough night. They'd been through a lot over the last few years. Kidnappings. Serial killers. Being wanted by the police. But that did little to prepare you for the next insane thing, like intermittent electro-shock treatments.

"You did confirm this dude is here, right?" Kathy asked. Her voice was hoarse. She leaned back into the car and grabbed her now watery jumbo iced coffee, slurping the drink as she closed the door.

"Define *confirm*," Pete said.

"I mean, did you set a meeting with him? Like we talked about with Harras?" Kathy said. "So you and I would be at the same place he was, ideally at the same time?"

"Not exactly," Pete said, getting out of the driver side and locking the car. "But not for lack of trying. He never got back to me."

"Okay, great," she said. "So what do we know?"

"Juan Carlos Maldonado—JC to his friends—is a member of this club. A pretty regular member," Pete said, referencing his notebook. "Odds are he's here, either taking his afternoon swim or a few rounds of golf. I'm guessing he paid his membership in advance, when he was flush, before his grocery app went under."

"Got it," Kathy said. "But it's safe to assume we can't just walk in and request an audience with the prince, right?"

Every place—restaurant, hotel, apartment building, movie theater, museum—has at least one back door. An employee entrance. A less glamorous, less visible way in. It was a lesson both Pete and Kathy learned in their early days as reporters. There was always another way in. In the case of the Miccosukee Golf and Country Club, it was a matter of finding it without being caught in the act.

The overpowering sense of being out of place hit Pete and Kathy right away. Even as they lurked on the perimeter of the club's massive front parking lot—which took up both sides of the driveway leading to the entrance—they could tell they were underdressed and wouldn't be able to blend in all that well: Pete with his T-shirt and worn-out jeans, Kathy with her massive sunglasses and wrinkled blue blouse and slacks. They wove through the parking lot, sticking close to the edge of the club as they cut across lanes of Porsches, Mercedes, and BMWs.

"Once we do get in here, assuming we do, without incident," Kathy said, her voice low, "what then?"

"We ask around and locate our friend JC," Pete said.

"You make it sound so easy."

They'd reached the midway point of the lot and had managed to go unnoticed when Pete crouched down and pointed toward the club's main building, past the security gate.

"There," he said.

"There what?" Kathy asked.

"See that guy?"

A man was walking around the edge of the main building, dressed in the all-white uniform of the catering staff, a box of some kind in his hands.

"Yes," Kathy said. "Do I get a prize?"

"Follow me," Pete said as he sped forward, picking up the pace. He glanced at the main entrance from time to time, making sure the stocky-looking guard remained at his post, oblivious to their movements.

They speed-walked through the remaining parking spaces and found themselves a few steps behind the kitchen employee, a short, tired-looking Hispanic man in his late forties. His uniform was mostly white in color, sporting a few food stains around the sleeves.

Before Pete could get any closer, the man had reached the end of the building and turned right. They waited a few moments, keeping vigilant in case anyone spotted them and wondered why two shabbily dressed adults were loitering in the club's parking lot.

They walked down the path behind the man and found the kitchen entrance.

Pete and Kathy made the short walk from the kitchen to a large, open space that gave members three options: a small gift shop sporting the usual golf and swimming gear, a largish restaurant that seemed to be half full, and an office that served as a doorway to the club's main attractions: the golf course, tennis courts, the gym, and the pool.

But the clock was ticking.

"I vote swimming pool," Kathy said.

Pete frowned.

"As much as I'd love to take a dip," he said, "I think our best shot is the golf course, at least to start. We can always backtrack to the pool and restaurant. Let's see if he's hitting the links first."

"You did not just say *hitting the links*," Kathy said.

The front desk employee manning the club's office directed them toward the golf course after a few awkward looks. Pete half expected him to ask for their IDs to cross-reference them with their member rolls, but the guy had been won over by Kathy's charm and a few well-placed smiles. Once past the office and outside, they looked out on the wide green expanse that was the club's main attraction. Even with the midday bustle, the club was quiet—and felt more like a retirement village than a hotbed of youthful activity. Pete didn't think he'd seen anyone under seventy since getting past the kitchen. A few yards away, under a long canopy, Pete saw a handful of men on the driving range, hitting golf balls out onto the practice green.

"That's him," Pete said, pointing at the man on the far left of the five men honing their golf swings.

"Are you sure?"

"Pretty sure," Pete said.

"I guess we'll have to make do with that," Kathy said as they began to walk toward the man they hoped was Juan Carlos Maldonado. They were intercepted by an older gentleman wearing one of the club's all-white uniforms. Maybe the internal alarm had been sounded and their time was up.

"Hello," the man said. "Are you interested in practice or playing the course?"

"We're actually meeting with a friend," Pete said, trying to step around the gaunt-looking man.

"Oh? Can I help you locate them?" he asked.

Pete shrugged.

"I think we can take it from here," Kathy said.

The older man gave them a smile, the kind a parent would give a petulant child.

"I'm so sorry, but I can't allow you to proceed," he said. "Unless you're a member or you're accompanied by a member—"

"He's right there," Kathy said, pointing at the figure Pete hoped was Juan Carlos Maldonado. "See him?"

Pete nodded. Kathy started toward Maldonado and Pete followed, sidestepping the host, who trailed behind them.

"Juan Carlos Maldonado?" Pete said.

The man turned around. He'd just finished another swing, which had sent a golf ball rocketing into the green void. He was in his mid-forties, tan, with sculpted stubble on his face and sunglasses over his eyes. He was handsome in a predictable Miami way. He raised the glasses to get a better look at Pete and Kathy.

"Who's asking?"

"I'm Pete Fernandez," Pete said, extending his hand. "And this is my partner, Kathy Bentley. We'd like to talk to you for a minute about your sister, if it isn't too much trouble."

He shook Pete's hand and looked at Kathy. The club employee was a few steps behind them, trying to get Maldonado's attention.

"Sir, I am so sorry. Folks, you need to leave. Now."

"It's fine," Maldonado said. "I'll take it from here, Frank."

Frank nodded and started to walk back to his post.

"You're the people who investigated the murders last year?" Maldonado said.

"That's us," Kathy said.

"So what do you want to know about my sister?" Maldonado asked. "What do you want to know so badly that you'd track me down to my country club and interrupt my day? Didn't you get the hint when I didn't return your calls?"

"We apologize for the pop-in," Pete said. "But we're looking into Carmen's murder and, while we did get the impression you weren't keen on talking to us, we felt it was worth the trip."

"Who are you working for?" Maldonado aked, his left eyebrow arching up. "I mean, you're pretty much catching me blind here."

"We're working for your brother-in-law," Pete said.

"He's not my family," Maldonado said, his voice sharp. "And you can leave now." He signaled to Frank.

Pete could feel Frank approaching. He didn't have much time to turn this conversation around.

"Before you kick us out," Pete said. "Take a minute and consider what I have to say. Gaspar is paying us, that's true. But we're not yes-men. We're not trying to get him out of prison. That's what he wants, sure, but that's not our goal."

"Oh yeah?" Maldonado said. "What's your goal, *compadre*?"

"The truth," Pete replied. "We want to figure out what really happened. And we want to write a book about it."

"The truth?" Maldonado said. "The truth is what the court said it was. He was guilty, now he's in jail, case closed. Put that in your fucking book."

"If that is the truth, based on what we discover, then that's what we'll write," Kathy said. "And believe me, people will read it. I've written two bestsellers already. This book will have an audience, and if, like you say, he's a murderer and killed your sister, then why not talk to us? Make sure the truth *is* what we discover."

Maldonado sighed. Kathy was hard to argue with when she got on a roll.

"Okay, fine. I can spare a few minutes," Maldonado said as he motioned toward a nearby table. "Have a seat. I don't think you can order food out here, but I'm sure Frank would be able to bring some drinks."

They took their seats.

"I'm fine, thanks," Pete said.

Kathy cleared her throat.

"As much as I'd love to mainline some more coffee, I don't think my body can handle it," she said.

Maldonado smiled—a polite, patient smile. Pete could see a slight resemblance between him and Maya. He was younger than Pete had expected, and seemed to be doing well in the finances department.

"So what do you want to know?" he prompted.

"We were just hoping to talk to you for a few minutes about Carmen," Kathy said, trying to smile. "And the terrible crime someone—"

"Gaspar Varela," Maldonado said.

"Pardon?"

"Varela. You said *someone*," Maldonado said. "It wasn't *someone*. It was Varela. Her husband. He killed her and tried to make up some crazy story. Bullshit. Total bullshit."

"That's what we're trying to prove—well, we're trying to figure out what happened, really, one way or the other," Kathy said. "Look—the evidence that made it to trial was slim. You know that. We want to revisit what's out there and discover what didn't get in front of a jury. We may end up with the same conclusion, but that's—"

Maldonado cut her off. His face was red. He took a deep breath and looked down at the table. "Okay, you want to talk? Let's talk."

It was as if no one had asked about his sister before. After the initial rough start, Maldonado dove into Carmen's story, no longer worried about who Kathy and Pete were beyond being two people who wanted to hear about his big sister. *Santa Carmen.* Saint Carmen. But he didn't want to just talk about the end—her end, the sad part. No, he wanted to cover everything. His first memories of her. Playing together. First communion. College graduation. First date. Her wedding day.

Pete was surprised at Maldonado's diplomacy. He avoided Varela until he had no choice but to mention him, trying his best to hover around the happy memories, as if by avoiding Varela he might be able to bring Carmen back. As the story went on, his telling got slower—he dwelled on more details—knowing he was getting close to the end.

He talked about Maya, his only niece, in an obtuse, distant way. Like a character who'd been written off the show of his life, not someone he was still concerned with.

As Maldonado steered the story closer to the murder, the telling became more disjointed and vague, like the first draft of a half-baked idea—plot and character intersecting but not in harmony, hinting at something more defined down the line.

"When did you realize it was him?" The words left Pete's mouth without a thought, filling an awkward silence.

Maldonado wrung his hands and looked up at the sky for a moment, as if to ask for guidance from some unknown higher power. The driving range had emptied by now, the golfers ready to tackle the real game.

"I believed him," Maldonado said. "At first. How could I not? He was my sister's husband. Who would do that to his own wife?"

He looked around, avoiding eye contact.

"He was so distraught," Maldonado said. "He was destroyed."

"But …?" Kathy said.

"The police came on strong in the beginning," Maldonado said. "'You always have to look at the spouse,' the cop said. They grilled Varela nonstop. I thought for sure they were going to pin it on him, evidence or no."

"But they backed off for a while," Pete said. "They weren't sure."

"Right," Maldonado said. "But that's when *I* became sure."

"What do you mean?"

"He lied to me," Maldonado said. "More than once."

Maldonado's nostrils flared as he looked out on the green, his eyes red and wet.

"He's a liar," Maldonado said, his voice cracking. "He gave me hope—said he was on the case."

"On the case?" Kathy said.

"He was going to find them," Maldonado said. "Find the crazy people he said killed my sister."

"But he didn't?" Pete said.

"Of course not. He told me he caught him," Maldonado said, his voice sounding almost comical in reaction to the absurdity of the story. "The one who did it."

"I thought he said he was attacked by two people," Kathy said.

"He did, but he said he found … the one …"

Maldonado stood up and walked a few paces away from the table. He jammed his hands into his pockets, his back to them.

"The one who …" he said, before letting out a quick, cough-like sound. "The one who finished her."

"How? Who was it?" Pete said.

"Gaspar was in Tampa—this was before they formally arrested him for murder. It took the cops a bit to get their ducks in a row and charge him," Maldonado said, turning to face them and walking back to his chair. He didn't sit down, instead hovering behind it. "Anyway, he was on a trip. Trying to get away from it all, he said. He was at a bar and he turned around and there the man was—sitting down a few seats away from Gaspar. One of the killers. The worst one."

"Why didn't he call the police?" Kathy asked.

"He followed him out of the bar," Maldonado said, "and down a few side streets. Then Gaspar confronted the guy. They fought and Gaspar said he lost control. He couldn't help himself, he told me."

"Lost control?" Pete said.

"He killed him," Maldonado said, his eyes wide. "He told me he murdered the man who helped kill my sister. He hid the body. He said I shouldn't worry anymore."

Maldonado laughed, a humorless, coarse sound.

"How could I not worry?" Maldonado said, waving his hand in a dismissive motion. "The second I started pressing—asking for details, trying to call the cops—he lost it. Got extremely upset. Finally, I did tell the police. They confronted him and he admitted he'd made it up."

"Why do that?" Kathy asked. "It makes no sense."

"He was annoyed," Maldonado said, his eyes half shut, each word a whisper, hiss-like. "He wanted me to leave him alone. Aside from Maya, I'm the only living member of the family, you see? Our parents are dead. It was just me, and I was a bother—pushing too much. He wanted to move on. Start a new life."

"That's what motivated you to testify?" Pete asked.

Maldonado gave Pete a curious look, as if he'd asked him the question in a foreign language.

"That's what got me thinking about it, yeah," Maldonado said. "It all made more sense. He was lying to me, lying to his daughter, to everyone. He's a murderer! He got what he deserved. If the judge had let me testify to that story, we wouldn't be having this conversation. What kind of a psycho says he murdered someone to calm someone else down?"

Pete leaned back in his seat. He wasn't sure what to think. Maldonado's hatred was fresh and strong, but Varela's move made little sense, especially if he was guilty. It seemed like the act of a desperate man. By all accounts Pete had read, Maldonado was a businessman with a spotty track record who, while not afraid of partaking in the pleasures that came with money, was also haunted by the death of his older sister. Pete felt that the man's anger was genuine, but was it Varela who Maldonado was angry with? If what he said was true, Pete could understand his resentment toward Varela. Pete could only imagine what it was like to have a sibling, much less to lose one so violently. And then to feel like the case had been closed, only to learn your own brother-in-law was just trying to get rid of you, like a pesky kid he didn't want to hang out with anymore? It was an act of unimaginable cruelty—enough to create a lifelong resentment, for sure. Then why wasn't Pete buying it?

Maldonado's cell phone rang, breaking the silence that had settled over the table like an early morning mist. Maldonado picked it up and took a few steps away from them. From what little Pete could hear—he was too far to make out the words—Maldonado seemed at first intrigued, then agitated, and finally resigned. The entire exchange took about two minutes.

Pete felt his own phone vibrate.

He was surprised by the name that popped up on the display— alerting him to a text message. But before he could mention it to Kathy, Maldonado returned.

"You have to leave," he said, his voice hollow. "Right now."

CHAPTER SEVEN

Pete hesitated before walking into the Thai restaurant. They'd been there before, years ago. He checked his watch and stepped in. The text message during the Maldonado interview had been a surprise, especially after almost a year of silence. He hadn't expected a response to his initial text message. But here he was, Pete thought, running at the first sign of anything.

She was sitting at the bar—having a cloudy martini. He tried to ignore the drink, but couldn't help it. She noticed him walking over and took a long sip—a last, almost desperate one, as if she'd be unable to have any more now that he'd arrived.

"Hey," Pete said.

"Hi," Emily said. Her bright blue eyes stood out against the grays and browns of the restaurant. He thought about leaning in for a hug, but decided against it.

"I guess this is weird," he said. *Lighten the mood. Make it less awkward.*

"I guess," she said. She took a short sip from her drink. "You reached out, I answered."

"I'm surprised," he said.

She let out a quick sigh and looked up at Pete. She seemed to already be tired of their exchange.

"Me too," she said. She straightened up on the barstool, brushing some invisible dust from her sleeve. She was dressed in an understated, dark pantsuit, her long blond hair pulled back in a tight bun. Her makeup was subtle and she seemed—well, fine. Pete felt a pang of disappointment at the thought that maybe she hadn't played out this meeting in her head as many times as he had on his way here. She'd put together a life that didn't involve him. A life he didn't know anything about anymore.

"Should we get a table? You hungry?"

"No," Emily said. "I don't want—I'm not hungry. Look, Pete, it's … good to see you. I guess. But we're not friends. We didn't stop talking because one of us moved or because I got a job that had me working weird hours. I never thought I'd see you again. But I guess I felt vulnerable and your text came at the right time, so I'm here."

Emily finished her drink and nodded at the bartender for another. Their eyes met for a moment and Pete was reminded of all the memories he'd allowed himself to wallow in, to try to savor, while darting through traffic to get to the restaurant. The past had a way of hypnotizing you, of whispering in your ear and spreading a feeling of tingling comfort over you like the warm buzz of a smoky, aged scotch. But memories weren't the truth, and Pete never sipped his scotch. Pete was a drunk, and things with Emily had ended—not in a clean way, but in fits and starts and too many raised voices and regrets.

"I heard about Rick," Pete said. "Like I said in my text, I'm sorry. It was a terrible thing to happen."

"That's nice of you to say," she said. "But you can't really mean it. We both know Rick was an asshole."

"What happened?"

"He was playing pool at that dive Duffy's on Red Road," Emily said. "That's the last time anyone saw him alive. He left with two guys around midnight."

Pete nodded and took the seat next to her at the bar.

"You've probably read the coverage on this already, but they found him stabbed to death near a park by Biscayne," Emily said. She didn't flinch. Her eyes didn't well up. "Some jogger saw it—his body."

"Jesus," Pete said. Not much of what she'd told him was new, but it didn't make the story any less depressing. Even a douchebag like Rick deserved a better finale, Pete thought.

"What are you going to do?"

She looked at her hands before responding.

"I'm glad you asked. Part of the reason I responded to you was because I need your help, and I hate that I even have to ask this of you," she said. Her shoulders sagged. "I need you to find out who did this."

"That's what the cops are for."

"Stories like this have a shelf life, even for cops," Emily said. "You know the drill about the first forty-eight. While it's in the headlines, the cops will do their due diligence, but after that, it drops off their radar. They told me as much when I talked to them. There's no strong evidence, and Rick wasn't exactly a stand-up citizen."

"Can I ask you a question without you getting upset?" Pete said.

"Go ahead."

"Why do you care?"

"What?"

"About Rick," Pete said. "About who killed him. About what happened. You weren't even living together. You've been living somewhere else for months. Your divorce must have been close to final when Rick got killed, right?"

"How do you know that?" Emily asked.

"I'm a detective," Pete said. "You don't think I did some research before I came to meet you? I was surprised you responded. It got me to thinking about why you did, after all this time."

"Rick was part of it," she said. "But I also wanted to see you and say goodbye."

"We've been through the 'I'm never talking to you again' routine before," Pete said. "I don't respond well to it."

"I'm leaving town," she said. "For good. Next week. All this place has brought me is pain and nightmares. You can imagine part of it. But I finally have the means to live life the way I want to, without having to be tied down to this hellhole."

Pete nodded.

"Rick had a lot of money, apparently," Emily said. "A lot of money I knew about, and a lot of money I had no idea about. Like, life-changing money. Never-have-to-work-again money."

"That's great for you, I guess," Pete said. "But I still don't get how this involves me or Rick's murder."

"Rick was in bed with some bad people, and I'm not talking about the whores he paid for," Emily said. "I mean criminals. I think that whole operation went south and that's why he was murdered. I could easily hit the road with his cash and not lose a wink of sleep, but I'm also worried. I mean, I had access to Rick's office and his computer. What if the people who killed him want to finish off anyone who might know what he knows? I need to find out who did this and why. That's where you come in."

"Slow down," Pete said. "Who was Rick working with?"

"I'm not sure yet," she said. She pursed her lips. "But I know what he was doing wasn't legal. I mean, you're right—we weren't talking much. The marriage was over. But that was part of the reason why, on top of the affairs and other bullshit that no one should tolerate, I knew he was doing something that wasn't legit. He was in over his head. That's what killed him."

Pete scooted off his barstool and stepped toward Emily. He noticed her tense up, as if expecting Pete to make an unwanted advance.

"I'm sorry your husband was killed," Pete said. "But I can't investigate Rick's murder. I can't be your fallback whenever Rick messes your life up. By the time any of Rick's cronies find out you looked into his stuff, you'll probably be long gone. You don't need my help."

Emily looked up and gave Pete a strained smile, followed by a sharp nod. "Goodbye, Pete."

He waited a moment, expecting her to say more. But instead, she turned toward her drink, like a reader flipping a page to the next chapter. He walked to the door, unable to shake the feeling that closure with Emily was just a shimmering mirage. No matter which direction he approached, it would continue to morph and pivot away, like a fast-moving shadow stretching toward the darkness.

CHAPTER EIGHT

Pete turned off South Bayshore Drive and parked down McFarland Road, near the street's dead-end finale on the fringe of Peacock Park. An evening wind hit Pete as he exited the car. Unlike the main drag of Coconut Grove, this stretch of park was quiet, far from the clubs and bars that littered CocoWalk, and made the Grove a destination for foodies and partiers on most nights. Pete appreciated the quiet for a moment before walking into the park, past a wide field and toward a cluster of trees near the small docks that littered the edge of this swath of Biscayne Bay. There was no police tape, but Pete knew this was the spot where Rick Blanco had died.

To anyone walking by, the area would seem undisturbed—a rare slice of Miami that was still tranquil and more nature preserve than metropolis, like a patch of grass growing through a crack on the sidewalk. Despite his stumbles and wrong turns, Pete wasn't just anyone—at least not anymore. He'd refined his reporter's eye for detail over time, tightening his focus and drowning out the background noise.

Pete noticed a cluster of fresh tire tracks on the street. A lot of people had gathered here to think about a man's death. Pete was the last one at the party. He wasn't going to find anything new—the scene was no longer a viable one, at least in terms of evidence, now corrupted by the reporters and peepers walking through the area after the police had moved on. But he wanted to get a sense of where Rick had been murdered.

Part of being a private detective was accepting that you didn't have all the answers. You might not get them even after a case is closed. With that knowledge came the acceptance that you had to trust your instinct to guide you down the right path. Pete had felt a shiver of unease as he left the restaurant and Emily. It'd led him here. The idea of Rick being murdered wasn't the kind of information that would, under normal circumstances, make him rush into action. But something about the news report had stuck in Pete's head, buzzing around like a dream forgotten too soon after waking up. The idea that Rick was dancing on the wrong side of the law didn't surprise him. What did come as a shock was that whatever he had been doing was enough to get him killed. Had *Los Enfermos* been responsible? The TV reporter seemed keen to make the connection, but Pete, forever a print guy at heart, took every bit of reportage he saw on TV with a significant grain of salt. Even if this jaunt turned out to be a waste of time, Pete had to find out for himself. Not for Emily. Not for anyone else.

"What were you up to?" Pete asked, his voice almost inaudible in the quiet night.

His eyes had adapted to the darkness, and he crouched down to look at a patch of ground bereft of grass and riddled with fading footprints and a crinkled McDonald's sandwich wrapper that stood guard on the fringe.

"You a cop?"

Pete stood up and turned around, his eyes locking in on the shadowy form in front of him, just a yard away. The man was hunched over a bit and seemed to be wearing multiple layers of clothing, despite the heat. His voice was more of a croak, and he was inching closer to Pete with an unhealthy and stilted gait.

"Who's asking?"

"This is my house," the man said. "Been too busy lately."

Pete didn't need to see the man to know he was homeless. The smell of cheap beer and dirt had already reached his nostrils.

"Sorry to disturb you, Mr. ...?" Pete said.

"Everton," the man said, stepping closer, into a crack of moonlight that had made its way through the trees. "Edward Everton."

Everton was stocky, his build augmented by the sweater and coats he'd piled on himself over time. His face was smeared with dirt and his shoes worn down and almost useless.

Pete extended his hand. "Nice to meet you," he said. "I can imagine this was a hectic corner of the park for a bit."

"Cops, reporters, rubberneckers," Everton said, ignoring Pete's gesture and counting each group off with a finger from his right hand. "They all been here too much. For what? Some drunk who probably deserved it?"

"You know how it is," Pete said. "Everyone loves a gruesome news story."

Everton nodded, his eyes expectant.

"Were you around when it happened?" Pete asked. "I'm not a cop, if that helps at all."

"I got nothing to say to you," he said. "Or to the cops. No benefit for me in talking. I just want to be left alone. I just want my home back."

Pete pulled out a twenty from his wallet and dangled it in front of Everton, who made his way toward Pete, snatching the bill away.

"I get you," Pete said. "I'd be pissed too. Maybe that'll help a bit, at least while you wait for people to stop invading your turf."

"Thank you kindly," he said.

Pete let the quiet unfurl for a bit. Ten seconds. Fifteen. Everton licked his lips, his hands fiddling with the twenty.

"I saw what I saw," he said. "But I ain't told the cops, and I ain't telling anyone, so if you're one of those busybodies running around spreading bullshit, I won't be here to repeat my story."

Pete nodded. "I'm not. This is between us."

The man cackled.

"Between us?" he said. "Who the hell are you?"

Pete extended his hand.

"Pete Fernandez. I'm a private detective."

Everton shook it. His palm felt chipped and coarse, like old wood.

"Good for you," he said.

"Sometimes," Pete said.

Everton let out a soggy cough, wiping his mouth with the sleeve of his long coat. Pete tried not to think about how grizzled and warm the man must feel in this weather, even with the minor dip in temperature.

"I saw it," he said. "I saw what happened. I wasn't right here, but I could see. I'd heard the car squeal in, so I know it was bad news. I got other hidey-holes. Other spots where I can set up shop while people stomp all over this here space. I'm not dumb. I know it's a good place. People want to be by the water."

"You saw them kill him?" Pete said. "Who was it?"

"I saw enough to know they'd done killed him," Everton said. "They pulled him down here and cut him up real good with their long knives. He was as good as dead when they dragged him here. But he was begging. Oh, he was begging for mercy."

"How many men were attacking him?" Pete asked.

"Just two," Everton said. "Couldn't see their faces in the dark, but both sounded young, talking that garbage Spanish to each other. Seemed normal in size, not too tall, not too short. One last slice and the man got all quiet, but they kept hacking away at him. I heard them laughing real hard all the way back to their car."

"Did you see what kind of car it was?"

"No way," Everton said, shaking his head. "No way in hell was I sticking around or getting seen. How that man screamed—I ain't ever heard before. Crying. Begging. He would've done anything. 'Sorry, I won't tell anyone.' 'Please, it was a mistake, I didn't want to see that.' Desperate. Like I said, I have me other places to go and hide. That's right what I did too. That's right what I'm going to do now. You just lucky. Lucky Pete Fernandez, private detective man."

Lucky was the last thing Pete felt as he watched Everton wander into the darkness of the park. He waited for the man to fade out of his vision before turning around and heading back toward his car.

Pete tensed when he saw the figure leaning on his car. He reached behind his back and felt the familiar shape of his gun. Nights like these tended to snowball and get worse, even in the tropics. He'd learned to be ready.

But as he got closer, the shape started to become more familiar. Now the question wasn't who was waiting for him, but why.

"You're getting better at this," Harras said as he pushed off Pete's car, taking a few steps toward him.

"Even *I* am bound to learn something after a while," Pete said.

"Though, I can't imagine you picked up on anything the cops missed," Harras said.

"You know better than most that's my specialty," Pete said.

"*Touché*," Harras said.

"Look—I need to talk to you," Harras said. "About Posada."

"Posada?"

"You interviewed him, right?" Harras said.

"Yeah, for a bit after my breakfast meeting with Maya," Pete said. He had an idea where this was going.

"What part of 'team' or 'partners' is eluding you?" Harras asked. "Did you at least tell Kathy you were crossing him off the list?"

"We talked for a few minutes over a hot dog," Pete said. "Not exactly a five-hour interrogation, so relax. We can all have tea together sometime soon."

Harras closed his eyes as he rubbed the bridge of his nose. "You don't get it."

"I get that you're annoyed, sure," Pete said. "But the opportunity presented itself and I took it. We have to be flexible."

"No, *you* get to be flexible," Harras said. "This is your way. You bump and trip and crash into things and eventually it comes together. But that's not how I operate, and I guarantee you it's not how Kathy operates. For Christ's sake, we're not in the Stone Age. Drop a text or call."

Pete shrugged. "Point taken. Can I get to my car now?"

Harras stepped to his left, motioning toward Pete's car like a limo driver welcoming a guest. "Don't let me stop you."

Pete walked around the car and opened the driver side door.

"One last thing before you jet off," Harras said.

Pete stopped himself from ducking into the car and waited.

"What did you learn back there? When you wandered off to stare at the trees and dirt by the bay?"

"It reaffirmed something," Pete said.

"What's that?"

"I hate coincidences."

Pete found Dave right where he'd expected to, sitting on a worn barstool in Churchill's Pub, a dingy old-school watering hole on the border of the nastiest part of Little Haiti and a wave of gentrification. Churchill's was a Miami epicenter to the punks and scenesters who were desperate for music with bite, jagged guitars and verve that didn't involve preprogrammed beats and Auto-Tune. Pete had seen many a band perform on the bar's stage when he was in college. The beer had been cheap, the music loud, and the energy high.

More recently, Churchill's had provided a bit of cloud cover for Pete. Wanted by the police and trying to pinpoint a serial killer's next move, Pete and Kathy had set up shop in a tiny shed near the bar's ragged patio, courtesy of Dave Mendoza, Pete's friend, boss, and pseudo-conscience. Dave was about Pete's age and had a fancy trust fund to live on. He also had connections on the wrong side of the street, which sometimes came in handy.

Pete hadn't known Dave long, but their friendship had cemented fast. They'd both grown up in the Miami suburbs, Pete with his widowed father and Dave with his real estate mogul parents. The Book Bin had been a rare property his parents couldn't flip for a profit. When their son, who'd collected a bit of a rap sheet over the years, asked to run the business, they were more than happy to write off the used bookstore and hand him the keys.

Churchill's main bar area featured a pool table, a collection of TV sets programmed to different soccer games, and the usual array of promotional posters for beers, bands, and vodka. The back room was what Pete remembered best—a ragged stage surrounded by seats you'd expect to find in a high school storage area. He felt at home here, the same nostalgic, comfortable feeling he'd feel wandering the halls of his old high school.

"This seat taken?" Pete asked as he slid onto the stool to Dave's left. They were the only customers. Pete remembered a time when he loved sitting in bars in the middle of the day. Even now, the novelty seemed romantic. But Pete knew the dark reality that came with those days and was in no hurry to revisit them.

"*Hola*," Dave said, lifting his bottle of Newcastle in salute. Pete could see he was a few rounds in. "What brings you here? Bored of the bookstore already?"

"It was quiet," Pete said. "Made an executive decision to close early. Book side and detective side. And I needed to talk to you."

Dave took a long pull and nodded. He didn't seem to care that Pete was playing hooky.

"Well, I'm here, so talk."

"I met up with Emily last night."

Dave groaned and took another long swig from the bottle. He spun his stool around, his head shaking in an elaborate show of disapproval. Dave never did anything subtly.

"Holy shit, man," Dave said. "Are we going down Bitch Avenue again?"

"Come on."

"No, you come on, dude," Dave said, stopping his chair to face

Pete, one hand on the bar, the other pointing a finger at Pete's face. "We've been over this before. She is bad news. Maybe not as a person, but bad news for you. She makes your head weird. She makes you do stupid shit, man."

"Rick is dead," Pete said.

"Who?"

"Emily's husband," Pete said. "You pulled a gun on him not long ago."

"Her ex? That guy?" Dave asked, a bemused look on his face. "That sucks, I guess. But so what?"

"So, she wants me to find out what happened to him," Pete said, turning to face the bar to avoid Dave's glare.

"Rick—the guy who cheated on her, who threatened to kick your ass too many times to count, and who struck me as a USDA-approved assclown—is dead?"

"Yes."

"Why would you want to find out who killed him?"

"Maybe I owe her something," Pete said, forming the words that had been hiding in the back of his head since last night, like an old photo stashed away, too painful to look at, but too important to destroy. "I mean, I've been fine not talking to her all this time. But I do feel guilty about what happened last year. She could have died because I was off somewhere hiding, a few bottles into a bender. Plus, she asked me to help …"

"Of course she did," Dave said. He finished his drink and motioned for another.

"I didn't say yes," Pete said. "I passed."

"Well, that's novel," Dave said, peeling the label off the empty Newcastle bottle. "Good on you. So you tell the woman no, but you're still sniffing around the dead guy. Am I getting warmer?"

"A little bit."

"Huh," Dave said, nodding to himself. "That's a little progress, I think. Maybe you'll evolve into a beautiful butterfly after all."

"Dare to dream."

"But you want your dear ol' pal Dave to give you the skinny on this guy anyway, right?" Dave said, his eyes looking Pete up and down. "Just for funsies, huh? Not for any kind of … investigation?"

Pete responded with a wry smile.

Dave was a rarity: a retired criminal who had no desire to step back into that life. He'd run drugs for years—cocaine, weed, pills, meth, the whole spectrum. He'd shot at people and been shot at. He knew the dealers and their distributors. He knew the gangs and what parts of town they staked a claim to. He'd also known when it was time to get out, cash in his chips, and run a used bookstore.

That life, in Dave's eyes, was over. He was a regular citizen now. Albeit one with a criminal record and a contacts list that was a who's who of Miami's most wanted. These days, he was content to enjoy his life and live off the money he'd saved. But retired or not, Dave still had some institutional knowledge Pete needed.

"Rick is low stakes," Dave said, his voice dropping to a whisper as the bartender slid another Newcastle in front of him. "Was low stakes. He was a dabbler. Nothing serious. He ran his real estate business but also did some stuff on the side. Low level. Some dealing. Some, uh, products—you know. He wasn't totally on the up-and-up. But I hadn't heard about him doing much lately. I know he cleaned cash for people."

"Cleaned cash?"

"Yeah, took dirty money, cooked the books—from drug dealers or other bad guys," Dave said. "And invested it in certain things so the numbers come out clean. Then, *voila*! The gangbangers can spend the money."

"The murder seemed gang related," Pete said. "He was stabbed to death. I found an eyewitness when I visited the scene—"

"The scene of the crime you're not really investigating."

"Right," Pete said. "And he said it was two guys with long knives, like machetes."

"Sounds like *Los Enfermos*," Dave said. "Or someone trying to pin it on them."

"Everyone keeps saying that," Pete said. "But what's their deal? Who are they?"

"*Los Enfermos* were started by Castro sympathizers in Miami," Dave said. "Militant thugs who were not part of the anti-Castrista majority of Cubans down here. They took down leaders of *el exilio* on orders from the Cuban government, and between high-profile stunts like that, built up a pretty impressive drug business, serving as the middle men to the cartels and other interested parties. You couldn't sell crack in Miami in the eighties without the permission of *Los Enfermos*. That still applies today."

"Wasn't that your scene for a while?" Pete asked.

"It was," Dave said. "I got permission."

"The knives thing throws me off," Pete said. "I mean, we live in a time where someone can walk into a club with a semi-automatic and kill a roomful of people. How does a gang of knife throwers survive?"

"Oh, they use guns and bombs and other stuff like everyone else—maybe better," Dave said. "But the machete kills are special. They're done that way for emphasis. To tell people, including other gangs, to back off. To let people know that this kill was important. Whoever got sliced up deserved it." He paused. "How hard was it to find Rick's body?"

"I don't think it was hard at all," Pete said. "They found him in Peacock Park. I mean, he wasn't faceup on the baseball diamond, but he wasn't chopped up and buried either."

"There you go," Dave said. "Rick must have really screwed up."

"Why would *Los Enfermos* do that to Rick, though, of all people?" Pete was thinking out loud. "What makes him special?"

"Find out where the money was going, who it was from, and you have your answer," Dave said.

"What do you mean?"

"The downside to cleaning cash is that you see two key bits of information. Where the money actually comes from—drug deal, robbery, murder for hire—and where it goes, pretending to be clean," Dave said. "If Rick was cleaning money for this gang, he must have been privy to a lot of shit. Probably more than the shit he was cleared to know. Knowing Rick, a smug asshole who always thought he was smarter than he really was, he probably slipped up."

"And someone caught him?"

"Rick pissed off the wrong people this time," Dave said. "And whoever did this to him wanted the world to know it got done."

The aging jukebox creaked to life, the discs scraping against machinery as the speakers unleashed the opening chords of the Clash's *London Calling* album. The bar was filling up with college kids, and high schoolers trying to act like college kids. Dave and Pete had moved to the other side of the bar, an adjoining room that faced a tiny stage. Had there been a band playing, they'd have been surrounded by sweaty, screaming punk kids. Since it was a weeknight, they still had an hour or two before things got too out of control.

"How's the other thing going?" Dave asked. He'd switched to bourbon. He still seemed all there, but there was a drag to his speech and his eyes seemed glazed over.

"What other thing?"

"Varela, the Varela case."

"It's going nowhere so far," Pete said. "I'm wondering why Kathy even needs my help. And Varela hired Harras to join us, which was a surprise."

"I'm sure Kathy loved that," Dave said.

"We were both caught off guard," Pete said. "But I think it'll be fine. We've talked to a few people, done some research, but nothing. Something doesn't fit right."

"What does your gut tell you?"

"I'm not sure."

Dave grunted and took another sip of his drink before looking at Pete. "What does that mean?"

"I mean, I'm still getting used to myself again," Pete said. "Not drinking … it clears your mind, for better or worse. I feel like I can see myself finally. But that's part of the problem. I can see myself and feel everything I was drowning out for years. It's really raw and weird, and I'm not sure if what I'm feeling is right or in tune with my brain. My instincts are off."

"Your instincts have always been good," Dave said. "Except now you're sober and not such a fuckup about it—your senses are clearer. So, again, what does your gut tell you?"

"I'm not sure Varela is innocent," Pete said. "But there's more going on. Either he had help, or someone was setting him up."

"Retrace your steps," Dave said. He poured the rest of his drink on the floor and set the glass on the table. Churchill's was that kind of bar. "Find that feeling again and follow it."

"That's very Zen of you."

Dave shrugged and stood up. He tossed two twenties on the bar and walked up to Pete, putting a hand on his shoulder. Pete could smell the beer and liquor on his breath. He tried not to enjoy it, but part of him did. This was as close as he could get—and it was probably too close for his own good.

"I gotta get home."

"You okay to drive?" Pete said. "I can drop you at the store."

Dave started to wave him off but Pete ignored him and stood up. He put his arm around his friend and led him to the exit.

A few years back, Miami International Airport could have been an honorary circle of hell: overcrowded, confusing, more flights delayed than on time, and a sense of gloom and defeat that felt thicker than the humidity outside. But after some much-needed remodeling, it almost felt like a modern airport.

Pete wasn't an expert. He hadn't flown much since moving back home to Miami from New Jersey. He didn't remember much about that flight, clouded by the news of his father's death and brined in a half dozen airplane bottles of vodka.

He felt awkward—standing by the JetBlue check-in area, looking around for a person he'd never met. His initial plan had involved conversation over *cafecitos* at one of the many Café Versailles mini-restaurants that were housed under the roof of MIA. But Pete wasn't about to buy an airline ticket just to get past security for a jolt of caffeine and an interview.

Pete felt a light tap on his shoulder and turned around, finding himself in front of a slim, thirtysomething JetBlue flight attendant with sharp features and long black hair. She looked at him expectantly and with a bit of hesitation.

"Are you Pete?"

"Yes," Pete said, extending his hand. "Pete Fernandez. Stephanie Solares?"

"That's me," she said, shaking his hand. "I'm surprised you came."

"Why's that?"

"I find that once you tell someone to meet you at MIA, you're probably going to get stood up," she said, a short laugh escaping her lips.

Pete smiled. People whirred past them, shooting dirty looks or exasperated eye rolls as they dragged their luggage around the only two people in the airport not scrambling to get to their departure gate.

"Coffee?" Stephanie asked.

"Totally."

They found a two-seater at Au Bon Pain, one of the few restaurants available to people before they had to take off their shoes and remove their laptops from their carry-on bags. Pete tried his best not to stare at Stephanie Solares. But he failed, mostly because she was stunning in a natural, almost effortless way. She didn't even seem to notice the smiles and glances from people as she walked by. Pete felt schlubby next to her, in his worn-out jeans and a polo shirt that might have been stylish in the late '90s.

But he wasn't here to swoon over an attractive woman, Pete reminded himself. He was here to talk to the friend Maya Varela had been staying with the night her mother was stabbed to death.

"Thanks again for meeting me," Pete said as he set down two medium black coffees on the small table. "I know you're probably busy."

"Busy is good. I like being a flight attendant, it keeps me entertained," she said, shaking a packet of sweetener and expertly pouring its contents into the beverage. "I fly a lot, obviously, but it isn't, uh, super-exhausting stuff like Europe or Asia. It's mostly the Caribbean and Mexico. Which is nice, because if I have time I can just stick around and hit the beach or see friends."

"That must be cool," Pete said.

"Yeah, totally," she said. "I can't wait to go to Cuba. That's my dream. I wanna see all the old cars and visit the house where my mom grew up."

Pete gave her a civil smile. He knew a political discussion would derail any chance of this interview being productive. The idea that Cuba, still under Communist rule and the thumb of a Castro, was now just another cool, hip destination for a second-generation Cuban like Stephanie Solares to add to her passport stamp collection irked Pete more than it should. He tried to let it slide.

"So, like I told you over the phone," Pete said, "I'm working for Maya Varela's dad. My partners and I are trying to re-investigate the murder of Maya's mother."

"Yeah, that's intense," she said. "Do you think he's not guilty?"

"I'm not sure," Pete said. "I'm just in the early stages. Trying to talk to key people and go from there."

"That must be cool."

"What?"

"Being a detective," she said, though her expression didn't match her words. She was being polite.

"It's a living," Pete said. He cleared his throat. "So, Maya slept over the night of the murder."

"Right, yeah," she said. "It was pretty normal for Maya to come over. We were best friends. We'd either go to my house or hers. Mine more often, I think. Maya liked our house more."

"Why's that?" Pete asked.

"Oh, it was nicer, I guess?" Stephanie said. "It was closer too. We both went to Lourdes and my house was super nearby, so we'd usually come back and watch TV or eat something, then her mom or dad would pick her up."

"Do you still talk?" Pete said.

"No, not in a while," Stephanie said. She hadn't touched her coffee. "We were like sisters in high school, but after, well, after everything, it kind of changed. We both moved. I went to UF and we stopped talking as much. I mean, I see her every once in a while. I saw her a few years ago at Bougainvillea's near Sunset Place, but we don't, like, hang out. Maybe I should call her."

"How did you feel when you found out what happened?" Pete asked.

"I was completely shocked," Stephanie said, opening her eyes, as if to prove to Pete her surprise at the time. "I loved Mrs. V. She was the best. It was scary to think someone would hurt her like that. So terrible. Everyone was crazy about it. It was like, I don't know, like we'd been infected."

"What do you mean?" Pete scooted his seat a bit closer, the din from the airport getting harder to ignore.

"That kind of thing didn't happen," Stephanie said. "At least not to us. To our families. It felt wrong. Like a monster coming to life or something you didn't think existed being real."

Pete let the sheltered comment pass.

"You said you spent a lot of time at the Varela home?"

"Yeah, I was there all the time," she said. "I was like their other daughter."

"Tell me about the night," Pete said. "The night of the murder."

Stephanie scrunched up her nose and looked away as if to collect her thoughts for a moment.

"It's funny, because I should remember more about it," she said, still not meeting Pete's look. "But I don't, because it was so, you know, normal for Maya to come over and spend the night. By the time we found out her mom was dead, that's what changed everything. The time before was just the usual."

"Were you surprised when Gaspar was arrested for the murder?"

Stephanie seemed to ponder the question for a moment, her lower lip sticking out slightly.

"I was, yeah, I was," she said. "He was such a dad, you know? Always around, fixing stuff around the house. He was a cop. He was just a good guy."

"Did you ever notice Maya's parents arguing?"

"No, not while I was around," she said. "But he worked late a lot, so I didn't always see them together. But they seemed happy. They were a tight little trio. Mr. V, Mrs. V, and Maya. Aside from the usual friction, they were okay."

"Friction?"

"Have you ever tried to raise a teenage girl?"

Pete chuckled. "I can't say I have," he said.

"That's what I mean," she said. "It was just the regular teenage stuff. Maya was independent, did her own thing. She'd act out. Stay out past her curfew, drink a little. Nothing crazy. I did the same stuff. We did it together most of the time."

"Did she get along with her parents?"

"Yeah, mostly," she said, a distant look clouding her eyes. "But we were both spoiled Lourdes girls. The big difference was I was from a rich family and Maya's was scraping by to pay for her tuition. So she probably resented that. It must suck to be spoiled and poor, right?"

Pete winced for a moment and then turned his attention to his watch. He had to go.

"Is there anything else you remember that you think might be helpful?" Pete asked.

"She loved her parents," Stephanie said. "Maya was so broken up when her mother was killed. Her father going to jail for it sent her to a really bad place. I can't imagine what she went through after we lost touch."

She could have called to find out anytime she wanted, Pete thought.

"Do you remember anything unusual about that night?"

"Not really," she said, looking around the empty restaurant. "It was the standard thing we always did—bad movies, bad food, talking about school and boys. The only thing that was different was the next morning. No one came to get her until the cops showed up, super-late."

Stephanie stood up, her coffee still untouched on the table.

"I have to get going," she said.

Pete followed suit and held the door for her as they walked out into the chaos of the airport.

"Thanks again; this was very helpful," Pete said as they shook hands. She gave him a cordial nod.

Stephanie turned around and took a few steps before wheeling back toward Pete.

"You know, there is one other thing," she said. "Something that happened a few weeks before—before Mrs. V was killed."

Pete motioned for her to continue. They moved back toward the restaurant, taking refuge from the swirling crowd.

"I'd cut class that day," Stephanie said. "I'm not sure why. I think I had an essay due and it wasn't ready so I needed to work on it or something. Anyway, I went to Maya's house, thinking that no one would be home and I could finish it there and wait until Maya came home and my parents picked me up. But the only way I could get in was through the back—they hardly ever locked the patio door, so all I had to do was cut through the backyard and come in. But the second I got into the yard, I heard screaming."

"Screaming?"

"Yeah, loud, frightened, and angry screaming," Stephanie said. "It was Mrs. V. I was scared. But I also felt like she might be in trouble, so I started running toward the house."

"What was she saying?" Pete asked. "What happened?"

"She was screaming into the phone, and crying," Stephanie said. "She was on the floor, rolling around like a kid. She kept yelling, 'How could you do this?' and, 'How could you do this to us? To our family?' "

Pete closed the heavy hardcover book and set it on the counter next to the register. He was sitting at the Book Bin's front desk, across from Martin Colón. It was a little past eight in the morning and they'd been chatting since seven. It had started out as a formal AA sponsor meeting—Pete walking Martin through some twelve-step work, sharing advice and experiences. It evolved into casual conversation and Pete asking questions about Martin's life and upbringing. It was the first time they'd met outside of the rooms, and Pete was trying to get a feel for how invested Martin was in the program—and in staying sober.

"I think we did a lot today," Pete said.

"Yeah, man, I appreciate this," Martin said. "You taking the time to show me all this stuff. It's overwhelming, you know?"

"All too well."

"Ha, yeah, I guess you're right—you haven't been dry all that long," Martin said. He was a jovial guy. Quick with a laugh and always smiling. Pete was optimistic for him. Hopeful this most recent attempt at getting clean was the one.

"You have stuff to do later today?"

"You mean, am I keeping busy?" Martin said.

"Yeah, you have to stay active," Pete said. "Keep doing stuff. Stay distracted. You don't want to be locked up at home thinking bad thoughts. Sounds silly, but it happens to all of us."

"I know it, man," Martin said. "I gotta get up and go to a meeting every day, or I lose a bit of, you know—what's it called, man?—momentum. I lose my momentum and start obsessing over stupid shit, like why that guy cut me off, or is this woman gonna call me, or, you know—dumb stuff. But it isn't stupid in my head."

"When you start to get like that, call me, call Jack, or hit a meeting. Or read from this book," Pete said, grabbing the book he'd set aside. It had a blue and yellow cover with *Alcoholics Anonymous* on the front.

"I am running low on funds, man. I can't buy this now."

"It's free. A gift. Pass it on to someone who needs it more when you're done, or when you can buy your own."

Pete's phone vibrated on the counter. Martin got up as Pete looked at the display. He didn't recognize the number. He pushed a button to send the call to voicemail.

"You gonna take that?"

"Nah, no worries," Pete said.

The phone started to ring again. Same number.

Martin started to walk toward the door, book in hand.

"Get your phone, don't sweat it," he said. "We'll pick up later this week. I've got some reading to do today."

Pete nodded. He waited until Martin was gone and then picked up the call.

"This is Pete."

"It's Juan Carlos." The voice on the other end of the line was quiet and rushed.

Maldonado.

"Oh, hey," Pete said, reaching for a pad and pen. "It's good to hear from you."

"I don't have a lot of time," he said. "I just wanted to tell you … that … to tell you that you need to stop what you're doing. You need to let things be."

"Stop? Why?"

"I don't have the time to explain it to you, buddy. But you're on a dangerous path, okay?" His words fell out in jumbles. "There's a lot of shit going on around the story—more than you can figure out on your own. More than I can tell you. Just leave it alone. For your own sake—and for your two friends."

"Okay, slow down—what's dangerous? Why should I leave it alone? What happened? You got a call when we were there—who was it?"

"No one—no, nothing happened," he said. "Just take a few steps back, okay? We can't talk anymore. Stop what you're doing, okay? Do not contact me again."

He hung up. Pete tried to call back a few times but each time someone picked up and ended the call. He saved the number in his contacts.

His phone rang again.

"Unreal," Pete said as he stuck his hand in his pocket. But it was Martin.

"Hey, man," Pete said.

"Hey, Pete, sorry to … sorry to call all of a sudden, man. I know we just hung out." Pete could hear the traffic sounds of the city in the background—Martin was driving somewhere. "But I had to talk to someone. It keeps happening. One of my boys just rang me up again to catch up with them and I know what that means, you know?"

"Hey, don't sweat it. You did the right thing. What did they want?"

"The usual," Martin said. "Go to a club, drink some beer, smoke a little weed. But I can't do that. I'm heading home."

"Good," Pete said. "Take it easy today. Do they know you're going to meetings?"

"Yeah, yeah, they don't know I'm seriously sober, not drinking. They just think I'm on a break or whatever," Martin said. "I used to roll with them a lot—shoot some pool, watch the game. They just wanted to see what I been up to. Haven't seen either of them for a while. They're not bad guys. I mean, some of them hang with people who do some shit. But that's the street, you know? The bad guys are everywhere. Shit."

"Well, it's good of them to check in," Pete said. "Maybe they're trying to understand where you're coming from. That's part of the process for some people."

"Yeah, I guess. They might want to find a meeting too," Martin said. "Those guys can pound, you know? But I just don't think I should be hanging with them anytime soon."

"Well, sometimes we lose friends when we decide not to drink. It's okay. If they—"

The store's front door chime interrupted Pete, and he turned to see Maya enter. She gave Pete a slow smile as she slid her purse down from her shoulder to her hand. She strolled over to the counter, as if she'd visited Pete at the store before.

"Martin, look, sorry, man, lemme call you back."

Pete heard Martin's response and clicked off the call. He looked up at Maya. She seemed relaxed and happy. She was wearing black jeans and a blue blouse. It was too hot outside for much else.

"Hello," she said. "I was expecting a fancy pants detective agency."

"Sorry, we're not open yet," Pete said, trying to keep a straight face. He watched her squirm a bit before cracking a smile.

"You jerk," she said with a laugh. "I didn't mean to interrupt. I was just in the area and figured I'd swing by and…"

"And?" Pete said.

"And see if you had time to grab a cup of coffee?"

INTERLUDE FOUR

Diego closed the studio doors and pulled out his key ring, heavy with similarly shaped keys for almost every office in the building. He found the right one and locked the door. He had a system. Like everything else in his life, he'd organized the keys so he would never struggle to find the right one. Even now, on a night when he should be sitting down to dinner with his wife, he knew where everything was.

Diego's ears still tingled from the show. It was a luxury he allowed himself. He knew it wasn't the highest-rated radio program on the station—his station—WHBA, Radio Havana. There were other, more popular shows. Other, bigger stations. But Diego was proud of his business. Proud of the signal he'd built in the years he'd spent here in his adopted country.

The show had been fairly standard. Diego—not Diego Fernandez, but Diego Angel now, clean-shaven and with shorter, grayer hair— had railed at Castro. The dictator's decision to name himself *presidente* after almost two decades of rule was laughable, Diego said. Another sign that Cuba was an enemy state and should be dealt with directly by the United States. The callers had been supportive. They'd cheered him on. Saluted the many hats he wore in exile. Businessman. *Anti-Castrista*. Father. Husband. Few people, only his closest friends, knew there were more ways to describe him. Batista man. Assistant to the Attorney General of Cuba. Fernandez.

Diego's son, Pedro, had rejected the surname Angel—because of what it stood for: a smokescreen his father had to put up to protect himself from the shadows he refused to explain, like a con artist moving pieces around to distract an oblivious sap. Pedro loved Miami. He loved the freedom they had. But he detested their adopted name. Cowardly, he'd called the idea once. That had been met by a swift smack across the face—one of the few times Diego had ever raised a hand to strike his child. Pedro understood. Perhaps he felt he deserved it. That was years ago, shortly after they'd been reunited in Miami. Pedro was a man now, with his own wife and their own home. He was Pedro Fernandez, a uniformed police officer protecting his adopted country.

The lights in the office hallway flickered for a second and went out, sending the building into darkness. Diego pocketed his keys and felt his way down the hall. He knew the offices well enough to navigate in the dark. The station was located on the northern fringe of Miami-Dade County, in an area that sported the illusory name of Miami Gardens. The neighborhood was not nearly as pleasant as it sounded. He'd have to call the super. He didn't want anyone getting hurt. He knew the offices were empty, though, because he'd given everyone the night off. It was *nochebuena*, after all. The night before Christmas. A holiday that should be spent with family.

He made his way down the two flights of stairs to the front doors. The light from outside made his journey a little clearer. His car was a short walk away.

Diego stopped short when he saw the silhouette of a man inside, in front of the double doors. The man was backlit, and Diego couldn't make out his features. He remembered locking the doors when he'd come in, alone, a few hours before. He didn't need a producer—especially for a show he knew few would even be listening to.

Diego was a few steps from the bottom of the stairwell.

"Who's there?" he called out.

The shape didn't move.

"This is private property," Diego said, his voice calm. He wasn't scared. Not yet. He knew this area wasn't the best, but the rent had been cheap and they'd lucked into a building with most of the equipment the fledgling station would need. Diego had to cut costs wherever possible to even hope to compete with more established—and well-funded—competitors like WQBA and Radio Mambi. While the station was home to Miami's top-rated radio show, hosted by local hero Madelyn Suarez, WHBA was still a distant third after five years in existence.

Diego took the final two steps and walked toward the doors. The man raised a hand. He was sporting a black mask over his face. Diego stopped.

"What do you want?" Diego asked, his hands up, showing he wasn't armed. "Do you need money? I can give you a twenty. Something to keep you going. I know it's a holiday—"

"Shut up, *viejo*," the man said. He sounded young, Diego thought. Around Pedro's age. He was calm. He wasn't yelling. "Stay where you are."

Diego saw a flash of metal. The man had a knife. A big one. Either this man intended to rob him—maybe he happened to see a light on and needed the cash—or he'd come here to do something worse. In which case, no offers of money would be enough to save Diego's life.

"*Oye, pero que tu te crees?*" Diego said. *What are you thinking?*

Soon, the man was next to Diego. He moved haltingly, but handled the knife with confidence. The man grabbed Diego's collar and pulled him close to his face.

"*Felicidades*, Fernandez," the man said. Diego felt the blade jam into his midsection, the sharp metal explode into him—pushing him down as the man pulled the weapon back and out of Diego, whose back slammed onto the stairs. Diego let out a frightened, gurgled scream—pain, fear, and surprise melding together to form an animal-like cry—and let his hands slide over his stomach, his body already slick with blood. He heard the man leave through the front door, the lock clicking shut behind him.

CHAPTER NINE

The attorney's office waiting room was bathed in blinding fluorescent light and smelled like a handful of air fresheners had just exploded. Pete tried not to sneeze as he took his seat next to Harras and Kathy, the three of them facing a distracted receptionist. Kathy flipped through a two-year-old copy of *Glamour* while Harras sipped a large black coffee and Pete rubbed his temples.

"I need caffeine," Pete said. "Especially before this."

"Well, that is something you should have resolved before we told them we were here," Kathy said, eyes focused on the magazine. It looked like a story about some starlet's struggles to get her basketball player husband into rehab.

Harras cleared his throat. "Maybe we can use this time to go over what we know," he said.

"Yes, excellent idea," Kathy said. Pete didn't like the look in her eyes as she glanced at Pete. "Anything you'd like to offer up to the group, Pete?"

"I tracked down Stephanie Solares," Pete said. "We chatted for a bit."

Harras clenched his teeth and let out a long sigh.

"And here I was hoping you'd decided to loop us in more," he said.

"*Mea culpa* on that one," Pete said, letting out a long sigh of resignation. "I'd reached out to her before we chatted and it came together after, but I should have let you both know. I'm trying to keep the going rogue to a minimum, I swear."

"How about keeping it to zero?" Kathy said. "Maybe try that. What did she say? Anything?"

"It was all pretty bland," Pete said. "The one thing that stood out to me was something she overheard while at the Varela house—she'd overheard Carmen screaming at someone on the phone a few weeks before she was killed."

"Guessing Solares had no idea who Carmen was talking to," Harras said, his interest piqued.

"Right," Pete said.

"I scream into the phone at least twice a day, so this means nothing," Kathy said. "At least without any more info."

"Do we know what we want to ask this lawyer?" Harras said, his tone sharp. "I get that you two like going on instinct, but I'm here to earn a paycheck too, and that involves some level of pre-gaming."

"Ms. Cruz will see you now," the receptionist said, interrupting Pete's answer, her tone subdued. She didn't bother to look up from her computer.

Kathy dropped the magazine, switching off whatever interest she had in the lives of the rich and vapid. The assistant led them past the reception desk and through another door. They turned into a long hallway.

"How'd you get on her calendar?" Pete asked.

"Barely. She says we have ten minutes. I also didn't mention you."

"Can't wait."

"Why wouldn't you mention him?" Harras said.

"You'll see," Kathy said, giving Pete a muted grin.

"Jesus Christ," Harras said under his breath.

They reached Jackie Cruz's door. Kathy rapped on it and they heard a voice from the other side. Pete couldn't make out what she said. Before he could think about much else, the door swung open. Jackie Cruz was on the other side, looking indignant and impatient. She was toned and athletic, her olive skin smooth and unblemished. She was in her early forties but probably got carded from time to time. She also didn't seem happy to see any of them.

"Kathy Bentley?"

"That's me."

"You didn't tell me who your partner was," she said, eyes locked on Pete. "Hi, Pete."

"Hi, Jackie," Pete said.

"Been a while," she said, moving behind her desk. "What was it? Two years ago? That messy case you tried to help me with but made even messier?"

Pete knew this was coming. He just had to ride it out.

"Did you tell your new girlfriend about us?" Jackie asked, taking her seat, a crooked smile on her face. "I wonder how that went over. I'm assuming the geezer is Harras?"

Pete cringed. He didn't need to turn to know Harras's reaction.

"You don't want to know what my assumptions are about you right now, lady," Harras said.

Jackie Cruz. When Pete first met her, she wasn't a hotshot defense attorney—and she was still reeling from the Varela case. They'd had a thing—Pete wouldn't define it as a relationship, because most of their time was spent at Jackie's place, in her bedroom or eating takeout in her kitchen. It lasted longer than it should have, mostly due to Pete's inability to be an adult, a byproduct of his drinking himself to near death. It felt like a decade ago. After their sort-of romance fizzled, Jackie asked Pete to help her on a case involving a grisly murder. It did not end well. Seeing Jackie now, in the flesh, reminded him it really hadn't been that long ago.

Pete, Kathy, and Harras grabbed the seats set up in front of Jackie's opulent desk.

Jackie folded her hands and rested her pointer fingers on her lips. "Well?" she said. "I only took this meeting as a favor to an old client. If I'd known I'd be forced to sit in a room with Pete fucking Fernandez and his two sidekicks, I would have passed, so let's get on with it."

"Thanks again for seeing us," Kathy said, trying to keep the meeting as cordial as possible.

Jackie shuffled some papers on her desk, put a few in a stack, and moved said stack onto a small file cabinet to the left of the desk. Her every action screamed annoyance.

"Fill me in," Jackie said. "Gaspar wants you to prove he's innocent? How's that going to work?"

"Well, that's what we're here for," Pete said. "To talk to you about the case."

Jackie glared at Pete, not interested in anything he had to say. Her brow furrowed. Her eyes reminded Pete of a predator's—the kind of wild animal who didn't waste time or energy unless it was going in for a kill. He tried not to break their eye contact.

"No shit," she said. "But what can I offer you? Gaspar said I should talk to you, which is fine, but I don't even work for him anymore. He can't afford me. I went through the trial and we thought we had it in the bag. But we lost. End of story. Even if he is innocent, he still needs to gather enough evidence to convince a judge to grant him a new trial. No easy feat. I mean, the guys burned through dozens of appellate attorneys. Big names too, like Sotolongo, Riesco, Otero and Kemp. Plus, people are over this."

"Over this?" Harras said.

"Yes, over it," she said. "It's shut. No one has an interest in putting in the work, money, or time to retry a case that's already closed, nice and tidy."

Jackie leaned back in her chair, as if to say, *There, what now?*

"So why'd you lose?" Pete asked. He heard Harras try to mask a chuckle with his hand.

She closed her eyes and pursed her lips. Pete didn't know Jackie all that well anymore, but he had spent enough time with her to know she was not the kind of person that appreciated being reminded of her losses. But Pete wasn't in the mood for posturing. Kathy fidgeted in her seat.

"Excuse me?"

"What happened?" Pete said. "If you're as good as the press says—and I know you are—why'd you lose this one? The one case that was ready to propel you to the next level? Garagos, Cochran—that strata. You'd be fighting off potential clients. What made this the one you lost?"

"Pete—" Kathy started, but she was interrupted by Jackie. She was laughing. Hard.

"You've got some major *cojones*, Pete, coming in here like this, talking like that," she said between giggles. "That was something. You almost got my goat, but I am too fucking old to get riled up that easy. Nice try though."

"Well, I had to do something," Pete said. "We're down to three minutes here."

Jackie waved her hand at the phone.

"Ah, don't sweat that," she said. "I make my hours. I just didn't know if I wanted to help Varela, much less that I'd be sitting across from you, of all people. It is kind of nice to see you again, I have to admit. You don't look as fucked up as you did the last time we talked."

She got up, cracked her knuckles, walked around to the front of her desk, and sat on the left corner, closer to Kathy.

"Why did I lose … let me count the ways," she said, her tone wistful but with a hint of resentment. "Like I said, it's always, always the spouse. Also, the judge hated my guts. Didn't seem like the kind of guy who was fond of strong, independent women, or women in general. The evidence the prosecution had wasn't much—it was all circumstantial. They didn't even have a murder weapon. But the jury bought it. Whitelaw was a viper too. He jumped all over us every chance he got. Gaspar's version of the story, that he and his wife were attacked by two random psychos for no apparent reason—was Charlie Manson thirty years too late, too crazy. And there wasn't enough evidence that pointed that way but didn't point the other. Get what I mean?"

"The evidence he was hoping would exonerate him was also hurting him?" Kathy asked.

"Sort of," she said. "All the evidence didn't make it to the trial either. There was no murder weapon, which I thought would help, but it didn't seem to with the jury. They figured Varela, as an ex-cop, would know how to hide a murder weapon. At least that's how Whitelaw played it. Varela's fingerprints were, yes, all over the scene—but he fucking lived there. Still, that seemed to help the prosecution more than us. The judge didn't let us focus on the fact that Varela didn't have blood on him consistent with the kind of splatter one would see in that kind of knife attack. Then there was Janette Ledesma."

"What about Ledesma?" Pete said.

"I'm guessing you've heard about 'the woman in the orange dress'?" Jackie asked.

"Yes, and Varela still stands by that," Kathy said. "That after he woke up from the attack, he saw a woman wearing a bright orange dress enter the house, and that woman also saw the two killers when they ran outside."

"Yes, and the supposed woman, Ledesma, testified at his trial," Harras said. "If you could call it that."

"Right, that testimony killed us. Straight up," Jackie said. "Her testimony took a shit over everything. We thought we'd won the lottery when she agreed to testify. But she ruined us when she took the stand. I'd call it sabotage if I had any evidence of it. Ledesma was supposed to confirm what she'd told the cops—that she came to the scene and saw the real murderers running off. She did the opposite, claiming she wasn't sure what she saw or if she was even there. That went over well, as you can imagine, especially with a shark like Whitelaw sitting at the other table. After that, the jury refused to trust anyone we presented, and the judge thought I was trying to make a mockery of the court."

"Why do you think Ledesma backtracked?" Harras asked.

Jackie looked at him. She seemed to be sizing him up.

"Why do I think she bombed?" Jackie said. "I wish I had evidence to prove it was something intentional, but I don't. All I do know is she was a junkie. Maybe she made the whole thing up and Varela *did* kill his wife. Anything's possible. If it created doubt in my mind, it certainly didn't help convince the jury that Varela was being framed."

"What I'm trying to say," Harras said, straightening up in his seat, "is, do you think someone got to her? After you talked to her and before she testified?"

Jackie raised an eyebrow.

"Yes, that's exactly what I think happened," she said. "But by the time the thought gained traction in my brain, I was off the case and I had paying clients to worry about."

The mention of Ledesma took Pete back to the day before. Coffee with Maya had been pleasant enough—work with an undercurrent of flirting, the atmosphere around them charged with electricity. Pete hadn't been sure how to respond, so he didn't. But somehow, the conversation that began at Versailles over two *café Cubanos* continued at Maya's Kendall townhouse, her shelves stacked with books, notepads, and accordion files loaded with trial documents, court filings, newspaper clippings, notes, and years of case law. With Jackie Cruz gone from the case, Maya had become her father's de facto lawyer. Pictures were tacked on the wall, along with maps and floor plans of Maya's childhood home. Red pins. Blue pins. String. Markers and circles of every color. This was what obsession looked like, Pete had thought. She would do anything to see her father freed. Maya was Gaspar Varela's last chance.

He felt conflicted about the quick, awkward kiss he'd shared with Maya before he left her house the previous night.

Pete caught a nasty look from Kathy—she could tell he was distracted.

"Pete, are you with us? Am I boring you?" Jackie said, bringing

Pete back to the now—the office, Kathy, and Harras next to him. Last night's kiss fading away.

"I'm here."

"Now you are," she said. "But your friends and I have been shooting the shit for what feels like hours."

"Sorry, I need some coffee," Pete said. "What did I miss?"

"Whatever works for you, dude," Jackie said, "Fibers from Varela's clothes—his PJs, basically—were found all over the living room, where he said he was sleeping, but not in the bedroom, where his wife was killed. Not game-changing, but interesting."

"Seems pretty definite," Pete said.

"Not if you have a good vacuum or got your clothes all bloody murdering your wife and changed, but yeah, it's helpful," she said before glancing at her Cartier watch. "Look, I have to go. I have to meet with some people who actually pay me money. Is there anything else I can help you with?"

"Ledesma," Kathy said. "Our research shows she died a few years ago. Any idea of what? Any family she left behind?"

"She was out of her mind on drugs," Jackie said. "She died alone in a crack house in Opa-Locka with a pipe in her hand and who knows what else around her."

Jackie opened her door and motioned for Kathy, Harras, and Pete to walk out of it.

"What about family?" Pete said.

"Family?"

"Yes, did Janette Ledesma have any close relatives?" Pete asked. "A husband? Brother? Parents? Anyone we could talk to?"

"There's a son," Harras said. "From a previous marriage—a brief one. But that's all I know. I never got a name."

"See?" Jackie said. "You don't need me. Silent but deadly over here has all the answers."

"Who is he? What's his name?" Pete said.

"I don't know. But I'll see what I can do," Jackie said. "My assistant will send over Varela's files to you—just let her know where you want them on your way out."

Pete lingered in the doorway for a second.

"Jackie," he said.

"Oh boy," she said. "Is this going to get awkward?"

"I need a favor," Pete said.

"Looks like it is," she said. Pete half expected Jackie to lick her lips in anticipation.

He leaned in and whispered a few words in Jackie's ear as Kathy and Harras looked on. Jackie gave Pete a curious look as she listened, nodding as he pulled back.

"We'll see," she said. "In the meantime, get lost."

Pete heard the door slam behind them as they headed back to the reception area.

"What is wrong with you? What the hell was that all about?" Kathy asked, her voice a low growl. "You went off to la-la land for a while there."

"Something she said got me thinking about something else."

"That is not in question," Kathy said, opening the door into the reception area and letting Pete walk out first. "I'm just asking what, pray tell, is more important than this?"

Pete kept walking.

"We got what we needed," Harras said. "I let Cruz's secretary know where to send the files. But we need to tighten up our game. That was sloppy. We had no plan and it showed. I'll see you both later."

"For once, you're right," Kathy said as the older detective walked on ahead of them. She wheeled around to face Pete. "Also, where were you last night?"

"What do you mean?"

"I called you around ten and you didn't pick up," Kathy said, her voice still quiet. "Unless you were fast asleep like the *abuelo* you sometimes are, you ignored my call. You know how I feel about that."

"I was out."

"Care to elaborate?"

"Not really."

"I see," Kathy said. "It's like that."

"I hung out with Maya for a bit," Pete said. He braced himself for Kathy's response.

"Well, okay," she said. "This is becoming a weird trend."

"What?"

"You and our client hanging out together without me, your partner on this case," she said. "Not to mention our assigned chaperone, Harras."

Pete could tell she was hurt. She hadn't expected this—whatever it was.

"It just came up," Pete said. "She dropped by the store and asked to grab a cup of coffee. We kept talking and it went on into the evening."

"Now you're bragging," she said, a petulant look on her face. "And from what I remember Emily telling me eons ago, you were far from king in that category."

"That is not what I meant," Pete said. He could feel his face reddening. "And what the hell? You and Emily shared stories about …? Oh Jesus. Never mind. We were talking about the case. We went over some of her files. Nothing like that."

"Then, my chaste friend, what did her files reveal to you?" Kathy asked.

"I think Ledesma is the key here. Maya didn't have a lot on her, though, just the basics Harras already shared," Pete said as they walked out of the office building and toward Kathy's car. "But Maya seems to think she was the great missing piece, and regrets how buried she got by the prosecution, and how her dad's defense didn't really develop Varela's theory on the killer. Not that it helps us much now."

Kathy let out a long sigh. "Wow, breaking news indeed. But Ledesma is dead—has been for a while. And this Cruz lady was zero help, beyond giving us her files. Let's hope the discovery has something useful in it. Anyway, at least our old pal Harras seems to be invested in us getting this right."

"We need to find Ledesma's son," Pete said, opening the passenger side door and sliding into the seat. "We need to know if Ledesma was actually in that room—and what she saw."

Pete stood at the far end of the freezer aisle in the Publix Supermarket in West Kendall. He gripped the handle of his green basket as he scanned the TV dinner options. The chill emanating from the glass doors was soothing, a nice contrast to the temperature outside, which felt more humid than usual, even for Miami.

He'd spent most of the morning at Kathy's Wynwood apartment, sitting across from her and Harras, going through the Varela files Jackie had sent over. A lot of it was stuff they'd picked up from news reports, conversations with Maya, and their preliminary investigation, but it was essential nonetheless. As Pete read through the lengthy trial transcripts, the major moments of the case played out in black and white, and the train wreck of Ledesma's testimony seemed that much more surprising—and devastating. But it was the discovery files that jumped out at Pete. They showed Varela starting off at an immediate disadvantage. He didn't yet have the benefit of Posada's checkbook to fund his legal expenses, so he was paying Jackie Cruz—at the time a somewhat inexperienced litigator—out of pocket. There was no real investigator tasked with proving Varela's version of the events, meaning all the defense had to support their case was the evidence the prosecution provided.

Jackie's notes also gave them some insight into the struggle she'd faced trying to formulate a viable alternative theory for the murder of Carmen Varela. Severely limited by a dearth of funds and support, Jackie had little to go on aside from the statements her client made to the police and what he told her. It resulted in a vague, inconsistent narrative that stood little chance against the more predictable tale of a desperate, angry husband trying to slash his way out of a loveless marriage.

Varela had been a narcotics officer with a solid arrest record. He'd brought in a lot of perps and busted up serious drug operations. He was not a friend to the Colombian cartels or their local partners, so it would follow that those powerful criminal organizations would target Carmen Varela. That was where the theory ended—unable to evolve into something concrete, supported by facts. By the time Posada started to help with the financial side, Varela had been convicted and had burned through a string of less-qualified appellate attorneys. Maya was also serving as her father's default legal counsel with chances of a new trial dwindling. Even double-checking the list of criminals Varela had brought to justice bore little fruit, Pete discovered. Most of them were either still in jail, dead, or too small-time to merit consideration. It was a wall Pete was having trouble getting around.

The shopping trip was meant to serve as a distraction—Pete needed to move and think on his own. It'd been a productive detour, at least. In addition to the files, Jackie Cruz had been helpful on another front: she'd delivered on her half-hearted promise and gotten them the name of Ledesma's son: Arturo Pelegrin, the product of a brief marriage. The kid, well, man—he was almost twenty—had been taken away to live with his father a few years before his mother's death. But finding out the kid's name was only half of it, Pete realized. They needed to figure out where he was and what to ask him. Pete needed to think before he sat down with his partners again. Thus, grocery shopping. It beat sitting at the bar.

He'd felt his phone vibrate in his pocket earlier, but hadn't bothered to check. He knew who it was. Maya. She wanted to talk about the case and about the night before. He hadn't done anything wrong—or, rather, he hadn't done anything he didn't want to do. He was trying to live a different kind of life from the one that had gotten him here—a more honest existence with fewer grays and much less black.

They had just kissed, that was all.

He could hear Kathy in his head. *Great, now you're going to sleep with our client? Why not just flush our case down the toilet?*

He ignored Imaginary Kathy and thought back to the night before. Maya's smell. The way the corners of her eyes crinkled a bit when she laughed and how she managed to look put-together and casual at the same time—like she'd slept in her clothes but still looked good, like crumpled velvet. He was rusty. He hadn't even bothered to consider anything romantic since he'd gotten sober. Sober this time, that is. He flinched at the thought of what had happened last year, and had the dark thought that maybe he didn't deserve anything beyond what he had.

No, he couldn't think like that. He'd worked too hard to be miserable now. He put the basket down and slid his hands in his pockets so no one would notice they were shaking. Even though he no longer craved a drink, he still had to deal with the stuff underneath the alcoholic grime and dirt, like the piles of wreckage in a long-abandoned house. He'd lived a cluttered life full of mistakes, wrong turns, and false starts. But it was still a redeemable one.

Pete felt his phone vibrate again. He pulled it out of his pocket and checked the display, his fingers poised over the ignore button. It wasn't Maya this time. The number was unlisted. He picked up.

An automated recording started.

"You are receiving a collect call from the Everglades Correctional Institute. To accept the charges, please press one. To decline—"

Pete pressed one. A voice came on the line—distant and faded, like someone calling from underwater.

"Pete?" It was Varela.

"Gaspar?" Pete said. He looked around. The grocery store wasn't too crowded, but the last thing he needed was a local reporter or blogger overhearing PI Pete Fernandez talking to the most notorious convicted murderer this side of Ted Bundy. He started toward the exit.

"Is this a good time?" Varela asked.

"Sure, sure," Pete said. "Is, um, is everything okay?"

"As fine as anything can be," Varela said. "But we need to talk."

Pete made it outside and walked toward his car.

"Okay, shoot."

"I know you've talked to my daughter," Varela said. "And to Orlando and Juan Carlos. But *we* need to talk again. You and me. I need you to get my side of things. I've been trying to reach you and I don't have a lot of time—"

"Okay, that sounds like a plan," Pete said. "I think we wanted to gather some information before we came back to you, you know, for a formal interview."

Pete opened his car door and started the engine. He made sure the AC was on and let out a long breath. He kept the car in park and let the cool air wash over him.

"I don't want to wait for a formal interview," Varela said. Even with the bad connection, Pete could tell his client was pissed off. He felt looped out. "You and your friends are working for me. What little bit of money my daughter has cobbled together from Posada or her own bank account is going to you—I want you to know my side of things before we go any further."

"Fair enough," Pete said. "Just keep in mind that anything you say on this call will probably be recorded, okay? I'm not your lawyer, so this chat isn't privileged."

There was quiet on the other end and for a second Pete thought Varela had come to his senses and hung up.

"Believe me, I know," Varela said. "Go ahead, ask your questions."

"I can't," Pete said. "This all instantly becomes admissible evidence. If you say the wrong thing—"

"Ask your questions," Varela said, his voice low, trying to keep his temper at a low simmer. "Okay? I know what the risks are."

"Did you kill your wife?"

"What? No, of course not," Varela said. "What kind of question is that?"

"You want to be interviewed," Pete said, one hand gripping the steering wheel. "This is it. No decorations. We talk straight. I ask direct questions, you answer. I need you to be honest with me. I'm the only chance you have. So, tell."

"No," Varela said, his voice softer. "I didn't kill her. I could never hurt Carmen."

"Tell me about that night," Pete said.

Varela took in a sharp breath.

"We'd had an argument," Varela said. "About work. She was tired of being a cop wife. Tired of the hours. Tired of me spending so much time away. We'd had arguments from time to time. This one got heated. I decided to sleep on the couch. Maya was at a friend's house, so it wasn't a big deal. Anyway, by the time we were getting ready for bed, things had calmed down. Carmen went in the bedroom and closed the door and I stayed up a bit longer on the couch. I fell asleep reading."

"Then what?" Pete said.

"I woke up with a start," Varela said, choosing his words with more care now, pacing his story. "It was dark, but I saw two people—two men—in my living room. We had a small nightlight—it was by the couch, so I could make some of it out, for a while. One of them was going into the bedroom, which was on the same floor. I heard my wife scream. A horrible scream. Pain, fear. I still hear that scream. She was dying. I tried to get up, but the other man hit me with something, a stick or a bat, and I was knocked out. I woke up on the floor, near the bedroom. That's when I saw Carmen … I saw her on the floor, at the foot of the bed. What was left of her."

Varela went quiet again. When he spoke next, he sounded shattered—his voice husky and hopeless.

"My beautiful wife was dead on the floor," Varela said. "There was blood all over the place. I hadn't been able to protect her. She was cut up—long, deep wounds all over. Her head was barely attached to her body. It was terrible. So much blood."

"Keep going."

"Jesus, man, this isn't easy for me," Varela said. "Have some regard for that."

"Believe me, I do," Pete said. "But I need to hear the unvarnished truth. It's the only way I can figure out if there's any evidence we can use to save you. So far, you've just given me stuff I know. I need your perspective. Your story."

"That's when I saw her," Varela said. "This woman, she'd walked into our home. She was wearing an orange dress, a loud one. She came in … asked if I needed help. I screamed. Told her to call 9-1-1. To please help my wife. She started to help but then turned and ran. I didn't see her again until the trial."

"That's not what she said. She said she was never there. That she didn't know you."

"She lied," Varela said, indignant. "I saw her. She was there."

"But what did she see that exonerates you?" Pete said.

"What do you mean?"

"Ledesma showed up, walked in on you looming over your dead wife's body," Pete said, pulling out a small notebook from his back pocket, flipping through the pages, scanning for information as he thought of his next question. "How does that help you? If you'd killed your wife, the situation could have been the same, right? I mean, the fact that you had an argument also doesn't help you."

A short silence followed. Pete could hear noise in the background—the sounds of a crowd, cursing and yelling.

"No, no," Varela said. "Ledesma saw the men. She saw them leaving the house. That cop, Vigil, saw her too."

"What about the two men?"

"What do you mean?"

"Did Vigil see them? What about Graydon Smith? Wasn't he on the scene, too?"

"I think so," Varela said, his argument losing steam. "I—I don't know."

"That doesn't help," Pete said. "I know she was going to testify to that, but she didn't. And now Vigil's dead, so he can't share his story in a courtroom."

"That fucking destroyed me, Ledesma's testimony," Varela said, deflated. "That was the end."

"What did the men look like?" Pete said.

"It was hard to see," Varela said. "They were dressed in black—masks, black pants. It was dark. I wish I could remember more."

"What about their physiques? Anything catch your eye? I mean, you're a cop," Pete said. "Isn't this what you're trained to do?"

Varela ignored the jab and continued.

"I wish I'd seen something, anything," he said. "But they moved fast, efficiently. They knew what the plan was ... it was almost like they knew how to avoid doing anything unique or obvious, if that makes sense."

"Okay, fine," Pete said. "But why would anyone—aside from you, for whatever reason—kill your wife?"

"To get to me," Varela said. "She never hurt anyone. She was a saint. She was too good for me."

"But who were these guys?" Pete asked. "If we can't find new evidence of you *not* killing your wife, we need to find evidence that someone else did—follow? So, think hard. Who had it in for you?"

"I-I can't think of anyone," Varela said. "I mean, there were perps I'd brought in, people I'd pissed off."

"That was the theory you had your lawyers pursuing, right?" Pete said. "The idea that someone with a grudge against you killed your wife. I mean, you've been sitting in a cell for a decade. Surely someone's come to mind?"

"Yes, of course," Varela said, sounding more desperate. "I made plenty of enemies. But it was all street-level stuff. I was a cop, they were criminals. It wasn't personal beyond that. Not enough reason to kill my wife, to destroy me. I was a good cop, ask Orlando or Harras. I did things by the book. I worked hard, went home, and tried to be a good father and husband."

Pete rubbed his eyes.

"Gaspar," he said. "I know what you're saying. But none of that stands up in court. Everything you've told me? None of it exonerates you. We gain nothing from suggesting other possibilities. Even if Janette Ledesma was alive and willing to testify that she was there, that doesn't disprove the theory that you killed your wife."

"Look—they're telling me to get off the phone," Varela said, sounding more distant than before, like a faded, automated recording. "I just want there to be a record. I want everyone to know I'm innocent before … I have to go. My time is up."

The line went dead, leaving Varela's defeated voice echoing in Pete's head.

INTERLUDE FIVE

Miami, Florida
June 11, 1984

Pedro Fernandez wheeled the chair down the makeshift ramp he'd installed to help get Diego in and out of their new house. His father liked sitting in the sun and reading. They were close to peak summer now, making today one of the few days they could sit outside and enjoy the weather without risking heatstroke.

He pushed his father into the front yard, to a small table set up near the carport. Diego waved his hand at Pedro, and Pedro handed him a copy of the newspaper—*Diario las Américas*. His father leaned back in his wheelchair and opened the newspaper. This was their routine. Quiet, calm, and hot.

Pedro pulled a lawn chair closer to the table and looked at his father. His body sagged into the chair, defeated. He looked older than his sixty-five years. Never fully recovered from a knife attack years before, Diego's health had then spiraled, leaving him chained to this chair as his life faded. It was on that day, when his father had been violently attacked, that Pedro went from son to caretaker. Pedro hadn't even become a father yet. That would come a few years later with the birth of his own son, Pete, who was now dozing in his bed in the house.

It'd been four years since Pedro's wife, Pete's mother, died during childbirth. Just as he'd received his greatest gift—a son—he'd lost his partner and best friend. That, coupled with his father's degrading health, had made for years of anguish, brightened only by watching Pete grow from baby to boy.

Pedro looked out onto the street, at his neighbors' houses. Westchester was a quiet suburb that almost lulled Pedro into thinking Miami was a safe haven. But that was bullshit. Miami was the nexus of the drug trade. Even pedestrians were at risk.

Pedro thought about the Dadeland Mall shooting just a few years back that had cost so many lives. He remembered speeding over to the scene with his partner, Carlos Broche, and being shocked by the bloodshed and carnage hitting the suburban shopping center. They'd gotten there too late. The bodies had already hit the pavement and the situation was under control. There was nothing they could have done to change the outcome, but Pedro still felt a weight on his chest. He didn't want his young son to live in this world—a world of guns and blood and drug deals. He tried not to think about the kind of place Miami would be in a few years.

"I made detective, Papi," Pedro said, trying to break the long silence that had become too routine for them.

His father nodded, not lifting his eyes from the paper.

"Does that mean better pay?"

Money. That's what it boiled down to for Diego: would he be able to create a better life for his family. Not about prestige or acclaim. Though Diego Fernandez had risen high in the Batista government in Cuba, his main concern had always been his wife and son, not his own political career. He had been content to be the assistant to the attorney general if it meant a good home and income. He could do without the hassle of fame or attention.

"Yeah, it's a better salary," Pedro said.

"Hours? Do you have to still work nights?"

"Yeah," Pedro said. "But not as much. I'm working homicide now. Carlos made detective too."

"He's a good kid," his father said.

Pedro felt an urge to say something then, something meaningful to his father. The feeling spread through his body like a quick electric shock. He wanted to thank his father for all the sacrifices he'd made to bring them here to this new country. For risking his life to make sure they were safe. For working long hours to ensure Pedro went to school and had every opportunity. For making the tough decisions that made the life Pedro now had possible. The thought fluttered away when he heard the car engine. Pedro turned his head and saw a beige Oldsmobile pulling onto their street, which rarely saw much traffic beyond the residential flow of people coming home or leaving to go to work. The car was speeding—even more rare in this quiet stretch of suburbia.

Pedro didn't have a moment to react. By the time he noticed the gun poking out of the passenger side window—held by a young man with jet-black hair and an overgrown moustache—the first shot had been fired. By the time Pedro knocked over the table and pulled his father down to him, trying to avoid another shot, two more bullets had penetrated his father's body. Diego shook in surprise, his eyes bulging open and his mouth trying to form words. The car was long gone.

"Don't talk, don't talk," Pedro said, clutching his father, trying to cover the bullet holes to stop the bleeding—but there were too many, the blood flowing too fast.

In the seconds it took to say the words, his father was gone—leaving Pedro holding Diego's bullet-riddled body and decades of regrets. Pedro's eyes, stinging from the dust and dirt, scanned the street and saw nothing.

CHAPTER TEN

"**J**ust, please, tell me you're not fucking our client."

Pete didn't respond to Kathy as he looked down the empty Florida International University hallway. They were in the public university's central building—the Graham Center—a testament to new money, adorned with bright colors and corporate logos. Pete wondered if his feet still remembered how to get to the Rathskeller, the school bar that had made up a large part of his own college curriculum. He wondered if it still existed.

They were standing outside of a classroom on the second floor of the building, down the hall from the university's student government office and newspaper. It had been too easy for Pete and Kathy to snag a copy of Arturo Pelegrin's class schedule. Just sounding like a cop seemed to work on the gum-chewing student manning the registrar's office front desk. Pete hoped that this little recon mission didn't go sour and point back to her.

Pelegrin was working on a BA in business, according to the academic transcript Pete read.

"I'm going to take this silence as tacit confirmation," Kathy said.

They could hear the discussion on the other side of the door—something about the Weimar Republic before World War II. Pete was trying to listen. Kathy wasn't.

All Jackie Cruz could dig up was a name. The rest was up to Pete and Kathy. In the flash of activity that followed, they hadn't had much time to formulate more than a vague plan of action for Arturo Pelegrin.

Pete checked his watch. The class would be over in a few minutes. He positioned himself off to the left of the door. The classroom was at the end of a long hallway, near a large window that faced the east side of the campus. Basically, you got a view of a giant peach-colored parking lot. *Miami in a nutshell*, Pete thought. Kathy inched over in his direction, still scowling.

"Have you heard from Varela?" Pete asked. His last conversation with their client had left Pete concerned. He couldn't pinpoint why. But the man had gone from energized to flatline in fifteen minutes.

"No, I don't think his cell is getting good reception *in prison*," she said, her head tilting with annoyance for the final part of her answer, emphasizing she hadn't forgiven Pete for his lone wolf interview. "I'd ask his daughter—you know, our client—but she's been strangely busy. I wonder with—"

"Jesus," Pete said. "We didn't sleep together. Happy now?"

"Well, not really," Kathy said, a frown forming on her face. "On the one hand, I'd be happy if you, my sad dove, did get some ass now and again that wasn't fraught with years of history or potentially riddled with selections from the STD Hall of Fame. That being said, I think canoodling with our boss is bad business."

"We just kissed," Pete said, surprised he was even sharing that much, but feeling relieved to get it off his chest to someone other than his reflection. "I don't think it meant anything."

"Oh, Pete," she said. "Of course it meant *something*. Even in this day of Instagramming your Tumblr Tweets, people still get emotional and want to make out. Just don't overthink it too, too much. Keep in mind we work for her—and for her father. And don't think I've forgiven you for interviewing fucking Gaspar Varela without me being present."

"I already apologized," Pete said.

"Apologies are garbage if they don't feel true," a voice said from behind.

Pete and Kathy turned around to see Harras walking toward them. He had known they were coming to question Pelegrin, but hadn't confirmed whether he'd take part. The fact he was here made it clear to Pete that the former FBI agent was going to keep better tabs on them moving forward.

"Gaspar called me," Pete said. "He wanted to be interviewed. What was I supposed to do? Put him on hold and call you for full sign-off?"

"You made your choice," Harras said, nodding. "I don't agree with it. From the sound of it, neither does your partner."

"This whole 'agreeing with Harras' thing has me worried," Kathy said. "What is the world coming to?"

Harras handed Pete and Kathy identical sheets of paper.

"What's this?" she said.

"Arturo Pelegrin," Harras said. "Thought it might be helpful to know what your target looks like. What were you planning on doing? Hoping he'd recognize you?"

Pete scanned the sheet—photo, date of birth, address.

"How'd you get all this?" Pete asked. "Did you run his name through the Miami PD database?"

"You'd be amazed what you can find via Google and a public Facebook page," Harras said, fighting back a smile.

Before Pete could respond, the classroom door opened and students began filtering out. Most of the college kids had made their way into the hallway when Kathy shot him a worried look—she didn't see Arturo. The crowd was too thick, the mass of people moving too quickly to the next thing.

Pete did the first thing that popped into his head.

He yelled "Arturo!" and waited.

A few kids turned and gave them strange glances. One guy, walking by himself, near the back of the group, looked at Pete a little longer. Pete zoned in on him. He matched the photo—skinny, tan, longish and unkempt hair to go with stubble masquerading as a beard. Bingo.

"Arturo Pelegrin?"

The kid walked toward Pete, Harras, and Kathy.

"Yeah? Do I know you?"

"No, not really," Pete said. "Can we go somewhere to talk?"

"Talk about what? Who are you?"

"I'm Kathy Bentley," she said, sticking out her hand. Arturo took it with a bit of hesitation. "We wanted to ask you a few questions. This is my partner, Pete Fernandez, and our colleague, Robert Harras."

"Holy shit," he said.

"What?" Pete said.

"I know you," he continued, his eyes bouncing from Pete to Kathy to Harras and back again. "You both wrote that book—about that Silent Death guy. Man, that shit was fucked up. You wrote another one too, right? More recent? I haven't read that one yet."

Kathy smiled. She loved this kind of attention. Pete wasn't so sure it was a good thing. Some jobs required a certain level of anonymity.

"That's us," Kathy said. "Always nice to meet someone who knows our work. Or, mine at least. Now, can we go somewhere to chat? Food or drinks on us."

"It's cool to meet you and all that, but what are we gonna talk about? Am I in trouble? I gotta get to class in a bit…"

Pete fought the urge to tell Arturo that they knew his next class, Survey of American Literature with Professor Arnold, wasn't until the following day, around three in the afternoon. But he understood why the kid was being evasive.

"We need to talk about your mom, son," Harras said, his tone flat. He met Arturo's eyes and saw them widen. The kid had been expecting something—anything—else. A parking ticket, late library books, a winning lottery number.

Arturo backed away a step.

"What about her? She's gone," he said. "Been gone a while. I got nothing to say about that."

"We know this is a hard subject for you," Kathy started. He didn't let her finish.

"You don't know shit about me," Arturo said, raising his voice. "You don't know shit about my mom either. You think you can just come in here—to my school, wait outside my class—and take me aside for some … what? Some article about my mom being dead? Is this about Gaspar Varela? No fucking thank you."

A few other students and a portly security guard, wandering over from the opposite end of the hall, had noticed the conversation, thanks to Arturo's rising octaves. They didn't have much time.

"I think your mother was murdered," Pete said.

Both Kathy and Arturo responded with the same word: "What?"

Harras shook his head and looked away, trying to hide his frustration from their target.

"It's just a theory," Pete said. "But I'd much rather talk about it somewhere less … public?"

They took four seats outside of the Graham Center—"the blue tables," as Arturo called them on their way over, past the cafeteria and information desk. The weather was gray but still hot, the clouds clinging to the rain, as if waiting for the right moment to let loose— like a kid with one water balloon left. Pete sat down, Kathy to his left, Harras on the right. She let Pete lead—this was his detour. He didn't miss the annoyed smirk on her face. He wondered if there was a chance it'd become permanent.

Arturo seemed anxious, drumming his fingers on the blue metal table. He shrugged his shoulders. He wanted to get on with this. They had the tables to themselves, aside from one student who was hunched over a *Chemistry and Society* textbook.

"Well?" Arturo said.

"Like I said, all I have is a theory," Pete said.

"That is not good enough, man," Arturo said. "You came here for something. You wanted some info from me. Why should I help you? You could just be saying that to get me to talk about my mom."

"Why would we do that?" Kathy said.

"I don't know, lady. I don't know what your motives are. And who's this other guy?" Arturo said, motioning at Harras.

"Name's Harras, kid," he said. "I'm a retired FBI agent. We're all working on this together. We're on your side."

"Working on what together? What do you want with my mom? She's been dead a long time."

"We're working for Gaspar Varela's daughter," Pete said.

"Say that again," Arturo said. He continued, not letting them respond. "You're working for Varela? Man, I got nothing to say to you."

He started to get up.

"Look, give us five minutes," Pete said. "Let me tell you what I think happened to your mom. If you don't buy it after five, then go."

Arturo plopped back into his chair. He crossed his arms and looked around the seating area.

"We were hired by Varela and his daughter to reinvestigate the case. The murder of his wife," Pete said. "Their goal is to exonerate him. But our goal is to find out what happened. To cut through the bullshit and come to a conclusion."

Arturo started to interrupt, but Pete raised his hand.

"Ledesma, your mother, was a key witness at trial," Kathy said. "For better or worse, her testimony changed everything. She had a rough life, we get that. We can only imagine how hard it's all been on you …"

"This isn't about what your mother said or didn't say on the stand," Harras said, cracking his knuckles as he spoke. "That's public record. This is about what else she knew—and what you might know."

Pete could see Arturo fidgeting from across the table. He was about to bolt.

"The way your mother died doesn't make sense," Pete said, cutting Harras off. "She knew something—whether it was the truth or part of it. Her addictions prevented her from sharing it at the right time, and it also prevented anyone from taking her seriously. But she knew something. Maybe she knew enough to get Varela out. Or enough to keep him there. Maybe she wanted to share that info, and maybe that got her killed."

Arturo's face tightened. His eyes seemed to water a bit. After a moment, he blinked and stood up.

"If I think of anything you can use, I'll let you know," he said, his voice raw, hoarse. "Do not contact me again."

Pete nodded. He handed him his card. Arturo took it, then turned around and walked toward the parking garage.

"I feel for that kid," Kathy said.

"Remind you of someone?" Harras asked.

"Me," Kathy said. "He just can't come to terms with where he's from—the people who made him, the circumstances he's dealing with. It takes a while."

"He was the closest we could get to Ledesma," Pete said.

"Do you think he knews something?" Kathy asked. "If he does, it didn't seem like he was in a let-me-bare-my-soul mood."

"They're not all winners," Harras said. "You tried. You're on his radar. Now we wait."

"For what?" Kathy said. "The Trix Rabbit to appear with a video exonerating our client?"

Harras ignored Kathy and looked at his watch.

"I gotta run," he said, standing up. "Wish I could say this has been fun or productive."

"As do I," Kathy said, following suit. "Guess you're on your own, Petey. Try to stay out of trouble for a change."

Pete knew he'd get in trouble for this. He was pushing it with his partners already, having gone off the reservation to talk to Varela, Posada, and, to a degree, Juan Carlos Maldonado. But as much as Pete relied on Kathy and Harras—for their knowledge, experience, and support—he needed to rely on his own gut to figure out what was going on with this case. To do that, he sometimes needed to go into the cave first, without a torch.

Matheson Hammock Park was just off Old Cutler Road, south of Coral Gables. Near Biscayne Bay, the large plot of land featured a large "urban pool," which was a fancy way of saying man-made lake. The view was stunning, pairing the sun and fun of Miami's best beaches with the quiet and calm of a neighborhood park. Families loved it because the waters were serene and you could let your kids run rampant without worrying about Mother Nature. It was a respite from the more manic pace Miami had acquired in the last decade. A reminder that the bustling city had once been more sleepy town than teeming metropolis. Late afternoon on a weekday seemed to fit the bill. The small restaurant-slash-snack bar adjacent to the beach was empty. Pete walked past the food stand toward the parking lot and found a batch of picnic tables near the fringe of the park. He took a seat and waited.

The call from Jackie Cruz had been short and cryptic, but Pete knew she'd deliver. He'd asked for a favor, half expecting her to tell him to fuck off. When she didn't flip immediately, he knew she'd help.

He saw a woman approaching from the same direction Pete had taken. She walked like a cop—her dark features and trim business suit in sharp contrast to the casual vibe of the park. Her black hair was tied back in a tight bun. As she got closer, she gave Pete a slight smile, as if to say, "Yep, I'm the person you're meeting,"

Pete stood up.

"Jackie Cruz sent you?" he asked.

The woman nodded. "That she did."

"I'm Pete Fernandez."

"I know," she said. "Nicole Purdin. Jackie said you needed some help. Here I am."

Pete's request had been a simple one: he wanted a forensics expert to look over the Varela case files. His reasons for asking to meet her alone weren't as clear to Pete, but he felt the need to see what she had to say about the case against Varela first—before bringing that info to the attention of the people paying his tab, or his partners.

Nicole took a seat across from Pete. She pulled a thin file folder from her purse and slid it over to him.

"Don't open it yet," she said. "I want to talk this out first."

She was all business. Pete could appreciate that.

Nicole tapped a finger on the table between them, as if pondering where to start. She looked at Pete.

"I wish I'd known Jackie when she was working this case," she said. "Because I think we might have been able to win."

"So you think Varela is innocent?"

"*Not guilty* and *innocent* are different things," Nicole said, raising her left hand, slowing Pete down. "But we'll get there. I do this for a living. I'm the expert who gets called to the stand to explain to a jury why the evidence the cops are harping on might not mean exactly what they want it to mean. I spent years as a forensic pathologist with the Miami PD. I know how they work. I know the shorthand they use, the loopholes they slide through, and the corners they cut. There was a lot of that here. A lot of stuff that was missed."

"Like what?" Pete asked. "Is there anything new? Anything we can present to a judge as grounds for a new trial?"

"No, sorry. There's no ace in the hole that's going to exonerate Varela," she said. "At least not in the forensics. The evidence the prosecution presented, though the messaging was off, was in the ballpark. It was a question of tone. Jackie's argument was undercut by two game-changing witnesses and a judge who could not stand her. If this were Varela's first trial we were aiming for, I think we'd have enough to get a not-guilty verdict. But I don't see enough to get him a new trial."

Pete's shoulders sank.

"Don't pout," she said. "We're adults here. I'll give you the top-line stuff and you can take that report and pass it along to your colleagues, assuming you want them to see it."

Pete scoffed.

"Yeah, Jackie told me about how you asked," Nicole said. "And, look, I don't care. You disseminate information to your people however you want. I'm doing this as a favor to Jackie. I've made a lot of money working cases with her. I can spare an hour here and there to look at files pro bono if it keeps me in her good graces. So, I'll give you my general thoughts, then you can ask me a few questions. Then I'm gone."

"Go for it," Pete said.

"The evidence against Varela isn't great—when the cops found him, he had blood all over him and his pajama fibers were only in the living room," she said. "But neither of those things mean he killed his wife. Like any concerned husband, he could've rushed to her when he found her on the floor, like he claimed. I think what we saw in the original trial was a very savvy prosecutor and a relatively inexperienced defense attorney butting heads and trying to present two different narratives based on the same evidence—standard courtroom stuff. Whitelaw wanted you to believe Varela was a bloodthirsty egomaniac who knew how to hide and disrupt evidence. Jackie wanted the jury to realize there just wasn't enough evidence to convict. Jackie—thanks to Janette Ledesma and, in a more damning turn, I think, Juan Carlos Maldonado—lost."

"What about the fibers?" Pete asked. "And the blood? From what I read, Varela's blood was on his wife and vice versa."

"That's true," Nicole said, pursing her lips as she grabbed the file folder and flipped through a few pages, looking for something. "But there's nothing that points to that as being a byproduct of a struggle, you see? If you, Pete, are stabbed and bleeding on the floor and I come to your body and try to resuscitate you and, as I've told the police, I've been in a struggle myself … well, it shouldn't be weird that I get my fibers on your body and you get blood on mine. But as you well know, seeing the evidence and understanding it are two different things. Whitelaw was able to present this evidence—which, in my expert opinion isn't completely damning—as if it was."

Pete closed his eyes. This wasn't the meeting he was hoping for.

"So, we've got nothing, then," Pete said.

"Don't lose hope yet," Nicole said, closing the folder. "One thing I did notice from the autopsy is that the medical examiner didn't do much with *how* Carmen was stabbed—or what she was stabbed with."

"Well, the murder weapon wasn't found," Pete said.

"That's true," Nicole said, her voice mellow, as if trying to rub some of her patience off on Pete. "But there are things you can determine based on her wounds—like the attributes of the kind of knife used, or the likelihood that it was a certain kind of knife."

"Okay, tell me," Pete said.

"The cuts and stab wounds were long, significantly longer than a kitchen knife or switchblade, and definitely deeper too," Nicole said. "She was basically hacked at, not poked at. Whoever did this to her seemed to know what they were doing."

"Can you determine the kind of knife used?"

"Not exactly," she said. "I can only guess, and that does you no good in terms of new evidence. But it might be enough to get you on track to *find* that new evidence."

"You're saying that if I have a better idea of what the murder weapon was, I could find that and use it to exonerate Varela?"

"I said no such thing," Nicole said, following her words with an empty, frustrated laugh. "Finding the weapon doesn't do much if the weapon has his prints on it, for example. But it is a major, major piece of evidence that no one has seen. That's the kind of thing that would lead to a new trial. And I think the kind of weapon you're looking for is a long knife, probably a machete. And, based on the evidence I looked over, I'm guessing an older one with a unique signature or marking, like a crack."

Machete. Pete's brain latched onto the word. Had Varela's wife been the victim of *Los Enfermos*? Or had Varela orchestrated it to seem that way? Pete didn't know—but he at least felt like he had a trail to follow now.

"That's definitely something," Pete said. "I'm impressed."

Nicole smiled.

"It's what I do," she said. Her phone rang. She pulled it out of her purse and looked at the display. "It's Jackie. Weird. Maybe she's checking in on us."

Her brow furrowed as she answered.

"Hello?" she said. "Yes, I'm here with him."

Pete could tell from Nicole's face that the news wasn't good. The call was brief. She put the cell phone back on the table. Her hands were shaking.

"What? What is it?" Pete asked.

"It's Varela," she said. "He's escaped."

CHAPTER ELEVEN

"How did this happen?"

Pete, Kathy, Harras, Maya, and Orlando Posada were in the lobby of a large office building off Biscayne, the home of Posada's postretirement security business, Posada & Associates. From the look of the digs, it seemed he was doing well for himself.

"Let's talk in my office," Posada said, moving his cane toward the elevator banks. There were already throngs of reporters converging on the building, and it would only get worse. They took the elevator up a few floors and ventured past another, less crowded lobby and made a few turns. Posada's office—the size of a luxurious conference room—was sparsely decorated. No photos on the wall, no plaques or mementos either. Just a calendar and a clean desk with a nameplate: *Orlando Posada, CEO.*

"Love what you've done with the place," Pete said, regretting the joke the second the words left his mouth.

"What's the use in decorating when you're blind?" Posada said, letting out a gruff laugh as he took the chair behind his desk. He seemed less hesitant moving around his office. He knew the space. "Take a seat."

Pete and Kathy grabbed the two chairs in front of his desk, Maya sitting on a more comfortable-looking love seat near the large windows that looked out at the ocean. Harras pulled up another chair and positioned himself behind Pete and Kathy. Maya looked shaken. She'd barely reacted to their presence. During the moments they had with her before Posada appeared in the lobby, she gave them a series of blank stares, as if hypnotized by something far off in the distance beyond the conference room.

"He was released," Posada said as they took their seats.

"Unreal," Harras said.

"How is that even possible?" Kathy said.

"It was fraud, of course," Posada said. "Someone from the outside managed to forge his release papers and was in contact with him. The falsified release papers passed muster. According to the cops, someone took Gaspar to a hotel in West Palm Beach. That's the last anyone's seen of him. He could be anywhere now."

"This is absurd," Pete said. "Didn't they realize what they were doing?"

"You ever have a mindless job, Fernandez?" Posada said, looking in the direction of Pete's voice. "These corrections officers just want to push paper from one pile to the next. They don't have time to cross-reference every release they're handed. I'm guessing this is something Gaspar's been working on for months—maybe years—with a contact outside. Someone who's familiar with the prison system and how prisoners get out."

"I should have known," Pete said. "He seemed off."

"You talked to him?" Maya asked, incredulous. "Jesus, when were you going to tell us?"

"He called me," Pete said, feeling his defenses go up. He'd already sparred with Kathy and Harras over the call. He wasn't in the mood for another round. "I was prepping a report about it—then he broke out of prison."

"While I appreciate your diligence in regard to paperwork," Posada said, "I'd think this is the kind of thing you'd alert us to sooner rather than later, don't you?"

"With all due respect," Harras said, "I don't think Pete's speed on the FYIs is really relevant. The big question is: *Where did our client go?*"

"He's all over the television," Maya said, her voice soft and confused. Whatever hopes she had of exonerating her father—or at the very least gaining him a new trial—were gone. "Channel 10 is calling it the biggest manhunt in Florida history."

"Doesn't surprise me," Posada said. "Gaspar was guilty in the eyes of the public. Now he's confirmed it to the world."

Posada stood up and faced the bay windows. He was in shape—well over fifty but he didn't look a day older than forty-five. He was Varela's closest friend, or had been. He seemed as disappointed as Maya, but was hiding it better.

"They found a disposable phone in his cell," Posada said. "He was using it to keep in contact with someone from the outside, coordinating this whole thing."

"All while talking to us about getting him out?" Kathy asked.

"Keeping his options open, I guess," Posada said. "I can't see how he'd be able to get very far."

"Varela's a resourceful guy," Harras said. "He's not an average street thug. He's an ex-cop with knowledge of weapons and the city. That gives him a head start."

"And, in the meantime, someone's leaked the news of his book deal—and our involvement in said deal," Kathy said. "My phone hasn't gone off like this since the months leading up to my senior prom. There's even talk that his escape is tied to that street gang—*Los Enfermos*—if you can believe that."

"You can't be serious," Posada said. "How would Gaspar align himself with *Los Enfermos*? It's ludicrous."

"Not really," Pete said. Kathy and Harras shared a "here we go" glance.

"What does that mean?" Maya asked.

"Varela's old lawyer, Jackie Cruz, connected us with an independent forensics expert," Pete said. He stole a peek at his partners and wasn't surprised to see Harras closing his eyes to contain his anger and Kathy's barely successful attempts to bite her tongue.

"You're just full of surprises today," Posada said. "I'm guessing this was going to be in the same report you were going to send us about your conversation with Gaspar?"

"Maybe, maybe not," Pete said. "Her actual analysis is quite detailed, but I'll just give you the bullet points: there's no real evidence that she can find, from the forensic side, to exonerate Varela. The only hope he has is finding the murder weapon."

Pete looked around the room. All eyes were on him, each expression a unique mix of anger and surprise, as if he'd told an off-color joke at a dinner party. Pete was used to that by now. He hadn't planned on sharing this info this fast, or this way, but he didn't have a choice. It was time to put all the cards on the table.

"But even finding it doesn't prove anything unless the weapon itself points to someone else," Pete said. "So that's a bit of a nonstarter. However, the pathologist, Nicole Purdin, did suggest that the weapon used to kill Carmen Varela wasn't a random kitchen knife. It was long and, based on the kind of wounds it left, most likely a machete."

"Like the weapons *Los Enfermos* use," Harras said.

"Right," Pete said. Despite his frustration, Pete could tell Harras was impressed by Pete's legwork.

"So what? A bunch of gangsters killed Carmen? Is that what you're saying?" Posada asked.

"If what Gaspar says is true," Kathy said. "Or if he wanted it to look like a gang-related murder. Or if he's actually connected to the gang."

"You can't be serious," Maya said.

"No, you're right," Kathy said, locking her eyes on Maya. "This is all a fun game and I'm waiting for you to laugh at my well-executed gag."

Maya started to respond but Pete cut her off.

"It's not just that—we have to present some kind of united take on all this. And it's not just about the reporters and what they write," Pete said. "I expect the police will want to speak with us too. They'll want to implicate us in some way."

"You don't have anything to hide," Posada said. "Tell the truth if they bring you in."

"*The truth*, unfortunately, isn't worth shit in this case," Kathy said, a humorless smile on her face. "The truth, according to you and Maya, was that Gaspar Varela was innocent. I don't think innocent men do this. So, no matter how often we tell the cops and the press that we had absolutely no idea this was in the works, they're not going to buy it. His escape has, in effect, ruined our reputation here. No one will believe anything we write—Varela participation or not."

Kathy, as was her wont, was exaggerating. But her words had the desired effect.

"I'm sorry we dragged you into all this," Maya said. "I'm completely blindsided. I don't know what we can do from here."

"We wait," Pete said. "Until they find him. In the meantime, we continue doing what we were doing."

"Are you mad?" Posada said, his tone almost mocking. "This is done. Gaspar has basically admitted he killed his wife. There's no coming back. It's worse than a slow-moving white Bronco."

"You didn't hire us," Pete said. He pointed at Maya, who was leaning back in her seat limply, her face red from crying. "She did. When she tells us we're done, then we're done."

Posada sputtered a bit before waving his hand in a dismissive motion.

"Christ," he said. "Get over yourselves. This is over."

Harras stood up first and made for the door.

"This conversation is over, that's for sure," Kathy said, following Harras's lead. She turned to Maya. "Keep us posted. Like Pete said, we'll keep collecting information, when we can shake the press off our asses. If you want us to stop, we will."

Maya and Pete also stood up. She moved toward him, stopping close—closer than Pete expected. He could see the cobwebs of red in her eyes, smell the detergent coating the rumpled clothes. Her mouth creased into a dry frown. *She isn't sleeping much*, he thought.

"I don't want to change anything yet," she said. "But we'll see what happens over the next few days."

"Sure thing," Pete said. He tried to smile before following Kathy and Harras out the door. As it closed behind him, Pete could hear Posada going on the offensive. Pete didn't bother lingering outside to listen to what he had to say. He could guess.

"We have a lot of catching up to do," Harras said as they filed into the elevator. "But for now, I need a few hours to myself."

"I'm sorry, I—" Pete said.

"You're not sorry," Harras said, not looking at Pete. "If you were, you would have stopped the first time you boxed us out. But this is your thing, your rodeo. We're just along for the ride. I get it. But I don't have to put up with it. I'll talk to you both later."

The elevator doors opened before Pete could respond. Harras darted toward the lobby without another word. Pete and Kathy cut the other way, heading toward the back stairs that led them to the parking garage, saving them an awkward walk through a phalanx of hungry reporters and bloggers. She gave him a quick hug and peck on the cheek before getting into her car.

"They can't all be winners, darling. At least it's been an entertaining three weeks," she said. She closed the door and lowered the window. "Get some rest. I'll give you a pass on another verbal lashing, seeing as how big bad Harras is already unfriending you. We'll see where we're at in the morning."

"Sounds good," Pete said. Kathy backed out and started speeding down the street before Pete could say anything else.

The text from Maya came a few seconds later.

"**I**'m a mess," Maya said as she poured herself another glass of wine. It was late—almost midnight. They'd just finished off some Chinese takeout and were lounging on her couch. She was in jeans and a black T-shirt. She looked exhausted. *She looks great*, Pete thought. He'd come over after she sent the text and basically listened for a few hours as she talked—about her dad, her life, her fears. She refused to believe her father's escape was an admission of guilt. He'd just had enough. He was done with being incarcerated for a crime he didn't commit.

They hadn't even bothered to turn on the TV. Pete had listened to the news enough on the way to Maya's townhouse.

"You're allowed to be a mess," Pete said. "But I hope Posada gave you some advice—because you're going to be getting a lot of questions about this."

"What do you mean?" she asked.

"Well, you're Gaspar's daughter," Pete said. "People are going to have a hard time believing you didn't know this was going to happen."

"I didn't," Maya said.

"That may be true—"

"No, Pete," Maya said. "It *is* true. I had no idea this was in the works. If I did, do you think I'd spend the better part of my life trying to get my dad out of jail? Do you even understand how this is wrecking my own belief system? I swore up and down to anyone who would listen that he was innocent. But it's hard to rationalize that with him on the lam like some deranged criminal."

"I get it," Pete said. "I'm just saying people will be asking you about this, probably for a good long while."

"Fuck 'em," she said, taking a long sip of wine. "Let them ask. I could care less what they think."

He tried not to watch the golden liquid in the stemmed glass. He hated himself for that. He felt his mouth watering and he closed his eyes. He said a quick prayer and opened them again. When he did, she was sitting next to him. A little too close.

"Getting tired?"

"Just praying," Pete said.

"Praying? What?"

"Never mind," Pete said. He leaned in to her a bit and then regretted it. She stiffened at his touch.

"I'm sorry," she said. "I must have sent mixed signals, inviting you here."

"No, it's fine," Pete said. "You didn't want to be alone."

She put her free hand on his, her fingers wrapping around his palm.

"It's true," she said. "I didn't. Shit. I just wish we'd met under different circumstances, you know? Because I do like you."

Pete steeled himself. He'd had this conversation before.

"Look, Maya, it's fine," Pete said. "I get it. We work together. Whatever happened before …"

"Was nice," Maya said. "I liked it."

She leaned in and kissed him. It was a quick, gentle touch. Pete didn't have time to close his eyes. Her face was still close to his. Their eyes met.

"Me too," Pete said.

She broke away from Pete, moving down the couch, her arms wrapped around her chest as if she were hugging herself.

"What a fucking disaster," she said.

"It's fine."

"You keep saying that," she said, still not facing him. "But it's not. My father just broke out of prison. He's all over the news. My voicemail is overloaded with messages from reporters. I don't know what to do. Is he coming here? Are they going to shoot him on sight? What do I do? I'm used to … I don't know … trying to fix things. Now all I can do is sit around and wait."

"You're allowed to be hurt by this, you know," Pete said, getting up. He took a seat across from her. "This is insane. And look, I have no expectations here. You called, I came over, and we chatted. You needed someone to talk to. Who am I to say no to my boss?"

She let out a quick laugh and nodded.

"Okay, I'll take that."

"See? That was easy," Pete said. "Why don't you crash? I can clean up here and head out."

"Where do you live, anyway?"

"Westchester," Pete said.

"It's up to you," she said. She leaned over and gave him a long hug. He could feel her breath on his neck. They clung to each other. "You can stay. Or go. I won't take it wrong either way. I'm not in the best state of mind now. But it was nice to have someone to talk to."

"Happy to do it," Pete said, his arms lingering around Maya before ending the embrace.

She exhaled.

"I would love for you to stay, here, with me, that way. But I don't think that'd be good for either of us now. My head's not on right," she said. "But I do want you to stay. I just don't think you stay-staying is a good idea."

"The couch looks pretty comfortable."

She smiled at him.

"Thank you for not making this weird," she said, walking toward the hallway. "I'll get you some sheets. I just don't feel like being by myself tonight."

After she set him up on the couch, they hugged again and Maya headed to her bedroom. Pete slipped off his shoes, lay on the couch, and stared at the ceiling.

He couldn't sleep.

INTERLUDE SIX

Pete Fernandez let out a long sigh. This fucking sucked. His father didn't look up from his desk, his eyes focused on the file folder open in front of him. It was almost nine and they hadn't even left the office yet. His homework was done and he was bored out of his mind. This wasn't a life, he thought. It was prison. How fitting that he was doing time at a police station with his dad as warden.

It'd been like this for months. Months that felt like years. Pete and his friend Javier thought it'd be hi-la-rious to walk into the 7-Eleven on Coral Way and steal some forties. It wasn't as funny when the cashier pulled out a shotgun. Since then, Pete had been under lock and key: no going out, no after school, nothing. He woke up, went to class, got picked up by his dad, and spent the night hanging out with him at his desk. It was hell. The only bright spot was watching the hustle of the police station—detectives talking shop, suspects being brought in for questioning, lineups being looked over. It got Pete's brain sparking. But those moments of interest weren't common, and most of his days involved long stretches of boredom. He was in exile.

But it wasn't like Pete had much of a social life to go back to. Javier wasn't talking to him—he'd gotten in deep shit and Pete was nowhere to help. All his friends were Javier's friends, and they'd all sided with the cooler guy. Whatever. A few months and he could go to college far away, and this would just be a weird footnote to his life.

Pete sighed again.

"I get it, you're bored," Pedro said, not looking up from the file. "We'll get some food in a few minutes."

Pete didn't respond. Any kind of confirmation or sign of agreement would imply that he was on board with this whole thing. He just wanted to go to his room, close the door, put on his headphones, and blast some music. Preferably something loud and grating. He tried to visualize his CD rack for inspiration. Maybe *In Utero*. Or some Dinosaur Jr. Anything at this point.

He was interrupted by the office door swinging open. Carlos Broche, his father's partner in the homicide division, walked in, barely nodding in Pete's direction. He laid his palms on the desk and leaned in to talk to Pete's dad. The whispers came fast, Broche's head nodding to the rhythm of what he was saying. Pete could only make out every other word. Something about forensics and shells being recovered. Broche said something in Spanish too—"*los enfermos.*" The sick? Whatever. Pete didn't care. He wanted to eat and go home.

Pedro nodded and motioned for Carlos to back up. Only then did his dad's partner react to Pete's presence.

"What's up, papo?" Broche said, mussing Pete's hair as if he were a toddler. "How's school going?"

"Fine," Pete said.

Broche grabbed Pete's shirt in mock anger.

"Poor baby still mad?" Broche said. "You know this wouldn't be happening if you hadn't pulled that dumb shit, right?"

Pete didn't respond.

"You should be on your knees thanking *Jesucristo* every day for your father," Broche said. "Not everyone has a dad like him, someone to make sure they don't end up becoming a hoodlum."

Pete pulled away.

"You'll figure it out at some point," Broche said.

"Leave him alone, Carlos," Pedro said. "Let him sulk. He's bored and hungry."

"Shit, I know I am," Broche said. "What're we doing tonight? What about that place on Coral Way? The American one?"

"Wags?" Pete said. "That place sucks ass."

"Hey, watch your mouth," Broche said, turning to face him, his humorous tone gone and his finger pointed at Pete's face. "Nobody asked you."

Pete walked toward the desk as his father stood up and shoved a file folder into his briefcase. He seemed to pick up the pace the closer Pete got. There were still a few loose pages on his desk.

"Pete, where do you want to go?" Pedro asked, his attention focused on the errant pages. Before Pedro could snatch them back, Pete caught a glimpse. The name on one of the forms: Diego Fernandez. His grandfather. Under the paperwork were photos of what seemed like the front yard of Pete's house. Except it looked like they were taken a while back. One of the photos near the top featured a covered body on the ground. He started to ask but was frozen by his father's eyes.

"Where do you want to eat, hotshot?" Broche asked, jamming up the gears turning in Pete's head.

"Whatever," Pete said.

"Whatever," Pedro said, collecting the errant papers in one quick motion and sliding them into his briefcase. "Whatever, okay, sure, I dunno, maybe … that's your entire vocabulary, *hijo*. I don't think that's enough to guarantee much of a career, do you?"

Pete started to say, "I dunno," but caught himself. He stayed silent instead.

His grandfather Diego had died long ago, when Pete was very young. An accident, his father said. The subject rarely came up. So why was there a report with photos of their house in a police file of some kind?

Broche tugged at Pete's arm, and next thing he knew they were walking out of the main doors of the Miami-Dade Police Department. Pedro couldn't meet his son's gaze as they moved toward the car.

CHAPTER TWELVE

Pete flicked off the television set. He put the remote down on the coffee table and paced around Maya's smallish living room. Her townhouse felt comfortable and clean. Family pictures on the wall—Maya and her parents, one with her dad in prison, another of Posada and her. Knickknacks on the shelf. The house smelled nice too.

Pete felt out of it. He ran a hand across his face, feeling the week's worth of stubble stab at his palm and fingers. With the television off, the house was totally silent. He couldn't hear anything coming from Maya's bedroom. It felt weird not to sleep in his own bed.

Maya was warm and kind. She was smart. She was also his boss. He wasn't sure where things would go after tonight, but he was curious and optimistic.

It was close to three in the morning. He hadn't expected to come here tonight, but it had happened. He knew he needed to spend some time thinking about this—relationship, affair—whatever it was. But that didn't have to be now.

Pete blew out the scented candle Maya had lit when they got in. That was when he saw the guy, as Pete leaned down near the windowsill. The streetlight illuminated the man's walk toward Maya's house, which sat at the dead end of the block.

Pete looked again. He couldn't make out the man's face. He was almost strolling. He seemed relaxed, casual. He was walking in the road—not on the sidewalk—toward the house.

Pete grabbed the glass of water he'd left on the coffee table and took a long sip. Who was he to judge? Everyone had the right to be out late, he thought. But the logic didn't calm him. He put the glass back down and paced around the living room.

He found his messenger bag near the door. Inside were his gym clothes, an apple, a book, a mystery by Lawrence Block—*Eight Million Ways to Die*—and his gun.

He pulled the gun out and held at his side, pointed down. Maybe he was being paranoid. *So what?*

His head began to buzz as his eye peeked through the door's peephole. The man was still moving toward the house. He wore a hat and glasses. Pete could hear his footsteps through the door. The man stopped as he neared Maya's porch. He reached for the doorbell.

Pete opened the door. The man seemed surprised and took a step back.

"Can I help you?"

"Are you Pete Fernandez?"

"Who are you?" Pete asked.

The man's face was lost in shadow. His skin was tan. He was wearing a lot of clothes—longish trench coat over a Chicago Bulls jersey, dark jeans. It seemed odd. Pete couldn't find the switch to turn on the front light. *Damn it.* The man's face seemed aged and pockmarked, an abandoned battlefield.

"You're causing some trouble for a friend of mine," the man said. His voice was menacing and melodic at the same time. His head moved from side to side with every few words.

"That's a shame," Pete said. "Let me know what I can do to fix that."

"Ain't nothin' you can do now," the man said.

The moonlight reflected off the shotgun as the man pulled it from behind him—with just enough time for Pete to drop backward. He felt a searing pain in his right shoulder. His ears were ringing.

Stay in bed, Maya. Stay in bed.

He yanked his own gun out from behind him before his back hit the floor. He fired twice. He wasn't sure if he hit anything. He looked at his right arm. Blood. Everywhere. Pooling around Maya's hardwood floor. He looked toward the porch, but couldn't focus. His vision was blurred. He saw the man on his back, his hand waving the shotgun in Pete's direction.

Pete tried to get up, but the pain shot through him like a jolt. He saw movement from the porch. He heard a scream. Not his own. Maya's. *Damn.*

Another shot.

He closed his eyes for what he thought would be just a second.

Kathy Bentley hated herself already. She tied her long hair back in an ad hoc ponytail and waited for the sound of the lock clicking into place. She took the three steps from the porch to the front yard of his house and reached into her bag for the car keys. This was the second time in less than a week and that was most definitely not the agreement. She shrugged to herself as she reached the driver side door. It was late in the evening—morning, whatever. It wasn't that she felt cheap, or any of that cliché, walk of shame bullshit. Those days were long gone. She was smart, attractive, and not bound by anyone's perception of what she should do, so there was nothing to feel bad about. It was just sex, and she was fine with that.

No, she was upset at herself for the cracks that were beginning to show—the ones only she could see—that indicated she was more invested in this every-once-in-a-while dance than she let on. That couldn't stand, and didn't really bode well for this continuing. It just wasn't how she operated. Not after her last serious ex turned out to be a hired killer for the various factions of the Miami mob. Not after she found herself tied up somewhere in the Keys and expecting to die. Those things put life in perspective. No. She was here to have fun and to let the serious stuff be serious. Fuck romance.

She noticed a man's shadow behind her as she pushed the key button to unlock her silver Jetta. She spun around, her hand still on the keys, and caught him by surprise—he hadn't thought she'd noticed him yet. He was a stocky Hispanic man, mid-thirties. That wasn't unique in a town like Miami. Or even here, in suburban Kendall, where every townhouse looked the same and every corner sported a Publix or TGI Fridays. The man seemed lost, standing just on the periphery of Kathy's vision.

"Hello?" she said, her voice raised to make up the space between them.

The man stepped into the light. It was Dave Mendoza.

"Well, hello there, Captain Creeper," Kathy said. "Are you following me? Is this your new thing? If so, I'd really appreciate it if you kept this little factoid to yourself—"

"Kathy," Dave said. His face was white, stricken. She'd never seen him like this before.

"What?" she said. "What's wrong with you? You look extra psychotic."

"It's Pete," Dave said, moving closer to her. "I couldn't find you. He's in trouble, he's—"

"Tell me what happened, right now," Kathy said, closing the gap between them, grabbing his arms, trying not to shake him. "Talk to me."

"He's been shot, more than once," Dave said as he fell into her arms, the words coming out of his mouth in quick jags. "He's … I don't know if he's alive. He was rushed to the hospital, he's there now. I don't … I don't think he's going to make it. I was trying to find you, but—"

"Who shot him?" she asked, yelling into his ear. "Where?"

"They got him," Dave said. "They finally got to him ..."

She screamed then, not a scream of fear or desperation but one of anger and anguish—for Pete, for herself, and most of all for whoever was responsible.

PART II:
TOWN CALLED MALICE

CHAPTER THIRTEEN

Titusville, Florida
Three months later

P ete drove the beat-up red Ford truck to the far end of the
Waffle House parking lot. He flicked off the car stereo playing
PJ Harvey's *Dry* and shut off the engine, allowing himself a
few moments of silence. The night air was thick with humidity, the
sounds of cicadas and cars whizzing by on Cheney Highway the only
noise disrupting an otherwise quiet evening. Titusville was a small
city on the eastern coast of Florida, close to Cape Canaveral and not
too far from Orlando and all its Disney trappings. There wasn't much
to do, aside from wandering Wal-Mart or knocking over mailboxes.
Though, in the town's defense, Pete had seen a record store on one
of his early drives around the area. It was a quiet, nondescript blip
of a town that most people wouldn't notice on the interstate, with a
population mostly made up of travelers, transients, people working
at the Space Center, and those looking to stay off the grid for as long
as possible.

He slammed the truck door shut. He pulled the military-green cap down on his head, the brim masking his eyes. He checked his phone as he walked across the dirt lot toward the restaurant. No missed calls. He dropped it back into his pocket and kept going. He took a deep breath. His chest and shoulder still ached, but he was feeling better each day.

The smell of fried food was strong, even outside the place, and he felt his stomach rumble. Waffle House was one of the few guilty pleasures he'd allowed himself these days. One of the few times he'd leave the house and risk it.

The door jangled as he opened it and walked into the restaurant. The bright lights coated the place's yellow and brown décor, giving the space a grimy, painted-on feeling. He took a seat at the counter and nodded as the waitress handed him a sticky plastic menu. Like most nights, the place was empty, except for a group of teenagers plotting their evening and an elderly couple sitting by the windows facing the expressway, finishing their dinner. The faint sound of the Eagles filtered through the overhead speakers, the bland, finger-picky ballad spreading over the evening like lukewarm gravy that needed a bit more salt. He motioned for the waitress, a woman in her late forties named Ruth. She had kind eyes and a cigarette-coated voice that made Pete feel at home, even here in the middle of nowhere. She nodded and walked over.

He didn't need a menu. He didn't even need to say his order, but the ritual was part of the pleasure of coming here.

"Hey, hon," she said. "How's your night going?"

"So far," Pete said, "not bad."

"You look tired," she said, pulling her notebook from her apron and clicking her pen.

"If you're perpetually tired, is that a thing?"

"It's the kind of thing you cure with either coffee, sleep, cocaine, or a doctor's prescription," she said. "What'll it be?"

"Just two scrambled eggs and a side of home fries."

Ruth smiled and moved toward the kitchen.

Pete wheeled his seat around and looked out toward the empty parking lot, unsure why. The feeling had followed him since he got into the car. A feeling that he wasn't alone. The low sounds of the diner—conversation, the soft rock music from the speaker, and the cling-clang of the kitchen—were soothing to Pete, but not enough to dislodge the growing unease. He looked out onto the parking lot again, toward his own car. That was when he saw the shape, moving behind his truck. Pete grabbed a twenty from his wallet and placed it on the counter.

"Keep the food warm for me, Ruth," Pete said, his voice raised.

He walked out the front door and stopped outside the restaurant. The night air felt good on his face, the small town silence was disrupted for a moment by feet stepping on dried leaves. Someone in a hurry hoping to get away unseen.

Pete didn't head for his car. That was where this person was coming from, not where he was going. The parking lot was mostly empty and each car could be accounted for. He turned and walked toward the back of the Waffle House, toward the garbage dump and employee exit. He was banking on his target not being as familiar with the terrain as Pete was. He was right. Whoever had been following Pete didn't know that while you could park your car behind the Waffle House, you had to come out the way you came in. If someone followed you there, you were stuck.

He kept close to the wall of the Waffle House, his eyes on the back area. Whoever was there was moving around now, pacing. He knew he'd been caught. Pete felt for his gun, tucked behind him. He couldn't risk the man getting in his car and speeding off. Pete picked up the pace.

When he reached the back exit of the restaurant, he saw a man leaning over a Hyundai sedan, trying to unlock the door. He was young, small, and seemed nervous. Pete couldn't get a good look at him in the dark parking lot. But he recognized the shape as the man who'd been around Pete's car a few minutes earlier. He was also certain the man had followed him here. Either way, Pete's secret life wasn't so secret anymore. He pulled the gun out and pointed it.

"Step away from the car," Pete said. "Right now."

The man stepped back, and that was when Pete saw him, the light from the restaurant illuminating his young face. Pete had expected a nameless thug. Someone sent to finish him off, to complete the job the man in the basketball jersey had not. He hadn't expected to see someone he knew.

"Arturo Pelegrin?" Pete Fernandez said. "Holy shit."

"You're alive," Pelegrin said.

"I am," Pete said, gun still locked on Pelegrin as he walked toward him.

"Didn't know you was living up here, man," Pelegrin said. "What a weird thing, I was just—"

"Cut the shit," Pete said. He motioned for Pelegrin to move away from the car. "Sit down."

"Dude, what is this?" Pelegrin said. "Do you always pull guns on people?"

"How'd you find me?"

"I didn't, uh, I didn't know you were here," Pelegrin said, his voice rising in pitch. Pete noticed a bead of sweat forming on the younger man's brow. He'd fucked up. He wasn't supposed to be seen. "I'm just driving through, was gonna get something to eat."

"Why would you?"

"What?"

"Why would you know anything about me?" Pete asked. He'd reached Pelegrin now—one hand pointing the gun at his head while his free one did a quick and rough pat-down. He wasn't armed.

"Hey, listen, don't get defensive," Pelegrin said. "I'm not trying to blow up your spot. I was just leaving. I wouldn't have even known it was you if you hadn't shown up with a gun, though. The beard's new. Glad to see you're alive, I guess. I heard you got fucked up pretty bad."

Pelegrin was talking fast, his eyes darting around, looking for any kind of way out of the situation.

"Arturo, I'm going to give you one more chance," Pete said, clicking off the safety. "I've had a bad year. I've been shot at. I was almost killed. So, I can't say I'm excited to see you. Now, are you going to tell me who sent you after me?"

"They know," he said, following the words with a quick intake of breath. He was sweating now, breathing hard. He wasn't sure what Pete was going to do next, and that worked to Pete's benefit.

"Who knows?" Pete asked, his hand on Pelegrin's collar, the gun in the other. "Who sent you?"

"I can't go back empty," Pelegrin said. "And I know you're not gonna kill me. That's not you. But listen to me, man, they know you're here. *Los Enfermos*. And they're after you. *He* is after you. They're not going to stop until you, your partners, and everyone you care about is dead."

Kathy was in a black robe when she opened the front door. Pete walked in before saying anything.

"We have a major problem," he said.

"Hello to you too," she said, closing the door and following him into the living room.

He fell onto the couch and looked at the large flat-screen TV on the opposite wall. She'd been watching some kind of police procedural on TV. Probably a marathon.

She sat down to his right and produced a bowl of popcorn. She offered it to Pete with a shake. Pete declined with a slight head shake. He'd lost his appetite.

They'd lived in this three-bedroom, prefab house—tucked away on the dead-end Crystal Court, off Cathedral Way, which led you back onto Cheney Highway—for about three months. It'd taken Pete that long to recover from the gunshot wound he had suffered at Maya's house. It'd taken him five minutes to realize he needed to leave town. Dave had put it into perspective during those first few hazy hours after the shooting.

"You have to run," Dave had said, sitting by Pete's hospital bed. "For a little while, they're gonna think you're dead. Eventually, they're going to find out you're not. When that happens, they'll come gunning again."

Things had moved fast after that, starting with a hasty departure from the hospital. After a few phone calls, Dave handed Kathy an address scribbled on a piece of notebook paper and keys to a used truck he'd purchased from an old friend in need of quick cash.

"Throw out your cell phones and get on the road," Dave had said.

Pete wasn't in a position to argue, and the next thing he knew, he was on I-95, Kathy at the wheel, riding high on pain meds and wondering where they were going. She was running too. Though she hadn't taken a bullet, it was clear *Los Enfermos* viewed her and Pete as a package—one they would deal with together if the opportunity ever arose. She needed a new area code as much as he did. She let certain people—Harras, Maya—know they were alive, but not where they were headed.

Nowhere was the answer: Titusville, Florida. The house was one of Dave's parents' real estate holdings, though definitely on the fringe of their portfolio. With a quick call, the renters had been booted out and the furniture replaced. Pete and Kathy walked into a new life and had a few months to figure out what to do next. Pete owed Dave—and he wasn't sure there was a way to pay someone back for this kind of favor.

While Kathy had remained productive, writing well-researched and click-worthy true crime pieces for a number of mainstream outlets, Pete's days hadn't amounted to much. The first few months involved hours of physical therapy and stacks of pulp novels. The recovery was made tougher when Pete kicked the pain meds a few days after arriving, feeling himself slipping back into a familiar, dark place. His routine had become fairly set and mundane: wake up, take a run, come home, shower, do some errands, make a simple lunch, catch up on Miami news at the local library, and get home to make some dinner. Some nights, like tonight, when Pete and Kathy were in need of some time apart, Pete would make the short trip to the Waffle House and kill a few hours. Every week he'd head to the basement of the local Methodist church to catch a meeting before swinging back home to maintain some semblance of sanity and to keep his new, record-setting levels of anxiety and paranoia in check.

Kathy pulled her legs up and folded them under her as she tried to get comfortable.

"Would Pete like to share with the group?" Kathy said.

"I ran into Arturo," Pete said. "Arturo Pelegrin. Well, more like I caught him tailing me and had to pull my gun on the guy. Remember him?"

"Vaguely," she said. "Janette Ledesma's son? He didn't seem keen on helping us."

"No, he wasn't," Pete said, his eyes moving over to the television screen. "He was following me around. I had to stick a gun in his face to get him to talk. We've been found out. They know we're here."

"Are you sure?" Kathy asked. "I mean, I guess it's a surprise to find anyone here in the butthole of humanity, but could it have been a coincidence?"

"No," Pete said, his tone grave. "By the end of it he made it pretty clear. *Los Enfermos* know we're here and they're not going to give us a pass. They missed one time. I don't think they're going to miss again."

The fact that the email was waiting for him when he closed his bedroom door and turned on his iPad didn't surprise him much. Today was that kind of day. The kind of day where your past peeked at you from the sewer and reached its hand out to remind you it was still there. Watching.

Pete turned on his nightstand light and slid into his bed—which was really just a mattress on the floor with a few pillows and sheets. He propped one up behind him and checked his email.

The subject line was brief—*Hello*.

Pete,

I hope you're well. Our last conversation struck me as pretty final, but I wanted to reach out after hearing about your injuries. While I'm not really sure where you are, Kathy assures me you're both doing alright. I didn't think you'd pull through this time.

I just wanted to let you know that the police have brought in a suspect for questioning in Rick's murder. His name is Gus Trabanco and it looks like someone who was at Duffy's that night can peg him as one of the two guys who walked Rick out of the bar and eventually killed him.

The other guy who killed Rick is a man named Nestor Guzman. You killed him in self-defense the night you were shot.

I know Rick was laundering money for bad people— shell accounts, false names, fake companies. I had my lawyer and his people look it over and he agreed it was not kosher. I don't know the specifics, nor do I want to. But just spending some time going through his paperwork shows me he was moving a lot of money from one place to another, with a cut going into his own pocket. Maybe more than he was supposed to? I can't tell. I'm not an accountant.

I'm leaving the country in a few days. I don't feel safe here. I don't think you are either. Whoever wanted Rick dead is also tied into whatever you're working on. They were upset with Rick and killed him for it. Now they're targeting you and Kathy.

Anyway, I don't expect a response. I just wanted to warn you.

Emily

Pete placed his tablet on the nightstand. He leaned back on the pillow. He wasn't sure what to make of Emily's note. He wasn't sure what to make of Emily, period. But her email confirmed two things

Pete had suspected. First, that Rick was cleaning cash—lots of it, like six- or seven-figure sums—for *Los Enfermos* and pocketing some for himself. Once the gang discovered this, he was gone. It didn't help that he was probably privy to way too many secrets. Second, it confirmed—at least in Pete's mind—that the Varela case and the *Los Enfermos* situation were one major problem. He just hadn't worked out the details yet. Was Varela running the gang now that he was out of prison? Did he have his sights on Pete? Did his relationship with the gang date back to before the murder of his wife?

He thought of Stephanie Solares and the yelling she'd overheard. Had Carmen Varela discovered that her husband wasn't the clean-cut cop he wanted the world to think he was? That he was actually tangled up with a band of murderers and drug dealers?

The police had been clear: a man named Nestor Guzman had been sent to murder him three months ago. Someone knew that he was at Maya Varela's house that night and wanted him dead. The fact that Pete was alive was pure luck. Doubly lucky that he managed to get off a few shots to kill the guy while falling backward. Pete had no idea who Nestor Guzman was then, and he had less of one now. But he no longer felt safe here, in the wilds of Titusville, in this secret house, living a secret life. He hadn't spoken to Maya since those first days immediately after the shooting—which he regretted, but also realized was a necessity. Pete knew she hadn't been shot that night, at least. He hoped she was fine otherwise too.

The AC window unit rumbled into action, startling Pete for a minute. He still hadn't gotten used to the quiet. The birds chirping. The wind. He missed loud car horns and fast, pitter-patter Spanish conversations. He missed Cuban coffee. He hated this weird limbo and hated himself for living in self-imposed exile.

He almost missed the call. He heard his phone vibrating. The display wasn't a number or contact he recognized. No one but Dave and Harras had this number, besides Kathy. Pete picked up.

"Hello?"

He heard muffled breathing on the other end.

DANGEROUS ENDS

"Who's calling?"

The voice came to life, low and creaky.

"We see you, Pete."

"Who is this?" Pete said.

"We see you."

The line went dead.

CHAPTER FOURTEEN

"Going back?"

Kathy was a few sips into her first cup of coffee. It was not the best time to bring up the fact that he was leaving, Pete realized.

"Our cover is blown," Pete said. "Varela is still missing, and we're as safe here as we were in Miami. We need to touch base with Harras and get this going again, or we'll just be sitting here in fear, waiting for them to hit us first."

"Harras is probably having a monthly party to celebrate us being gone," Kathy said. "And I haven't heard a peep from Maya in months. Maybe she's glad her dad is AWOL, or maybe she's pissed you haven't told her where you are, being her secret boyfriend and all. I mean, it's not like Varela had a lot of hope in terms of the judicial system. I'm impressed he got away, though."

"This is all connected somehow," Pete said. "Varela, the attempt on me, Rick's death."

"Shit," Kathy said, getting up. "I need a cigarette."

"Come with me," Pete said. "You can work from anywhere."

"Working isn't my top concern now," Kathy said. "This is very bad. I know you hate the urban tumbleweed that is Titusville, but we snuck away in the dead of night because you were 'at risk' in Miami. Now we need to go back? It doesn't scream 'stability' to me."

"I'm at risk here too," Pete said. "We both are. They know we're here."

Kathy turned around and opened the fridge. She grabbed a diet soda and dropped it in her purse, which was resting on the counter.

"Emily says the guy who tried to kill me was one of the guys who killed Rick," Pete said.

Kathy paused for a second. She turned toward Pete, who was leaning against the far wall near the coffeemaker.

"Explain."

"Nestor Guzman," Pete said.

"Yes, the man who thought it'd be cool to turn you into Swiss—or should I say, Cuban-American—cheese while you were sleeping with the boss," Kathy said. "That has been established."

"I wasn't sleeping with her."

"About to, just finished, whatever, bro," Kathy said, emphasizing the last word. "You wanted to get with that. Real professional, you are."

Pete ignored her.

"He and an associate, Gus Trabanco, murdered Rick," Pete said. "Emily confirmed that Rick was moving money around for *Los Enfermos*. She's leaving the country now."

"Goodie for her," Kathy said. "I'm sure she's being really indecisive about that too."

Pete loved how protective Kathy was of him in regard to Emily. She said the things he couldn't let himself speak aloud.

"I think we need to figure out where all this stuff stands," Pete said. "How it all relates. If Varela is still around, orchestrating this, he's much more dangerous than we thought—and showing his true colors more and more."

"That'd be easy, now wouldn't it?"

"Easy?"

"The Big Bad Villain breaks out of prison to take the throne of his evil *Los Enfermos* criminal empire," Kathy said. "That'd be easy."

"It makes the most sense."

"Why would he want you dead, Pete?" she asked. "He hired you. Haven't you learned by now? The easy answer is very rarely the answer. I don't disagree, though, something does seem to be going on. I apologize for not joining your chorus of panic immediately."

"I appreciate your humble recanting," Pete said.

"So what shall we do if, say, I join you on this random trip back to the bong-water swamp that is South Florida?" Kathy said.

"You're coming, then?"

"I can't let you dive back into this by yourself," she said, trying not to smile.

"I can't believe I drove to Florida City for this shit."

Harras yanked off his sunglasses and wiped them on his shirt. The shade from the tree in the house's front yard provided little cover from the sun, which was at full blast. It was early afternoon and Harras's white dress shirt was already mottled with sweat. Pete sipped his giant glass of water and sat up straight in his chair. Kathy looked like she was asleep, leaning back, her eyes covered by giant sunglasses and a straw hat casting a long shadow over her face. They didn't bother to get up for the new arrival.

Pete motioned for Harras to take the empty seat across from them, also in the shade. He sat.

"Can you please tell me why you and Bernstein over here invited me down to the Everglades?" Harras said as he wiped his brow. "What is this place, anyway?"

"It's one of the many properties in the Dave Mendoza family

portfolio, apparently," Kathy said. Once they'd decided to come back to Miami, Pete's first call was to Dave. They needed a base of operations that was as off the grid as you could be in Miami. Pete's second call had been to Harras, who let them know that *Los Enfermos* had put a bounty on their heads and were spreading the word through the Miami underworld. "His parents use this as a summer house, when they're bored of their Brickell apartment or Gables mansion. Who needs a summer house in fucking Miami? But hey, they're rich and didn't seem to care about us using it, so I'm grateful, as they say. Also, we're not in Florida City. Your geography is rusty. We're in the unexplored pocket of Miami known as South Miami Heights. Which is perfect, because it seems like Pete wants to stay incognito for as long as possible. Go figure."

"Smart," Harras said. He seemed less grumpy now that he was in the shade, which was maybe two degrees cooler than the ninety-plus action happening in the sun. "Trying to avoid getting shot again? Good luck with that."

"I'm stubborn, if anything," Pete said.

"Can we get on with this, seriously?" Harras said. So much for being less grumpy.

"What's going on with Varela?" Pete asked.

"Nothing since we last spoke," Harras said. "He disappeared. It's a huge embarrassment. The paper-pushers are bouncing off the walls. Couldn't think of a better organization to be feeling it than Miami-Dade Corrections. The whole department's going through a massive external review. I'm sure jobs will be chopped and new paper-pushers will be brought in. But aside from that, nothing. No credible reports or sightings, and they've had his daughter and buddy Posada under surveillance since he broke loose, in case he tries to reach out. Nothing. I've been trying to keep a low profile too. I can't just assume the people who went after you didn't notice I was working the case as well."

"What do you think?" Kathy said.

"About what?"

"His escape, what it means, your horoscope, anything?" Kathy said. Harras and Kathy weren't super-simpatico, but Pete figured that was because they were a lot alike—no-bullshit alphas who wanted all the answers. Ten minutes ago.

"I think he's long gone," Harras said. "And he'd been planning it for a long time, stringing everyone along into building this campaign to prove his innocence, including his daughter, Posada, us. It was all cloud cover while he figured out how to escape, and I'm still trying to nail down just how extensive his network got to be while he was in prison."

"Network?" Pete asked. "Like *Los Enfermos*?"

"Yes," Harras said. "That's a built-in network of people. This kind of an escape doesn't just happen with a spoon and a hole in the prison laundry room. Varela has people under his thumb who helped him get out and are now helping him stay hidden."

"You think Maya is involved?" Pete asked. He hadn't told Maya he was back. He wasn't sure where they stood—if anywhere.

"I doubt it," Harras said. "She's smart, but she doesn't strike me as the type of person able to orchestrate this kind of thing, or to take part in it. She's been quiet—even with the press hounding her. But she did come in and talk to the police, which was a show of good faith."

"We're going to pick up the case again," Pete said.

"What case is that?" Harras said, a humorless laugh escaping his mouth.

"Varela. Whether he did kill his wife or not," Kathy said. "That's what we were hired to figure out."

"You two are incredible, you know that?" Harras said. "There is no Varela 'case' anymore. He's gone. He broke out of prison. If that's not proof of guilt, I don't know what is. Also, do you think his daughter still wants you two on retainer after that disappearing act you pulled? You're lucky she didn't sue you to get whatever she paid back."

"That may be, but someone tried to kill me, and whoever wanted that to happen figured out we were in Titusville," Pete said. "And I think that's connected to Carmen Varela."

"If you asked me to list the people who want you dead, I'd run out of paper," Harras said, standing up. "Anything else you want to clue me in on, aside from your T-ville escapades, which I'm already tired of hearing about?"

"We want your help," Kathy said, looking up at Harras from her seat. "We need to pool our resources and figure this out."

"You say that like I have all this other work coming in," Harras said. "I'm retired, remember? I'll help, but we have to set up some ground rules. The kind you ignored when this was more official. Understand?"

"Not really," Pete said.

"Don't play stupid," Harras said. "No more flying solo. No more surprise interviews. No more detours. We all talk, we're all on the same page. That's how it has to run. Let me know when you find anything and I'll do the same. That'd make my life a bit easier, grading on a steep curve. I can at least try to run interference for you."

"You got it," Pete said.

"Also, you both need to be careful," Harras said. "This isn't just a pretend threat out there. There are people—bad people—out to get you. I'd think twice before you leave the house. This isn't funny ha-ha wearing a wig and sunglasses shit either. They're pros. And they want to get paid."

Harras motioned for Pete to get up.

"Follow me to my car, I've got something for you," Harras said.

"A present?" Pete said. Kathy waved limply as they walked away.

"Depends."

Harras opened the backseat of his car and pulled out a box of files. His back blocked Pete from seeing what was in it. He turned around with a single file in hand and passed it to Pete. It was heavy and held together by a few rubber bands.

"What is this?" Pete asked.

"Don't open it yet," Harras said. "Do you have somewhere we can sit for a while?"

"Sure," Pete said, heading back to the house. He waved at Kathy as they opened the front door. "I'll be out in a bit."

"Whatever," she said.

Pete made a quick right and another right into a small office. There was a desk adjacent to the far wall with two chairs nearby. Pete placed the file folder on top of the desk and sat down. There was a small TV on a rickety-looking stand. The Dolphins game was on, muted. It was the first quarter of the early afternoon game. They were losing to the Bills.

"Okay, are you going to tell me any more about this before I crack it open?" Pete asked.

"That was your father's," Harras said.

"Okay," Pete said again. "Are you going to give me breadcrumbs or just spill?"

"It's a case file, sort of. Open it up," Harras said, closing the office door before he took the free chair.

Pete took off the rubber bands that held the file together and opened the folder. He felt a rush of emotion as he flipped through the first batch of handwritten notebook pages. His father's penmanship was clear and blocky, unlike Pete's sloppy cursive. The notes were meticulous and concise, a series of journal-like entries chronicling a murder investigation that seemed familiar to Pete, like a name he couldn't put a face to. Years ago, while tracking the mob killer known as the Silent Death, Pete had discovered his father's case files, tucked away in the back of Pete's own car. He thought that was all he'd ever have, in terms of his father's work. This was an unexpected addition.

"How'd you get this?" Pete asked. "I thought I had all his files, before his house was destroyed—but I've never seen this."

"It's not an official file, so it probably wasn't with the ones you had, I guess," Harras said. "It's not a case your father was assigned to, but something he was doing on his own time. Whatever little of that he had, with you running him ragged."

Pete smiled a bit. He'd been a tough kid to handle.

"Why would he be working on a murder case off the books,

though?" Pete said. He flipped through a few more pages in the file and found his answer. Written in large letters above another sheet of notes were the words *Who killed Diego Fernandez?*

"Do you remember your grandfather?" Harras said.

"Not really, he died when I was a kid," Pete said. "My dad had just made detective. They said it was a heart attack."

"Sorry to break it to you," Harras said, reaching for the file and flipping to a later page, "but your granddad died from multiple gunshot wounds. It happened on your father's front lawn, what would eventually become your front lawn before it went boom-boom a while back."

Pete felt himself going back farther than he'd allowed himself to remember in a long time. The memories were cloudy. A scream from outside the house. Rushing to the front window and seeing his father hunched over a body. The smell of burnt rubber and smoke. Being pulled away. Days later, his father in a dark suit. He'd been about four years old, so the memories felt like dream fragments—vague, undefined. But as he cobbled them together in his mind, it began to make sense.

"He was killed in the middle of the week, on a hot summer day that was probably a lot like this one," Harras said. "The only reason I even found it was because I spent a lot of time researching gangland murders—like the one you almost became—while you two were off hiding, and this popped up. Looks like your father left it with his partner, Carlos Broche, when he retired. He knew he couldn't chase it off the books. After Broche died, his wife turned it in to the PD. Then I found it."

Harras waited a beat, his eyes on Pete.

"Your grandfather's death wasn't just a robbery or accidental homicide," Harras said.

Pete clutched the case file tighter.

"He was assassinated," Harras said. "And your father spent whatever time he had trying to find the man who killed him."

They spent the rest of the afternoon going over the file, pages stacked and spread out on the small desk, a few other piles of paper around the room. The total file wasn't large, but it was a lot of information to digest. For Pete, it was also something that ran counter to the story he'd believed for years, at least when it came to his grandfather.

His grandfather hadn't spent a lot of time with Pete as a kid. The older man had moved into their house for the final year or two of his life, which overlapped with the first few years of Pete's own. The file had explained why he moved in. Diego, the owner of a fledgling talk-radio station, had been attacked while leaving his office. It had been written off as a mugging at the time, though nothing was stolen. His father's notes told another story: that Diego Fernandez had been attacked by an agent for Cuban dictator Fidel Castro, an act of vengeance meant to punish Diego for his "betrayal" of the regime. Castro was no stranger to political hits or violence against old enemies, Pete knew, but the method of this attack jumped out at him.

"Seems like my grandfather wasn't very popular," Pete said.

"Not with Castro, no," Harras said. "Or his agents in Miami."

"He was stabbed," Pete said.

"No, he was shot," Harras said.

"Yes, when he died," Pete said. "But before that—according to the file—he'd been stabbed. Outside his office."

"Where'd he work?" Harras asked, not turning from the stack of papers he was looking at, his back to Pete.

"A radio station," Pete said. "He owned one of those anti-Castro talk-radio setups, like WQBA. It was late and he was leaving."

"Gimme the details."

"Huge knife wound to his stomach, he barely survived," Pete said. *Deep knife wound. Click, click. "Los Enfermos*—they were a political gang, no?"

"Yeah, to a point," Harras said, turning to look at Pete. "Pro-Castro. This fits."

"The stabbing fits too," Pete said. "Maybe they tried to off him their usual way."

"Then waited for the right time to finish the job," Harras said.

"There isn't a lot on the actual gunman," Pete said. "It's hard to really even confirm that the guy who stabbed him at work was the same guy who killed him. But I think it's a safe bet."

"Yeah, the people in the neighborhood said the guy doing the shooting was pretty young," Harras said, "from what I remember reading. But that's it. The car he drove—lots of people said it was a beige Oldsmobile, but that doesn't narrow it down. Everything else, from the guy driving to the direction it sped off toward, didn't really materialize. The evidence points to someone working for Castro's government, though, trying to take down one of the more vocal and successful exiles in Miami. It was a win for him, even if he couldn't take credit."

"How fucked am I?"

"What do you mean?"

"With *Los Enfermos*," Pete said. "I need to get out of their sights. What do I need to do?"

"Well, they've tried to kill you twice—that we know of," Harras said. "They've tracked you down to the armpit of the state and back. I'm not sure this is something that can be resolved peacefully."

Pete ran a hand through his hair. He was tired. Normally, he'd have a target—a husband who needed to be followed, a killer's patterns that needed to be analyzed. This was an entire gang of killers with the shared goal of wanting Pete dead. Were they really taking orders from Maya's father?

"These guys don't quit," Harras said. "They're blood brothers and they run the streets here. They do what their boss says, they kill who they're told to kill, and they skim and steal and threaten when they need, just to keep things rolling. It's been this way for a long time. You're just the latest target."

CHAPTER FIFTEEN

Maya pulled out her cell phone as she walked out of the Posada & Associates offices. She tapped it a few times and brought it to her ear as she made her way toward the parking lot on the building's east side. It took her a moment to register that Pete was blocking her path. She muttered something into her phone before dropping it into her large purse. Her attire was no-nonsense—dark blue pantsuit, her hair tied back, not a lot of makeup.

"Pete," she said.

"Hey," Pete said. He hadn't thought this visit through, he realized. His mind was all over the place following his meeting with Harras and the revelation that his own grandfather might have been a victim of *Los Enfermos*. The news had served as a stark reminder of the bloody past that still haunted Cuba-U.S. relations. *Los Enfermos*, in addition to being a cabal of bloodthirsty gangbangers, were also an elite hit squad, serving Castro and his lieutenants. While it did seem like the last vestiges of the Cold War were melting away, the murderous orders from Cuba's now-retired dictator were more recent than people would like to think.

Pete was sporting dark sunglasses and a cap pulled low, his best attempt at going incognito on short notice. He hated the idea of not being able to walk the streets of his hometown freely, but with a bounty on his head he also had a strong desire to avoid another run-in with *Los Enfermos*. He wasn't sure he'd survive.

"You're back," she said. "I tried to call you."

"I know," Pete said. "I'm sorry. We had to go."

"Is that what you do?" Maya said. "Pick up and leave in the middle of the night?"

"No," Pete said. "But I had to in this case."

"Well, I'm glad you're alive," she said, tilting her head, as if trying to ensure it was Pete. "But—look, whatever. I know we didn't have anything real, or whatever the hip term for it is, but you should have called. Even if personally you didn't feel like you needed to, you guys were working for me. What the fuck? Did Harras know where you went?"

"He knew we were fine," Pete said.

"Great, great," she said. "Guess he couldn't be bothered to give me that heads-up either? Were we not paying you enough?"

"I'm sorry," Pete said. "I came by to let you know we're back. We're okay and we want to keep working on this. We just had to go away for a while. I didn't feel safe here. Hell, I still don't—so please keep it under your hat that we're even back. But we want to finish the job we started."

"Is this a joke?" Maya said. "Pete, my dad is gone. He broke out of jail. It's pretty clear whatever hope we had of proving him innocent disappeared into the night with him. There's no point in investigating anything anymore."

"Stuff is still going on," Pete said. He was looking around them. "Can we talk somewhere more private?"

Maya looked at her watch. It was close to three in the afternoon. She started walking toward the parking lot. Pete followed.

"I get that you were injured and scared for your life," Maya said. "I was scared too, Pete. You were shot in my house. For all I know, they were gunning for me too. Thank God, seriously, that you were there. It's insane. So, on some level, I understand why you had to run. But what makes you think I'd even want to hire you and Kathy after all this? There's no work to be done and, mitigating circumstances aside, I can't trust that you'll stick around to finish the job. I don't hire a lot of private investigators, so I may not know how this works, but I don't think that's it."

"It's not how it works," Pete said. "Let me explain."

Maya reached her car. She opened the driver side door and shook her head before looking back at Pete. "Get in."

"So this Rick Blanco is somehow connected to my dad?"

Maya's eyebrows crashed together. She seemed confused. Pete was not doing a great job of explaining, well, anything. They were sitting in a booth at Swensen's—an ice cream and burger place on South Dixie Highway. They'd driven for a while, mostly in silence, until Maya blurted out a desire for ice cream, fries, and a good burger. Swensen's delivered that with gusto.

"I'm not sure yet," Pete said, grabbing a fry from Maya's plate. Pete's was empty. "But the guys who killed him—killed Rick—one of them tried to kill me. Nestor Guzman. He's dead. But his buddy, Gus, is part of *Los Enfermos*."

"It's almost like those guys don't like you much, huh?" Maya said.

They laughed. Pete felt some relief. They'd gotten through Maya's understandable anger over Pete and Kathy's disappearance and settled back into something resembling a friendship. Or so he hoped. Maya took a sip from her strawberry shake.

"So are you and Kathy on complete lockdown?" Maya asked.

"Yeah, basically," Pete said. "I shouldn't even be here. We've got a house in South Miami Heights—my friend Dave let us crash there until all of this gets sorted."

"I can't imagine what that must be like," she said. "Not being able to even walk outside. Have you learned anything else about these guys since you snuck away?"

Pete ignored the dig.

"If *Los Enfermos* are after me and they killed Rick," Pete said, "it could mean that everything—including your dad's case—is linked."

Pete mentioned the strange encounter with Arturo Pelegrin, while explaining where he and Kathy had been living for the past few months. Maya frowned for a second.

"He was in Titusville? For what?"

"They sent him to get us," Pete said. "I caught him tailing me, so we got lucky. He made a rookie mistake."

"That's a lot to process."

"How so?"

"Everything, really," she said. She pushed some of the fries on her plate around. "My dad, this gang, the knives, this Rick person. It's hard to take it all in. Do you think my dad was working with these people, *Los Enfermos*, to get out of jail? Like, he's some kind of gang lord?"

Pete's silence said more than he could ever hope to with words.

Duffy's Tavern looked like any Irish Pub—in Miami, New York, or Kentucky. Clover leaves decorated the establishment's dirty green awnings, which hunched over the dark brown double door entranceway, like a warped architectural gargoyle. Inside was a cramped and smoky bar that provided patrons with a special kind of sensory overload: photos covered the walls, touching on every shadowy corner of the city—from Miami Dolphins quarterbacks, to mayors on parole, to actresses from *The Golden Girls*, to city commissioners who blew their own brains out, all smiling with Duffy's owner. The place also had piss beer on tap and watery well drinks to boot—the total package.

Pete gave his eyes a second to get comfortable with the lighting—

dim and gray in stark contrast to the blinding sun outside, which boasted the kind of heat that made it hard to even breathe. No wonder people crowded into dives like Duffy's. The AC alone was reason to stop by. Pete knew he was pushing it. Stepping out with a bounty on his head wasn't the safest bet he could make. He was pretty sure that dark shades, a Pere Ubu shirt, and a Miami Heat cap would do little to hide his identity from *Los Enfermos*. But there was work to be done.

Duffy's was empty aside from the bartender—a thin older man with a salt-and-pepper moustache and faded Dolphins cap—and a stocky woman in a too-tight tank top and sweat pants sitting at the bar, nursing what looked like a Midori Sour. The bartender nodded as Pete came in, and the woman grunted, stirring her drink with a red straw.

The bar was located to the left of the entrance, with the rest of the space taken up by high-top tables, booths, and a jukebox that probably still had tracks by Gloria Estefan, Willy Chirino, and Jon Secada. Near the back, Pete saw a pool table that had more stains on it than pockets and balls combined. He sat at the bar. The bartender dropped a coaster in front of him.

"What's it gonna be?"

"Seltzer."

"Guess it is kind of early," he said, a tinge of disappointment in his voice.

The bartender brought him a yellow glass with bubbly water in it. No lime.

"Three bucks."

Pete dropped a twenty on the table and kept his hand on it while looking at the bartender.

"I have a few questions," Pete said.

"I hope I have a few answers for you, pally." He nodded and took the cash.

Pete extended his hand but the bartender shook his head and went back to the register, which was down at the far end of the bar.

He grabbed a towel and returned to where Pete was sitting. He started to wipe down the counter in front of Pete, not making eye contact.

"This place is loaded with cameras, but they just record visuals, not audio," he said, his voice low. "So, thanks for the Jackson, I do appreciate it. But I'm not going to answer any questions from my boss about our conversation if I can help it. And you look like the type of guy people are going to ask me about later."

"Is that right?" Pete said.

The bartender slung the towel over his shoulder with a flourish and gave Pete a once-over.

"Name's Winslow," the bartender said. "Keep the questions simple and quick and I'll give you what you paid for. If that's not enough, I imagine you took out more cash before you came here. Probably wasn't all for seltzer either."

Pete ran a finger over the condensation that had already begun to form on the tiny glass. The lady across the bar finished her drink with one long, gurgly slurp. She slammed the glass on the counter and looked around before putting her head down on the bar, her arms serving as the pillow. Down for the count before noon.

"I'm Pete Fernandez," Pete said. "I'm an investigator. I wanted to ask you a few questions about something that went down here a few months ago."

Winslow stuck his hands in his pockets and leaned into the bar.

"I have an idea what you're going to ask about, kid," he said. "So let me save you some time. Number one, there's no video from that night. Camera tapes over the previous night's, and by the time the cops came by the footage was gone. Number two, I already spoke to the cops about the guy they found in Peacock Park and what he was up to before."

"Could you tell me the same story?" Pete asked.

Winslow grabbed Pete's glass without asking and sprayed another seltzer into it with the soda gun that rested under the bar. He placed the refilled drink in front of Pete and turned to look at the lady across the bar. Realizing she was already spending some quality time with the Sandman, he swiveled back and straightened his apron, splotched with grease and food stains.

"Easy enough," Winslow said. "I was working that night. I usually don't. I'm more a day shift kind of bartender. Work is slower, easier, and the regulars know how to tip. Night crowd is full of young assholes. The pace is faster too. Plus, these kids order drinks I'd need a handbook for. Don't even get me started on the kind of shit they put in their mouths. Me? I'll stick to Early Times or a cold beer. Rum if I want to get crazy. That's it."

"Good to know," Pete said.

Winslow smirked.

"Listen, buddy, you need me more than I need you," he said. "So bear with me, okay?"

"You got it," Pete said. "You were working the night in question, then."

"Right, I was," Winslow said. "It was late. Near closing time. Still pretty busy, but I could see the sea parting, if you get what I mean. Three guys—one of them I knew, the other two I didn't—were playing pool in the back. Pretty standard. But based on the mood of the two guys I didn't know, it looked like the wrong side was winning."

"They were upset?"

Winslow rubbed his chin.

"They seemed upset, yeah," he said, letting the words hang out there.

"Seemed upset?"

"It seemed like they wanted the regular—Rick, nice guy—to think they were pissed," Winslow said. "Then they went outside. That was that."

"So you knew Rick?" Pete asked. "He came here a lot?"

"Yeah, I knew him," Winslow said. "But like I said, I worked days mostly. He'd come by to get lunch or have a few if he had a meeting in the area. Guess his offices were way south, in Homestead. But yeah, I knew him. Good guy. I talked to him that night for a bit too. Said he had to entertain these guys. They were like clients. Worked for his big boss. Never seen business clients like that myself, but what do I know?"

Pete let the information simmer for a bit. Rick had been trying to entertain two gang members for business. Emily had mentioned that Rick's dealings were not fully on the up-and-up, that'd he'd been cooking the books for *Los Enfermos*. One of the two street thugs had tried to kill Pete. He was now dead. The other guy was in jail for his part in Rick's murder. The puzzle pieces were floating in front of Pete but not yet connecting to form a picture.

"Was there anything else that you remembered after you talked to the police?" Pete asked.

Winslow sighed. He was put out, having to think this hard so early in his shift.

"Y'know, not really," he said. "Maybe one thing. But it wasn't even that night. It was a few weeks earlier. Rick had come in to grab a bite and we got to talking. Place was pretty empty, like this—so why not? Gotta work the regulars, I say. Become their guy. Anyway, we're talking and he seems stressed and overworked so I ask him, 'What's wrong, amigo?' He was complaining about work. How this one guy he was in business with was pissed at him. How he—Rick—had paid a little too much attention to something he shouldn't have, and now he was worried it was gonna come back to bite him. What he was doing, according to him, was stuff that wasn't—how'd he phrase it?— 'in the lines.' He said something else that stuck with me. I didn't think to press him on it. Not sure why it's the part I remembered most. I sure as hell forgot it until you asked me that."

"What'd he say?"

"'Sometimes, Winslow, I just feel like bait,'" Winslow said. "'A smaller fish being used to trap the big one.'"

Pete winced as he walked out of Duffy's, the bright sun making it hard to see much beyond what was right in front of him. One thing did jump out in Pete's line of sight: someone was standing by his car, which had been one of three in the parking lot. It was now one of four, and the driver of car number four was watching him approach.

Pete was armed, as was the norm for him now. But even that knowledge didn't really calm him. He started to walk toward his car. Whoever was waiting for him was leaning on his vehicle with little concern, his eyes locked on his phone and his back to Pete.

"Can I help you?" Pete said. He let out a long breath of relief when he realized who it was.

Martin from AA turned around, stuffing his phone in his pocket, startled for a moment.

"Shit, hey, man," he said. "Didn't hear you creep up like that."

"That's good, I guess," Pete said. Martin seemed jittery. He was shifting his weight from foot to foot, scratching his neck in an effort to seem casual.

"Man, it's good to see you," Martin said. "Been a while. Beard's new, huh?"

"Yeah, I'm sorry for falling off the map," Pete said. He kept his distance. He wasn't sure of what Martin was after—or if he was sober—and he didn't want to get too close. Not until he figured out how Martin knew where to find him.

"It's cool, man. Shit, you got shot," Martin said. "Tried to see you in the hospital, but that place was on lock, you know? Glad you made it, though. Lucky man."

"Very lucky," Pete said, scanning the parking lot, trying to seem casual. "How'd you know I was here?"

"You're gonna be mad at me," Martin said, his face trying to smile, but twisting into a frightened scowl. "I was thinking of going in. Going into this place."

"Thinking and doing are different things," Pete said. "Are you okay, Martin?"

"Nah, man," Martin said, looking at his feet. "I'm not okay. Haven't been going to meetings, haven't been reading the literature.

I haven't been doing shit. Seeing the wrong people. Snapped at my boss last week, next thing I know, he calls me to say, 'Don't bother coming in anymore.' Can you believe that?"

"Bosses can be dicks sometimes," Pete said. He didn't fully buy Martin's story. "But you need to train yourself to handle the bad times—like these—better. Minus the drinking, you know?"

Pete felt like a hypocrite, having not hit a meeting in weeks, but he'd also learned to gauge himself. Sitting in a bar just now didn't help, but he had built tools over time that would allow him to understand his body and his own problem. Martin was still too new to the program to know that.

"Yeah, I feel that," Martin said. "But it sounds easy when you say it. Ain't easy when I do it. Plus, what were you doing in there, Mr. Pete?"

"I'm working on something," Pete said, keeping it brief.

Martin was moving faster now, shoving his hands in his jacket pockets—*why was he was wearing a jacket?*—and stepping from side to side. He looked tired, haggard.

"Martin, are you okay?" Pete asked again.

"Pete, man, I am sorry—" Martin said.

He raised a hand, as if to brush Pete off—but never completed the motion. The bullet tore into his chest. Another shot came soon after, hitting him in the forehead and sending brain matter and skull fragments in every direction. Bits and pieces hit Pete across the face as the bullets continued to come—pouring onto Pete's car, shattering the driver side window—loud pops echoing in the empty parking lot.

Pete fell back, landing on the warm asphalt a few seconds after Martin did, who now didn't look much like Martin anymore—his face a red, clumpy pile of skin and bone. Pete couldn't hear anything, the gunshot blast negating all other sounds. He inched away from the body—using his elbows to drag himself toward his car for cover. Was he still in the shooter's sights? He tried to get up, but his legs gave way at the sight of Martin, his friend—someone he'd worked with and tried to help—lying on the dark street, a pool of blood forming around what used to be his head and chest. He rolled to his side and threw up. He tasted the burn in the back of his throat and felt his nostrils fill with the copper smell of death.

CHAPTER SIXTEEN

Pete felt a shiver run through his body, his clothes drenched from a brief rainstorm. Miami was known for sun and heat, but the city was no stranger to the skies opening up. The rains would usually fade out as soon as they started. Pete sat on the parking lot pavement, a lukewarm paper cup of coffee in his hand, his back leaning on the rear bumper of his car.

Rain didn't help crime scenes. Under normal circumstances, Pete would take some pleasure in seeing the Miami PD scramble around like crumb-starved pigeons. A number of officers were milling around Duffy's parking lot—a few clustered by Martin's torn-up body, the rest cordoning off the area and splintering into smaller groups. A handful of them had wandered in the general direction of the gunfire.

Pete closed his eyes and tried to center himself. For the second time in a few months, someone had come after him with a gun. Both times he'd been lucky. But how long would that last? And if they could find him on a random detour to Duffy's, what was to stop them from finding out where he and Kathy were holed up? Was he safe anywhere? Before he'd gotten sober, it was during times like this that Pete craved a drink. He made a note to hit a meeting after the cops let him go. For himself and for Martin.

"Pete, you with us?" Harras's voice sounded far away, like a radio playing across the street.

Pete opened his eyes, taking a moment before looking up at Harras, squinting in the early afternoon sun as it peeked through the remaining rain clouds.

"Pete?"

"What're you doing here?" Pete said. The question came out with more bite than he'd intended.

"Buddy of mine got the call," Harras said. "Once he found out you were on the scene he gave me a ring. I was around."

Pete took a sip of his coffee. He couldn't think of anything to say. He felt numb.

"I think the PD got everything they need from you," Harras said. His expression was soft, his usual sharp tone muted. "I'm not sure it's a good idea for you to be out in the open like this any longer than you need to be."

"What's your take on this?" Pete asked, waving the cup of coffee toward the police tape and Martin's body.

"How well did you know this Martin guy?"

"Not very."

"I mean, how does an ex-journalist turned PI like you run in the same circles as a street thug like this Martin kid?" Harras asked.

"He was a friend."

"Well, your pal had a rap sheet that lines him up with people who run with *Los Enfermos*," Harras said. "So maybe he thought he was relaying a message, but in reality, he was the message."

"What do you mean *a message*?"

Harras scoffed.

"Boo," Harras said with a straight face. "That's what this was."

"Boo?"

Harras scanned the crime scene and scratched his balding head. His suit was rumpled and his body sagged. He'd been at this a long time. His life was crime scenes and murder talk.

"Whoever was after you before—those people who made you scurry away to Nowheresville, Florida, for a few months?" Harras said, not turning to face Pete. "They still want you dead, and they know where you are."

The Sunny Palm Room was a mid-size lounge space tucked behind a dentist's office on 107th Avenue, a few blocks south of 101st Street in South Miami, a long stretch of half-empty strip malls, shiny Aldi supermarkets, empty storefronts, and chain Cuban restaurants. The lounge was not tropical. It was not well lit. It featured a small table near the back wall with a microphone. A few couches lined the other walls. There were slogans and posters hung around the room—*Put Some Gratitude in that Attitude, One Day At A Time*, and *Easy Does It* caught Pete's eye as he walked in.

He nodded at the older woman standing by the fridge, which was surrounded by a counter that resembled a bar—a discovery that would have made Pete chuckle under better circumstances. She smiled and welcomed him. He self-consciously wiped at his face, worried that there were still streaks of blood on him. He'd had an extra shirt in his bag, but that didn't fix everything. He still looked like he'd been in a scrap.

The meeting was set to start in ten minutes. There were only a handful of people floating around, some in their chairs, already watching the clock, others socializing with friends, in no hurry. Pete took a seat on the end of one of the couches to the right of the front table.

He was used to this routine. It'd been well over a year for him this go-round—longer if he counted the time before his relapse. He liked the program's simple approach and listening to fellow alcoholics share battles with booze. You could have a meeting in a shack in the Everglades as long as you had two drunks talking to each other. He wasn't perfect—his problems weren't limited to having been a blackout drinker. Pete knew there was room to improve himself. But like the yellowed sign said, he took it a day at a time. He was optimistic that with practice, he'd get better at being better.

Martin would never have the chance to realize that. He'd been struggling before Pete left Miami—getting a few days dry, then falling into bad habits. But Pete had been hopeful. Now Martin was gone, his body shattered in a spray of gunfire. Something had pulled him into Pete's other world, the world that dealt with murderers and kidnappings and violence. Pete needed to find out how that happened.

"… or anyone just coming back?" The question from the middle-aged man sitting at the table hung over the room. Pete realized a few people were looking right at him. He raised his hand. The speaker nodded in his direction.

"My name's Pete, and I'm an alcoholic," Pete said. "This is my first time at this meeting."

A slow, sloppy round of applause hit, followed by a collection of "Hey, Pete!" and "Welcome" greetings. The speaker continued. Pete looked around the room. This had been Martin's home group. None of the faces looked familiar to Pete. He felt strange, blending his half-baked day job with his sobriety, but he'd learned over the last few years that few things were absolute. Life was gray—sometimes darker, sometimes lighter, but always gray.

Pete walked through the parking lot to a quiet corner that was maybe two degrees cooler, thanks to the shade from a few banyan trees. There were two younger guys talking and smoking—fast. Pete knew the type. Early twenties. One was lanky, with a buzz cut and acne scars. His friend was heavier with longer hair and crooked teeth. Both were Latino but native. Their English was impeccable. Pete figured their Spanish was rusty or nonexistent, like his. They were new to the AA game and still not sure it was theirs to play. It was the kind of lesson you either learned right away or discovered after a lot of bumps and bruises, if you learned it at all.

They both pivoted as Pete approached. He tried to smile, but it came off wrong.

"Good meeting," Pete said.

"Yeah," the lanky one said.

Pete extended his hand to the lanky one. "My name's Pete."

"Eric," he said, then pointed to his beefier friend. "This is José."

"Hey," José said.

Pete cut to it before the awkward silence could set in.

"You guys come here a lot?"

"Depends," Eric said. "I try to come to the afternoon meeting."

"This place is open all the time," José said. "So, yeah, I try to, like, be here once or twice a week."

"How much time do you guys have?" Pete asked.

"Not long," José said, looking at his shoes. "Been in and out."

"I hear you," Pete said, looking from José to Eric. "It takes a while sometimes."

They nodded but offered little else.

"Do either of you guys remember Martin? Martin Colon? He used to come around here."

Eric and José backed up a bit.

"You a cop?" Eric said.

"No, just a drunk like you guys," Pete said. "Looking for info on my friend here."

"Sure sound like a cop, though," José said.

"I'm an investigator," Pete said. "He came to this meeting. Did you know him?"

"I don't think that we can talk about him," Eric said, looking at José to back him up. "I mean, that would hurt his, like, secret or anonymous-ness."

"His anonymity," José said, nodding in confirmation. "We can't out him, even if he did come to this meeting."

Pete appreciated the brain trust's adherence to the rules of the program, even if it did slow him up a bit.

"Martin's anonymity doesn't matter anymore," he said. "He's dead."

After twenty minutes, Eric and José had burned through a pack of Marlboro reds and had given Pete very little to work with. They both recognized Martin from the meeting and had spoken to him a few times, but not much else. The daylight was fading and the temperature was going from surface-of-the-sun hot to somewhat stuffy. Pete wiped his forehead with his arm and felt it get slick with his own sweat.

"Did he have any friends?" Pete asked. "People he talked about?"

"No, I don't think so," José said. "I mean, like I told you, man, I spoke to Martin maybe three, four times in my entire life. Guy was cool and all, but we weren't best buds or anything. I didn't even have his phone number."

"I'm trying to figure out who he may have pissed off," Pete said. "Or if he knew anyone who might want to hurt him."

"He kept to himself, mostly," Eric said. "Only spoke up when it was a round robin, where the mic gets passed around and you have to share. He was really shy, I guess."

"Did you ever see him outside the meeting?" Pete said.

Both got quiet, pondering Pete's question. José spoke first.

"Only once, months ago," José said. He seemed ready to go. "At the movies over by International Mall. He was with some friends. But we didn't say hi or nothing. What am I gonna say? 'Hey, did you drink today?' I didn't want to blow up his spot."

"What'd they look like?" Pete asked.

"Who?"

"His friends," Pete said. "What did they look like?"

José thought for a second. Eric's attention span was waning. He lit another cigarette and walked a few paces toward the parked cars.

"Not great, I guess, you know—tough guys," José said. "The kind of thugs who go see a movie at International Mall. Shady guys. I was a little surprised that was his crew, but like I said—I never talked to the dude."

"Anything else?" Pete said.

Eric's gaze returned to the conversation.

"Yeah, I know who you're talking about," he said, sticking his hands in his pockets and looking around. "But I ain't got a lot to say about this. I'm trying to get my shit in order, y'hear?"

"I'm not quoting you," Pete said, meeting his eyes. "Just trying to help—"

"I get it, man, I do," Eric said. "I ain't worried about Martin. He was a good guy. I just mean I know who he was running with. Guys like Nestor, Gus, and some others."

Pete felt a box being checked off in his head.

"What about them?"

"Like José said, they're trouble," Eric said. "Not nice people. I saw them a while back, they pulled up here, actually. To pick me up, to hang out. Whatever. No big deal. I still see my friends, even though the AA book says to give up people, places, and things. I don't buy that."

Pete nodded. He wasn't interested in Eric's hot take on the program.

"So they get me, I get in Nestor's car, and he asks me, 'Yo, do you know that guy?'"

"Meaning Martin?" Pete said.

"Yeah, yeah, exactly," Eric said. "He points his finger at him."

Eric mimicked the movement, his pointer finger directed at Pete, like the barrel of a gun.

"'That guy, we got plans for him,' Eric said. "'Big plans.'"

He pulled his hand back, his finger still extended, as if recoiling from a gunshot.

The call came in as Pete hit the expressway south, his car now sporting a shattered window and a few extra bullet holes. He'd spent too much time out today and it'd resulted in his getting shot at, losing a friend, and wondering what to do next. The car's Bluetooth picked up the incoming call and routed it through the speakers.

"Hello?" Pete said.

"It's Harras. Where are you?"

"In the car, heading back to the house," Pete said. "What's going on?"

"Have some intel for you," Harras said. "Ready?"

"Yeah, hit me."

"They found a clearing near Duffy's," Harras said, his words coming out methodically. "Rifle parts, footprints, the usual— whoever was there didn't care about their shit being found. The rifle being there pretty much confirms it's where the shooter took Martin out from."

"What else?" Pete said.

"They got some prints, checked out cell phone records, you know the drill," Harras said. "And if this leaks anywhere, you are a dead man. More than usual."

"Understood."

"This Martin kid had a record," Harras said. "His phone was pretty busy in the days before the murder too. Lots of calls from one place in particular. Ever heard of the Vida Club?"

"Part of that new casino on 37th Avenue?" Pete said.

"Yes, that's the one," Harras said. "Nice, shiny new casino—also a known hangout for your friends, *Los Enfermos*. They own part of it, some think. See the dots I'm connecting here?"

"Almost," Pete said. "So they sent Martin to take me out?"

"Doubt it," Harras said. "Martin was unstable. Seemed like a fringe part of the organization at best. But they knew he knew you. My guess is they asked him to relay a message to you. Probably what they'd had in mind with Pelegrin before you caught it."

"But then they killed him," Pete said. "Just to get to me. Shit."

"There's more," Harras said. "Like I said, we got prints on the rifle that killed the kid. The person who did this wanted us to know it was him."

Pete was quiet. He knew Harras wouldn't need any prompting to get to the point.

"It was Varela."

CHAPTER
SEVENTEEN

"What now?" Posada said.

His deep voice cut through the large Posada & Associates conference room. Most of the seats were empty and Pete wondered why they'd chosen this massive space, inside Posada's swank offices, to have their come-to-Jesus meeting. Kathy was seated to his left, Harras to his right, with Maya at the far end of the table near Posada. No one looked happy to be there.

"We can't really continue to work on this," Pete said. "I mean, the guy you want us to exonerate is out to get us."

"We don't know that for sure," Posada said.

"I guess you don't read the newspaper, watch TV, or have an Internet connection," Kathy said. "Or believe in fingerprints either. I know it's a relatively new form of evidence."

By now, the news that the police were looking for Varela—not just for a brazen prison break, but for taking out Martin in an attempt to kill Miami private investigator Pete Fernandez—was out there, and the city was abuzz. Pete had held onto the news as long as he could, not even telling Maya after Harras called. That had driven a slight, but hard to ignore wedge between them. Pete was okay with that. He and Kathy were in survival mode. They were under siege from the press—even more than before, which Pete could not have fathomed. Martin's murder made for a fairly juicy story the press wasn't going to ignore, twenty-four-hour news cycle or not.

"I can't believe he would want to do this," Maya said. She looked disheveled. Her clothes were wrinkled and the bags under her eyes had gotten a shade darker.

"Well, that's a real shame, because he did do this," Kathy said. She pushed off from the table, the rolling chair moving her back toward the meeting room wall. "When we came back into town, we tried to pick things up because we felt like something was off with the case, but that's not the reality. Varela escaped and he's gunning for us. We have to side with self-preservation here. This has dragged on for months and we've only gotten deeper in the shit. In fact, I'd safely say Gaspar Varela has figured out his own way of exonerating himself—by escaping from fucking prison."

"There's no need for that now," Posada said, walking toward Kathy, his hands up, trying to be conciliatory.

"For what? Fucking reality? Because that's all I'm dropping on this table right now," Kathy said, her voice rising. "There is zero hope here. Your client-dad-friend-whatever is out, he has a gun, and he wants to kill us. From what it looks like, he's also the kingpin of some Miami drug gang. So, cool, he can add that to his criminal CV. Excuse me if I don't think proving his innocence is high on our general to-do list. It's safe to say you do not need us anymore."

"Are you suggesting we're the least bit happy with this?" Maya asked, her eyes on Kathy. She hadn't said a word to Pete since the meeting started.

"No one's happy with this, believe me," Harras said.

"Of course not," Pete said, looking at Maya. "But this is done. Kathy, Harras, and I have to worry about staying alive now. No one is going to help us investigate a crime from a decade ago when the guy we're hoping to vindicate just murdered someone in cold blood."

Maya's face was stricken.

"My father, you mean? You can say it," she said. "You think my father tried to kill you. And you think he killed my mother."

"I didn't say that," Pete said.

"You might as well have," Maya said.

"So fucking what?" Kathy said, moving toward the exit. Harras was already up and at the doorway. She shoved Pete's shoulder and he stood up. "The evidence is there. I'm very sorry reality offends your delicate disposition, but your dad took a shot at Pete and he escaped from fucking jail—because he had no hope of getting released, because he is fucking guilty. Let's just call it what it is. Now, we're going to leave, we're going to stop working on this case, and if there are any financial issues you want resolved, please consult my attorney."

They walked out—Pete didn't meet Maya's stare. He felt sheepish, but he didn't have much to add to Kathy's rant—he rarely did.

The door clicked shut and they walked down the hall toward the main elevators.

"That was fun," Kathy said.

"Was it?" Pete said.

"Of course," she said. "How often do you get to slam your hand on a table and yell—plus keep your retainer?"

"Well, let's see if that happens," Pete said, pushing the button summoning the elevator.

"They won't chase us for money," Kathy said.

"And now the path is clear," Harras said.

"What do you mean?"

He turned to Pete and smiled.

"Now we work."

Before they could step onto the elevator, they heard rushed footsteps. It was Maya, looking frantic and rattled.

"Wait," she said.

"What is it?" Pete said.

"Calvin Whitelaw is dead," she said, trying to catch her breath. "Orlando just got a call."

It took Pete a second.

"The prosecutor in the Varela case," Harras said.

"Yes, yes," Pete said. "What else do we know? What happened?"

"There aren't a lot of details," Maya said. "But Orlando's contact on the force said it was bad. One of the bloodiest scenes they've seen in a long time. Whoever killed Whitelaw did it with gusto."

CHAPTER EIGHTEEN

Walter's Coffee Shop in Perrine, about ten minutes from Pete and Kathy's temporary compound, was more diner than coffee shop. It was just past ten in the evening, so the place was empty, except for what seemed like a few regulars. At least that was how it looked from the outside, where Pete and Kathy sat in the front seat of Pete's rented car. They didn't turn around as they heard the back passenger side door open and close.

"What do you want to know?" Harras asked.

"Whitelaw," Pete said, meeting Harras's eyes through the rearview mirror. "What happened? Did you hear anything from your people?"

"Messy," Harras said, his eyes scanning the car. "Knifed in the stomach as he was leaving his office for the night. Throat slit after that. He bled out in the hallway. Whoever did this was not fond of the guy."

"Varela?" Pete asked.

"The forensics team was able to drill down on the murder

weapon," Harras said. "Which we can either look at as a lucky break or intentional on the part of the killer."

"What was it? A *Los Enfermos* machete special?" Kathy asked.

"Yes and no," Harras said. "According to my guy on the scene, it was a machete, but a specific kind, an antique from World War II—a Bolo machete. This version is not extremely common. So, it's similar to the one used to kill Rick Blanco, but so are all the machetes the gang uses."

"It might be the same one used to kill Carmen Varela, though," Pete said. "Or to stab my grandfather."

Kathy nodded. Pete had updated her on what his father's files contained after going over them with Harras. That impromptu research session seemed like it'd happened years ago, Pete thought.

"Or someone wants us to think that," Kathy said. "Someone may want us to think Varela is settling old scores."

Harras cleared his throat.

"We can't presume," Harras said. "What we do know is whoever killed the man who put Gaspar Varela in jail really didn't like him and also knew how to use a knife. The wounds were messy and the crime scene was a horror show."

"Meaning?" Kathy asked.

"They were going for a kill," Harras said. "They weren't just poking the piñata, hoping it'd burst. This one was as much for show as it was for effect. The scene was as important as the murder itself."

Pete gripped the steering wheel.

"Something's not working for me," Pete said. "Does Varela have any pro-Castro track record? If we're trying to line this all up, then he took out my grandfather, Martin, and now Whitelaw, in addition to killing his own wife."

"We don't know he did each kill," Harras said. "But the motive is there for Whitelaw, at least."

"Oh, you mean the fact that Whitelaw put Varela in jail?" Kathy said.

"But that's no longer relevant," Pete said. "Varela's free."

"Do you erase all resentments when they stop being relevant?" Kathy asked. "Is that the AA way?"

"It's a valid point—doing something like this puts him, as an escaped convict, at risk," Harras said. "But no, I have no idea if Whitelaw had anything else on Varela that would give him reason to slice and dice him."

"What else?" Pete said, turning to look at Harras for the first time. The exchange lacked the verve or energy of the last few days. They'd cashed out whatever humor they had left. Things were not looking good.

"I have an address for Whitelaw's now-widow," Harras said as he passed a folded piece of yellow notebook paper to Kathy. "Why don't you make yourselves useful?"

"I like this new Harras model," Kathy said. "It's like we're part of a power trio, if a bit weak on the harmonies."

"I'm not a cop anymore, so you can do whatever you want," he said. "Just don't use my name or get me implicated in this bullshit. Consider all this a favor."

Harras's jaw clenched and he opened the car door.

"Whether you meant to or not, you saved my life when that psycho put a bullet in my stomach," he said, sliding out of the seat. "I owe you for the years I've got left. Doesn't mean I'll be nice. Doesn't mean I'll be a cheerleader while you and Veronica Mars here break the law and make things harder for the real police. But I will help you if I can do it with a clean conscience. We work well together. So far, so good."

He didn't wait for their response. He got out and walked down the street.

CHAPTER NINETEEN

Before his recent demise, Calvin Whitelaw had lived in a large, six-bedroom house in Weston, an affluent city in western Broward. The suburban community was loaded with gated complexes that were nicer, shinier, and boasted more golf courses than their Miami counterparts. On top of that, most of the brand-name food spots and clothing stores were well within reach. It was a whiter, less diverse version of Kendall.

The drive from West Perrine to the address Harras had gifted them had been long—thanks to morning commute traffic and lack of sleep. Wired after their chat with Harras, Kathy and Pete had talked into the wee hours—strategy, fears, and next steps. It was all they could do to not lose their minds, a way of exerting control over a chaotic situation with no clear solution. Their every movement, especially those taken outside of the supposed safety of their secret lair, was loaded with fear and anxiety. A drive like this one, which would have previously just been an annoyance due to the time it took, now featured deadlier stakes for them to contend with. Even mundane Miami traffic felt like a deadly obstacle course: A sudden bout of traffic. A car that stayed behind him for a minute too long. An unexpected lane change. It all seemed far from trivial now. Pete was in their sights every second he spent outside. But this was an important meeting, and, if successful, might help them reach a point where they weren't running for their lives.

The houses got bigger the further into Weston they drove, until they reached the Whitelaw compound. The first gates led them to a security anteroom, where they signed in and Mrs. Whitelaw was alerted to their presence. Then they drove down a narrow path, past trees and ornate lawn furniture and fountains, until they arrived at the front driveway, which wove around a large swath of bright flowers and small trees. Kathy parked the car in front of the main door, only to be met by a previously unseen butler, who offered to take her keys and valet the car. She agreed, but not without some hesitation. A minute later they were standing at the front door, notebooks in hand.

They'd hashed out their plan the night before, over coffee and cigarettes. Get a sense of Whitelaw as a person and his life after the Varela trial. Try to suss out who might want him dead and hope Mrs. Whitelaw was willing to part with any strand of evidence or information that hadn't yet made it to the public. Any kind of head start on the person gunning for them could save lives. Including theirs.

"I'm starting to think it's too easy for Varela to have done this," Pete said.

"That sounds familiar. Almost as if *I* said the same thing before we came back. But to play devil's advocate, maybe he's crossing people off his shit list," Kathy said as she pushed the doorbell. They heard a loud, gonglike chime come from inside the house and exchanged glances. "First you, then Whitelaw. Not sure who's next."

"Maybe, but—" Pete didn't get to finish. A thin, birdlike man with a trim white moustache greeted them on the other side of the door.

"Mrs. Whitelaw will see you now," he said. His jacket—also a crisp white, like his slacks, tie, and shirt—featured a fancy nametag befitting his fancy name: Rutherford.

"If you'll follow me," Rutherford said, motioning to them with his left hand.

He walked them into a large, hangar-like living room adorned with an almost wall-size portrait of Whitelaw. It reminded Pete of something you'd see in a museum, though it lacked a powdered wig. Pete and Kathy sat on the lengthy white leather couch and waited. After a few minutes, a woman—early forties, slim, dressed in a sharp dark blouse and long red skirt—entered. She made a beeline for them, hand outstretched. Pete shook it first.

"Miranda Gomez-Whitelaw," she said. "You're Pete Fernandez and Kathy Bentley."

She sat down on the love seat across from the couch and crossed her legs, her back straight, her hands resting in her lap. All business. The use of her full name jolted Pete's brain, and explained how a prosecutor like Whitelaw, successful or not, had been living the high life. The Gomez clan was old Florida money, high-rolling Cuban investors who owned a stake in most major Miami land deals brokered after 1975. Only Dave's parents came close, and they were a distant second. Maybe Weston wasn't so white after all.

She continued before Pete could interject. "Save your condolences, please," she said, no sign of emotion on her face. "I loved my husband. He didn't deserve to die so painfully in his final years with us. But I know he had enemies. What I don't know, to be quite honest, is why you're both here."

"Well, Mrs. Whitelaw," Kathy started.

"Call me Miranda."

"Miranda," Kathy said. "We're working on a case that may be connected to the death of your husband."

"So, you're not here to offer your services?" she asked. "To figure out who did this, I mean."

"No, not exactly," Pete said. "We don't want to interfere with an existing police investigation."

"Well, that'd be a first," Miranda said.

Pete stammered for a second before Miranda spoke again.

"Did you think I would just take a meeting with anyone the day after my husband was stabbed to death?" she said. "I know who you are, both of you. I know about the Silent Death, I know about Julian Finch, and I know about the case with that poor child. I know your rep. I talked to friends. I'll admit, I wasn't sure why you'd be here, but I was hoping it was because you wanted to take on my husband's case. Lord knows the Miami police aren't up to the task."

Pete took a second to compose himself before responding.

"Well, both cases are connected, we think," Pete said, avoiding Kathy's eyes as he veered off course. "It's true, your husband had enemies—any successful prosecutor is going to incur the wrath of the people he's tossed in jail. But we wanted to get a sense of who his enemies were, and see if they overlap with our existing case."

"The Varela case?" she asked.

"Wow, you've got us all covered," Kathy said, her sarcasm percolating under each word. "Yes, Varela. We're trying to reinvestigate the murder of his wife."

"Snippy suits you." Miranda seemed unmoved by Kathy's tone. "I am probably not the first person to wonder aloud why you'd ever think investigating that murder was a good idea. Especially now."

"I'm starting to think he's innocent," Pete said. He avoided looking at Kathy.

"Do tell, Pete," Kathy said. "I must have missed that tidbit at our morning strategy session."

"Yes, this meeting has suddenly gotten a lot more interesting," Miranda said, folding her hands over her knee.

"I said *I'm starting to think*, not that I'm convinced," Pete said. "And it's more a gut feeling than anything else. I mean, this guy has been in prison for years, helping his only daughter build a case for his innocence. Why not cop a plea? Why continually insist you're innocent if you're not?"

"With that rationale, our prisons would be empty," Miranda said.

"Also, the man broke out of his cell. If I had to rank signs of guilt, that would be pretty high up there."

"Fair enough," Pete said. "But suddenly we're supposed to believe Varela has ties to *Los Enfermos*? And he's out to get me for investigating his wife's murder? That doesn't fly—we spoke to the man. He was on board."

Miranda stood up. She smoothed her skirt down before walking toward the living room's main doorway. She turned to them. "Follow me."

Unlike the rest of the house—or at least what they'd seen on the way in—Calvin Whitelaw's home office was cramped, disorganized, dusty, and lacking an iota of style or personality. It was closer to a dad's garage than a working space—file cabinets stacked together, a desk covered in papers, accordion files, legal pads, and folders. It smelled musty—of old paper and printer ink.

Miranda held the door open for them and nodded toward the office.

"This is where Calvin actually worked," she said. "His office downtown was for show, a last vestige of a career spent in the spotlight. He'd put in a few hours during the week to maintain appearances. If he had an actual case to work on, it'd happen here."

"Do the cops know that?" Pete asked.

"I may have forgotten to mention it," Miranda said, frowning. "I imagine you can find your way out? I'll just assume you got lost on your way to the bathroom and ended up in here. You know, client confidentiality and all that boring stuff. There should be a copier under some papers in there."

"Got it," Kathy said as they entered the crowded workspace.

The afternoon dragged into the early evening. They split the space—Pete took the files on the left side of the office while Kathy took the right.

After a few hours they'd discovered very little beyond realizing that Calvin Whitelaw, renowned prosecutor and community leader, was a serious packrat. They found multiple versions of the same files, dinner receipts from the mid-'90s, and legal pads packed with Whitelaw's vague notes to himself. They worked in silence—the house providing an eerie, quiet backdrop to their paper shuffling. Their only contact with Miranda had been through Rutherford, when the butler came in with a platter of sandwiches and water, his feet padding down the long, dark hallway that led to the office.

"I've hit a wall," Pete said, sitting cross-legged on the floor, piles of papers surrounding him.

"You look like you're about to cast a spell to the gods of paper clips and staples," Kathy said, glancing over her shoulder as she continued to rummage through a last cabinet on the other side of the room. "I'm amazed we even got in here."

"She doesn't seem to be a fan of the police," Pete said.

"She didn't seem to be a fan of ours," Kathy said. She pulled out a fat folder and scanned the first document inside.

"This could be something," she said, walking over to Pete's mini-shrine. He stood up and leaned in to see what Kathy had.

The tab on the folder was more vague than ominous: *Collected*. It appeared to be printed-out emails and records of payment sent to Whitelaw's personal account from Samael@hotmail.com.

"Samael? Is that the dude's name?" Kathy said. "Like, Samuel but not, right?"

"No, it's a Hebrew reference," Pete said. "Samael was an evil archangel."

Kathy gave Pete a look.

"Well, and here I thought you were a good Catholic boy," she said.

"Hey, I went to school, okay?" Pete said. "Let's see what Whitelaw said to Mr. Samael."

The exchanges between Whitelaw and "Samael" covered a period of years, with the two exchanging emails every few weeks. The tone from Whitelaw was veiled and threatening. He referenced "what happened" and "when things shake out." He knew something that Samael wanted kept under wraps.

The last email Whitelaw had printed out was dated the previous year.

My dear friend,

You'll find your bath water is getting a bit warmer these days. See what I did there? I'm not the only one hot on your trail. The reporter and her sidekick are sniffing around—she even came by the office tonight. Nice trick trying to scare her off. If I dare to hazard a guess, I think you did—for now.

But what happens when smarter—richer—people do the same and offer me more in return for what I know? Or, even better, for what I have? That'll be problematic for you, I'd wager.

Yours,
Calvin

"Seems Mr. Whitelaw knew something—or had something— this Samael person didn't want others to know, and was making a nice chunk of change from it," Pete said, taking the email from Kathy and reading it again. "But what?"

"What's also disturbing is that he knew who attacked me that night," Kathy said. "But what did Calvin Whitelaw have?"

"And was it enough to get him killed?"

A side from the emails, Whitelaw's folder held a few other gems— including a receipt for a storage space in Broward under the names *Samael* and *Arturo Pelegrin*. Pete took note of the address. Collected at the bottom of the file were newspaper clippings dating back to the early to mid-'80s. Crime reports, mostly, or local *Miami Times* stories discussing gang-related activities, including those involving violence against anti-Castro groups in Miami. Whitelaw, in his own weird way, was building a case against *Los Enfermos*. But why?

"CYA," Kathy said. "He was covering for himself. In case whatever he had that *Los Enfermos* or this Samael guy wanted wasn't enough to keep him alive."

"He was trying to build a case that *Los Enfermos* were behind these murders," Pete said. "It doesn't look like he finished doing it, though."

"Death tends to interrupt things, yes," Kathy said, standing up and dusting off her skirt. "I think it's time to go. Don't you?"

Pete nodded and followed her out of the room, carrying the copied file with him and closing the door behind them. Kathy started toward the long hallway, but Pete grabbed her by the elbow.

"Wait," he said.

"Yes?" she said, yanking her arm away. "Did you leave your wallet or something?"

"Let's see what else we find here," Pete said, turning around, going in the opposite direction from the one they'd originally come from.

"I like this," Kathy said, whispering. "What's more fun than wandering around rich people's houses?"

There wasn't much to see, as the hallway ended a few doors down. One of the rooms was a small linen closet, another a bathroom, and there was a larger room that seemed to be a screening area of sorts—with a couch, big-screen TV, and more DVDs than Pete thought possible. That left one door, at the tail end of the hall, for them to try.

It wasn't locked. Pete stepped in first, expecting a small library area or work shed. Instead, he found himself yanked into a museum of sorts. It was dark, even with the handful of lights that spotlighted certain areas of the space. The room was a celebration of Miami and Florida, but not the beaches, celebrities, and sights. It was an exhibit dedicated to the city's dark underbelly. Memorable photos lined the walls: Ted Bundy, Arthur Teele, Versace, the McDuffie Riots, the Dadeland Mall massacre, Elian, the Mariel boatlift. There were even pictures of Javier Reyes, the Silent Death, and serial killer Julian

Finch. Pete wasn't sure whether to feel honored or disturbed.

But the room wasn't limited to photos. There were glass cases that housed an array of handguns, knives, and assorted weaponry—some of them fairly old. It would take a few hours to go through it all, Pete guessed.

"This is fucking weird," Kathy said. "But also makes sense, I suppose? Guess he was a true crime maniac, in addition to putting people in jail."

"We all have our hobbies," Pete said, wading deeper into the room, which didn't seem to end, perhaps due to the dimmed lighting.

Near the far wall, past the more current photos and memorabilia, next to photos of American gangsters partying and living it up in pre-Castro Cuba, was an ornate glass case taking up a central spot. It was wide and long with a small nameplate under it.

"Guess he never got to hang his special phallic pistol," Kathy said from behind Pete. He felt her breath on his neck as he stepped closer, trying to catch the light to read the inscription on the thin gold label under the space where something should have been.

When he was able to read it, he felt a cold jolt hit him and spread over his body, like jumping into a pool of frigid water, headfirst.

WWII Cattaraugus USA Folding Pilot's Bolo Machete Knife

"Holy shit," Kathy said.

"Did you lose your way?"

Pete and Kathy wheeled around with a start and saw Miranda Whitelaw standing at the other end of the room, leaning on the doorframe. She didn't seem surprised, as if she'd wanted them to find the space on their own, and was pleased that the lab rats she'd allowed in the maze were pushing the boundaries of the experiment.

"What is this room?" Pete asked.

"It was my husband's testosterone chamber, I guess," Miranda said as she walked in slowly. "He liked collecting junk. Especially junk that had something to do with famous trials or crimes. You'd think he would just leave this shit at the office, right? It became a bit of an obsession once he retired."

"Where did this machete go?" Pete asked, pointing to the empty case.

"How should I know?" Miranda said. "My husband liked rearranging his little museum. He would often take things down and bring them back later."

"It's the only empty case here," Pete said. "And it just happens to be the same kind of weapon as the one that killed Carmen Varela."

"And your husband," Kathy said.

Miranda raised an eyebrow, but her expression remained unchanged. She was processing, pondering next steps.

"My husband collected a number of things, one of them being weapons," she said. "Just because he owns a machete and Varela's wife was killed by one is coincidental."

"It's a hell of a coincidence," Kathy said.

Miranda shrugged.

"Varela's wife was killed by this exact kind of machete," Pete said. "Which, while not impossible to find, isn't exactly sold at Target. Did you know that your husband was exchanging emails with someone tied to the case for months, maybe years? That he was basically blackmailing this person with some insider knowledge and evidence?"

"My husband and I didn't keep secrets from each other," she said, more matter-of-factly than defensively. "But say your little theory is true. What of it? What does it change?"

"Why hide the weapon?" Kathy said. "It's the kind of thing that would help convict Varela in a second."

"Assuming the weapon proves Varela used it," Miranda said.

Pete felt his mouth go dry.

"Say it did prove Varela was the killer," she said. "Nothing could kill an appeal faster than a weapon with Varela's prints on it that matched the forensic evidence on his wife's death. Whoever was paying my husband did not want this knife to go public. Desperately."

"But why would he hide the weapon either way?" Kathy asked. "He wanted Varela to go down. He sent him there."

"My husband sent him to jail without a weapon, he was that good," Miranda said. "But by discovering it later, Calvin saw an … opportunity. He found someone willing to pay a lot of money to prevent him from showing an antique off to the wrong people."

"Maybe so," Pete said, growing tired of the back and forth, and of Miranda Whitelaw's detachment from the entire affair. "But that doesn't answer the big question."

"What?" Miranda asked.

"Where's the knife that murdered Carmen Varela?"

PART III:
THE DEVIL'S RIGHT HAND

CHAPTER TWENTY

Pete pulled out the beat-up vinyl copy of Sonic Youth's *Washing Machine* and flipped it over. It wasn't in great condition, but for a few bucks it might be worth it. He scratched at the beard he'd continued to grow. A few months of stubble and a hoodie wasn't much of a disguise. But he needed to get out. The store, Sweat Records, was located catty-corner to Churchill's, on the fringe of the Little Haiti area. He needed a break. It'd been a few days since their confrontation at Posada's office and the Whitelaw visit, and Pete felt off-balance. He needed to focus on something else for a few minutes, even if "something else" was digging through the USED bin at his favorite record store.

The door chimed as he slid the record back into the bin. He'd revisit the album on his second pass. He turned around and found himself facing Maya Varela.

"Hey," she said.

"Hey," Pete said. "Record shopping?"

"Not really," she said. "I called Kathy and she said you might be here—'getting his Wilco dork on,' she said. Then I remembered you had the Sweat bag at breakfast. That made me think my chances of catching you were above average."

"Are you sure I'm the detective?" Pete said. The quick joke didn't have the desired effect. Maya responded with an awkward, strained smile.

"This your first time here?" Pete said, cutting off the silence.

"I … um, I'm ashamed to admit this."

"What?"

"I'm not a huge music person," she said, looking around the small space, taking in the various posters, boxes full of records, and the display of coffee and vegan treats.

"I'll forgive the blasphemy you just uttered for now," he said. "I'm guessing you want to talk?"

She nodded.

"But not here," she said.

The outside seating area at Tobacco Road, a landmark downtown bar in Miami's Brickell neighborhood, was at half capacity—a mix of hipsters and early-bird drinkers who hoped to make people think they were getting caffeinated or fed instead of sloshed. Pete and Maya had found a small table on the quiet fringe. After some pleasantries and a few rounds of beverages, the crowd had grown, and Pete saw a band setting up on the outdoor stage, closer to the bar entrance.

"I'm sorry about how we—"

Maya raised a hand. Stop.

"Not yet," she said. "I called this meeting."

"Very formal."

"Hey, it's true," she said. "I'm happy to accept your apology later, but for now, I just wanted to let you know that I understand."

"You understand … what?"

"Why you have to drop the case," Maya said. "I get it."

Pete waited a beat.

"I'm trying to come to terms with it," she said.

Maya looked away, toward the restaurant, breaking her eye contact with Pete. "I've got to come to terms with the fact that my father did what he did to my mother, to your friend, and to Whitelaw."

She fiddled with her silverware before looking at Pete. "I don't know how to explain what he did," she said. "What he tried to do."

"It's hard to wrap your head around it," Pete said. "I can't imagine what you're going through, or what you're thinking. Currently, I'm a little nervous about being out in the open like this. That's my new status quo."

"To live in fear?"

"Something like that," Pete said.

She cracked a slight smile.

Their next round of drinks arrived—a Bloody Mary for her, another seltzer for him. Pete felt his energy dwindling, and he wasn't sure how long this talk would go on for. Maya seemed defeated, deflated, off. Pete knew what that was like—when everything you had banked on somehow went backward. He wanted to reach out his hand, but held back.

"What if I told you we weren't dropping it?" Pete said.

She took a long sip from her drink. She put the glass down and leaned back in her chair before responding.

"I'd ask you why not."

"I still have a lot of questions I need answered," Pete said. "Like, why is your father working with a violent Cuban street gang? Why does he want me dead?"

"It might have something to do with you investigating the murder of my mother," she said. Her tone was flat.

"I guess," Pete said. "But then why let you continue to investigate this?"

"Well, it's probably not easy to tell your only child you murdered her mother," she said.

"Why ask us to reinvestigate the whole thing?" Pete said. "He was basically at the end of the line, fourth quarter, two minutes, not even in the—"

"I get the metaphor," Maya said. "Look, Pete, you and Kathy are going to do whatever you think is best. I don't see the point in you going rogue now, not to mention doing it for free. I'm not paying you to do this anymore."

"I also think we have a lead on the murder weapon," Pete said.

"That … that would change everything," Maya said. "Holy shit. Where is it?"

His wasn't sure why he was doing this—opening up the case to Maya, who was very clear in her desire not to be their boss. But part of him wanted to lay down a foundation of trust with her. He wanted to salvage things with her.

"Not sure yet, but it could be a big thing if we get our hands on it," Pete said. "I wanted you to know we're making progress. It seems a little pointless, with your father out there and Whitelaw dead and everything crumbling down. I realize that, but … I'm not sure how to say this."

She didn't respond. Not a word or a nod of recognition. This was not going well.

"I know I just dropped a whopper of info on you, but can we put this on pause for a second?" Pete said. "I just wanted to say that I was happy to see you. I've been thinking about you a lot. Maybe now that we're not, what's the word, financially tied together …"

"Pete Fernandez," she said. "Are you asking me out? Right now? Nice gear shift, buddy. Wow."

They were silent for a few moments, looking each other over, as if both analyzing what was going to happen next, even if they knew where it was heading.

"You are a true man of mystery," she said.

"Am I?"

"It's funny you picked this place," she said, leaning over the small table, her breath hot on his face. She swung her arm around, motioning toward the bar. The drinks seemed to be kicking in. "This is my spot. I hang out here. Didn't you get the memo?"

"It must have gotten stuck in my spam," Pete said, raising his voice as the in-house speakers started to blast Springsteen's *Out in the Street*.

"This is strong," she said, pursing her lips as she took a long sip of her drink. "I think I'll be done after this one."

"It's good to cut loose sometimes," Pete said.

The waiter came back with two half-filled glasses of water.

"Why are we here, Maya?" Pete asked. "Why'd you want to talk to me?"

Maya leaned back in her chair. Pete watched her as she scanned the expansive outdoor seating area, a silly grin on her face. She started to talk before she'd turned to face him.

"I followed you," she said. "To the record store, I mean."

"Oh?" Pete said.

"Yes," she said. "Don't be mad at me. I mean, I knew you liked that place, but it was more than just a casual bumping into you. I needed to talk to you."

"Why would I be mad?"

"I dunno, because it sounds stalkerish and crazy," Maya said.

She moved her hand over his.

"I agree with you, Pete. I wish we could go backward," she said, looking at their hands. "I feel like it's all gotten really complicated. I wish we didn't have all this shit to sift through with me, my dad, you ... it's too much sometimes."

The crowd had thinned, as the band—a six-piece ska-type group—had started packing up their gear and leaving the stage. Pete finished the rest of his water and stood up.

"You wanna get out of here?"

"That was nice," Maya said, rolling over, her face next to Pete's.

It was close to three in the morning. They were lying in Maya's bed, in her house. Pete couldn't say he was surprised, or that he hadn't wanted this to happen. It had progressed naturally—and without him in a fog of alcohol, which he wasn't fully used to—from the flirtatious conversation at Tobacco Road, to an all-night Denny's on Miracle Mile, to Pete following Maya home so they could watch a movie. They didn't get through the first act before they were tussling on the couch, hands groping around, exploring, their mouths doing the same.

"Yes, nice," Pete said. "More than nice."

He leaned in and gave her a long kiss, trying to be present—to savor the moment and not get lost in bigger things, like what this meant or how long it would last. He'd defer those anxieties until he was alone, later today.

"I wanted this to happen," Maya said, propping herself up on her elbows, facing Pete on the bed. "I want to be honest with you about that."

"Just about that?"

"What do you mean?" she said, her eyebrows popping up in concern.

"It was a joke," Pete said. "It's fine that you wanted this to happen. I've wanted this for a while."

She gave him a wistful smile. Even in the dim light of her bedroom, he could tell it was laced with some regret. For what, he wasn't sure.

"I meant what I said at the bar," she said. "Even though I was probably a little tipsy. I wish we could start over. Have a cleaner break, I guess."

"From what?"

"From the past," she said, lying back on the bed, staring up at the ceiling. "Yours and mine."

"I think the past has broken with us," Pete said. "Whether we want it to or not."

"I guess you're right," she said. "My father made his choices. I have to come to terms with who he is now, or always was."

Her words lingered over them, their bodies sweaty and still tangled together. Pete wanted to savor this moment. He didn't want to talk about Gaspar Varela, his past, or anything, really.

It was rare for connections like these to match the build-up, the flirting. Especially the kind of sex that's been danced around, prodded, and teased at for too long. But he felt good, happy. It was an unfamiliar sensation, and she seemed to be sharing it with him. It'd been a brief respite from the grave world they lived in, like a light switch flicked on, illuminating a pitch-black room.

"Did you and Kathy ever date?" Maya asked. "You seem to have, I dunno, chemistry. Like exes or people who know each other intimately do."

Maya rolled toward Pete, her arm under her head and pillow, her warm body closer to his. He met her move, facing her in the middle of the bed.

"No," Pete said. "We're friends."

"Sorry," she said. "I know that's not the kind of thing you talk about after … well, after this. You don't owe me your dating résumé."

"It'd definitely fit on one page," Pete said. "But no, Kathy's not on the list. She's my friend—probably my best friend. She's stuck with me through some tough times."

Maya let out a frustrated groan.

"I'm really making a case for myself here, huh?" Maya said. "Giving you the third degree after just one night together?"

Pete gave her a peck on the mouth.

"It's fine," he said. "Don't worry about it."

She didn't respond right away, looking at him as he leaned over her naked body. Pete noticed her eyes were watering.

"What's the matter?"

"I just want this to be over," she said, then stopped. "Not this-this, no, not us, but 'this' as in my dad and the case and the reporters. I just want to get back to a normal life. Or something close to that."

Pete sat up and rubbed his eyes. The night was taking a sharp left. He knew what she was asking. But he wasn't ready to have that discussion. Too much was happening too fast. He swept those thoughts away for the moment and allowed himself a few more hours of pleasure. He pulled her toward him, kicking the sheets off the bed in the process.

"Let's not overthink this," he said.

She hesitated before kissing him again, a smile widening on her face.

"Smart boy."

CHAPTER
TWENTY-ONE

Arturo Pelegrin placed the slim bouquet of flowers next to the tombstone. It was early afternoon, but the sun was hidden behind a cluster of clouds, sparing Arturo from some of the heat. Caballero Ribero North was a fairly nice cemetery, as far as those things went. His mother's grave was well kept. Arturo wasn't really sure what to judge the place against. It was the only cemetery he'd ever been to.

He said a silent prayer, bowing his head and closing his eyes. He was starting to forget her. What her voice sounded like. How she smelled. Her expressions and how she reacted to things. He knew it was part of getting older. But he also knew that she'd been taken away too soon.

She had been an addict. There was no denying that. But she did the best she could under those diseased circumstances. Arturo remembered many weeks where groceries came second to copping. Hungry nights or dirty nights or nights spent at friends' houses because they were too anxious to send him back home to his junkie mother. The lady from that trial. The crazy one. He'd heard it all. He built a thick skin around it.

He did the sign of the cross and turned away from her simple, modest grave. He would be back next week. He would see her every week, just like he did as a younger man—even when she was curled up in a fetal position, sobbing about this or that, begging him for a couple bills so she could get a shot, her lips chapped and bloodied, bruises and scratches in odd places. He would never stop.

He thought about the detective—Fernandez—for a second. He knew he was back in Miami. His benefactor had told him. Fernandez was trying to fly under the radar and failing. He and his girlfriend were digging around, making themselves a nuisance. It was their way. Arturo wasn't sure why his boss had such a hard-on for them. He wasn't really even sure who his boss was. He had come to him last year, a day or two after he'd first run into Kathy and Pete, and offered to fix Arturo's life in exchange for small favors here and there. It seemed too good to be true. It was. But Arturo was short on cash and on the verge of being kicked out of school for nonpayment. He was getting desperate. He had never considered cutting corners or selling drugs, but those were his only other chances to stay afloat. He couldn't risk losing everything. He needed to stay in school. He needed to graduate and start a life for himself. Everything would resolve itself once those pieces were in place. He had to believe that.

First, the requests weren't anything serious. Pick up this package. See this guy. Research that. Then the big one: drive to bumfuck Florida, find Fernandez, and give him a message. Let him know we see him. Arturo knew what that meant. He wasn't finding Pete so his boss could deliver a mislabeled package. But he did it anyway, and got caught with his pants down. He'd been lucky. His boss seemed so pleased that Arturo had found Pete that he didn't seem to care about the rest of the operation going sour. Now Pete was back in Miami, and it seemed like the entire world was gunning for him. Whatever. He had his own problems to deal with. Fuck that guy.

He walked to his car, parked on the east end of the main lot, and slid into the front seat. He flipped on the satellite radio and played with the dial. That was when he felt it on the back of his head—the gun barrel, cold and heavy. He didn't dare turn around.

"Don't say a word," the voice said.

Dave Mendoza felt hot and itchy under the black ski mask. It'd been a while. The thick cloth felt awkward and unfamiliar. Even silly.

He felt less silly about the gun he was holding to Arturo Pelegrin's head. That was serious. It had been the only solution that came to mind as he was thinking about his friends and their situation, and what he could do to help. There was a bounty on their heads, and Dave had traced the info back to Pelegrin. He hadn't discovered who from *Los Enfermos* wanted Pete dead, and he didn't really care as long as he could make it go away. If Dave was good at anything, it was making things—or people—go away.

"Who are you working for?" Dave said, his voice muffled by the mask.

"What—who—what are you talking about?" Arturo said, trying to meet Dave's eyes via the car's rearview mirror.

"Don't look at me, asshole," Dave said. "Answer the question."

"I'm a student, man," Arturo said, his hands on the steering wheel as Dave had instructed. His voice cracked on the last word. "I don't have a job."

"Cut the shit," Dave said. He was having trouble maintaining his deepened voice. "*Los Enfermos*. Talk now or get ready to meet your mommy in hell."

Arturo hesitated. Dave increased the pressure of the barrel of the gun on his head.

"Shit, fuck, okay, man, Goddamn!" he said. "I barely know those guys, okay? I'm not even a member. I just ran with some of them from when we were kids."

Arturo stopped talking.

"You're not getting out of this car alive until you tell me everything," Dave said.

Dave felt his blood rise. He felt a familiar tingle in the back of his skull.

"One of my buddies, Gus, one of the guys who's part of the crew," Arturo said, licking his lips, nervous. "He came up to me a few months back. Said he wanted info on someone. Pete Fernandez. The guy who was in the news a while ago for that serial killer shit. He'd just come up to me with his partners, talking to me about my mom and the Varela case. I guess they weren't too happy Fernandez was sniffing around it again, causing trouble and headaches for people who thought that shit was long gone, you know?"

Dave didn't respond. Arturo nodded and kept going.

"So, I told him, Gus, Gus Trabanco, what I knew, which wasn't a lot," Arturo said. "But next thing I hear, his boy Nestor—Guzman— tried to take Fernandez out but got killed and Gus got busted on something else, some shit at a bar. But he's out now. He's out and he wants Pete gone, yo. Please, man, I don't know anything else. You gotta believe me. I don't want any more trouble."

"You told them Fernandez was in Titusville," Dave said. "You tried to set him up."

Arturo gulped.

"Shit, yeah, look, just tell me what to do, I don't want to die …"

"Just answer my fucking questions and you might not die," Dave said.

"Okay, cool, okay," Arturo said, his words jumbling together. "Yeah, I went to Titusville, but I was just driving through, it was a coincidence. I didn't want to get anyone in trouble or nothing."

"Bullshit," Dave said.

"For real," Arturo said. "I'm not lying."

"No one stops in Titusville," Dave said. "You knew he was there. Or you had an idea. Quit lying to me or this gun goes off fast. They put you up to it."

"Fuck, man," Arturo said. "Alright, you're right, alright. I told them I could find him."

"Who asked you?" Dave said.

"I don't know who it was, man," Arturo said. "He called me, said he was Gus and Nestor's boss and that he had an errand for me … said to find Fernandez and hold him, but I fucked up. I should have left him alone."

"But you didn't," Dave said. "You knew you had valuable information. You told them where he was."

"Yeah, yeah, I did, I did and I'm sorry," Arturo said. "But I had no choice. I thought they'd kill me for fucking up and being seen. I thought I was done for."

"What happened?" Dave asked. "Who did you talk to?"

"I told one of my boys and he told Gus, and then he told the boss and they were on him."

Dave swung the muzzle of the gun across the back of Arturo's head—hard enough to bruise, but not hard enough to knock him out. Arturo clutched his skull and let out a pained yelp. When he looked at his hand, it was covered in blood.

"Oh Jesus," he said. "Fuck, man. I need a doctor."

"You won't need a doctor if you don't talk," Dave said.

"What else do you want? I got nothing else," Arturo said, his words coming out between high-pitched sobs.

"Names, I want names," Dave said. "Who is the boss? What boy?"

Dave felt his hand tighten around the weapon, now back to its original spot, digging into Arturo's head, sending zaps of pain every time it jabbed the bloody gash down the back of his skull. Dave licked his lips. This had to end soon. He'd tried hard to leave this life behind. He'd rationalized this instance to himself. He was helping a friend. He was on the side of the angels for once. But his trigger finger was slick with sweat and the car felt much hotter than when he'd first snuck in. It all felt too right.

"I don't know his name, man," Arturo said, his voice getting whinier the more he spoke. "I just know Tito, my boy from back when we were kids, he's with that crew. I told him about Fernandez being alive when I got back. Then Tito took it to Gus, his boss. I don't get any access to the real boss. No one does."

Dave believed him.

"Tell me about your mom," Dave said.

"What about her?" Arturo said. "She's dead. She died."

"Was she lying about the Varela case?" Dave said.

"How should I know?" Arturo said. "I was, like, a sperm when that happened."

"Quit joking," Dave said, bumping the nozzle on Arturo's bruised head—a warning tap. Dave didn't want to hit him again, but he would if he needed to.

"She was an addict, man," Arturo said. "She would do or say anything for another hit off that pipe. What does that tell you? You think she thought twice about making shit up on the stand if it meant getting some cash in her pocket? Maybe she was in that room. Varela was hoping she was the one who could save him. But once that jury decided my mom was lying, thanks to that prosecutor, everything else went out the window. She sunk it for Varela."

"What about her boyfriend?" Dave said. "Fermin? Where is he?"

"Fuck, I don't know," Arturo said. He was moving around, getting impatient. "He barely dated her. They weren't together long before she died. The guy was a scumbag. His beat my mom to death. *Cabrón*."

"Why is the boss obsessed with Fernandez? Why does he want him dead?" Dave said.

Arturo shook his head, he started to look up, then stopped himself. The gun was still pressed against his skull.

"It's all connected, that's the thing, and Fernandez is getting too close," Arturo said. "He's stirring up shit and putting the light on some old stuff, man. That Rick guy, stabbed in the park, Varela, Whitelaw, everything. It's all one big problem and the boss doesn't want those dots connected, you hear? He upset the structure of things, and now they want him gone, like, yesterday. If Fernandez had just stopped and backed away, it'd be fine, but now the only way to fix it is for him to die, because he knows too much, and *Los Enfermos* are foaming at the mouth to get your boy. But I'm out, done with this shit. I'm just trying to go to school now, man. I don't want any part of this any—"

Dave clocked him with the gun's handle. Arturo shouted from surprise and pain—dazed by the blow. It gave Dave enough time to slip out of the car and head for his own, parked beyond the lot on the street.

"**Y**ou're nuts. You know that, right?" Pete said, no sign of humor in his voice. They were seated outside a recording studio at the offices of WRGE—RAGE 95.7—Miami's local hip-hop and pop music station. Dave had given Pete a brief recap of his run-in with Arturo Pelegrin. Pete had been surprised—not that Dave was capable of that kind of violence and intimidation—but that he'd backslid into it so easily. Pete would have felt almost honored if he wasn't worried his ex-thug friend was moving closer to just being a thug again, and on account of him.

"Do you think he recognized you?" Pete said. He was whispering, hoping to avoid the attention of the secretary sitting a few feet away from them, manning the office front desk.

"How could he, bro? I've never met the twerp in my life," Dave said. "You're in a bind. I had to help. These guys can't just put you on blast and expect it to be no big deal. They don't run this town."

"What'd Pelegrin say?"

"A few things that stuck out," Dave said. "He was definitely put up to it, finding you, that is. He seemed like he was in over his head. Someone is pulling the strings, but he had no names. He kept harping on about everything being connected."

"I'm getting that feeling too," Pete said. "Are you planning on telling me why we're here?"

"I want you to meet someone," Dave said. "She's tapped in and might be able to give you a sense of the baggage the Varela case has."

"I'm just glad to have you in my corner. You're our lifesaver," Pete said, stretching his arms. "So, tell me—who is this lady?"

"Madelyn Suarez," Dave said.

"The DJ?"

"Yes, the radio personality," Dave said. "You realize this is where your grandfather's radio station used to be, right?"

Pete looked around. He hadn't realized it. He knew Diego Fernandez had started a radio station in Miami, but little else—only what his father chose to tell him, and if he believed Harras and the file he'd handed Pete, that was only the beginning.

Above them, a lit RECORDING sign shut off, and the studio door swung open. A short older woman with a bleached-blond bouffant hairstyle and a lime green business suit stormed out, cigarette dangling from her mouth, and what looked like a gallon-sized travel coffee mug in her hand. She stopped and turned to look at Pete and Dave.

"Which one of you is Dave Mendoza?" she said, her voice a croak.

"That's me," Dave said, standing up, hand extended.

She ignored the gesture and moved toward the front desk. She slammed her mug on the counter and waved goodbye to the assistant. She reached into her large, tote-like handbag and pulled out a massive pair of dark sunglasses. Once she had the shades on, she turned her attention back to Dave.

"My manager says you want to talk to me," she said. She looked at Pete. "Who's this guy? Your boyfriend? Everyone has a boyfriend now."

"I'm Pete Fernandez," Pete said, skipping the handshake attempt but walking over closer to Dave and their new friend.

"Good for you," she said. "Madelyn Suarez. You should know me. If you don't, something's wrong."

She looked up at Dave.

"Where are you getting me drunk?"

Dave smirked, his chubby face turning a slight shade of red, even through his thick brown beard.

"You know of a place to party in Miami Gardens?" Dave said.

"Miami Gardens? Get me out of here, Davey boy," Madelyn said. "Let's class things up. You want info? You want my time? Neither is free. You're driving too."

DANGEROUS ENDS

The Clevelander was a beachside nightclub bar on Ocean Drive in Miami Beach. It was not the kind of place Pete would frequent, even during his drinking days. The music was loud and obnoxious, the people were plentiful and overdressed, and the lighting had probably caused its fair share of brain aneurysms. Pete hated the beach—at least the trendy, overcrowded, and grimy tourist trap slice of it known as South Beach. Nowadays, unless he was working a case, he made it a point to avoid the area. He wasn't the venue's target audience. The Clevelander had it all—bar, pool, dance floor, and outdoor seating a few feet from the water. This was where tourists came to live it up, be loud, and party hard. There was no room for Pete here, and he was slowly getting priced out anyway. The last time he'd been around, a rum and coke at a trendy spot like this would clock in at double digits. Pete didn't want to think about what it'd cost now.

They managed to find some space at the main outdoor counter, which faced the beach and Ocean Drive. The music wasn't as loud outside, which was a tiny blessing, but that was overshadowed by the swarm of drunk millennials swaying and grinding with each other. It'd only been a few minutes and Pete had already been jostled and had narrowly missed having a fruity drink spilled down the front of his T-shirt. He gave Dave a dirty look as they took their seats. Madelyn sat between them. She was already on her third cranberry and vanilla vodka—all of which was taking up residence on Pete's bar tab. Her voice had begun to slur.

"You're Diego's grandson? That is something," she said, pointing at Pete, her finger wavering, then finally dropping with the rest of her hand back onto the counter. "You don't even look like him. Your dad was cute. Cute kid. Smart kid. Good cop."

She took a long pull of her drink.

"I knew it was over after they stabbed him," she said. "In our own offices, *Dios mío*. I knew it was over. He lost himself after that. Sold the station. Retired. By the time those *Castristas* shot him, he was already half dead."

She raised her glass toward the beach, toasting to a fallen friend.

241

Pete and Dave exchanged a glance. Better to get to some questions in before she was completely soaked and sentimental.

"Madelyn, I know you've been hosting your show for a while now—"

"Thirty-five years," she said, straightening up a bit. "It's an institution. Every government official listens to *Hoy en Miami.*"

Pete knew this wasn't true. Sure, the show had enjoyed a lengthy heyday, but now it'd been reduced to a monthly, pre-taped thirty-minute program that aired in the wee hours, when people were either asleep or asleep at the wheel, driving back home from the club, bar, or whatever had taken up their evenings. Still, for a time, Madelyn's program was essential listening—to get the gossip and feel the pulse of the city and its various backroom deals and corruption scandals. Madelyn Suarez was a Castro-hating conservative firebrand who loved Cuba and prayed for the day she and her family could sail back and reclaim what was once theirs. Little had changed since the day Pete's grandfather had stolen her from his top competitor to anchor his fledgling talk-radio station.

"What do you know about the Gaspar Varela case?" Pete asked.

"Varela?" Madelyn said. Her eyes narrowed. "The cop who killed his wife? What is there to know? He's guilty and he ran away because he was tired of being in prison."

"Do you think he did it?"

"Doesn't matter what I think," she said before draining the rest of her drink. She started to look around for the waitress.

"That's a first," Dave said.

She gave Dave a sluggish look. The waitress returned, took her glass, and had a refill ready in the time it took Madelyn to formulate a response. Dave got up and wandered through the sweaty, gesticulating crowd toward the bathroom.

"Okay, you wanna know what I think? Here's what I think—the guy probably did it or he's not telling the whole story," she said. "There were too many holes in his version. Still, who remembers everything they did on a boring day or night? I don't. I don't even remember what I had for breakfast. His story—about the two people coming in and killing his wife—is crazy enough to be true. But now we get into the part the cops don't care about because they had someone behind bars: motive. Why would anyone else kill his wife, who, from what I heard, was a nice, pleasant housewife with a lovely kid and not even a blemish on her record? There was no political angle either. Varela wasn't a hard-line Castro lover or hater, he was a cop in good standing."

"So you're on the fence, basically?" Pete said. He was trying to goad her—to help shake off her cobwebs from drinking and from old age. It was a gamble. She might just tell him to fuck off.

"Watch yourself, *mijito*," she said, wagging her finger again. "I'm not your *abuelita*. I don't have to take any shit from you."

"Sorry," Pete said.

"Don't be sorry. Jesus," she said, "that's the worst thing in the world today. Everyone apologizes for fucking everything. So you said something rude? So what? Own it. Anyway, am I on the fence? I guess so. I'm not sure if he did it. I'm not as sure he did it as some people are. The escape doesn't help. Innocent people don't break out of prison. Even that doesn't explain the lack of any real motive or strong, condemning evidence. Where's my drink?"

She looked around, noticed the refilled drink, and took a long, hungry sip, closing her eyes to savor the liquor as it went down into her aging system.

"Feel terrible for the daughter, so young," Madelyn said.

Dave returned from the bathroom, carrying a tall glass full of a clear liquid that was probably gin.

"It's impossible to walk through this place, man," he said. Pete didn't respond.

"What about the daughter? Maya?" Pete said.

"Sad, s'all," she said. Madelyn was drunk. She'd graduated from a little sloppy to completely shit-faced in less than a minute. It was all hitting the older woman at once. They had to take her home.

"Her, Varela's partner Posada, the brother who ended up

testifying against him," she said. "They were good people. Still good people. Even with the brother's problems."

"What problems?" Pete said. He hadn't thought of Maya's uncle since they'd returned to Miami.

"He's broke," she said, waving her hand toward the beach. "Or he was broke, from that stupid grocery app business. Now he's back on top of the world. I hear he doesn't even have to work anymore."

"What put him back on top?" Pete asked.

Madelyn ignored his question and tilted forward, her hands stopping her from hitting the counter at the last possible moment. She lunged for her drink. It was empty in seconds.

"What about Janette Ledesma?" Pete said. He still had questions, but his window for asking them was closing. "Do you think she was lying?"

"She was—she wasthn—" She didn't finish the sentence, her eyes sliding shut and her body leaning back in her seat. Dave tapped her on the shoulder. She moved a bit to the left.

"We have got to get this lady home, man," Dave said.

"Can you pour her into a cab and find your way?" Pete said as he stood up. "There's somewhere I have to be."

CHAPTER TWENTY-TWO

J uan Carlos Maldonado didn't notice Pete sitting on his front porch steps until he almost tripped over him as he tried to get to the front door of his Aventura house, a few blocks south of Barry University. The darkness combined with a faulty porch light was part of the problem. Maldonado being drunk off his ass explained the rest.

"What the shit?" Maldonado said as he stumbled forward, his legs trying to avoid Pete.

"We have to talk, Juan Carlos," Pete said.

It took Maldonado a second to fully register who was there. His expression evolved from frightened to enraged. Maybe he was expecting someone else—someone with more than a conversation on his mind.

"You again?" Maldonado said. "I thought I told you to leave me alone? You're not a great listener, Fernandez."

"Guess not," Pete said, standing up, looming over Maldonado from the top porch step. "Are you going to invite me in or should we air your dirty laundry outside, so the entire block can hear?"

Maldonado looked around. The streets were quiet and it was late. He ran a hand across his face, as if he were trying to shake off the evening's drinks. Finally, he motioned to the house with his chin.

"Inside," he said. "Sure, let's talk."

Pete was far from the style police, but one could only describe Maldonado's sense of interior decor as tropical and tacky. The walls were painted a loud orange and featured movie posters—mostly mediocre gangster films—and garish religious paintings, with the exception of a massive map of Cuba on the far side of the large living room. Maldonado motioned for Pete to take a seat on the black leather couch that was stationed across from a huge flat-screen TV set.

"Let's make this quick," Maldonado said. "I'm tired and I have work tomorrow."

"Seems like you had a rough night," Pete said, sitting on the edge of the couch.

"None of your business," he said. "What do you want?"

"I want to know how much *Los Enfermos* paid you to turn on your own family," Pete said. He watched Maldonado's expression, which remained hard and unchanged except for a darting look.

"Who told you that?"

Pete ignored the question.

"I guess I just find it weird that someone like you—a guy who ran an online grocery app that went belly-up six months after launch—can afford to live in a pretty nice house like this one," Pete said. "And not be hounded by the collection agencies that forced you to file for bankruptcy. Maybe I missed the story where you announced a new venture that's been successful?"

Maldonado remained silent.

"Not to mention the nice car you drive, the country club that you're a member of," Pete said. "I could go on."

"So what?" Maldonado said. "I have money. Just because something failed doesn't mean I can't get back on my feet."

"It's funny," Pete said. "Because it seems like your fortune started to improve right around the time you testified against your brother-in-law. Weird, right?"

"You got nothing on me," Maldonado said, a sneer creeping onto his sweaty face. "Now get the fuck out of my house before I call the cops."

"Maybe you should," Pete said. "I'm sure they'd be interested in looking at some files I got from the office of Rick Blanco."

Pete thought he saw Maldonado's jaw drop for a second, but chalked it up to wishful thinking. Still, the man's entire demeanor changed from blustery bravado to a more subdued sense of defeat, a ringside announcer gone quiet.

"Remember Rick Blanco, JC?" Pete said.

"No idea who you're talking about," Maldonado said, but it was clear he was lying, the words coming too fast, as if he'd prepped himself to say that when Rick's name first came up.

"Really? That's funny," Pete said. "He sure knew you. Hell, he knew your bank account info. He knew enough about you to wire you a lot of money on the regular for a long time."

Maldonado's eyes widened. The information had started as a hunch for Pete, which required an awkward call to Emily, asking her to check her dead husband's scattered records. But it was there, albeit camouflaged as investments toward Maldonado's failed grocery business.

"Yeah, he was your money man," Pete said. "And, well, he's dead, as I'm sure you know. I don't think that's affected your Thug Chic lifestyle, but it will soon. Especially if the right people get to see some of these wire transfer forms."

"So what?" Maldonado said. "You with the IRS now? You think I'm gonna go to jail for unreported income? Rick Blanco was just a patsy, moving piles of cash. There's no proof of anything."

Pete let out a slow, thoughtful sigh. He was enjoying this. Yanking Maldonado down from his high horse to wrestle in the dirt for a while. He just needed to deliver a final blow and crack the coconut open.

"There is proof, though, that's what I'm trying to tell you, *consorte*," Pete said, standing up and walking toward Maldonado. "I wouldn't be here if there wasn't. And it's not just proof you took money, Juan Carlos. I mean, who wouldn't, right? Free cash? It's where the money came from that'll get people excited. Shell accounts that can easily be tied to *Los Enfermos*, and a timeline that happens to dovetail really nicely with your game-changing testimony during the Varela trial. Coincidence? Sounds like big evidence to me. The kind of evidence that might lead to a new trial for Varela."

"Varela's gone," Maldonado said.

"Sure is," Pete said. "Still, I dunno, call me crazy, but I doubt your bosses want that kind of evidence out there in the press, Varela or no Varela."

Maldonado closed his eyes, his breathing growing louder.

"What do you want?" he said, almost too softly for Pete to hear.

"Who is he?" Pete asked. "The man behind it all."

"I'd be dead if I told you," Maldonado said. "Even if I did know."

Maldonado turned around and took a few steps toward the large Cuba painting. He placed his hands on his hips and cursed to himself.

"I didn't know what was happening right away," Maldonado said, his voice almost pleading, hopeful that Pete would understand. "But I was in trouble. This stupid business was failing. It was too late. The idea of ordering groceries online was old, I was just playing catch-up. I was bleeding cash. I had to go bankrupt and hope I could keep my house and car and start again. But I'm not young. Starting again with no idea what to do is not what I wanted. Then this guy comes to me and says he knows someone who wants to invest, who wants to help me get back on my feet. At first I thought he meant in the company, which would have been fine. But eventually I just start getting these envelopes of cash and I have, like, no fucking clue what to do with them. I kept pressing the guy for more info on the business proposition he promised, but it never came. 'We'll be in touch,' he keeps telling me. So, in the meantime, I'm paying off my debts. I gave up on the business. Who needs it when the money is coming in, right? Then

I'm buying new clothes. Then I'm buying a house. It was so surreal I just went with it. It was like a dream. But then the call came. The one I knew was coming sooner or later. They sent that guy, Rick, to meet me. He told me his bosses had a strong interest in Varela going down. That he was a bad man. That there was a lot of money in it for me, and, that, hey, we've given you a lot of money already. I'd already made the deal by spending the money. They owned me."

"What did you say?"

"I'm not total garbage, man," Maldonado said. "I pushed back. Said I could pay it all back, that I wasn't like that. I don't do my family like that. But the truth was, I couldn't pay any of it back. It was gone. I was living paycheck to paycheck, working a make-believe job. Then they stopped the money. Now I was really sunk. My house was about to get foreclosed on. The debts I paid were coming back. All of a sudden, my old business partners were looking to sue me. I was drowning. So I took the lifeline. I thought I was saved. That's when they hit me with the big ask, though."

"And that's when you found out who was behind it?"

"It's not who, but what," Maldonado said, turning to Pete now, his eyes red, face stricken.

"*Los Enfermos*," Pete said.

Maldonado nodded.

"How do you even look at yourself?" Pete said. He'd met terrible people over the years and often tried to turn the other cheek, to find the strain of good that still remained. He was having trouble doing that here, or even wanting to understand Maldonado's reasons for destroying so many lives.

"I don't," Maldonado said. "I can't."

"You abandoned your entire family," Pete said. "Varela, Maya, everyone."

"Life is all about tough choices, man," Maldonado said, more to himself than to Pete.

He walked to the door and opened it.

"Go ahead and post those documents," he said. "I don't care

anymore. I don't care if they kill me either. It's not worth it."

Pete left without saying anything else. The zingers he had ready to fire would do no more damage than Maldonado's own self-loathing. Pete was fine with that.

He heard the door click shut behind him as he walked down the street toward his car. He dialed Jackie.

"I need another favor."

CHAPTER TWENTY-THREE

If someone had told Pete he would be dressed in black, sitting in Kathy's car somewhere in Lauderhill at two in the morning, he probably would have doubted them. But that's what was happening. Not surprisingly, Harras passed on joining this particular excursion.

The bright, flickering STORAGE EXTREME sign loomed over the wide expanse of garage-like units. The place looked decrepit—half the storage areas were empty, doors open and welcoming vagrants and animals to set up shop. The parking lot they were sitting in was equally desolate. Pete wasn't sure what, aside from the lack of care, was "extreme" about the place. He turned to Kathy.

"It's number three fifteen," she said, checking her iPhone.

"Is this what people refer to as a 'career low'?"

"Oh, stop with the whining," she said. "Do you think I want to be on the news for breaking into a cheap-ass Broward storage facility? But here we are. Living the dream."

"Why do you hate Broward?"

"I don't, I just needed something to be angry about," she said, putting a black skullcap on. "Suit up, partner. Let's break the law."

Pete had gone back home after his confrontation with Maldonado. It was early enough that Kathy was still around and asleep. He'd barged into her room, woken her up, and recapped the conversation. Maldonado's confession cemented—at least in Pete's view—that Varela was not the one pulling the strings of *Los Enfermos*, even if it didn't explain away why he'd broken out of jail or whether he was actually innocent of his wife's murder. The fact that Maldonado had been bought off was enough information for a retrial on its own.

Kathy tried to be enthusiastic, but also put a cap on Pete's jubilation—there was still work to be finished, and she'd done some research of her own while he'd been talking to Maldonado. She'd focused her energies on the storage slip they'd discovered in Whitelaw's office, which happened to be in Arturo Pelegrin and Cain Samael's names. It had sent her down a research rabbit hole that she'd just climbed out of an hour before Pete's return. She was by far the better researcher, and it showed. She knew how to sift through data and come to conclusions. Pete knew his gut and what it told him. Kathy had keyed in on Arturo's vague comments about his mother and had started to not only investigate her, but him. It seemed that someone had been funding not only Arturo's academics, but the storage space. With the supposed murder weapon missing from Whitelaw's house, the space seemed like a logical next step, Kathy concluded.

After some debate, they chose the most direct route: breaking into the space to see just what was being kept there.

Storage Extreme was dark. Aside from the main sign, lighting was minimal. Every few minutes Pete would hear a solitary car drive by. If "Cain Samael" was looking to keep whatever was in the storage space in a desolate, unremarkable place, he'd done a good job.

Pete could barely see what was in front of him. Kathy was a few steps ahead, flicking her tiny mini-flashlight on and off to guide them.

"Here," Kathy said. "This is it."

She flashed her light up above the space's bay—like door and confirmed it—315.

"What now?" Pete said.

She unzipped her black backpack and pulled out a crowbar.

"Are you just going to whack it with that thing?" Pete said

"What would you like me to do? Knock?"

She turned and took a swipe at the lock—it gave. A few moments later, they were lifting up the door and entering the space.

"Success," Pete said, pulling the door down behind them and turning on his phone light. The space was the size of a small bedroom, empty except for a small plastic bin in the far right corner. Kathy headed straight for it. If they found a machete inside the case, they'd make a beeline for the police and call Maya on the way. Though her father was still on the lam, knowing he would be exonerated for the murder of his wife might be just enough to entice him back, Pete thought.

Kathy knelt in front of the bin and yanked off the lid. Pete hovered over her, shining his phone light into the box. It was empty.

"Shit," Pete said.

"What the fuck?" Kathy said, standing up. "This is bullshit."

"Looking for something?"

The voice came from the other side of the space, near the entrance. Kathy and Pete wheeled around and pointed their respective lights toward the sound.

The man was about their age, Latino, with a shaved head, muscle shirt, tattoos on his arms and neck, and a well-kept goatee. He probably worked out a lot. He had a gun—pointed at Pete and Kathy.

"Who are you?" Pete said.

"Trabanco," he said. "You killed my boy, Nestor."

"Your boy was rolling up to me with a shotgun, if I remember correctly," Pete said. He tried to inch his hand to his lower back, where his own gun was resting, but Trabanco noticed.

"Keep your hands where they are, both of you," he said, stepping toward them. "You two are pretty fucking annoying, you know that? Making me sit here and wait for your dumb asses to show up," Gus Trabanco said, frowning. "I could be out with my lady, up in the club, doing anything but this dumb ol' shit. I mean, who parties in Lauderhill?"

He stepped closer to Kathy, pushing the barrel of the gun into her chin. "People are not happy with both of you right now," he said.

Pete went through his options. He could try to tackle him and risk the gun going off and killing someone. He could wait and see how this would play and risk Trabanco killing them. Or he could try to talk his way out of it.

"Who's pissed?" Pete said.

Trabanco turned to Pete, pulling the gun back. Kathy sighed in relief, rubbing her face. She locked eyes with Pete, her eyes saying, "Be careful with this psycho."

"Who do you think, bro?" Trabanco said. "The boss. Mr. Cain. The man you guys have been sweating since day one. I'd say lay off, but there's no point, you're way past that. He wants you dead—so I'm here to make that happen."

"Is this Cain guy real?" Pete said.

"What do you think, man?" Trabanco said. He was moving from amused to annoyed. Pete's window was closing.

"How'd you get out?" Kathy said. "Weren't you under wraps for killing Rick Blanco?"

"Lady's smart," Trabanco said, nodding. "Nah, I got a good attorney. Nestor, may he rest in peace, is taking the—what is it?—post-humorous fall for that one. Say hi to him for me, will you?" Trabanco started to raise the gun.

"You think your boss is going to let you live with what you know?" Pete asked.

Trabanco hesitated. His smirk faded.

"The fuck you talking about?" he said.

"You've taken orders, directly from him, to kill other people," Pete said. "You basically have a get out of jail free card now. That's gold if you decide to testify against him. You don't think this guy knows that? Now you're going to kill two more people for him. Do you think he's going to set you up with a nice retirement plan in Boca?"

"You're talking mad shit, man," Trabanco said. "Funny the things people say when they have a gun on 'em."

"We're not stupid," Kathy said. "We know your crew is after us. Do you think we came here without telling the cops?"

Trabanco took a short step back, the gun still on Pete.

Then everything went to hell.

The voice seemed to be coming from above them—loud, hoarse, and angry. Trabanco jumped back at the first word, then wheeled around, pointing his gun at the ceiling.

"Attention, this is Fort Lauderdale PD—we have the area surrounded," the voice said through the megaphone. "Come out with your hands up. Repeat—we have the area surrounded."

"Fuck, fuck," Trabanco said as he stepped around the small space, trying to figure out what to do next.

Pete didn't hesitate. He lunged at Trabanco's feet, taking him down hard. Trabanco's hand hit the cement floor, sending the gun rattling out of his reach. Before he could get his bearings, Pete delivered two quick punches to his face, leaving Trabanco dazed and bloody. He pinned Trabanco to the floor and pulled out his own gun.

"Do not even think about moving," Pete said. He could hear Kathy in the background, scooping up Trabanco's errant weapon.

"You're dead," Trabanco said. "You're both fucking dead. You have no idea who you're fucking with."

Pete swung the gun barrel across Trabanco's face and heard a soft crunching sound. Trabanco groaned as a long gash opened up across his nose, blood pouring out of the fresh wound.

"Shut the fuck up," Pete said. He was exhausted. Tired of running. Tired of dealing with two-bit thugs when he wanted to nail the top boss.

The storage facility's rolling door inched up, a hand tugging it open. Harras walked in, alone, a megaphone in his hands.

"Funny the things you keep from your old job that come in handy after you retire," he said, unable to keep the smile off his face.

CHAPTER TWENTY-FOUR

"An archangel?" Harras said as they drove down Oakland Park Boulevard in his black Escalade. Kathy was in the front passenger seat with Pete in back. It was past six in the morning and the sun was beginning to peek through the clouds to launch its daily assault on Miami and Broward.

"Not just that—but the Jewish archangel of death," Kathy said as she looked out the passenger side window. They were all working on a few hours of sleep, none of it gained after the encounter with Trabanco. They'd spent most of the early morning hours at the Lauderhill police station, explaining why they were in someone else's storage unit with a known felon, and why said felon had been beaten severely.

Harras had smoothed most of it over and Trabanco was detained—but that would only last for a short time, and soon they'd be back where they'd left off: with no new leads on the murder weapon, Gaspar Varela still on the loose, and the deadliest gang in

South Florida looking to put Pete and Kathy six feet under. Happy Monday.

"Whatever," Harras said. "Whoever this guy is, Varela or someone else, knew Whitelaw had that storage space and they put two and two together when they realized you talked to his widow. It was too easy. A trap you two walked right in to."

"Luckily, you knew where we were going," Pete said. "And trap or not, I'm pretty sure it's not Varela who wants us dead."

"The second you mentioned what you two were doing, I knew it was a bad idea," Harras said. "But I didn't need you thinking I was part of your Scooby gang or whatever."

The first gunshot shattered the car's front windshield and sent Harras backward, clutching his right shoulder. Kathy dove in front of him and tried to steer the car, but the big SUV veered into the left lane of traffic, followed by honking horns and scrambling commuters.

Pete ducked. His ears were ringing and he felt glass on his face, blood trickling down. He couldn't hear. The car had screeched to a stop. Through the smoke, Pete saw that the car in front of them, a black Jeep Wrangler, had also stopped.

"What the fuck?" Kathy yelled, crouching down below the windshield. "What was that?"

Pete crouched behind Kathy's seat, but not before sneaking another peek at the Wrangler—and the two men stepping out of the car with guns in their hands.

"Ambush!" Pete said. "Stay here."

Harras was gasping for air, his hand trying to stem the bleeding from the wound in his shoulder. Pete prayed the bullet hadn't hit anything vital.

"Stay here?" Kathy said. "Where are you—hey!"

Before she could protest any further, Pete had opened the right backseat door and bent down next to the SUV's rear tire. He could see the four feet approaching the car as traffic whizzed around the accident scene. The cops would be here any second. He slid the gun from his back and rolled away from the car, getting two quick shots off. One connected—he knew this because he heard the thug yelp in pain. The other hit the Wrangler.

Pete scrambled back behind the car. The man he'd pegged was on the ground, but not down—he could still fire. Fuck. These guys worked fast. Just a few minutes out of the police station and they were already getting heat.

He heard more gunshots, coming from Harras's car this time.

He looked through the Escalade's back windshield and saw Kathy—holding Harras's gun—firing at the approaching thug. Her delivery was good but her aim wasn't anywhere near where it should be. All she was doing was keeping them at bay—and serving as a distraction.

Pete slid around to the left side of the car and onto his belly. He was out of their line of sight. He could hear sirens in the distance. He needed to disable these assholes before things got more treacherous. His top priority was making sure Harras got through this alive. He inched down and stretched out his arms, holding the gun upright. He sent off one shot at the more mobile gangbanger and connected with his shin. The scream he let out was unlike anything Pete had ever heard.

The other disabled hoodrat was now scrambling away from his fallen comrade, aware that Pete was coming at them from below. Thug #1 was down for the count. Pete got up and moved toward the two men—his back against the left side of the car, his gun held up and out, pointed at the downed gang members.

"Put your guns down and kick them away," Pete said, his voice loud and slow. He didn't want to be misunderstood. The second one, the one who'd been hit first, complied. The other one was passed out—from shock or blood loss.

Pete heard rustling behind him and saw Kathy in the car, hovering over Harras, her hands pushing down on his shoulder, trying to keep the pressure on. His eyelids fluttered closed.

She reached over and lowered the driver side window.

"He's lost a lot of blood," she said. Her face was smeared with blood and dirt, her eyes wild. It reminded Pete of when he first found her years ago—bound and trapped somewhere in the Keys, desperate to survive.

"I hear sirens," Pete said. "What the fuck just happened?"

"We almost got killed," she said, out of breath, her eyes on Harras, who was emitting a low moan now. "That's what happened. Shit."

Pete turned at the sound of squealing tires, expecting to see a handful of police cars and an ambulance circle around the disabled SUV. Instead, he caught the rear of the Jeep peeling out, one of the two thugs behind the wheel—not interested in sticking it out with his comatose comrade as a sign of *Los Enfermos* solidarity.

"Shit," Pete said.

The Jeep was still a few feet away. Pete broke into a sprint and pointed his gun. He wasn't going to let this bottom-feeding gangster get away so clean. He pulled the trigger. The bullet missed the driver, but managed to make contact with a back tire, sending the Jeep into a tailspin, the car flipping onto its side. The driver managed to crack open the driver side door, enough room so he could slither out and collapse.

Pete started to jog over, gun in hand, but he was intercepted by a Lauderhill police car cutting in front of him. An officer burst out of each door and they both pointed their weapons at Pete.

"Put the gun down," the driver said. "And put your hands up, asshole."

Pete complied. He dropped to his knees and said a silent prayer for his injured friend, for his partner, and for himself.

CHAPTER TWENTY-FIVE

The Florida Medical Center was a short drive from the scene of the shootout. Once the cops cuffed and disarmed Pete and Kathy, they loaded Harras into an ambulance and got him into surgery. From what Pete could gather, his friend had lost a lot of blood but would survive. The bullet had gone clean through. Harras was lucky.

That had been the easy part. Explaining to the local PD why he had a loaded gun and was shooting at Miami gang members on a crowded street in Lauderhill during the early morning commute was a bit more difficult. The fact that they'd spent hours talking to the same officers about a different incident with a different member of the same gang wasn't helping their cause. Still, Harras being involved gave them a decent amount of cloud cover. Pete just wasn't sure for how long.

Pete's only phone call was to Dave. His friend was sending a lawyer. At least that was going their way.

Kathy, asleep in the police station waiting room next to Pete, repositioned herself, her body inching closer to him. It'd been a surreal twelve hours, and he wasn't sure they had much to show for it. Maldonado had confirmed that his testimony was false, but they still had no murder weapon, and Varela was still in the wind.

"They're not pressing charges," a voice said.

Pete looked up. Jackie Cruz.

"Excuse me?" Pete said, trying not to move.

"I talked to the cops, explained the situation, noted the bad PR that would hit if they arrested a vocal critic like you and that, in fact, you helped apprehend two wanted felons," she said, rattling off each point on her fingers. "So, you're free to go. They're okay with looking the other way on this one. You're welcome, Fernandez."

"Jackie," Pete said, still processing. "What the hell are you doing here?"

"Dave called," she said. "Well, Dave's mommy called."

"You know Dave," Pete said, more a befuddled statement than a question.

"Dave's parents keep me on retainer," she said. "Small world, huh?"

"That's one way to put it," Pete said.

"Let's head to the hospital—they got Harras his own room," Jackie said. "Maybe then you can sneak away from your girlfriend and take an ex-flame out for a cup?"

Pete and Jackie grabbed two coffees and sat in the hospital cafeteria by the windows. It was early afternoon, right after the lunch rush, and not crowded.

"I'm sorry I was such a bitch to you and your *novia* when you came by with Harras," she said.

"Kathy's my partner, not my—well, not my life or sex partner," Pete said. He was fried. The words weren't coming out right anymore.

"Whatever," Jackie said. "I don't care. You and I—that was just a summer fling a million years ago."

Pete nodded and took a sip of his black coffee.

"But it was fun, right?" she said, a sly smile on her face.

"Jackie, it was definitely fun," Pete said, not laughing, but curious to keep the conversation going. "And, look, don't get me wrong—it's great to see you, but I'm really freaking out. I don't think I can go anywhere without these psychopaths trying to destroy me. I've pissed off the biggest gang in South Florida and it doesn't seem like they're interested in reestablishing diplomatic relations."

"Save the whining for the *gringa*," Jackie said. "I'm not here to be your pity party coordinator, okay? I want to talk to you about a few things."

"And I thought you were just here to be my get out of jail free card."

"That's a given," she said. "But you called and asked for something. I haven't forgotten."

Jackie looked around the empty cafeteria before turning back to Pete, her voice lowered.

"So I made a few calls," Jackie said. "I connected Nicole Purdin, the forensic lady you met with a little while ago, with the people investigating the Whitelaw murder. She suggested they compare his wounds to those of Carmen Varela and the attack on your grandfather."

"And?" Pete said.

"Well, the Diego files weren't as detailed as the murder books, which is understandable, since the stabbing wasn't a homicide," Jackie said. "But the knife wounds were too close to have come from different knives. The machete that killed Carmen Varela was probably an antique, and it had a specific crack in the blade that made the wounds unique. That trait was also present in the other two cases. So you're looking for one weapon—potentially one person."

"That's huge," Pete said. "But what does it do for Varela? I mean, this has got to be enough for a new trial. We got what he wanted."

"Slow down, kiddo," Jackie said. "This doesn't mean shit. Varela is gone. You think Miami PD is going to open up the Carmen Varela case now all of a sudden? Make a plea for her husband to come back? Now, if he were sitting in prison, his fingers crossed for a new trial based on this evidence, I could get him one."

"Yeah," Pete said. He'd let his hopes rise too high. "Plus, he could have just been the person using that knife, though I doubt it."

"He could have been, sure," Jackie said. "That's the argument I'd put up if I was the prosecutor. But I checked Varela's duty record. Which took a lot of digging, but most of it was put in as evidence at his first trial. Gaspar was out on patrol the night your grandfather got stabbed. He was with his partner, Posada. They were in the field, working a case for narcotics, when your grandfather was murdered."

"Those people could have lied, though," Pete said. "I mean, the Miami PD doesn't have a sterling record. I could see the opposition going for that."

"Maybe," Jackie said. "But this case has been such a shitshow that I'm not betting on the DA going after his own police force, even if it's a past, more corrupt iteration."

"So, if all this lines up, we have someone who wants us to think Varela is running *Los Enfermos*, killed his wife, and more," Pete said. "But why? Why pay people like Maldonado to betray Varela?"

"And why pay Janette Ledesma," Jackie said. "You and your *amiguita* came by asking about Ledesma, and it got me to thinking— once I got past the white-hot rage I hold in the depths of my soul for that dead junkie whore."

"I get it," Pete said. He'd read the transcripts. He wanted to move this along. Talking about Ledesma seemed like small fry compared to Jackie's news.

"Well, here's the thing—Ledesma was shit-poor at the time," Jackie said, pulling out a file from her big brown purse and laying it on the grimy cafeteria table. She opened it up and pulled out a few printouts. "She didn't have a steady job, most of her money went to the pipe, and she was about to be evicted from her studio apartment."

She pushed one of the pages across the table to Pete and flipped it over.

"Look at this," she said, pointing to the middle of the page. "A few months after the trial, she's suddenly flush. She bought a house—a piece-of-shit house in a piece-of-shit neighborhood, but a house nonetheless. She got a new car."

"Just like Maldonado."

"Right."

"She also got a new boyfriend," Pete said. "Gilbert Fermin."

"Yes and no," Jackie said. "But you're on the right track. Fermin came later. He beat the shit out of her on the regular. He beat the shit out of her the night she died too. Never charged. But if two dots ever needed connecting, it's those two: abusive boyfriend and dead girlfriend. Especially after things got suddenly better for her."

"What's Fermin's background?"

"That's the blind spot," Jackie said, collecting her pages and putting the file away. "I never got a bead on him. By the time Janette Ledesma died, I was done with Varela and wanted to move on. But your call got me thinking."

"Jackie, this is really helpful, on so many levels," Pete said. "I'll check in on Fermin."

Pete started to get up. He needed to stretch his legs and check on the rest of his wayward crew. His brain was at full speed now.

"I've got a line on Varela," she said, turning her head to look out the window.

Pete sat down again.

"What did you just say?" Pete said, trying to keep his voice down.

"You heard me," she met his glare. "I can reach him. I will never admit to having had this conversation with you. But he wanted me to tell you. He also wanted me to tell you to be careful what you believe."

"Holy fuck," Pete said. "Is that the real reason you're here?"

"That, and I take weird pleasure in bailing you out of shit," she said.

"Where is he? Can you get me in touch with him?"

"You're not understanding me," she said, leaning across the table. "Be careful about your information—about Varela, about how it relates to you, about anything. Even the twists are twisted up."

"Cryptic much?"

"Look, it's not like I'm on Gchat with the guy all day," she said. "I've spoken to him once since the shit hit the fan and I don't have a number where I can text him emojis. He made a point of asking me to come to you and relay that message. What you do with it—that's up to you."

CHAPTER
TWENTY-SIX

Follow the money. If, like Juan Carlos Maldonado, Janette Ledesma had been paid off to botch her testimony, then Pete had to find out where that money came from, and how far it reached. He knew the money probably had been moved around by Rick Blanco, but what mattered was the source. That was how Pete would find out who was really in charge of *Los Enfermos*. The only link to that info—and it was a stretch—was Gilbert Fermin.

He was alone. Harras was recovering in the ICU at the Florida Medical Center and Kathy had rented a hotel room nearby, not comfortable with going home to await a gang of wild criminals looking for blood. Pete couldn't blame her. She needed to rest after the last forty-eight hours. So did he. But something was gnawing at him.

After an awkward ride home, courtesy of Jackie, Pete stuffed a duffel bag with his essentials and a few of Kathy's—clothes, toothbrushes, laptops, deodorant, and credit cards. The rest was expendable. They'd be able to move quickly now. They were officially on the run again.

He didn't like making the call, but he couldn't think of another way. Miranda Whitelaw had been friendly enough when he rang, peppering their conversation with references to Pete and Kathy's recent string of bad, violent luck. She'd dug up the info Pete needed fast from her dead husband's files. Fermin's last known address was a tiny studio apartment on Sunset and 137th. Peak West Miami suburbia. Where restaurant chains went to multiply and commingle with hair salons, gyms, and pharmacies.

The apartments at Kendale Lakes were nice enough—each building in the complex was painted the same tan and brown and the trees and hedges were well kept. But beneath that was a layer of dirt and shoddy craftsmanship that hinted at a decaying structure. These apartments had been nice once, Pete thought. Now they were just places to live. *Faded* was the word that came to mind.

He pulled into the small lot adjacent to the address Miranda Whitelaw had given him and walked toward the elevators. There wasn't a main entrance—it was open-air and you could enter at any time. There was little breeze to speak of, Miami's stifling, year-long summer in full swing today. Pete pushed the up button.

When he got to the third floor, he made a right and knocked on Fermin's door. He heard some rustling inside and then a muffled voice.

"Yah?"

"I'm looking for Gilbert Fermin," Pete said.

"Who is it?"

"This is Pete Fernandez," Pete said. "Let me in, Gilbert."

Before he finished the sentence, he knew the door wasn't going to open—the rustling grew louder and Pete heard what sounded like a balcony door opening.

"Fuck."

He had a decision to make. He could either run down the stairs and try to intercept Fermin—a man he'd never seen or met—on the other side, or he could take a more direct route. That would involve going through his apartment.

Pete was always a fan of the direct route.

He positioned himself in front of the door. His kick hit under and to the right of the doorknob. The crack of cheap material was good, but the door didn't give. Pete delivered a second kick and the door swung open, revealing a mess of an apartment: pizza boxes, ripe takeout containers, empty cases of beer, and the smell of over-used cat litter mixed with really skunky weed.

Pete cut through the living room and onto the balcony. Aside from two pieces of cheap, off-white patio furniture, the area was empty. He leaned over the railing. Gilbert Fermin, a pudgy, fiftysomething man with a thin black mustache and a few wisps of hair remaining on his head, was clinging to the balcony's edge, his face red from the strain. He didn't seem inclined to look down, having underestimated just how steep a drop three stories would be.

"Gilbert Fermin?" Pete said.

"Y-y-yes," Fermin said. "Please, I don't want to fall."

Pete grabbed one of Fermin's meaty arms and leaned back, hoisting the large man up and over the railing. Soon, they were both lying on the balcony, gasping for breath. Pete got up first.

"Let's talk," he said, walking into Fermin's squalid apartment.

Fermin followed him and headed straight for the kitchen.

"Stop right there," Pete said.

Fermin turned around and saw the gun pointed at him. His mouth creaked open and stayed that way.

"Don't get out of my sight," Pete said. He motioned with the gun for Fermin to sit on a gray, stained futon. Of course the guy had a fucking futon.

Fermin sat, placing his hands on his knees.

"What is this about?"

"Janette Ledesma," Pete said. Recognition flickered across Fermin's face for a moment. He tried to hide it by looking at his feet.

"Remember her, Fermin?" Pete said. "I hope so. You used to

knock her around pretty good way back when."

"Of course I remember her," Fermin said, almost to himself.

"What can you tell me about her?"

"She's dead, man," he said. "That was a long time ago. Forgot a lot of what happened back then."

"Who paid you to kill her?"

The fact that Fermin didn't even feign surprise confirmed that Pete was on the right track. The question was a gamble—a leap based on a few strands of speculation that might not tie into anything substantial. But he'd made contact.

Fermin hung his head. "I didn't kill her," he said.

"Close enough, though, right?" Pete said, stepping toward Fermin. "Close enough for it to seem like an accident, but enough to collect, right?"

Fermin's head shot up. He was angry now.

"What do you want from me? What the fuck is this about?"

"Answer the question," Pete said, keeping his tone flat and his gun pointed at Fermin.

"If I talk to you, I am a dead man," Fermin said. "How do I know they didn't send you to test me? Why would I risk my life and talk to you?"

"I'm not here to make this easy on you," Pete said. "But I have the gun and you have the answers. So let's speed up the knowledge transfer, okay?"

Fermin let out a long sigh and leaned back on the couch.

"I never liked her," Fermin said. His words dribbled out in a slow drone. "But the ask was simple and the upside was big, man. So big. Like, I'm still living off it big. I don't need to work today. May not for a while."

"You must be so proud," Pete said.

"I used to run with those guys, when I was younger," Fermin said. "The older generation was calmer. More thoughtful. They didn't do all this crazy shit. The top guy needed me to work this angle, Janette Ledesma. Make sure she didn't blab to anyone. Keep her in line.

Maybe get a little sugar out of it. She wasn't bad looking, after all. But man, that woman was a junkie. She would suck your dick for a dollar if it meant she could cop with it."

Pete didn't realize he'd swung the gun handle at Fermin until the man was clutching his face, blood pouring from the gash on his lip. The burst of violence surprised Pete. It came fast and felt right, but it was not the kind of thing he was used to. Had Fermin hit a nerve? Did the clarity that came with being sober also mean he had to do a better job keeping his own emotions in check? Possibly.

"Motherfucker," Fermin said, not looking at Pete.

"Listen, you piece of shit," Pete said. "I don't care about her being a junkie, or what an upstanding citizen like you thought of her. I want to know who put you up to it and where I can find them."

"You really don't know, do you?" Fermin said, his voice muffled by his hand covering his mouth.

The explosion came from behind Fermin, and sent the fat man hurtling forward. Pete moved out of the man's flight path and knew Fermin was dead before he landed, face down. His back was charred and already soaked in blood. Pete tried to avert his eyes, but he still caught glimpses of tissue and bone. Smoke and dust cloaked the tiny apartment—making it hard to see clearly and harder to breathe. Pete dove to the right, away from the open balcony window and toward the kitchen, crawling to reach the wall. The futon was on fire, having caught on when the small explosive went off. Someone had planted the device in Fermin's apartment. But how did they know when to set it off? Pete looked out of the studio through the balcony and realized he was being watched.

He tried to crawl to the kitchen, keeping his body low. His ears were ringing from the blast and everything felt like it was moving at hyperspeed. That was when he heard footsteps.

Someone was sprinting down the hall outside the apartment. The steps were getting louder.

Pete ducked inside the main hall closet and closed the door behind him. He waited. He heard the front door open. He heard someone walk in and stop. Pete felt sweat pool on his hands as he gripped the closet doorknob. The killer was now inside the apartment, walking around the small living room. The steps were slow and thoughtful. The intruder didn't want to interfere with the scene or leave evidence. Someone aware of law enforcement, Pete thought. He heard some rustling and then a voice—gruff, older.

"Yeah, it's me," the man inside the apartment said, not bothering to keep his voice down. "We dealt with our problem, but the other one is gone."

A pause.

"He's gone, okay? He must have gotten spooked," he said, annoyed at whoever was on the other end of the call. "Yeah, I get it. I'm out the door. The cops will be here any second. Yes. Bye."

A long sigh was followed by a few more footsteps. He heard the killer shuffling papers at the far end of the apartment. Then things went quiet. A few more steps and the front door opened and closed. Pete waited a moment before stepping outside. The apartment was empty.

Pete pulled out his gun and opened the apartment door. He could see the killer heading for the stairwell. Pete followed. The killer was about half a flight ahead of him and had noticed Pete was in pursuit. Pete couldn't get a good look at him, but the man could hear Pete's gaining ground. The man was well built, perhaps a bit older than Pete. He cursed himself for being out of shape.

Stepping out of the stairwell and into the lobby, Pete almost tripped over someone—an older lady knocked down by the killer as he tried to escape. No time to help her up. He chased the guy through the apartment building's main double doors—the figure was still too far off to identify, but Pete was getting closer. He'd have to hop in a car at some point.

Pete turned a corner that led to the main parking lot, expecting to see the figure on the fringe of his vision. He was gone.

Pete cursed and looked around. The parking lot was half full and he saw no signs of someone having sped off. Whoever he'd been chasing was still here. But Pete didn't have time to linger. The cops would eventually show up and wonder what he was doing on the scene of another murder, and Pete had dealt with more than his share of cops over the last two days. He did a quick lap around the lot and saw nothing out of the ordinary. Shit. He heard a few sirens in the distance.

He hopped in his car and sped out of the lot. He took a moment to look himself over in the rearview mirror and realized he was covered in dirt and Gilbert Fermin's blood.

CHAPTER TWENTY-SEVEN

"**Y**ou weren't being honest with me."

Madelyn Suarez almost jumped out of her designer heels at the sound of his voice. She turned around and saw Pete and Kathy and let loose with a barrage of Spanish obscenities Pete hadn't heard in years. It felt almost comforting.

"The hell are you talking about, you little *pendejo de mierda*," she said, spittle flying out of her mouth. "Who the fuck do you think you are, coming at me in a parking lot in the middle of the—"

"Cut the shit, lady," Kathy said. "The 'tough old broad' act is very 2003."

"Who's this pelican-looking slut?" Madelyn said.

Pete ignored the insult and pressed on.

"Gilbert Fermin is dead. So's Calvin Whitelaw," Pete said. "*Los Enfermos* have tried to kill me and my partner a handful of times too. Someone wants us to think it's Gaspar Varela calling the shots. I think it isn't. You got jammed up when I asked you about the case. I need you to be honest with us. It could save our lives."

Madelyn hesitated, then leaned on her car, a black Nissan in need of a new paint job. She seemed decades older now.

"I was hoping this would blow over," she said.

"Well, it hasn't," Kathy said.

"Where can we talk?" Pete said.

"Here's as good a place as any," Madelyn said, motioning for them to get in the car with her.

Pete sat next to Madelyn in the front and Kathy slid into the backseat.

"Better I not be seen traveling around town with you two," she said, lighting a cigarette. "So, tell *Tía* Madelyn why you're angry at her."

"You know more about the Varela case, I can tell," Pete said. "You gave me the press-release answer. Dave says you know everything about this town. That was one of the biggest scandals in Miami history. I was amazed you didn't have even one tidbit."

"Well, I don't work for you, *papi*," she said. "So, what's my incentive?"

"You worked for my grandfather," Pete said.

Madelyn met Pete's eyes and smiled.

"He was a good man," she said. "Didn't deserve to go out like that."

"We know Ledesma was in the room after Varela's wife was killed. Someone paid her to tank her own testimony," Kathy said. "Then someone paid to have her beaten to death when it seemed like she might flip. We also know Whitelaw was in contact with someone nicknamed Cain Samael. He was blackmailing Samael with information and the actual murder weapon, threatening to reveal some truths about the case, along with the kind of evidence that would certainly lead to a new trial. Now Whitelaw's dead. Whoever this Samael is, he is after us and is running *Los Enfermos*."

"Varela's no *pandillero*," Madelyn said. "I promise you that. Miami doesn't want that story, though. Too easy, not as sexy. They don't want another situation where the police fucked up, even if it exonerates one of their own. Follow the cops, follow the money, follow the motive, then you'll have your answers. To both cases."

"Both cases?" Pete asked.

"You're trying to figure out who killed Diego, *el pobre*, right?"

"Yes, my dad was investigating it before he died," Pete said. "It looks like whoever killed Varela's wife may have been the one who stabbed my grandfather."

"Jesus, do I have to spell everything out for you, *niño?* Read the notes, you *comemierda*," she said before taking a long drag of her Parliament. "Your dad was a great cop. The best. He worked on that case for years. He knew who the killer was. What do you know about how your grandfather died?"

"Just what was in the files," Kathy said. "So, very little. We know that, years after a deadly knife attack left him in poor health, someone drove by and shot Diego Fernandez and sped off. The only descriptions noted he was a younger, well-built man in a beige Oldsmobile."

"Okay, think," she said. "Who were his enemies?"

"No one in Miami," Pete said. "But Castro? *Los Enfermos* have a history of hitting people for the Castros."

"There you go," Madelyn said. "You're not so dumb after all. *Los Enfermos* were as much a political hit squad as a gang. They made money from drugs and murder and the usual, of course, but they were also an elite attack force for Fidel and Raul. *Los Enfermos* got to the people Castro couldn't reach in Miami. Diego was one of them. *Esos hijos de la gran puta* killed a good man. Killed many good people. The big man you're looking for on the Varela thing? He's the same guy behind your grandfather's death. I guarantee it."

"So, what, we just start searching pro-Castro databases and see who drives a beige Oldsmobile?" Kathy said.

"If you're an idiot, yes," Madelyn said, turning to look at Kathy. "But if you're smart, you'd consider that maybe some Castro agents infiltrate anti-Castro groups. It's not the answer, but it's a start. You should put me on your payroll."

"I need more than that," Pete said.

"I guess this baby needs a bottle, then?" Madelyn said, licking her lips. "Okay, let me make this easy for you. I'm going to say a name and you tell me what you know about him."

"I am not in the mood for this," Kathy said.

"Shut up for once, *mija*."

"Go ahead," Pete said.

"Graydon Smith," Madelyn said. "What do you know about him?"

"He was one of the first cops on the scene of the Varela murder," Pete said. "He was part of Varela's crew, with Posada and a few others. Young guns of the Miami PD."

"Very good," Madelyn said. "What else?"

Pete shrugged. He hadn't thought of Smith in months.

"Look at those files again," Madelyn said. "See where Officer Smith pops up."

Madelyn started to cough—a long, wet, hacking sound that stopped after a few interminable minutes.

"What do you know about Smith?" Kathy asked.

"Bad," Madelyn said.

Another flurry of coughs followed. Madelyn took a moment before speaking again.

"Varela was an honest cop, though, so think about it," she said, wiping her mouth with her sleeve. "What does that make him? A minority in Miami. Like your father. Someone wanted him out of the way. Other cops were okay with that because it meant more pie for them. Someone saw an opportunity. Now you and your *hermana* start asking questions. Start digging around. Then suddenly Varela escapes. What better way to confirm his guilt to the world, right? Even if he wants to go back, he can't just walk into the prison and ask to be re-arrested. He'd be doomed. No one would buy a story about being forced to escape. Just like no one bought his story of people coming to his house and beating the shit out of him and killing his wife. Look at the cops—look at the evidence. Then you might see a different picture."

"**Y**ou're trouble, Fernandez," Harras said, squirming on his hospital bed. "Every time we hang out, I get shot. It's not a trend I want to continue."

"Hello yourself, Mr. Cheerful," Pete said, sitting down by the bed. Kathy leaned on the wall behind him.

"Any word on when I can get the hell out of here?"

"Nurse said at least a day or two, when I badgered her for info earlier," Kathy said.

"Ah shit," Harras said. He scooted up on the bed and winced, his left hand reaching for his bandaged right shoulder. "What's the latest?"

"Gilbert Fermin is dead," Pete said. "*Los Enfermos* knew I was heading there and killed him before he could talk. Jackie's forensic expert also thinks, based on the evidence, that the knife that killed Carmen Varela also finished off Whitelaw and was used on my grandfather."

"Any leads on the weapon?" Harras asked. "Now that would be something. Even if it doesn't automatically exonerate Varela, it definitely counts as new evidence."

"Not since we went all B and E on the storage space. We talked to Madelyn Suarez. Again," Kathy said. "She seems to think Varela is innocent."

"Does she?" Harras said. "Not surprising. She's a contrarian, through and through."

"She told us to follow the cops—across the board," Pete said, pulling out a reporter's notebook from his back pocket. "So Kathy and I did some research, made some calls."

"God help us all," Harras said.

"It's frightening, I know, but once upon a time, we were—well, at least I was—a decent newspaper reporter," Kathy said. "I still have contacts in the Miami PD. They had a few interesting things to say."

"Remember Graydon Smith?" Pete said.

"What about him?" Harras said.

"Well, it seems this guy was not only around when Varela was arrested," Kathy said, "but also when Martin Colón got his head blown off and, strangely enough, when Diego Fernandez was murdered. He retired recently and no one's heard from him since his goodbye drink-up at Club Deuce."

"So? Multiple cops show up at crime scenes, and one cop visits many over the course of a long career," Harras said. "Are you saying he also killed these people? The guy served for over thirty years—he should have retired a long time ago. Now you want to drag him into this? Let him ride off into the sunset."

"We're just asking if you know him," Pete said. "Have any sense of what kind of guy he is."

"He was an asshole," Harras said. "There? Happy now? The guy was a prick. He was probably on the take to some degree. Like everyone else who was working in the PD. He was difficult, and he didn't make things easy for me when the FBI needed something. But he was around and he made his arrest quota and everyone was copacetic. I wouldn't peg him as a killer."

"That's what I heard too," Kathy said. "Plus, he was part of that crew—with Varela and Posada. They were the three amigos, basically."

Harras grabbed the remote from the small table connected to the bed and flicked the TV on.

"Well, there you go," he said.

"You don't think that's a coincidence?" Pete asked. "I mean, for all we know, he was there when Gilbert Fermin died."

"Listen, kid, the less you talk about that, the less likely anyone's going to realize that you—Mr. Tough Guy PI—were actually there," Harras said.

"Were where?"

The three of them turned to face the entrance. Maya had walked in, a small plant and a *Get Well Soon!* balloon in her hands.

Pete stood up and took the stuff from Maya and set it on Harras's nightstand.

"Nothing, we were just going over some stuff," Pete said.

"For the case?" Maya said.

"Yes, the case," Kathy said, looking at her nails.

Maya ignored Kathy and turned to Pete.

"I wanted to see how everyone's doing," she said. "Do you need anything?"

"We're fine," Harras said. "Just recovering from attempted murder. Another day in paradise with Dumb and Dumber over here."

Maya let out a dry laugh. She grabbed Pete's hand and leaned in to him. "Can we talk?"

She let go and left the room before Pete could answer. He followed a few paces behind.

She turned around when they got to a small seating area down the hall from Harras's room.

"You seem upset," Pete said.

"I am upset," she said. "And it sounds really cliché, but I'm pissed off that I haven't heard from you in days. I don't understand what you're doing—with me, with this case, with anything. I mean, I only figured out what was going on when I got in touch with Kathy, and she wasn't exactly super-helpful, Pete. If you want to try to be together, let's do it. I'm in. If you don't, that's fine—I'm not a teenager. But give me some kind of idea what's going on."

"That's fair," Pete said. "I've had a lot on my mind lately. The case is getting convoluted, but I think we're on to something. And hey, I don't mean to argue, but I've been shot at a handful of times, so I can't say being social was atop my to-do list."

Maya frowned. "Fine," she said. "I get that. But it's not like we're just a random couple that went on a few dates, okay? We're tangled in all this together. Us, the case, and everything that's coming up with it. Were you planning on updating me on what's going on?"

"I just told you," Pete said. "There's nothing concrete to share. I mean, if Kathy were here, she'd remind you we don't work for you anymore."

"But you're fucking me," Maya said, her voice raised. The solitary nurse at the main desk turned her head toward them in response. "Okay? We had sex. We are at least somewhat together. Okay? So, I'm not your boss, but you think it's cool to keep things that directly affect me or my father from me?"

"Look, there's nothing new to report," Pete said, lowering his voice, hoping that would calm her a bit. "We're just following some leads to see where they go. All we know is your dad is still out there and hopefully he'll turn himself in."

Maya let out a long sigh. "Fine," she said. "Can we get back to why I'm here? I don't want to have weekly state of our union chats. This is not what should be happening this early."

"You're right," Pete said. "I—how do I say this?—I don't have a good track record with this. With relationships. So, my first response is to ignore. It's something I need to work on. Are you free tonight? Do you want to get a bite?"

"Sure, yes," Maya said. "Come over and we can order something. Keep it simple. Just text me when you're on your way."

She turned and started walking down the hall toward the elevator bank.

"That sounded totally awesome," Kathy said. "What did your hot new lady have to say? Complaining about being overdressed in a hospital?"

Pete turned around.

"Were you snooping?"

"I don't snoop, dear," Kathy said. "I happened to come out to use the lady's room when I noticed *Melrose Place* was filming by the nurses' station."

"Funny," Pete said.

"I thought so," Kathy said. "Can we talk about work now?"

"Sure, shoot."

Kathy pulled out a tiny Post-It note from her back pocket and handed it to Pete.

"What's this?"

"Graydon Smith," Kathy said. "I called my guy. Pressed a little more. He works the desk at the PD and is also about to retire. He's one of the few people who's managed to keep in touch with Smith. He's not at home and he's not hanging out where he usually does. But he's here."

F ox's Lounge had seen better days. But that was part of the charm. Slotted in next to US 1 near the University of Miami, Fox's was a drinker's dive. Dark, cool, nary a trendy jukebox in sight, and a wait-staff that would as soon smack your hand as bring you a bowl of French onion soup. Pete was no stranger to the place—he'd propped himself up at the smooth bar many a time. Now he felt anxious and tired, and the last place he wanted to be was in a bar. He needed to stop meeting sources at bars, he thought. A park would be nice. Maybe a fancy restaurant.

It was midday, but when they walked into the dimly lit Fox's, it could have been early evening. An older couple sucked face at a booth near the bathroom and a big older man sat at the far end of the bar, twirling an empty glass. Kathy sat down to his right and Pete to his left. His reaction—slow and annoyed more than surprised—was proof that he was already half in the bag at lunch.

"Who're you?"

"You're Graydon Smith, right?" Pete said.

"So? Who's asking?"

Pete extended his hand. "Pete Fernandez," he said. "This is my partner, Kathy Bentley."

"Aw shit," Smith said. "Pedro's boy."

"Can we get you a drink?" Kathy said.

Pete didn't like plying a drunk with more alcohol, but didn't know how else to approach him. He also saw a glimmer of light in Smith's eyes that told him they'd asked the right question.

"Seven and seven," Smith said, twirling his glass again, as if to show them he was done. "Make it a double."

Kathy waved at the bartender, a thin, short-haired hipster kid who could have passed for thirteen or thirty. He nodded and started making the drink.

"One drink gets you a question or two, then we're done," Smith said.

"What about two drinks?" Kathy said, leaning into him. He leaned toward her, making no effort to hide the fact that he was breathing in her perfume. Pete felt nauseated.

"Well, let's do one first and see where the night goes," Smith said.

Pete didn't bother to correct him on what time it was.

"Mr. Smith," Pete said.

"Call me Gray," he said as the bartender brought him a new drink. "Everyone I know does. Gray. Mr. Smith was my dad. Fuck him."

"Okay, Gray," Pete said. "I'll cut to the chase, so we can leave you to the party here."

The older man nodded, missing Pete's sarcasm.

"We're working on the Gaspar Varela case," Kathy said. "We're trying to investigate whether or not he actually killed his wife."

"Was in jail for it, wasn't he?" Smith said. "What more do you need?"

"Well, believe it or not, police and law enforcement sometimes make mistakes," Pete said. "There's a lot of evidence that's fuzzy in the case."

"Not to me," Smith said. He sounded sober all of a sudden.

"Can you tell us anything about it?" Pete asked. "You were one of the first cops on the scene."

Smith looked around and took a long sip of his drink.

"Okay, sure, let's talk," Smith said. "I got nothing to lose. I'm a dead man walking."

"Why do you say that?" Kathy asked.

"Don't gimme that shit, sweetie, you're no innocent," Smith said. "You know as well as I do that someone's cleaning house. People are dying. Anyone connected to Varela—even Varela himself—is ending up dead or missing. Whitelaw. Fermin. Just the tip of what's going down."

"Is that why you finally punched out?" Pete asked.

"I'm old, that's why I punched out," Smith said. "Overstayed my welcome. The PD doesn't have my kind of cop anymore. They're younger, meaner, more by the book."

He wiped his mouth with his sleeve and Pete caught a whiff of him—stale, dirty, reeking of a few days without a shower and lots of booze. He tried his best not to recoil and noticed Kathy was already inching away from the other side.

"I've done some bad stuff, we all did," Smith said. "Your father, he was the golden child. But I bet he cut corners too. His partner, Broche, was as slanted as any of us. We all have to pay the price at some point. But I won't lie—for a minute there, I thought I was going to get away clean."

"Who's after you?" Pete said. "Why are they after you?"

"Aren't you listening, kid?" Smith said. "Someone is mowing down the people that mucked with the Varela case—and others. I'm next in line. I held on as long as I could. But you two showing up proves it's over. I've been sleeping in my car, drinking myself blind, driving around, and trying to keep moving. But I don't have that in me anymore. I'm stopping here."

"We can try to get you protection, if you testify," Kathy said. She was stretching. Pete wasn't sure what Smith could even say to warrant that kind of guarantee.

"Gray, you were at not only the Varela scene, but also at a few other ones," Pete said, speaking in a slow, calm voice. "Diego Fernandez, my grandfather. How do they all piece together? Calvin Whitelaw. My friend Martin. Maybe even Gilbert Fermin. What's the connection?"

"Beyond me being a cop?" Smith said. "You're not that dumb, I guess. Figured that'd give me cloud cover for a while. By the time anyone sussed it out, I'd be dead or in Mexico, sipping a piña colada on the beach. But at a certain point, when the guy you're working for is killing everyone who works for him, you have to wonder if you're the exception or just last in line."

"Who is it? Is it Varela?" Kathy asked. She was getting impatient. They both were. Smith was dragging it out as long as he could.

"No, Varela's a patsy," Smith said. "He was a good cop, too good. Like your father. Couldn't crack those two. After a while, we had to figure out a way to crack them to keep getting our cut. Sooner or later, they were going to rat on us. So we had to send some messages. We had to take care of them."

The pieces started to click together in Pete's head. Varela and Pedro Fernandez. Two good cops in a sea of corruption. Graydon Smith was working for someone else, who would be threatened by anyone finding out about their side deals, extortion, and skimmed money. Pete's dad had started as a beat cop before moving to homicide. Varela did as well, before moving to narcotics.

Pete grabbed his phone and dialed Harras. Before he could launch the call, Smith slammed Pete's wrist onto the bar, sending a shooting pain down his arm. By the time he recovered, his phone was in Smith's pocket and a gun was trained on Kathy's head. The bartender—and the couple sitting in the back—were gone.

"You're smart, but you're not that smart," Smith said, stepping away, pushing Kathy toward the bar next to Pete.

"Gray, look, we can help you," Pete said. "It doesn't have to end this way."

"Pete—" Kathy started to speak before the sound of the main door opening interrupted them. They were facing the far wall. They couldn't see who was there yet.

"It will end this way," Smith said. "But not for me. Did you think your source suddenly just knew where I was? You really bought all that talk about me being last? The exception? That's bullshit. I'm still around because I didn't pussy out. Like Varela. Like Gilbert Fermin. Like Janette Ledesma. Like Whitelaw. Like your friend Martin Colón, that idiot Rick Blanco, and Arturo Pelegrin. They're all dead. One by one, people start to get scared. They get a taste and want more until they realize how deep they've gone; then they want it to be like a job where you give two weeks' notice and everything is fine and dandy."

Pete started to say something, but stopped when Smith raised his gun-free hand.

"Sit down," he said. "And shut the fuck up."

Pete and Kathy complied. Smith walked up to Pete and patted him down, removing the gun from his back and putting it in his own pocket. He seemed to take pleasure in sliding his hands over Kathy, despite a look of disgust on her face.

They heard footsteps. Smith backed away from them, as if to make way for the arrival of a king.

A looming figure entered. The boss, Pete realized. He wore a long black jacket over a tailored gray suit, his salt-and-pepper hair was closely cropped, and his face clean-shaven. A golden half-heart pendant hung on a chain around his neck. Pete didn't gasp when he saw him. He'd figured it out. But it'd been too late. Kathy cursed under her breath.

"You don't seem surprised," Posada said.

"If this was twenty minutes ago, I would be," Pete said.

"That's a shame," Posada said, a smile on his face. "I was so hoping to catch the great Pete Fernandez and his partner by surprise."

"Maybe next time," Kathy said, her face defiant and angry. "Congrats on the whole being able to see thing. You got better fast, Cain Samael."

"Yes, yes. *Samael*, the blind, fallen angel, and *Cain*, the original traitor. I'm surprised that didn't tip you off. The whole blindness thing was a necessary ruse, if a bit annoying to keep up," Posada said, walking closer to them. "I have to say, you've both graduated from marginal pains in my ass to genuine threats. So, no. There won't be a next time."

"Do you really think this is it?" Pete said. He was trying to keep everyone talking while he tried to think of anything that could slow things down. "You don't think we've talked to other people? Better detectives than us? Harras has our notes."

"Harras will be dead within the hour. There's a nurse at the hospital who owes us a few favors," Posada said. "Now, I'm not one for lengthy chats. You got close. We tried to steer you off and you kept digging, so now we're here. And at what cost? Your drunk buddy with gangster aspirations is dead. Everyone you touched while researching this case is dead or will be shortly. That's on your shoulders, not mine."

"We'll find the murder weapon," Pete said. "And then it's over. Then you're sunk."

"I admire your tenacity," Posada said as he reached into his coat, pulling out a long blade. "Did you mean this? I really missed it. Calvin Whitelaw was so fucking annoying toward the end there. It was nice to get it back. I hadn't used it in so long. That might have been why Calvin's body got so hacked up. Rusty, I guess."

"You are nuts," Kathy said. Smith took a step in her direction, but she ignored him. "I haven't added it all up yet, but you're the psychopath here. You killed an innocent woman and blamed your best friend. You helped his daughter try to prove he was innocent for almost ten years. And all this time you've been a cop *and* a drug lord? If you think killing us will make it all disappear, you're truly mad."

Posada's smirk didn't waver during Kathy's speech. He reached into his coat with his free hand and pulled out his own gun, looking it over with admiration.

"Well said, Ms. Bentley," Posada said. "But let's do the math. The only people who've made the connection—who've realized that a former cop who's carved out a fairly nice life for himself in retirement after a blinding accident is actually running *Los Enfermos*—are right here."

He pointed the gun at Pete. "You …"

At Kathy. "You …"

At Smith. "And you," he said.

He pulled the trigger, sending Smith lurching forward, blood spreading around his stomach, the ex-cop's body spinning from the bullet's momentum. He landed at their feet—his head at the base of the bar, his legs splayed out, and a pool of blood spreading out under the barstools that Pete and Kathy had just been sitting on.

Posada looked down at his dead lackey and shook his head. He pocketed the gun.

"He was losing it," Posada said. "His sob story—the one I'm assuming he shared with you—was getting too close to reality. Oh well. He had a good run."

"It doesn't have to be like this," Pete said. He inched forward a bit. He could see his gun behind Smith's; it had fallen out of the dead man's pocket. He glanced at Kathy. She saw it too.

"Is this when you start to beg?" Posada said, the blade raised again, poised to strike at Pete's head. "That makes my stomach turn. You make my stomach turn, Fernandez. Just like your father did. Watching him cry like an abandoned baby when I murdered *his* father is something I'll always cherish. Those few bullets paid off so many times. I got your golden-boy *papi* off my ass—his father's death derailed him enough he didn't have the time or energy to look into a corrupt narco cop—and I got paid by Castro's people to murder a traitor to *la patria*. Now I get to put you in the ground too. I get to make three generations of Fernandez men suffer."

As Pete saw the ex-cop's grip tighten around the hilt of the machete, Kathy leapt off the barstool and crashed into Posada, knocking him off-balance. But before she could reach him, Posada slashed at her midsection. The blow only slowed Kathy's momentum as she tried to tackle Posada, and the few seconds she'd bought Pete allowed him to drop down and grab his gun.

Posada and Kathy were tangled, the machete held between them, each one pushing for control of the weapon. Pete couldn't get a clear shot. He tried to move around to get a better angle, but they were tussling—with Posada gaining ground. Kathy was strong but injured, and Posada seemed to have the better hold on the weapon, though Pete couldn't get a good look at it. Kathy was getting weaker, her wound spilling blood over both of them as they pushed at each other.

Then Posada took a calculated risk—pulling his right arm away from the disputed blade and jabbing his palm at Kathy's chin. Pete heard a cracking sound and saw Kathy stumble back. Then Posada went in with the blade, slashing at her already bloody midsection. Kathy fell back, screaming in pain. She collapsed on the floor. Posada took a few steps away from her and tried to regain his composure. Pete didn't hesitate.

He pulled up his gun and fired. The bullet blasted Posada's chest; a look of surprise formed on Posada's face as he stumbled backward. Pete fired again, this time blowing off a chunk of Posada's neck. The cop-turned-druglord crumpled to the ground and landed with a wet, sloppy sound.

Pete rushed to Kathy, curled up on the floor. Her breathing was strained and Pete couldn't tell where she'd been cut—her chest and midsection covered in blood.

"Don't worry, don't worry," Pete said, digging in her pockets for her phone. "I will not let anything happen to you. Kathy, stay with me, okay? You're going to be okay."

She mumbled something and closed her eyes, her head dropping back.

Pete pulled her to him and found her phone. He dialed 911. She wasn't breathing. A chill swept through the dark, blood-spattered bar as Pete screamed for help.

CHAPTER TWENTY-EIGHT

Pete took a sip of the scalding coffee and grimaced. He looked around the half-empty St. Brendan's church basement. It was locker room hot in the cramped space, and only a few people had shown. A few were busy stacking chairs and returning the room to its previous state after the weekly AA meeting.

"Another good one," Jack said, pouring himself a cup of coffee from the pot.

"They're always good," Pete said, nodding to his sponsor.

"Getting back into the swing of things?" Jack asked.

"Yeah, it feels good," Pete said. "Been an intense few weeks, to say the least."

"The reporters are outside for you," Jack said. "I can help you get through if you need."

"I'm sure I'll be fine," Pete said, a sad smile on his face. "Thanks, though."

"My pleasure," Jack said. "Just know you can call whenever you need. Don't go trying to fix everything by yourself."

"Not possible," Pete said. "I've broken too much already."

He tossed the paper coffee cup into the trash and nodded to Jack as he headed up the flight of stairs that led to the small parking lot next to the church. As Jack had promised, there were a few stray reporters waiting for him. The number had dwindled over the past week or so, as newer, sexier stories took up valuable TV and Internet real estate. But there were still two or three dedicated vultures waiting for him to say something.

"Pete, Pete, what can you tell us about Orlando Posada?" a Channel 7 reporter said. She was young, dark-haired, and looked fresh out of college.

"Nothing," Pete said, sidling past the small cluster and getting into his car. He felt a tap on the passenger side window. Another reporter. This one older. Gray hair thinning but still in the game. Pete brought the window down an inch.

"Pete, gimme something, will ya? We're dying here," the man said. Narvaez was his name. Pete had seen him on TV now and again. He was new in town.

"No can do, my friend," Pete said. "I have to be somewhere."

A text message appeared on his phone display. Pete hadn't thought of her in weeks, maybe more. Stephanie Solares.

Can we meet?

Pete backed out of the parking lot and turned north on Galloway.

Harras found Pete in the lobby at South Miami Hospital. The ex-FBI agent had a large bouquet of flowers in one hand and an equally large coffee in the other. He didn't seem any worse for wear from his injuries.

"You're late," Harras said. "Thought you'd be here an hour ago."

"Something came up," Pete said. "Sorry again."

"Don't worry about it. How're you holding up?" Harras asked as he motioned for Pete to push the elevator button.

"Been better," Pete said, holding the door for Harras.

"That's an understatement," Harras said. "Where'd you snag that Cruz lady? She really saved your ass."

"She's a friend," Pete said. "She also reps Dave's family, and for some reason they like me."

Jackie Cruz had indeed saved his ass—in more ways than one. Pete had avoided any charges related to interfering with a police investigation, leaving the scene of a crime in relation to Gilbert Fermin and, most importantly, the death of Orlando Posada. In fact, the Miami PD had been uncharacteristically swift in moving things along. It probably helped that Pete had already pulled the rug out from under the department a few times. In exchange for the speedy handling, plus a nod and a wink from the detectives in charge, Pete was keeping things mum in regard to the press, even though the case felt far from closed to him.

"Reporters still hassling you?" Harras said, pushing the button for the fifth floor.

"They're just curious," Pete said. "And Varela's still out there. It's too complicated for the news. Too much to explain, even with the Castro connection. They want the easy headline and a sizzle reel."

"Just keep your head low," Harras said.

Pete nodded. "I'm trying. It's hard not to flinch every time someone moves toward me. I'm wondering if they've been sent to take me out. *Los Enfermos* didn't go away with Posada. Hurt, sure. The head is gone, but the body lives on."

"Shame about the Pelegrin kid," Harras said. "Never stood a chance."

Pete wasn't sure what to feel about Arturo Pelegrin. Like his mother, he had lived his life as an enigma, trying to play all sides— the police, Pete, *Los Enfermos*. He wasn't surprised the kid ended up dead in his car, a bullet hole behind his ear. Pete felt some regret over not having had the chance to talk to Pelegrin and let him know he didn't have to end up that way—he could make his own path.

"At least your ex finagled her way out, whatever that's worth,"

Harras said. "She's probably traipsing around Europe, spending all of her dead husband's money."

Pete shrugged his shoulders. He had nothing to add.

The elevator chimed as they reached the eighteenth floor. The doors opened and Pete and Harras cut left to room 575. Dave sat outside, looking dazed and tired. He'd probably been there most of the night.

"Welcome back, amigos," Dave said, getting up. He pointed at Pete. "I have a bone to pick with you, my man."

"Oh?"

"Pregnant?" Dave said. "Was anyone going to tell me?"

"Are you the father?" Harras said.

"Well, no—I mean, no, definitely not," Dave said.

"Then it's none of your business," Harras said.

"We didn't know until they wheeled her in here," Pete said. "She'd kept it quiet."

"That's Kathy for you," Dave said. "But who's the *papi*? That's what I wanna know."

"It doesn't matter anymore," Pete said. He walked past Dave and Harras and opened the door to Kathy's room. She was asleep, hooked up to machines. The beeping and blinking were not reassuring to Pete.

He pulled up a chair next to her bed and took her hand.

Her eyes fluttered open. She turned her ashen face to Pete. "Hey," she said.

"Hey there," Pete said. He could feel his eyes welling up. They'd gotten so close to losing her, he wasn't going to take any of these small moments for granted. He gripped her hand.

"I feel like shit."

"You'll get better," Pete said.

She'd been like this for the last day or so—popping in and out of a deep sleep. A marked improvement over the coma she'd been in when everything was touch and go. Now, all signs pointed to a full recovery. The knife wounds were bad—lots of blood loss, some emergency surgery—but she would make it. The baby didn't. It was gone before she got to the hospital.

"You're not going to ask me," Kathy said.

"You'll tell me if you want to," Pete said.

She didn't respond. She gave him a weak smile and let go of his hand, turning to face the other wall.

"I think I'm going to take another twelve-hour nap," she said, sniffling. "Thanks for being here."

Pete stood up and rested a hand on her shoulder.

"Of course," he said. "Just get some sleep."

He felt his phone vibrate and checked the iPhone display. Maya.

> **Hey you! How's Kathy? Still up for dinner tonight at my place? I'll even try to cook :)**

Pete smiled and replied with a quick **Yes.**

His phone vibrated again. This time from a different, unknown number. The message was short and vague, but Pete knew what it meant. And who it was from.

CHAPTER TWENTY-NINE

Sergio's Cafe was the best Cuban food available past 87th Avenue heading west—once you cleared La Carreta. Pete knew it well. The food was heavy, loaded with flavor, and the portion size was impressive, making the restaurant a regular stop for most Westchester and Kendall residents.

Pete walked in and scanned the packed restaurant. He didn't have time for this. But he also didn't have a choice.

Servers wove around Pete as he made his way to the back of the restaurant. He found him sitting at a two seater near the bathroom, Dolphins cap worn low, the brim of the hat hiding his newly bearded face and sunglasses. He wore a black polo shirt and light khaki shorts. Basically, he looked like every Cuban dad scarfing an early dinner. Pete pulled out the seat across from him and sat down.

"Wasn't expecting to hear from you," Pete said.

"Welcome to Sergio's," Gaspar Varela said.

Pete looked around. Everyone seemed immersed in their food,

conversations, or whatever was happening on their phones.

"Not exactly a low-key spot to meet," Pete said.

"Hide in plain sight," Varela said. He took a sip of a Corona and looked at Pete. "I figured we should talk."

"Let's talk," Pete said.

"I wanted to thank you," Varela said.

"For what?"

"What do you think?"

"Let's move this along, okay?" Pete said. He tapped a finger on the menu in front of him. "I could alert the cops that you're here. They'd have this place surrounded."

"But you won't."

"You don't know that."

"When's the last time you worked with the cops?" Varela said. "But you're right. It's not fair to play games. I got distracted. I don't get out much, as you can imagine."

"How'd you get out of jail?"

"It was Posada's doing," Varela said. "Orlando had a connection on the inside. A few keystrokes and a 'clerical error' was born. He guessed—smartly—that I would walk through the open door."

"But you've been exonerated now," Pete said. "You can come back. Your daughter is going out of her mind wondering where you are."

What Pete said was mostly true. The justice system worked slowly. While Varela would eventually be exonerated of the murder of his wife, thanks to the evidence Pete and Kathy had presented to the police after the death of Posada, it was by no means a certainty. Varela could still face charges for the crimes he did commit, like breaking out of prison.

"I'm not spending another day behind bars," Varela said.

"So what's your plan?"

"I don't have a plan," Varela said. "If I don't know my next move, no one does."

"Tell me about Posada," Pete said.

"He betrayed me," Varela said, taking a long pull of his beer. "In more ways than I can really describe. I wasn't playing along with him, so he wanted me gone. We went from close friends to enemies in a matter of months. He was getting dirtier as time wore on—skimming, taking drugs, selling drugs, taking hits on assignment. He was a mobster in a police uniform. On the outside, he danced the dance. Cop, good citizen, *anti-Castrista*. But that was a front. He killed for the Castro regime—right here on American soil. Your grandfather was one of many. He was by far the biggest trophy for Posada, but not the only one. He had to try twice to take the old man down, though."

"There's that, I guess," Pete said.

"He murdered my wife to send me a message," Varela said, his stare going long and distant. "Then he framed me for it. He paid off Janette Ledesma. He used his money to bribe people to keep his story going—Whitelaw to keep the murder weapon, Maldonado and his bullshit story about me killing someone, your friend Rick because he needed someone to clean the money, Fermin—you name it. If they pushed back, found out too much, or threatened him, he killed them. He spent decades hiding in the shadows. On the surface he was an honorable, blind ex-cop. But that wasn't the truth."

"And you had no idea?" Pete said. "Why not say something? You spent years in prison."

"I didn't know it was Orlando until it was too late," Varela said. "Until it was time to walk out of prison."

"So you took the bait?" Pete said. "Just like everyone else?"

"I had no choice," Varela said. "I couldn't do anything. He had access to Maya. He could kill her."

"That's no longer the case. Posada is dead. You need to come back," Pete said, no rancor in his tone. He was too tired for that. He flipped open his menu.

"How's my daughter?"

"You should ask her," Pete said.

"What do you want me to say?" Varela said, his palms open.

"It's not what I want you to say," Pete said. "It's what I want you to do."

"Tell me," Varela said, taking his sunglasses off.

The man crept up behind Varela. He was dressed similarly, but had the gait and build of a rookie cop. He put his mouth near Varela's ear.

"Put your hands behind your back and walk out of this restaurant with me," the officer said. "Let's not make a scene. This can be easy or it can be very hard."

He put his arm on Varela's shoulder and held it there as Varela stood up, his eyes locked on Pete, wide with anger.

"You set me up," Varela said.

"You owe it to your daughter," Pete said. "She gave up a decade of her life to see you walk free. Why not let her have it?"

"You don't know anything about this," Varela said. "Even now."

Pete shrugged his shoulders as the officer led Varela out the door. He thought about apologizing, but let the feeling pass.

"Don't forget to look at the menu," Varela said, forcing a humorless smile on his face. "They may have added some dishes since your last visit."

Pete lifted his menu and found a piece of notebook paper underneath, sloppy handwriting covering most of the front and back. A note from Varela to Pete.

He checked his phone. The evening was just starting.

CHAPTER THIRTY

Pete walked in through the unlocked front door. He could hear the kitchen sink running.

"Back here," Maya said, her voice cheerful. "Just finishing up dinner."

"I'm gonna drop my stuff in the bedroom," Pete said. He felt a great ache in his body. He was beyond tired. He felt spent. Defeated.

He made a quick right as the entranceway led to the main hall and entered Maya's bedroom. It was tidy and well decorated. A print of Edward Hopper's *New York Movie* hung over the bed. A gift from Pete.

He dropped his duffel bag on the bed and turned to the chest of drawers across from it. A jewelry box rested atop the cabinet. Pete opened it and sifted through the necklaces and rings until he found it. The words in Varela's note kept echoing in his head.

If you're reading this, we didn't get to talk much.

Something must have gone wrong.

He took the piece of jewelry out and looked it over. Even in the dark of the room, the gold glimmered—the moon's light shimmering off the gold half-heart pendant. Pete slipped it into his shirt pocket and left the bedroom.

> **There's something I need to bring up that I doubt I'll**
> **be able to in person, even after all the trouble it took**
> **to meet you, face-to-face.**

She heard his footsteps as he got to the kitchen entryway. He leaned on the frame.

"Hey, you," she said, turning her head to look away from the dishes. "How's Kathy doing?"

"She's doing better," Pete said, looking at his hands. "All things considered."

"I'm glad she's going to be okay. Though I can't imagine what she's dealing with after losing the baby," she said. "Poor thing."

"Yeah, it's crazy," Pete said. "I had no idea."

"What have you been up to?"

"Nothing," Pete said. "Well, not nothing."

"Pete," Maya said. "Are you okay? You're all somber tonight. But you should be happy. You guys solved my mom's murder. I can't believe you did, but you did. Now all we need to do is find my dad and …"

> **I know you're with my daughter. I think this is good.**
> **She needs someone like you in her life.**

"I saw your dad today," Pete said. Flat.

"What?" Maya said, turning around and wiping her hands on a dishrag. "Tell me. Why didn't you call? What happened?"

> **She's my life. She fought so hard for me while I was in**
> **prison. She's my legacy and part of me.**

"He's in custody," Pete said, looking up to meet her eyes.

"But how … how did the police find him?" Maya asked. She was standing close to Pete, almost leaning into him.

"I led them to him," Pete said.

But she's also my biggest disappointment.

"What do you mean?" Maya said, stepping back from him, her face not understanding.

Not only has she spent—maybe wasted—her entire life trying to set me free, but she's harboring a dangerous problem. A problem even a father's love can't solve. Something that cuts deeper than the death of her mother.

Pete didn't respond. Maya grabbed his arm, as if she wanted to drag him into the kitchen's light.

"What the fuck happened?"

"I spoke to Stephanie Solares today," Pete said. "Remember her?"

Maya responded with a confused look.

"Sure, yeah," she said. "That's really odd. I haven't talked to her in years, since high school. Why would she reach out to you? I didn't even know you knew each other."

"She felt guilty. She needed to talk to someone. To tell the truth. She told me about how things really were back then," Pete said, his voice distant and cold, because it had to be now. "The gifts, the late-night meetings with him. How she'd cover for you. How she found your mom screaming into the phone when she learned about you and him."

"What is this? What are you getting at?"

Orlando Posada sliced my wife to bloody shreds. He lifted the machete blade and cut her throat open while I lay on the floor, unconscious and unable to defend her. Her blood splattered on my face. I know now that he did it. My best friend murdered my wife.

"I know what you did, Maya," Pete said.

"You are freaking me out," Maya said, trying to smile—trying to change the tone. To yank things back to how she thought they were a few minutes before.

He pulled the half-heart-shaped pendant from his pocket. He'd seen the other half before, on a chain around Orlando Posada's neck.

Her eyes focused on the golden piece of jewelry. They fluttered, then closed. She let out a long, defeated sigh.

"Stephanie Solares covered for you that night, the night your mother died," Pete said. "You were at Orlando's house, waiting for him to come home. You'd let him know that your parents would be there alone. Your father told me, Maya. He learned the truth when Posada got him out of prison. He ran because he couldn't face the truth."

She backed up a few paces, her hands on the kitchen sink. She turned away from Pete. He couldn't see her reaction. Couldn't read her face.

"Stephanie told me about your fights with your mother over him, how she refused to accept that you were with an older man like Posada," Pete said. "You asked Posada to do it. Because your mom found out."

"She was going to tell my dad," Maya said, sounding jagged—like she was in excruciating pain. "It was going to ruin everything. She didn't understand."

But it was Maya who had her killed.

"Understand what?"

"That I loved Orlando," Maya said. "He took care of me. He paid attention to me, took me places. I felt special and nice. It was forbidden, which was also part of it. He was handsome and charming. I was a kid. My mom and I were always arguing, fighting. She didn't let me do anything. When she found out about us—a neighbor of Orlando's told her, showed her—she told me she was going to send me away, tell my father, and destroy everything. I was scared. I told Orlando. He said he'd fix it. He said he'd make the problem go away. But I didn't know he was going to kill her. When that happened I was destroyed. He said he was going to talk to her, maybe scare her, but nothing like what he did. But by then it was too late. I was tied into it. All I could do was try to get my father a new trial, and even then I knew it was impossible, not with Orlando watching, his fingers in everything."

"He used you, tricked you into falling for him," Pete said. "He wanted your dad gone. He manipulated you to get him off the board."

Her knees buckled and she fell to the ground, curling her body into a ball.

CHAPTER THIRTY-ONE

New York City
Five months later

The red traffic light display said six seconds. Pete was halfway across Dyckman Street, and made it to the other side with a second to spare. He was late. He undid his tie as he walked up the steep hill on Payson Avenue. It was chilly now—even in his full suit Pete felt underdressed. He had yet to master layering for the cold. It looked like it was going to be a brutal, frigid winter.

Kathy was midway up the hill on Payson, two giant bags of groceries in each arm and a look of complete exhaustion on her face. Pete took the bags from her hands.

She gave Pete a friendly peck on the cheek and turned to continue their walk home. Pete followed her up the rest of the hill toward their apartment—a roomy two-bedroom steal of a place in the north Manhattan neighborhood of Inwood, just south of the Bronx. It had its quirks—like most New York apartments seemed to—but it was starting to feel more comfortable. For the first time in a long while, Pete was calling a place outside the Sunshine State home.

"Your lawyer called," Kathy said. She never referred to Jackie Cruz by name.

"Yeah?"

"Looks like Varela will be out soon," she said, then paused. "Gaspar, that is."

Pete nodded. There was nothing to add. Gaspar Varela's only crime was walking through the door Orlando Posada had opened for him. Once he was captured and word of his false conviction spread across the national and international news, his trial on those charges sped through the system and he was met with an acquittal and a formal apology. Pete wondered if that apology would keep Varela from suing the City of Miami for damages. He doubted it.

Thinking of the swift resolution to Varela's legal entanglements reminded Pete of his friend Martin, apparently gunned down by Varela himself. Those facts soon unraveled, as Varela explained to the authorities that the damning fingerprints found on the murder weapon were placed under duress after his escape, Posada forcing his old partner to give him one last bargaining chip. A stray fingerprint belonging to Graydon Smith—the man Varela pegged as Martin's actual killer—supported this. The news made little difference for Martin, Pete thought.

"She asked that you call her, in reference to Maya's possible trial," Kathy said, speeding through the sentence, her patter faster than usual. "My guess is she's going to ask you to go back to Miami to testify, which, in my humble opinion, is too risky."

With Posada dead, the district attorney's office was focusing all its energy on Maya, to make up for the mistaken conviction of Gaspar Varela, the latest black eye on the Miami PD, courtesy of Pete and Kathy. The case against Maya was thin. Maya hadn't been present at the murder and the evidence linking her to the plot was tenuous and hard to prove. But the DA was pushing for a conviction. Pete hoped Maya's lawyers found a way to settle and allow everyone to move on with their lives. The people left alive, that is.

"That's fine," Pete said. He understood Kathy's hesitation—he didn't want to talk about Maya. The trial. The last year.

"Except for that pesky bounty on your head," she said.

"It'll take *Los Enfermos* a beat to reorganize," Pete said. "I doubt I'm their top priority."

"It's been five months, dude. For starters, we derailed their entire operation," she said. "And you killed their leader. You are most definitely their top priority. Or did you forget why we are living in another state?"

She was right. *Los Enfermos* had suffered a paralyzing blow after the death of Posada. But the gang lived on, their powers weakened but not gone forever. Pete and Kathy felt safe enough in New York, watching from a distance. But a return to Miami was out of the question and would be for some time.

Kathy saw him first and stopped walking toward the door. Not upset or happy—just on pause. Harras was standing in front of the double doors that led to their apartment, atop a small set of stairs that made up the stoop. He looked rough.

"You two weren't that hard to find," Harras said. He walked down the steps and stood in front of them. His eyes rested on Kathy for a few extra seconds.

Pete went in for the hug and, for once, Harras was receptive to it. The embrace was brief. Kathy stayed back, her arms folded.

"I've got to put these groceries away," she said. "Then maybe you'll come inside and explain why you're here."

They sat on opposite ends of the large sectional couch that took up most of the living room, Pete sipping from a large glass of water and Harras holding a can of diet soda. Kathy had sped down the main hallway and into the kitchen. Pete could hear her slamming cabinets with more force than usual, cursing under her breath.

"Is this when I ask you what's new?" Harras said, deadpan. "I'm still figuring out this small-talk stuff."

"Things are fine," Pete said, leaning back into the soft couch.

He'd tugged the tie off seconds after entering the house and now unbuttoned the top button of his long-sleeved shirt. His suit jacket had landed somewhere near the dining room chairs.

"That sounds riveting," Harras said.

"We're starting over," Pete said. "We had no choice."

"So, what are we talking about?" Kathy said as she entered the room and took a seat between them.

"Just getting the update," Harras said.

"Well, Pete's got a nice gig as an investigator for one of the local New York sportsball teams, thanks to his former fuck buddy," Kathy said. "We lost the Varela book deal because—well, no case means no money, and Varela wasn't keen on talking to me after Pete had him arrested. But my agent got me an even better deal, sans Varela. I'm looking over page proofs this weekend. Should be out in a few months. It's just a straight true crime book without the interviews we wanted from Varela, but I think it'll do nicely. That's a long-winded way of saying Pete's paying most of the rent for now. Oh, and the subway smells a lot worse than the MetroRail. But no one rides the MetroRail, so there's that. Not much else has changed, aside from our zip code."

Harras winced at Kathy's dismissive tone. Pete realized he hadn't been in a room with both of them for a while.

"I think the better question is what brings you to our doorstep," Pete said.

"Nothing good," Harras said. "But it also gives me a chance to let you know what's going on."

"Yes, do tell—what *is* going on?" Kathy said, looking at Harras.

"Well, I talked to some of my contacts and they gave me the quick and dirty of it all," Harras said, clearing his throat. "This isn't pleasant, so let me know now if you want me to skip it."

"Go ahead," Pete said.

"Okay," Harras said. "After the Varela murder, Posada allowed Maya to play the part of crusading daughter, to a point. If she got too close, he'd either buy the person off or have them killed. Posada killed Carmen Varela because he saw it as an opportunity to frame his partner so he could continue doing what he was doing—namely, using his job as a cop to profit and murder."

"Because Gaspar had started sniffing around Posada's not-legal dealings, right?" Kathy said. She seemed impatient.

"Right, but Gaspar hadn't figured it out yet. So it was a two birds scenario," Harras said. "Maya couldn't tell anyone she actually had her mother killed, but things fell apart with Posada romantically. He didn't seem to care, since he'd already gotten what he wanted, but he kept her involvement hanging over her head. He used her to keep her dad docile in prison. Gaspar didn't really see the entire picture until he walked out of prison and Posada told him. Maya didn't expect you two to actually figure it out."

"So, she hired us because we were idiots?" Pete asked. "And Gaspar pushed to have you join because he didn't have faith in her choice?"

"I wouldn't look at it that way," Harras said. "But she wasn't expecting you to do as well as you did."

Pete nodded for Harras to continue.

"Eventually, Maya started feeling worse and wanted to be discovered," Harras said. "She *wanted* you two to solve it. She was conflicted, or so she's told the police. Posada and she had a falling out and he turned his energies on getting you two gone. But she pushed back, so we saw some hesitation, like Martin getting shot as a warning. But Posada won that tug of war. He stopped humoring her. Instead, he forced her to help him by providing information on what you were up to."

Harras cracked his knuckles before continuing.

Pete stood up.

"She wouldn't do that," Pete said. "She made a mistake as a kid, but helping Posada while we were investigating it? I don't know if I buy that."

Kathy looked up at him.

"She *did* do that, Pete," she said.

Pete closed his eyes for a moment and sat back down.

Kathy rubbed his back.

"It's over now," she said.

"Is it?" Pete said. "I can't even go home. We're living this exile life and playing house, but if we step foot in Miami, we're dead."

Kathy recoiled.

"What would you like to do, then? Risk it?" she said. "Take the next flight to MIA and see if *Los Enfermos* remember who we are? Hope for the best?"

"Well," Harras said. "That's why I'm here."

"You've got to be fucking kidding me," Kathy said.

He looked at Pete and leaned in, his palms up.

"We need you back," he said. "We need you in Miami."

"For what?" Pete asked. "I don't work for the police. Hell, the police have never even recognized me as anything but a huge pain in the ass."

"FBI, not police," Harras said. "A case you worked a while back has cropped up again."

"FBI? What, you're un-retired now?" Kathy said. She was gunning for Harras today in a way Pete hadn't seen before.

"That's irrelevant," Harras said, turning to look at Kathy, his tone softening. "This is about something Pete did years ago. A case he was directly involved in. We need him back."

He looked at Pete, his eyes pleading.

"Pete, we're not just politely asking here," Harras said. "There's new info on the case—you know the one I'm talking about. The dead kid? There's more to it. I know it. You worked it when it all started. You could have some insight into this that they don't. They're begging. The FBI does not beg. Try to understand that. You know something they need to crack this case."

As a PI, Pete hadn't worked many major cases, aside from the Silent Death and Julian Finch. He knew exactly what Harras was talking about. It flashed back to him now, all at once. Stumbling drunk in the rain. A dead child. Screams of fear and anger. He wanted nothing to do with it.

"No," Pete said. "The case is closed. They found their man."

"You know there was something fishy there," Harras said. "It's more complicated than that. Come back and help me look it over again."

"I said no."

"You're not even going to ask me about it?" Harras said. "You're just going to turn your back on this? On me?"

Harras knew the case haunted Pete. He knew the guilt Pete felt about his role in how it ended. He knew what this meant. It was a big ask. Pete was surprised Harras was even going there. It made him wonder if the man before him was truly a friend or just someone who had repaid a debt and was now back to being an adversary.

"Nothing to ask, and it's nothing personal," Pete said, standing up. "I'm not going back to Miami. That's it."

"Fucking Miami," Kathy said as she left the room.

Harras slapped his knees and also stood up.

"Looks like this is gonna be a short visit, then," Harras said.

He made a beeline for the door. Pete followed, a few paces behind. Harras turned around to face him in front of the doorway, his hand on the knob.

"You can't hide here forever, living in this pretend world with your pretend wife and pretend job," he said. "There's no escaping this. You had a life in Miami. You affected people—for good and bad. Your demons will find you wherever you go. They have before."

"It was nice to see you," Pete said.

Harras nodded.

"You're a good detective—you solved a murder the entire city thought was closed. Hell, you've solved a few of them," Harras said, gripping Pete's shoulder. It was more affection than Pete was used to from the ex-agent. "Your father would be proud. I'm proud of you. You picked up the shreds of your life and made something of yourself. But there's another side to that coin, you know? It means using those skills when they're needed. Risking your life for something instead of sitting back and sitting out. That's not like you. You have my number if you reconsider. We could use your help. A killer is on the loose."

Harras closed the door behind him as he walked out of the apartment. The sound of his heavy footsteps faded as he made his way down.

ACKNOWLEDGMENTS

It never gets easier.

That's the big lesson I've learned while writing these Pete Fernandez mysteries, of which you now hold the third installment in your hands. While, as a writer, you get better and (hopefully) refine your craft, each new book comes with its own set of challenges and pitfalls. If you're lucky, you have great people around you to help you avoid those traps and focus on what matters: writing a good book.

In that regard, I'm very lucky.

The fictional story of Gaspar Varela owes a lot to the (still unfolding) true crime saga of Jeffrey MacDonald, a US Army officer accused and convicted of murdering his wife and two daughters in 1970. It was after reading Errol Morris's excellent *A Wilderness of Error* that the idea for Pete's latest case came to me: *What if MacDonald had been innocent? What if his Manson-esque tale of drugged-out hippies was true? What if one of the kids survived—and had even been to blame?* That got my mind riffing, and the next thing I knew, Gaspar Varela had appeared in my mind's eye, along with his crusading but conflicted daughter, Maya. I'm very much indebted to the work of Morris, Joe McGinniss's *Fatal Vision* (and its short epilogue, *Final Vision*), and the incomparable Janet Malcolm's *The Journalist and the Murderer*.

While *Dangerous Ends* is still very much a book about Pete Fernandez's Miami, unlike its predecessors *Silent City* and *Down the Darkest Street*, it zooms out a bit in terms of place and time—looking back at Cuba during the early days of the Castro revolution and at Miami during different moments leading up to the present day. During the writing of this book I thought back on and pulled from my own memories of Miami and the Cuba stories that were passed down from generation to generation and eventually to me. I also relied heavily on a number of books, both fiction and nonfiction. Most notably, Ann Louise Bardach's well-researched and engrossing history of the Castro regime and the Miami exile community, *Cuba Confidential: Love and Vengeance in Miami and Havana*; Carlos Eire's beautifully-crafted memoir of his boyhood in Cuba in the 1950s, *Waiting for Snow in Havana: Confessions of a Cuban Boy*; Richard Gott's *Cuba: A New History*; Cristina Garcia's evocative novel *Dreaming in Cuban*; and T.J. English's pre-Castro Cuban mob chronicle *Havana Nocturne: How the Mob Owned Cuba...and* Then *Lost It to the Revolution*. Despite the stack of books, very little could top those actual stories that made their way from Cuba to Miami, usually told to me by my grandparents (Margot and Guillermo on one side, Angel and Olga on another); parents; and my dear aunt Alina, who regularly implores me to not forget where I come from. I hope this book proves I haven't, *tia*.

Like any novel, the version you hold in your hands is vastly different from the author's first draft, and I'm thankful for that. I owe a great deal to my crack team of beta readers— Elizabeth Keenan-Penagos, Austin Trunick, Meg Wilhoite, Angel Colon, Justin Aclin, Paul Steinfeld, and Andrea Vigil, Miranda Mulligan, Rebekah Monson and Amanda Di Bartolomeo—who managed to be both supportive friends and effective critics during the process. Not an easy feat. My mother-in-law, Isabel Stein, was once again an invaluable source of editorial (and moral) support, which I can never truly repay. There are also many authors and publishing industry friends who shed a little light on this winding path for me, either through a friendly bit of advice or a kind word. I'd list them all here if I could, but I'm only allotted so much space. As always, you know who you are.

I'd also like to thank Erin Mitchell for her all-purpose help that always goes above and beyond what's required or expected, Meredith Jones for her sage legal advice and a big thumbs-up to my bosses, Jon Goldwater and Mike Pellerito, and my colleagues at Archie Comics for letting a noir writer into the Riverdale city limits. I am also keenly aware of how lucky I am to have an agent as sharp and thoughtful as Dara Hyde of the Hill Nadel Literary Agency—thank you for your advocacy, steady hand, and guidance. I'm also extremely grateful to my stalwart editor Jason Pinter and the entire team at Polis Books for giving Pete and his band of misfits a home. I'm honored to be part of the Polis team.

This book would surely not exist without the loyalty, care and kindness that my friends and family regularly show me. It keeps me humble and thankful. My heart is full.

And, finally, I'd like to thank my wife, Eva Stein Segura, for her unflinching support, love, and honesty. Thank you for being my ideal reader, fearless editor, co-conspirator, and an amazing mother to our little boy, Guillermo (who will hopefully read this one day and smile). I'm an extremely lucky man.

Alex Segura
Queens, New York

ABOUT THE AUTHOR

Alex Segura is a novelist and comic book writer. He is the author of the Pete Fernandez novels *Silent City*, *Down the Darkest Street*, and *Dangerous Ends*, all available from Polis Books. He has also written a number of comic books, including the best-selling and critically acclaimed *Archie Meets Kiss* storyline, the "Occupy Riverdale" story and *Archie Meets Ramones*. He lives in New York with his wife and son. He is a Miami native.

Visit him online at www.AlexSegura.com and follow him on Twitter at @Alex_Segura.